BLUE HOLE BACK HOME

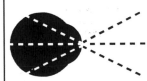

This Large Print Book carries the
Seal of Approval of N.A.V.H.

BLUE HOLE BACK HOME

INSPIRED BY A TRUE STORY

JOY JORDAN-LAKE

THORNDIKE PRESS
A part of Gale, Cengage Learning

Detroit • New York • San Francisco • New Haven, Conn • Waterville, Maine • London

GALE
CENGAGE Learning™

Copyright © 2008 by Joy Jordan-Lake.
Thorndike Press, a part of Gale, Cengage Learning.

ALL RIGHTS RESERVED
This story is a work of fiction. All characters and events are the product of the author's imagination, although some are based on real-life events and people.
Thorndike Press® Large Print Christian Fiction.
The text of this Large Print edition is unabridged.
Other aspects of the book may vary from the original edition.
Set in 16 pt. Plantin.
Printed on permanent paper.

LIBRARY OF CONGRESS CATALOGING-IN-PUBLICATION DATA

Jordan-Lake, Joy, 1963–
   Blue hole back home : inspired by a true story / by Joy
Jordan-Lake.
     p. cm. — (Thorndike press large print Christian fiction)
   ISBN-13: 978-1-4104-2274-3 (alk. paper)
   ISBN-10: 1-4104-2274-7 (alk. paper)
   1. Large type books. I. Title.
PS3610.O6623B55 2010
813'.6—dc22   2009039728

Published in 2010 by arrangement with David C. Cook.

Printed in Mexico
1 2 3 4 5 6 7 14 13 12 11 10

*For
my husband, Todd Lake,
whose unflagging encouragement kept
this novel alive,
and for
my brother, David Jordan,
who, at a time in my younger years when
I had few friends
of my own, shared his own friends
with me*

My love and thanks always

ACKNOWLEDGMENTS

As always, I owe a thousand thank-yous to my husband, Todd Lake, and to my kids, Jasmine, Justin, and Julia Jordan-Lake, for their support, their love, their gracious tolerance of and laughter in the midst of nutty writing deadlines, and for all they teach me every day.

My parents, Diane and Monty Jordan, my brother, David Jordan, and his wife, Beth Jackson-Jordan, their kids, Christopher, Catherine, and Olivia, my mother-in-law, Gina Lake, and brother-in-law, Steven, have been thoughtful encouragers, sometimes in a well-timed word or hug, sometimes in the gift of an obscure and incredibly relevant book.

A circle of far-flung but always-dear friends offered enthusiasm, comfort, and reminders to laugh at myself at every turn. Susan Bahner Lancaster, my childhood chum, fellow English professor, and lover of

7

books, read this novel in its earliest stages and offered invaluable insights. The unsinkable Kelly Shushok would not rest until this book was published. Throughout every book deadline, Ginger Brasher-Cunningham has called with a word of grace or good humor just when I needed it most. Laura Singleton, herself a writer, has been an inspiration and encourager for years. The multitalented Milton Brasher-Cunningham has been there — if a thousand miles away — to share the writing life, help celebrate good news, and help mourn the bad. Susan and Kyle Matthews and their kids have been cherished companions for my family and me as we've thought and dreamed together about faith and words and music. It was their son Christopher who reminded me how much I loved Earth, Wind & Fire, and still do.

I am so grateful, too, for the writing-specific encouragement and good counsel of Tammy Bullock, Kitty Freeman Gay, Mike Glenn, Regina and Bryan Hall, Elizabeth and Scott Harris, Kelly Monroe Kullberg, Anne Moore, Julie Pennington-Russell, Dorrie and Ramon Presson, Elizabeth and Jason Rogers, Mary Anne and Roger Severino, Christy and Jim Somerville, Susanne Starr, Benita Walker, Gloria White-Hammond and Ray Hammond, and a host of others I'll hate myself in the morning for not specifically naming.

I also wish to thank Katie Boyle of Veritas Literary Agency and the good people of David C. Cook who made this book such a pleasure to publish: my particular gratitude to Don Pape, Andrea Christian, and their fabulous gun-for-hire, Nicci Jordan Hubert. If this novel has any merit, it's thanks to Nicci's heart and instincts for the rhythm of story.

And finally, I'm thankful for the kind-hearted people of my hometown, Signal Mountain, Tennessee, who are, by the way, not the same as the people of the fictional Pisgah Ridge. The people of Signal Mountain taught me my earliest lessons on faith and risk and redemption, and I am indebted to them for not giving up on someone so painfully shy and homely.

1. BACKSTITCHING TIME

Likely it was only two dreams crisscrossing paths, one snagging on the other in passing, but somehow the face that walked by me this morning, not four feet away, got tangled up with one from my past. The way-back and way-faraway, all quiet and almost forgotten, got yanked up and placed alongside today, where two minutes before I'd have told you I was: in Boston. At the Public Garden. Not a stone's throw from Beacon Hill, where I live and work, and pay as much for my own private parking space as folks back home do for a decent slab ranch and enough acres for the dogs to tree themselves something other than city-soft squirrel.

I was cozied up on a park bench in the Garden to cool my espresso and pry off the pumps I despise and I wear every day. Then the face passed by my bench. I lurched forward to stare, then back — to cover for staring — and splashed espresso clear down

11

my front.

And I swear time backstitched on itself, and at that very moment, I was barefoot — not with black pumps stowed under a park bench, but the right kind of barefoot. The kind of barefoot that went with the truck bed of a pickup. I was back with the wind standing my ponytail straight up over my head, the Blue Hole just around the next curve. And I was tracing my cheek where a kiss had just landed.

So there I sat in the garden this morning, tracing my cheek, feeling my heart seize up in my chest, and the ache stabbing down to my toes, and my toes going cold in the wind off the truck. In that moment, the smell of espresso got overpowered by the scents of my past: pine needles and boy-sweat, salted peanuts and Coke. I heard bluegrass guitar and banjo all mixed up with rhythm and blues and a rope swing ticking forward and back, keeping time. I was barefoot in the back of a pickup, believing that it was love that makes people brave and gorgeous and clever and kind. Believing, and being wrong.

I haven't often — or ever, actually — told the story of that summer, because its beginning, when the new girl lifted her brown legs up over our tailgate, never connected up with the end, with the goodness or the fire. Brown was what that leg was, back at the beginning, and not just tanned into dark. It was me who'd said we should stop for her, and me who knew first that our troubles had just dug in deep, a fat tick way down into fur.

"Shoulda known better" was what people said. "You mix up your colors like 'at and you got yourself mud's what you got."

Thing was, I *did* know better. Brought up in those mountains where the pines grew tall out of clay the color of blood, I knew what was what, and who was who, and who was not.

Plenty of folks said what happened that summer was my doing, and plenty said it was all Jimbo's fault. But I'm saying it was the fault of the Blue Hole.

"All sunk sweet and sacred" was what Jimbo called the Blue Hole back then.

The son of the First Baptist Church preacher — a kind of Little League pope in a small Southern town — Jimbo handled words like electrical wires he just might dip into water. And though he favored the peculiar or crude, he'd often come out with something like that — some musty old word like *sacred* — and make us all jump.

Sacred's not a word I've ever much liked

13

— says to me bad organ music, the celesta stop out, and sopranos with skin like cheap parlor drapes hung from their jaws. But maybe some things, and some places, just are. And maybe the Blue Hole was one of those places. Even more so, perhaps, after that one August night when men in white bedsheets paid house calls all over Pisgah Ridge, and made sure we all understood that although times had supposedly changed, some kinds of thinking, and some kinds of hate, had not. It was the men in white bedsheets that changed us — them and the Blue Hole changed us forever.

I've learned, now, not to speak of these things to folks here in Boston, especially the men that I date. Early on, before I'd learned better than to talk of back home, they would fumble their lobster forks into their chowder. "How *old* must you be?" they would ask — the ones whose mommas must not have harped much on manners. Like living through one race of people not being real kind to another takes a whole lot of age. Sometimes inside the main course, I might try to explain George Wallace, the before and the after repentance — was that what he called it? — and Reconstruction and Rosewood. Then they had to know why, did I think, Huey Long got himself shot and

14

Strom Thurmond didn't.

"Pass the drawn butter please, sugar" is how I come back.

So I generally don't talk much of the past anymore, my own or the South's. I don't stamp myself with stories that might limit my shelf life, making me sound even older than these Boston winters already have made me look. I rarely refer to Carolina at all, or to the mountains, or to my little town on the Ridge. If I mention the Blue Hole, it's only in passing, and I take care to skirt real far around the topic of riots and rope swings. I skirt further still around the story of Jimbo and us and the new girl who tore up our calm, or the good that snuck up on us in the dark. I don't mention crosses, either burning or strung up by the neck in a church. I don't mention Mecca or Jesus, or why just yesterday driving the Pike, when Daniel Shore on NPR said "Sri Lanka," I let go the wheel and made a map with my hands, just like I have now for twenty-five years, every time I hear the country's name spoken.

They all — these men who buy me dinner at Legal's — once read O'Connor and Tennessee Williams and Faulkner at Harvard. That was years ago now, back before their first marriages — but it's clear they've looked ever since for Misfits and Snopses and Stellas, for lovely, loose women who smell of magnolias.

I don't line out for these men, or for anyone else, why my adult life takes place a good thousand miles from the only place I'll ever call home, or how no manner of grace — a word Jimbo used — can undo what gets done. I don't say this either: that my home is a beautiful place, a terribly beautiful place that gives birth to traitors and cowards and heroes, sometimes all in one skin. And I never say why — because I don't know — I long like I do to go back.

They say you can't go home again, ever, can't relive the past — and until this morning I would have said that was true. But something about the face I saw in the garden got me to wonder if maybe time does have its backstitches and snags like the physics professors all drone on about, though no one believes them. Maybe some parts of your past don't stay just where you thought your life left them all shredded in pieces.

This morning I wondered, nearly knocked to my knees with the scent of espresso and pine needles and peanuts and sweat all at the same time, if maybe there's some other end to my story still to get made.

16

■ ■ ■ ■

In that summer of 1979, we all ran together in a mangy pack — that's what Jimbo's mother called us, *y'all's mangy pack,* and she liked us better than most. My brother Emerson and his best friend, Jimbo, had started their landscaping business — their work always centered on Miss Mollybird Pittman's impossible yard — and I helped out some when Momma allowed. It was the summer when everyone else bought albums and '45s of the Bee Gees and Eagles and Peter Frampton, but Emerson's white pickup truck held only an eight-track tape player, which soundtracked our shoveling and planting and hauling manure. The only tapes the three of us owned came from Jimbo's purchase at a garage sale down in the valley where a woman was unloading her entire eight-track collection, the tapes' slick paper labels already bubbled. Jimbo loved his collection, and we loved Jimbo, so we labored under a Southern Appalachian sun to decade-old Motown. Diana Ross and Marvin Gaye oversaw our planting magnolias; James Brown set the beat for our sinking azaleas into peat moss and mulch.

That summer the temperatures soared,

even up on our mountain, and stayed there — and I, ever since I'd studied Icarus that spring at school, was sure we'd all just melt and plummet on down to the valley.

"If I keep sweatin' like this," Jimbo would moan every morning while he flopped himself into Emerson's truck bed, "y'all gonna have to call me a lifeguard." Or sometimes, "Can't hardly stand to strap on underwear."

"Gave it up yesterday myself," Emerson would tell him, or "I'm saying we give up the pants, too" — which was likely why my momma didn't much like my going along.

We survived the heat that summer by piling into Emerson's pickup and heading into the woods. We carted along a cast-off Styrofoam cooler pieced back together with electrical tape, and Emerson's Big Dog, a remarkably chubby golden retriever with a weakness for pork barbecue scraps and Dr Pepper, which she drank straight from the can. Jimbo was learning to play Em's guitar, and from the truck bed, he fingered out strange medleys of "Stairway to Heaven" and "Holy, Holy, Holy." In four-wheel drive, we jolted down old logging trails — Jimbo fumbling chords as we went — through tangles of loblolly pines and post oaks that hid the secret we teenagers had found — or maybe created. They were deeply eroded, those old logging trails, ragged gashes in that dark red clay, like a knife had gone slashing through flesh.

"You comin', Turtle?" Jimbo'd call from the truck, Emerson slowing enough for me to fling myself in over its side. My parents christened me Shelby Lenoir. Shelby Lenoir Maynard — not too bad as Southern names go — but it was Jimbo's nicknaming me "Turtle" that stuck. Back when we were kids lined up on the vinyl bench seat of our father's Chevy Impala, I'd taken my turn steering the car on a two-lane dirt road. Jimbo and Em, in giggle-fits over my barely keeping the car out of the woods, had first seen the truck coming our way and, laughing too hard to speak, only pointed, while my father, beside me, gave the order to straighten the wheel. Instead, I'd covered my face with both arms. My new name was born that very day, along with the sad realization I live with even now here in Boston that sometimes when life barrels at me head-on, I hide my head and hope the crash doesn't land on my own little shell.

I had no female friends in those days: Girls struck me as backstabbing and shallow and silly, compared with the brutal, straight-in-front put-downs of my brother and his buddies. I never much fit in with the girls' fingernail-polishing parties. I was skinny and awkward, and carried whatever smarts I had then like a warning, like a Jew's yellow star, or a leper girl ringing her bell. It was the smarts, Emerson said, that messed me up most — as a girl, I reckon he meant.

The new girl in town might have counted as my one female friend. Except that she didn't count. She'd come just the last month of school. I was a sophomore — Jimbo and Em, loud, cocky juniors — and the new girl and I had met, briefly, after nearly colliding in front of the water fountain down by the old gym.

Naturally I knew who she was, her being the only one in our school even close to her color — though I can't say I knew anyone who'd spoken with her. At the fountain, the new girl motioned for me to drink first.

"Before me, you may proceed," she told me, and nodded her head real formal.

"No, really, you go ahead."

"Please, I insist upon it." She stepped aside, and held out her hand to me, like we were both there on business. "If I may present myself, I am Farsanna Moulavi."

I'd heard people say she was strange — more than her color, I mean — and just that one stiff, stilted speech was enough to make me wonder if people weren't right. And her face was odd too — her expression, that is. Because — and here was the thing — there wasn't any expression at all. Except in her eyes. And they looked out of her paralyzed face a little too dark, a little too deep, maybe a little unsteady, like they were black pits that might or might not be hiding explosives.

"Shelby Lenoir," I told her. "I'm Shelby Lenoir Maynard." And I almost added, "There's some call me Turtle." But that was reserved for friends.

I drank, and to cover for the water dribbling down my chin, said the first thing that poked into my mind: "Cool accent."

"The accent is to you the strange thing, no?" She asked this with an almost-smile, some kind of not-smile hanging at the edges like shadows.

"Well . . . your skin's a nice color," I told her then because it was true — though it sounded peculiar somehow, saying it out loud to her face.

Farsanna Moulavi was the color of the hot cocoa Jimbo Riggs' mother made from Nestlé dark chocolate, powdered sugar, and dried milk. The kind the Riggses drank in their basement rec room when they played

21

Parcheesi on Friday nights.

"I come from Sri Lanka," she said, watching me. "You perhaps know it as the former Ceylon." She held up her right hand flat against the air, as if it were a map. "If this would be India, then this," she placed her left fist by the lower thumb knuckle of her right hand, "is Sri Lanka." She turned to drink, then rose up straight, all in one piece, like her spine didn't bend. "The accent and the skin, they come both from Sri Lanka."

"Sri Lanka." I nodded to show I'd recognized the map she could make with her hands, and that I knew where it was — close enough, anyhow. My father was the city desk editor of our local newspaper and he was a Yankee, so he likely knew all about Sri Lanka, or would sound like he did anyway — which, I've learned by living in Boston, is pretty much the same thing.

Now Momma, had she been there with the new girl at the fountain, would've offered up quick something sweet — maybe a second cousin's having seen that part of the world lately and loved it. Just *loved* it. Momma made certain everyone in her path felt affirmed at all times, even if she had to perjure herself, or her second cousin, to do it.

But I stood staring at the new girl's

homemade-cocoa color, and thinking how Momma would whisper that *a lady does not stare* or that *Jesus would make a stranger feel welcome.*

But I was not Momma or much of a lady or Jesus, and "Oh" was what I managed instead.

I turned then to leave, but Emerson and Jimbo's baseball team was just burrowing up from the locker room. I'd had a crush all spring on both the shortstop and pitcher, Quincy and Quirt, identical twins, and one of them — I never could tell them apart — had smiled at me once from the dugout. So I dropped to retie a shoelace that hadn't come undone, and with a quick flick of my tongue, popped my retainer clear out of my mouth and straight into my gym bag.

I flashed a smile up at the new girl but mostly at the shortstop and pitcher cleating up behind her. "You liking the school and everything okay?" I asked the new girl, just like I wanted to know.

She looked startled, like our little exchange had been suddenly tossed, then retrieved — and no reason for either. But she took — after a second — the rope-end of talk I held out.

"This mountain for you has always been home, no?" she asked. I sure couldn't see how that answered my question.

"Me? Shoot. Six generations on Momma's side. But my father's a Yankee."

She cocked her head, and I noticed how still her hair lay on her shoulders. Dark as I'd ever seen. And so thick. I wondered if it were heavy as it looked.

My shortstop-pitcher matching pair had already passed — without so much as looking my way. Emerson gave me a punch in the gut. And Jimbo gave out his signature wave, his whole arm flapping, and winked. Only at me. His one dimple dug in deep.

I winked back, just like always, but then he was waving again, a little barely-there wave, and not looking at me. And he grinned, right at the new girl, and drilled in his dimple again — which was like him, giving that smile out to just anybody happening to be standing in the same hall.

At the back of the herd moved Morton Beckwith, a Clydesdale behind skittish ponies. The other boys' cleats clattered and pinged against the hall's tile, but under Mort's bulk the hall echoed like a blacksmith's hammer against a draft horseshoe. He played catcher, and while he missed a wide world of think-quick plays to the first baseman and pitcher, he excelled at scaring runners headed home with his size and his snarl. He had the build of a fullback and the mind of one too — one who'd taken all hits with his head.

He nodded at me — it's not in the Beckwith nature to wave — and then his eyes latched onto Farsanna. He passed not more than three inches from her and never took his eyes off her face. His bottom lip jutted out nearly straight from his gums, the skin more or less permanently distended from the tobacco he dipped. For some reason, lips like his defined manly good looks on our Ridge — reminding me always of *National Geographic* full-page photos of remote island natives who weight their earlobes, stretching them down to the base of their necks. So the bulge of Mort's bottom lip in particular might have brushed up against the new girl had his head not towered above her.

Then, just past her, as if in slow motion, he spit.

It was nothing but normal, a boy — a Southern boy, and a baseball player at that — dipping tobacco and needing to spit. But brown juice did land near the sandaled feet of the new girl, and maybe spattered a little like hamburger grease onto her toes. They were brown too, though, so it didn't show.

I told myself it didn't mean anything.

Though a chill did run down my neck into my hands, and maybe that's what stood the hair up on my arms as it passed.

Swinging his big head only once to glance back, the whites of his eyes always too yellow and the skin around them puffy and dark, Mort hoofed back into the herd. Quincy and Quirt were slapping each other on the behind and Emerson and Jimbo had disappeared: So the whole team had passed by, and my purpose for standing by the fountain seemed pretty much passed too.

"Well," I told the new girl, "see ya."

And I left . . . those eyes, flammable-looking, just watching me go.

It did occur to me, at least once or twice, to feel guilty for walking away so awfully fast, and a little defensive, too — like the new girl might lump me with everyone else. Like I was one of those on Pisgah Ridge who might spew brown spitjuice on her bare toes, or ignore her because she was different. Far from it, though. I ignored her because she might be the same — like every other fifteen-year-old female I'd found not much worth knowing.

So the new girl walked on alone down our high school's concrete-block halls, the late spring air hot and thick, smelling of locker

26

rooms and chalk dust and fried okra and greens, tobacco dried in linking rings on the tile floor.

I went to a public school, which probably goes without saying, since my father, who'd gone to Dartmouth, marched with Dr. King, sat in at a Greensboro lunch counter, and settled South only to marry Momma, who'd been shopping, right through the sit-in, at the Greensboro Woolworth's. My father believed in what he called The Enunciation, and clung to precise, Dartmouth-man diction like a lifeline, like if he let one "g" go unsounded, he might be sucked whole, quicksanded into the slurred Southern culture around him. "What I'm saying," my father pronounced, "is quite simply that no child of mine will be part of any white flight to the monochrome elitism of private schools."

But there were no blacks on Pisgah Ridge, in the town or the schools, public or private. Sure, there were the ones who cleaned our houses and mowed our lawns, but they all left on the last bus every evening down to their homes in the Valley. And they knew enough to never miss that ride down.

Yet here in my fifteenth summer was Farsanna and the Moulavi family come to our Ridge, plain as Pete, just smiling, polite.

And all of us wondering if they knew they'd broken the rules.

Even after school let out for the summer, my having walked away from the water fountain — the new girl left standing alone, her and brown spit — kept me uneasy. So maybe, then, it was guilt that made me bang on the back of Emerson's truck cab several weeks later, asking him to stop at the new girl's. Or maybe I was just too hot to think straight.

The Moulavis' house sat on our mountain's main road. The house — more of a box — was more painfully ugly than just nondescript, and I was cringing all over as we drove by. I saw the new girl staring out a plate-glass window onto a lawn where red clay showed through the grass like worn spots in old carpet. So from my usual spot in the pickup bed, nestled among boys, shovels, and mulch, I thumped on the cab's glass.

"Hey, stop! Turn around, Em."

Emerson stuck his head out the driver's-side window without pulling over. "How come? You forget the cooler again?"

"No. Just saw the new girl back there in the window. She looked hot."

"You know anybody in town who's not?"

28

"But, come on, that yard — you see it?"

"Yeah? So what?"

"So it's . . ." I reached for something he'd tap his brakes for, "it's like the scorched plain in Dante's *Inferno*." I'd not read the *Inferno* — only skimmed the back jacket, which I'd reckoned was plenty — but I was guessing Emerson secretly had. I'd recently found our father's college copy, not at all dusty, behind Em's dirty clothes hamper. Me, I'd devoted my summer to the Brontës.

Emerson and I came from a family of readers. But my brother billed himself as a bona fide jock and hid books, old poetry mostly, in issues of *Sports Illustrated*, like Pisgah's drugstore wrapped *Playboy* in brown paper. No kid sister was going to blow his cover in front of his friends.

"The what?" he yelled back. "In who's where?"

"Nothing. You reckon she'd want to come with us?" I called.

Em likely hadn't thought to form an opinion one way or another, which naturally argued for ignoring his sister. He opened his mouth to say so.

But Jimbo stopped his strumming on "ye saints of the Lord," and spoke up. "Oh, go ahead. Stop," he called up to Emerson.

"Why?"

"Why the howlin' hole not?" Jimbo said, with a lopsided smile, because there were plenty of reasons why not, and we all knew it.

Emerson must have decided it was too hot to oppose his best friend, or to avoid appeasing his sister, so he U-turned back to the Moulavis' house.

I poked my head around from the truck bed to the driver's-side window. "Em, you can be real nice when you want."

"Go jump," my brother told me.

"I love you too, Emerson, hon."

The house itself, a small, red brick warehouse affair, was a rectangle — and so was the front plate-glass window and the narrow, pine veneer door and the little plot of seared, treeless lawn — all of the rectangles sharp-sided and bare.

The bed of the pickup held Jimbo and me and my cousin L. J., the pack's resident genius, and Bobby Welpler, whose daddy walked out years ago but whose momma still sometimes showed up for Bobby at their trailer home. The boys kept the back of the truck full up with talk they traded like baseball cards, all about girls and cars and sports, and more girls. They curbed their comments not at all for my sake.

"You're not much of a girl," Emerson

explained to me once, "as girls go." Which I reckon he meant as high praise.

But when Emerson's pickup rattled into the Moulavis' straight-gravel drive, all the swaggering talk suddenly — too suddenly — hushed. We watched the new girl, wearing a long-sleeved blouse with a high neck even in this broiling heat, and a long red cotton skirt that fell to her feet, emerge from the box. A black and white spotted dog, not much more than a pup, sat at her feet and she crouched to pet him. The dog, a not-very-lucky toss of genetic dice, had the gangly black legs of a Lab and the long, silky ears of a Springer Spaniel, and his nose bobbed up and down as he wagged, like his head had to agree with his tail on being just real glad to see you.

Bobby Welpler — we called him Welp — shook his head as Farsanna began approaching the truck. The stick he'd been whittling snapped clean in two. "Y'all can't be thinking of taking her with us. *Can you?*" He raised his voice. "She don't need to be coming with us. Y'all gone crazy on me?"

Jimbo put his index finger up to Welp's lips. "Cork yourself, Welp. You're bordering on sounding unneighborly. And put that knife away before you go shishkabobbing somebody."

Emerson looked back through the cab window. "Girl's got a dog," he said, like that was some kind of powerful argument either way.

Truth was, I don't remember much caring one way or another, and then coming to think of Jimbo's grinning at her that time by the fountain, and her following me with those way-too-black eyes when I left her alone and walked on off down the hall, I was starting to wish I'd kept my mouth shut about stopping the truck. But I'd have had my nose crocheted shut before I'd been caught siding with Welp.

Jimbo reached for my hand and squeezed it. "Go ahead, Turtle. You got a bead here on the right thing to do. So you shoot."

I no longer much wanted to shoot, but it was Jimbo asking me to, and there wasn't anything much short of illegal — and maybe a good bit of that — I wouldn't have done for Jimbo.

I made the new girl the offer from where I sat — it was too hot to get out of the truck or stand. "We're going four-wheeling and swimming at the Blue Hole." It wasn't much of an invitation — or an apology either. "Wanna come?" I threw in to be clear, since her English wasn't so good.

She nodded, but didn't move for the

truck. Instead, she went on scratching the dog behind his long, silky ears.

She looked over the boys, one at a time, first Emerson, nodding to her from the driver's seat, then Jimbo, who waved, then L. J. who nodded, then Welp, who huddled down into himself, his arms crossed.

Em swung his legs out of the cab and walked toward Farsanna. "That your pup?"

Farsanna shook her head no. "A lost."

"Stray," L. J. corrected from the truck bed. Correcting was what L. J. did best — or if not best, at least a whole lot.

"However, I gave to him food this week. Now he sleeps there," she pointed, "beside the door."

Emerson knelt beside the new girl to stroke the dog's head. "Reckon he's yours now." He stood. "You know, he can come too, if you'd like. Big Dog — she's mine in the truck — never misses a trip to the Hole."

She thought about this as she rose. "Thank you. But he is most safe here. Do you think?"

Then she stepped toward me. "I have nothing for the swimming. Would these," she nodded down at her clothes, "be to this place acceptable?"

I could smell curry and onions on her breath — or maybe it just reeked from the house — from where I sat in the truck bed, and could feel the boys' eyes all on me — all of us wondering in what sort of world a person eats curry in her own home smack in the middle of the day, and owns not one single swimsuit.

But this was how I came back: "Why, shoot, nobody'll notice."

It was what Momma would have said — I wouldn't know about Jesus — and it wasn't even remotely true.

She cocked her head at me, like she was deciding whether to peek around the curtain of what I'd said to see whatever really sat behind it.

"You will follow me?" she asked, already retracing her steps back up the chipped sidewalk to the front door.

"Inside?" I looked from one of the boys to the next, hoping one of them would explain why I couldn't possibly go inside with the new girl. They studied the bed of the truck. All except Jimbo, who grinned and stood to offer me a hand to help me out of the truck.

I followed Farsanna in and saw a woman standing at the kitchen sink looking out the back window. She did not turn as I slunk barefoot after Farsanna through the living room, unfurnished except for a small, shabby couch.

Perhaps it was the sight of her mother's headscarf, covering her wrists and ankles in addition to the top of her head, that reminded Farsanna to glance back at me — me and my cutoffs, my dirty bare feet and stork-skinny legs and tank top. She held up a hand for me to wait by the door.

I watched Farsanna approach her mother from behind, lay a hand gently on each of her mother's shoulders, and kiss the back of the headscarf. Her mother turned then, one hand reaching to stroke her daughter's hair. Then both hands cupped the curve of Farsanna's jaw. Their foreheads touched, and the two stood like that for a moment. Their touches had spoken so clearly, I was a little startled when the mother said something I couldn't make out.

Farsanna answered in English, mostly. "I am with —" she glanced over her shoulder, "with a girl from the school, *Mata.*"

The mother's hands went to Farsanna's eyes, feeling their shape. The mother faced in my direction and said something.

Farsanna shook her head. "Yes, she is there at the door. What? In English, *Mata.* You know he wishes for us to speak in English, no? You know he wishes for me to know friends of my same years."

Farsanna's mother took two steps in my

direction, her body pitching heavily to the right as she swung her left leg forward. Holding one hand before her, she groped for the kitchen door frame and stopped there, still facing in my direction. Though I'd no idea what she could see of me. Me and my cutoffs.

Smoothing her mother's headscarf, Farsanna kissed her mother on both cheeks. "You will not weary yourself this day, no? What? Yes. I will. Safely, yes, *Mata.*"

Not sure if I should speak at all, I waved good-bye, then dropped my hand. Who knows if she could see me? I backed into the pine veneer rectangle of a door, and into the outside.

"Thank you," I mumbled from the front stoop, then added louder, "ma'am," because even if the Moulavis were odd, and not just their color of skin, and even if my stomach was flapjacking over onto itself, I'd not been raised by a pack of wolves.

I waited until Farsanna pulled the pine veneer back into place — or as much as it shut, its having warped out of alignment with the door frame. "So," I said as we walked toward the truck. I made sure my voice had a casual shrug to it. "So she . . ." I stopped there, a little stumped, wondering how Momma would've asked about how come Mrs. Moulavi limped, or whether or not she could see or hear like regular folks. "She . . . ?"

Farsanna knelt to scratch the stray dog behind his ears, then looked me dead in the eye. "She did not wish it, to go away from her home. She does not wish for her daughter to cease in wearing a hijab." She swept her arms over her head and I gathered she meant the scarf. "She does not wish to speak English or Sinhala, the languages of business in our ho— in Sri Lanka. Rather, she wishes to speak only in Tamil. She has," Farsanna glanced away from me toward the trees as she felt for the word, "fear."

It was more than I'd asked for, and still didn't answer what I'd intended to ask. I tried again. "Is your momma, um, can she see?"

"She had sickness as a child. That made her see and walk not well. Although I think perhaps," she glanced my way quickly, "I think perhaps her fear makes it more."

The mutt licked Farsanna's hand and as she stroked the dog's ears, her eyes moved to the truck bed. "He likes me," she said, "no?"

I watched the new girl swing her leg out from under her red skirt — a brown leg, darker at the knee than the thigh, and darker still more at the calf. And I watched the boys watching the brown, or maybe the shape — I wouldn't know what boys see when they watch — of first one leg then the other, and not a one of them — Emerson or Jimbo or L. J. or Welp — able to talk. Except for Em to the stray: "You stay here, now. You hear? You be good."

Me, I had a spasm of wanting to stay put myself, of fear that tripped up my feet and made me wish desperately I could miss this one trip to the Blue Hole with our mangy pack and the new girl. Because I was beginning to think what a bad, what a truly remarkably bad idea this whole thing might be.

2. A Shot Over the Bow

We always relied on Jimbo when some occasion called for gallantry. Maybe it was his name — James Beauregard for the Civil War general on his momma's side — that made him seem like he was bowing when he smiled and shook your hand.

It was Jimbo who reached for Farsanna's arm — her having struggled to climb, what with her skirt, into the truck. She floated in with the balancing help of Bo's arm, one of her hands holding the side of that skirt like some dark Cinderella climbing into her coach. It occurred to me then, and not for the last time, I might not much like her.

"You're from," Jimbo kept hold of her hand to shake it, "somewhere — some island." He pumped her hand and let go.

"That is correct. If this would be India . . ." She flattened her right hand against the air and placed her left fist beside it, but stopped. "Probably you know where is Sri Lanka."

I doubt Jimbo Riggs passed a geography test in his life. Or if he had, it was only because the teachers all thought the same thing about Bo: "What a sugar." Jimbo nodded at the new girl — and then winked, like he'd just arrived back from the place, and it was a secret between them.

But I knew it wasn't just her. It wasn't that she was special so much, or singled out with his wink. That was Bo's way. That was all.

Emerson leaned out the left window of the truck cab to touch his hat, a filthy Boston Red Sox baseball cap he wore backwards and rarely ever removed, and Big Dog, who always rode shotgun, stuck her head out the right side and retriever-grinned and panted. Em put the truck into gear and pulled out, the tires spitting white dust and gravel. We settled ourselves down into the truck bed, taking some care — not too much — not to stretch our legs on flakes of mulch or manure. Welp sulked at scrub pine out over the sides of the truck bed.

Jimbo braced his feet against the tailgate. Because he'd slumped back onto his elbows, and because his Adidas were size 14, his stern stuck up as high as his bow, like a canoe. Bo rested the guitar on his chest and strummed from a nearly prone position.

The new girl seated herself in a right angle and then, multiplying right angles, folded her legs under her skirt and her arms over her chest, like she'd set up some sort of shield.

"Sri Lanka. The island nation," L. J. said, all smug, "formerly known as Ceylon." L. J. wore his disdainful smile, which seemed to scare the new girl a little: She started, and blinked. But I could have told her he meant nothing by it. Emerson, who'd camped out with him, swore L. J. even slept with a disdainful smile. It was as part of his face as the slope of his nose. "Under British rule prior to its independence." Then he shrugged, like he could've reeled off major crops and annual rainfall too if he'd wanted.

I can speak ugly of L. J., his being kin. His daddy was my momma's brother, and L. J. was the oldest of his siblings, the smartest, and the least well-liked of four brothers: Matthew, Mark, Luke, and L. J. — born before his daddy got religion. Folks outside family avoided L. J., mostly because he made people nervous by saying what he thought when he thought it, like he'd been raised in New York.

"How are you finding the Ridge," L. J.

asked, "and its inhabitants?"

Farsanna's face registered nothing.

I'd seen that expression — the one that wasn't one, really — before. At least twice before. First, in front of the water fountain, brown spit at her feet, and then again later at a baseball game just before the school year had ended.

It was our last home game of the season, and Pisgah had the field in an inning that was whimpering to an end. Even the first baseman was yawning — that was Jimbo, his hair poking straight up from his head each time he whisked off his cap.

It was an afternoon game and they'd let us out early from classes to watch — sports being the primary purpose of Pisgah's schools. I'd attended sixth-period typing class less than a half dozen times that whole May, and still couldn't tap out *The red fox ran from the hound* without fumbling keys. I loved these afternoon games, if only for the view. At the far end of the ball field, hemlocks sawtoothed into blue sky, and off in the distance, the haze of more mountain ridges. From the trunk-skirts of those hemlocks, the earth drops three thousand feet to a ribbon of river called the French Broad. Emerson was a Red Sox fan, and rabid — I've learned now in Boston that all of them are — and he liked to think of that line of hemlocks as our own Fenway Green Monster. He'd once whacked a ball through it, during a high-tension ninth inning. Sometimes on rainy days in the porch hammock, Em and Jimbo and I would make up stories about just where that ball had floated by now.

"The ball washed ashore," I once suggested from deep in the hammock, "near Highlands, at the dock of a house on Lake Toxaway." Highlands and Toxaway, we'd heard, catered to tourists from outside the South, served hash browns and unsweetened tea, and, unthinkably, sold no local newspaper but only the *New York Times.*

Bo, sprawled full length on the wide white planks of the porch and popping peanuts into his Coke, lifted his head. "What then, Turtlest?" In the big wicker chair, Em paused in picking out "Dueling Banjos" on his guitar, and waited for me to decide.

"Well . . . the lake house belonged to . . . let's see . . . to Bucky Dent."

Em spit violently to the side.

"Remind me," Bo asked, too innocently, "who that was."

"The Yankees' shortstop," I told him, "who hit the three-run homer last year during a tiebreaker and won the game *and* the American League pennant for New York. Remember? And prolonged the Curse."

Emerson hurled a handful of peanuts at me. "C'mon, Turtle. Bo watched the game with us. He just enjoys seeing me suffer. So go on with your story."

"So Bucky Dent picked up the ball," I continued, "just to see, and it was still so hot from Em's hit that the ball burned the man's hands."

Em considered this hopefully. "How badly?"

"So badly he fell to his knees in unspeakable pain, and in his agony, begged forgiveness for his sins, especially his playing for New York, and pledged an everlasting oath of allegiance to the Red Sox."

Satisfied, Em sighed and Bo, grinning, popped more peanuts into his Coke.

Jimbo lifted his Coke in a toast. "Revenge and repentance go real nice together."

But that particular afternoon at the ball field, I sat on the bleachers with L. J. and Welp while Jimbo and Em played ball. I was sucking in deep the scent of the mountains, like incense maybe for people who pray. I was basking, too, in the glory — if only reflected — of having a brother and a brother's best friend star on the team. They

44

were mine: my Emerson, my Jimbo, and I roused myself between snow cones to make that clear, their being mine, by clapping extra and calling their names that I shortened for show — because they were mine and I could: *One more, Em, one more! 'Atta boy, Bo, 'atta boy!*

Above me in the bleachers, I noticed Jimbo's daddy. He sat there sunk deep into rolls of dark suit, there in full sun. He was sweating into his necktie, a wide, faded yellow triangular flag hanging limply, wearily, from his neck as if it were begging to be relieved of its duty. Reverend Riggs, his round face made rounder still by a balding blond head, resembled his son in nothing but the dimples. And unlike his son's impish green glint, Reverend Riggs' pale blue eyes above round-apple cheeks always looked eager — even desperate — to please. He waved to me tentatively. Come to think of it, Reverend Riggs always waved tentatively, as if he were asking permission to say hello.

When I turned back to the field, Jimbo was tipping his catcher's mask to his daddy. I wondered if Bo saw in his daddy what everyone else did: the colorlessness that defined the man — his washed-out eyes, and worn-out yellow and off-white of his skin, his ties, his hair. The way neither his flesh nor his thoughts seemed to take on a firm substance, never seemed to push back against whatever happened to poke into him.

But Jimbo adored his daddy, and we all adored Jimbo, so I made a habit of stealing glances at the Reverend whenever I could, hoping to see whatever Jimbo saw there. Once again this day, though, I could see nothing much but that yellow triangular flag of a tie.

Sitting beside me, L. J. was scowling into a calculus textbook — the first time our school ever offered the class, and only because L. J. insisted. It had to be hard for a boy to be clumsy and stringy and smart in a school that cared nothing for schooling. He sat in that heat, the sweat on his nose making a slide for his glasses, him pushing the horn-rims back into place once a page.

Beside L. J. was little Welp, who'd never been smart or athletic or cute. Like always that year, he'd gone out for the team — he'd puppied after Emerson and Jimbo since we were all small. But he'd not made even the first cut, and muttered all through every game I remember about how the coach didn't like him, had something against him, that life was unfair. And sometimes when he thought no one was paying attention to him — we rarely were — he'd fuss over how maybe if he'd had a dad to defend him, or even a mom, a mom who was sober . . .

In fact, it was Welp, occupied with carving "Bobby" into the chocolate top of his Snickers bar with his pocketknife, who first noticed when the new girl came walking alone toward the bleachers.

"Well," he said through a mouth full of Snickers, "who let the black panther out of her cage?"

"Shut up, Welp," L. J. and I said together, without looking at him. Welp was the sort you learned to handle that way.

But he got a good flutter and flap from the gaggle of girls sitting down the bleachers from us. They were the Miss Pisgah types, with Neesa Nell Helms as their leader, their hair in identically angled Farrah Fawcett swoops they recurled and resprayed between classes. Here in the bleachers, deprived of mirrors and plugs, they calmed themselves with strawberry lipgloss they passed like a pipe.

The girls turned and looked at Bobby and laughed, even as we all watched the new girl approach.

"Where do you s'pose she thinks she'll sit?" Neesa asked, with her volume cranked up to full. "I'd real gladly let her sit here —

47

except for my having a nose." She sniffed high in the air then, and crinkled her face.

Passing behind home plate, the new girl paused, like she was watching the game for real, and not just stalling for time because she had no place to sit.

"I don't reckon they learn them to shower in . . ." Hayley Neal held up her palm and one fist, "wherever the place is she comes from."

"My folks say," another one offered, "her kind's got overdeveloped glands of some sort, bless their hearts. Been proved. Our yard man's so bad you can't hardly stand close enough to give him instructions."

Hayley squealed. "Look, Neesa. Emerson Maynard's staring at you again, I'm swearing. I been saying he likes you."

Neesa's eyes sliced back to me. "Lands, who could tell that all the way from left field?"

Hayley Neal must've forgotten Em's kid sister two rows behind to bear witness. Or maybe she'd calculated, like most every other girl at our school, on my not much counting. "Lord, Neesa, *look!* I'm swearin', I swear I'm swearin'!"

I gave them both glowers of utter disgust meant to slay them right there on the spot. But they lived. Lived, and even flipped on

Hayley's transistor. Three Dog Night crooned from her purse: *The ink is black, the page is white, together we learn to read and wr— .* Hayley wrinkled her nose, and she shut the thing off.

"I swan," Neesa was broadcasting, "I do believe Jimbo Riggs is the one staring this way. At *you,* Hayley Neal. You know, I sure see what you mean: He *is* awful cute."

The bill of Bo's cap ticked toward us, but then back over the plate — someone was at bat.

Hayley played at gasping and smacking her friend. "You hush, Neesa, or I won't tell you nothing, not ever again."

Neesa Nell held her hand out, arm straight, for the lip-gloss, and then stiffened, like a pointer back onto her prey: All she lacked was a tail. "Don't look now, girls, but *somebody's* coming. Hold your breath, ladies."

The new girl had to have heard this. From that distance, she couldn't have missed it — *no one's* English is that bad.

But on she came, the new girl did, like she'd take us all out in one fast punch from those eyes. She walked straight up to where the Miss Pisgahs huddled. And sat down.

They were so stunned — we all were — that nobody spoke. L. J. even shut his

49

calculus book and made a point of cleaning his glasses, like he didn't want to miss anything. The girls cut their eyes right and left at each other, shredding the air between them. But Farsanna Moulavi sat still, right there in the tatters of silence.

In fact, she sat still through the end of that inning and the whole limping next one and into the last. Then she rose, not hurried, not one little bit, looked slowly around her, those eyes looking short-fused and burning — then descended the bleachers.

I wondered when they'd go off, those eyes, and blow us all clear off the Ridge and down the French Broad. Never seen anything like it myself, the new girl's way of behaving. It was like she'd had the great gate of teenage social approval clanged shut in her face — and in public. And yet she'd walked away from it all in one piece. Even defiant.

Me, I couldn't help but like her a little — a *little* — for that, even if she was strange like they said, like I'd seen for myself.

A *kethunk, kethunk* behind me signaled Reverend Riggs making his way down from the bleachers one step at a time, his spherical body balanced, just barely, on each metal step. His head was bobbing in Bo's direction, both arms already beginning to rise as if he could hug his son clear through the fencing that guarded home plate.

Farsanna had stopped walking just around the back of home plate which Jimbo had just crossed for our final run. She stood still, Jimbo turning toward her. He grinned.

"Good game," he said to the new girl.

Her back to me, I couldn't see her expression, only that her head cocked, unsure maybe what Jimbo meant, his words or his grin. I could see that she nodded, and walked on.

The *kethunk* behind me had ceased, Reverend Riggs' round body motionless there on the third-to-last bleacher step. Perspiring from his balding blond head down into his yellow necktie, he was watching his son, who was watching the new girl walk away from the field. Reverend Riggs' eyebrows crinkled together over the bridge of his nose.

So there we sat in the back of Em's truck, and there came that look of the new girl's again, her eyes swinging to L. J., who never much liked repeating himself but was saying again, "Are you currently finding the Ridge at least marginally inhabitable?"

She stared at him hard, her eyes stickpinning him onto the side of the truck till he squirmed, a stabbed bug with glasses.

When she finally responded, he got only

51

this: "My father says it will be to us a hospitable place, no?"

Silence followed — jarring silence, like potholes in paved road.

"It's, um," I tried, thinking of Momma, "what we're known for. Hospitality. That's us. The South."

Jimbo helped me from there. "Hospitality," he assured the new girl, "and charm out the wazoo. And, as you can see for yourself," the sweep of his arm included us all, as well as the landscaping mulch and manure we were hauling, "cleanliness-next-to-godliness and golly-gorgeous good looks."

Farsanna cocked her head at him as if she were deciding whether Jimbo's charm could be trusted. "We have," she said at last, "for many years dreamt about America. Of coming here one day."

"Here?" L. J. blurted out rudely. He'd always had trouble respecting anyone who tolerated our town. He was certain he'd been misplaced at birth, he'd once confided in me: Though raised in a green vinyl-sided split-level on Pisgah, he was surely conceived someplace else, by someone else, on the city wall of Jerusalem, maybe, by vacationing foreign diplomats, unmarried, stationed in Nepal. He kept gaping at the new

girl. "Dreamt of coming *here?*"

"In America, it is everywhere the land of opportunity, my father says." Farsanna looked around then, unsure of herself, unsure of us, like she'd covered herself in a coat she could tell didn't fit.

L. J.'s sneer had sunk, if possible, deeper. "Yeah? 'Bring me your tired, your poor, your naive, huddled masses . . .' So, what else does your father say?"

Farsanna raised her chin, but her eyes tipped, unsteady. Her voice bunched into clumps. " 'It is the . . . end . . . of the rainbow,' he likes to say," she told L. J. — though she seemed not to like saying it herself.

Despite the blow of her saying she liked our town, L. J. granted the new girl another chance. She was after all someone who had seen the world, seen something beyond the too-warm, maternal arms of our mountain.

"Why don't you relate pertinent facts about your home?" he suggested.

Rising from the floorboards of the pickup bed, Farsanna's line of vision leveled out with his. "This now is home," she said. And then tried it again, like she was convincing herself, or trying: "*This* now is home."

L. J.'s sneer dug itself into a scowl. He sat back. I could always read L. J.'s face —

most everyone could. It was a shame, he was thinking: He knew little about that part of the world, and he might've added it to his Places to Visit Real Soon. Just as Real Soon, our mangy pack knew, as he could break the news to his father, *the* owner of Waymon's Feed and Seed (known in three counties), about not sticking around to inherit that millstone of a family business.

Then L. J. leaned forward, across Jimbo's body-canoe, nearly in the new girl's face. "Does anybody peruse, oh, I don't know, any, say, American *history* books in Sri Lanka? Or the newspapers, perhaps? Anybody inform your family they were relocating to the *South* end of the rainbow?"

Little Bobby Welpler yipped in with "Pisgah Ridge, North Carolina: Pot of Gold, USA."

"Sure," L. J. shot back, "*White* Gold."

With his left elbow, Jimbo rammed L. J.'s chest back against the pickup's metal wall. "I hope . . ." he interjected, "*we* hope you like it here." He reached over to pat Farsanna's forearm, adding, "Welcome." Then his arm stretched back over his head through the truck cab window to scratch the Big Dog on her remarkably chubby neck.

We rode for awhile without the social padding of chatter and none of us liked it, not

54

a one of us able to find a comfortable place to set down our legs or our eyes. But the pickup's bucking over the root-clogged trail down to the Hole gradually knocked loose our tongues. Or maybe it was just approaching the Blue Hole itself.

Little Bobby Welpler, of all people, saved us that day with his forgettable blather. We laughed with him and at him — and he laughed some too. Even Farsanna joined in once or twice, that iron spine of hers melting almost soft.

In the Clearing — our clever name for it — just before the logging trail funneled to a single-file path, Emerson pulled alongside a cluster of other pickups and Jeeps. He was blocking in at least three, and we'd soon be blocked in by others. But no matter: Everyone left their windows rolled down and their keys on the seat, and shuffled each other as needed.

We scrambled out from the truck bed, Bobby Welpler hitting the ground before Emerson put it in park. Propping Em's guitar against bags of manure, Jimbo turned back to offer a hand to Farsanna, but she'd already lowered her skirt and herself to the ground.

Her eyes weren't on Jimbo anyhow. She was watching the truck that had pulled in behind us.

From out of the driver's side, Mort Beck-with unpacked his beefy self, sinewed and bunched tight at the shoulders and thighs. I sometimes wondered if, raw, Mort would look nice and marbled like Momma'd taught me to look for in meat.

Ducking his head, he reached back into his truck.

Jimbo had turned to watch him. "Howdy there, Morton. Top o' the evening to you."

Mort reversed himself slowly, a riverboat paddle wheeler changing direction. When he'd fully backed himself out of the front seat, he spit to one side, then: "Howdy, Bo."

I followed the new girl's eyes to the gun, a .22-caliber rifle which Mort twirled under one arm like a baton: the beefiest majorette ever to spin a stick.

"It's okay," I whispered fast to Farsanna. "He doesn't mean anything by it. Mort car-ried a GI Joe doll till he was seven and his older brother — the Beckwiths are every one of them bullies — called him a pansy. Very next day, Mort was carting that gun, and every day since, like Linus's blanket. For all we know he sleeps with the thing. He'd take it to school if it'd fit in his gym bag."

Jimbo had pulled back from the path at

the opposite side of the Clearing and was making his way closer to Morton.

"How 'bout you snuggle that gun there back in the saddlebags where she'll be warm?"

"Her name's Jemima." Mort spit again, aiming to bull's-eye the same circle of brown he'd made before.

"Look, Morton Man, it ain't hunting season for deer, dove, or platypus, that I heard. So how 'bout you just put her on up."

Mort hauled himself up on the hood of his truck. He fondled the gun. "Only wish I could do that there thing, Bo. But she's been hankerin' for a good cleaning. You don't want to let things go getting too dirty on you." Mort's eyes might have been on Farsanna, or might have been just generally back on the woods.

"You just make sure for certain," Jimbo said, trying to sound unconcerned, "that you recollect where they put the safety on those things, you hear?"

Mort ran his hand down the butt of the gun and he spit again to one side. I turned my back to him too and followed Jimbo toward the head of the path.

The late-afternoon heat had gone violet and soft — because of our day jobs, we almost always arrived at the Blue Hole at the tail end of the afternoon — and I watched the ends of Jimbo's black hair flip at the back of his neck in curls that looked soft, like they needed someone to wrap her fingers inside them.

We started to maze our way among the parked Jeeps and trucks, toward the path that led toward the Blue Hole. No breeze granted relief, or at least the trees that circled the clearing had blocked it, and a Southern summer day settled like wet gauze on our skin.

Then the air around us split open, ripped by the sound of what Mort said with a flick of his trigger finger, our bodies knocked flat with a blast from behind.

3. HOLY OF HOLES

Jimbo was the first to raise his head from the ground. "*MORT!* You *idiot!* You could have killed somebody with that little display!"

"Killed?" Mort chewed on that for awhile, along with his tobacco.

"Look, you got something to say, you say it! With your own big mouth and not some long-barreled excuse for a brain."

Mort ratcheted the safety into place. "Reckon ever'body slips up sometime or another. I didn't scare nobody, did I? Grace of God I didn't shoot none of y'all."

Jimbo climbed to his feet and offered his hand to Farsanna. "Grace of God's got some kind of kick to it."

I could see Farsanna was trembling.

But then, we all were.

Mort was still propped where he'd arranged himself on the hood of his truck, and had flipped his .22 to peer down into

59

the barrel, like he might find inside it what he wanted to say.

The boys, all except Welp, approached Mort and the upturned mouth of his gun. Welp slumped off to the side.

"Beckwith, you *jerk* —" I could hear Emerson start in, but Jimbo motioned for him to lower his voice.

That left Farsanna to me. "Well," I said, "I reckon accidents happen." I had no earthly idea if I was telling the truth, and the truth was beside the point just then. "And you gotta know that had nothing to do with you." I could see from her eyes that consolation was a mistake, that it might not have occurred to her to think the shot *could* be about her. And now I'd put the idea in her head.

The boys walked back to where we stood, none of them, Emerson or Jimbo or L. J., looking too much at ease, and L. J. was all but staggering, his glasses perched cockeyed and low on his nose. Bobby Welpler tagged behind.

Jimbo must've caught the new question on Farsanna's face. "Reckon it wasn't too much on purpose, as much as a Beckwith ever purposes anything much," he told her. "Don't reckon that old son of a swamp sucker was aiming to hurt anybody. Mort's too mean to let life alone, and too soft to much injure it up. He's just expressing his views."

What the new girl made of that, I couldn't say.

We now had nothing to do but walk on — a little closer to each other than we might have done ten minutes before — like we knew now what we hadn't before: that we were moving somewhere underneath a bullet's spiraling run, or inside whatever kind of grace explodes and leaves you seeing things for what they are but hoped they weren't.

From the Clearing, the footpath to the Blue Hole threaded through boulders in a slow descent and then, without warning, tilted cliff-steep almost, tumbling hikers into a slide from tree to tree and rock to rock. Every summer, we'd dared each other to run down it and we'd later signed each other's plaster casts.

At the top of the tilt, last in line behind me and the boys, the new girl studied L. J.'s and Emerson's and Bobby Welpler's descents.

I kicked off my flip-flops. "Here's where the shoes come off," I said to the new girl.

She looked from my bare feet to the

jumble of sneakers and sandals beside me to the vertical path, covered in root webs and rocks, that dropped like a slide from where we stood.

"It's what we do here," was how I explained.

But Jimbo wouldn't leave it at that. "Gotta go barefoot on holy ground," was how he tried to make it make sense. Stomping on his sneaker heels to remove them, he flung them with a swift kick over his head to the heap of unclean shoes behind him.

The new girl just stared at the drop, then back up the path to the Clearing.

I could guess what she was thinking, that her choices just then both looked pretty bleak: to return up the path where a gun might go off any minute, or go forward, where the path fell away now in a nearly ninety-degree angle. So I tried to help. "Now don't be letting Mort Beckwith bother you any, him and his toys. He's always pointing that thing at whatever's smart enough to look scared. He's harmless, though."

Jimbo had fallen in beside me. "Ain't none of us harmless," he said — like that was helpful somehow.

So I pointed down at Bo's huge feet, for something to say. "How in heaven's name do you run on those things?"

"Turtle, you wound me. You don't reckon the glass slipper'll fit when my prince comes someday?"

"Glass-bottom boat, maybe. One for each foot."

He grinned at me before starting down and then, holding a towel out to the new girl, glanced back over his shoulder at her. "You all dine and fandy?"

"Fine and dandy," I translated without looking at her, and gave back Bo's smile.

And my heart pinged in my chest, an engine all off rhythm, when he reached one arm back to pat the back of my calf.

Farsanna accepted the towel Bo held out to her, but shook her head at his offer: "Haul on down beside me if you're feeling scared."

"This," she said, "I can do by myself."

Which, I had to admit, was a point in her favor. And that was with her still a little shaky from the gun going off.

Jimbo flashed her the dimple that said *that* was the right answer.

But I wasn't missing the chance to get the jump on Jimbo's getting his usual jump on me. "In that case," I said to them both, "Geronimo-o-o!" And I flung myself on my backside before I'd finished the word.

The proper, and unused, path down to the Blue Hole wound slowly, switching back on itself to avoid erosion. But the one we all took threaded straight through the trees and the outcroppings of rock, the course always slick with a carpet of leaves and loose soil. From the top, a good eighty yards up, just before the path tipped into descent, hemlocks and oaks blocked any view of the water below. But even from high up above, even if you weren't listening for it, you could hear the rumble and rush of the stream that fed into the Hole. On a hot summer's day, the mere sound of the stream spoke coolness and mercy, pulled on us, tumbling, helpless, to where the water pooled for us, waiting.

Well into my slide, I slammed feet-first into an old yellow poplar on the way down, and Bo rolled in next and, shoulder first, hit the boulder before me. We crashed and careened the next several lengths of the path, Jimbo cursing me and my future offspring all the way down. We landed in the usual heap, bruised in the usual places, at the mud beach on the north bank, where the stream indulged itself with a final flourish of small waterfall before becoming the Blue Hole. Panting, we rolled on our backs to watch the new girl, sliding — stiffly, of course — on the towel, her long red cotton skirt tucked around her ankles as she descended.

I clapped a couple of times for her. Then, noticing the sweat blossoms flowering on my tank top, I began shedding my clothes down to my suit.

Still on his back, Jimbo made the baseball referee's sign for an out in the new girl's direction. "Disqualified!"

"What?" I laughed at him.

"We can't be allowing that kind of behavior. Look at her."

I looked at her. "What about her?"

"Way too smooth and clean. What would it lead to if we all did it that way?"

The new girl levitated to her feet without the use of her hands, and dusted off her skirt, which was not anywhere dirty from what I could tell. And I came close to saying, disgusted, how behavior like this — this princess act — wouldn't likely turn Em's truck into a pumpkin, or a proper coach, either.

Her gaze swung out toward the Hole, whose clay sides and black bottom silt had been churned up all day, suspended now in water that was deep rusty brown. Granite boulders rimmed the pond, and mountain laurel and hemlock provided shade like umbrellas at street cafes: The Blue Hole was a study in greens and grays and browns and rust-reds, with round punctures of pink where rhododendron blooms still hung on to life, badly wilting.

I followed Farsanna's eyes. "Okay, so nothing here at the Blue Hole's blue except sky. It was never officially named, really," I told her. "We just call it that."

She examined the scene. "There are many crocodiles here — or no?"

I laughed at her, laughed out loud at the thought: a croc slithering out from under a pink rhododendron. "We get a water moccasin every once in a while — and nobody tells their mommas. That's rule number one. And we get mosquitoes as big as a baby's fist. They attack in a swarm, like the moccasins will. But just make sure you look where you land when you jump in, and you'll be all right. *Before* you jump in." I waited for her to go big-eyed or back away from the edge.

But she nodded, taking it in, not even rattled. I couldn't help but like that about her. Bo saw it too. His head swung around with interest at her not squealing or acting squeamish. She had just earned herself points.

"So," I asked, "does this look anything like

where you come from?"

She glanced down at her toes, already sunk into the red clay that lined the banks of the Blue Hole. "In Sri Lanka, there is sand, beautiful sand, gold, and some brown, the color of king coconuts in my country. The color of . . ." She paused, searching for a more local example. Her gaze resting on me, she brightened. "Yes, the color of Shelby's hair. Like this, the sand of Sri Lanka is beautiful."

Jimbo winked at me.

"You see," I told him, while pretending to pat my wheat-sheaf of ponytail into place, "I have one friend in this world."

Farsanna was inspecting the scene before her. "Who discovered it the first, this place?"

Discovered it? I raised both eyebrows at Jimbo, who took up the question.

"Well now, I don't reckon nobody first discovers a place like this. You just know about it. Or don't. Average folks don't. And most folks are average." He winked at her. "You got to have someone show you the way."

"What if," her head came up then, like she was trying to keep a bead of sweat from falling off the end of her chin, "I had come by myself here?"

Jimbo, who was struggling to strip off his

landscaping khakis without losing his swim trunks beneath them, paused for a moment to consider the question. He held out his hand to Farsanna. "Then I reckon you wouldn't be our honored guest."

She examined his face. And then smiled.

I don't suppose I'd seen her smile before, not a real one — maybe she hadn't smiled since she'd moved to the Ridge. It was strange, that smile, and slow coming. Like a dark wave that swells and then crests, and splashes everything in its path. Her smile had that splash to it, whether or not I'd been looking to like her.

It took me a minute to recover from the force of that smile. And maybe Jimbo a minute longer, or two. But I tried not to let this nettle me much, since Bo was a man, or almost, and they're all weak, Momma said: the first lesson every Southern momma teaches her girls, just before the Why We Let a Man Think He's Won.

So I ignored Bo and took charge myself. "Follow me."

I led the way, a half-circle around the pond, leaping boulder to boulder, to where Emerson and the other boys had spread out their towels. We joined them out on the palm of our favorite rock, which could cup us all in close.

As usual, the games had already begun for the doctors' and lawyers' and CPAs' kids who didn't work in the summers. Between Em and Jimbo's landscaping and L. J.'s daddy's Feed and Seed, our mangy pack rarely arrived during the most miserable heat of the day.

Already well established for the day, then, were the rope swing competitions. Boys from all over Pisgah Ridge conducted wild contests of masculine prowess from the rope on the sweetgum tree. Scrambling up the scrap wood nailed to the trunk, the boys hurled themselves to the rope and down into the water from branches higher and higher.

"Be a man about it," they taunted each other.

"Put some hair on your chest!" they called out to the arc of an upside-down spin.

The day Farsanna first showed up with us, the banks of the Blue Hole were heavy with teenagers conducting the business of life from where they lay: long, lean bodies like big cats, stretching and sleeping and sunning and occasionally striking a particularly gorgeous pose for anyone who cared to admire. Farsanna Moulavi, walking last behind all of us, stepped from the shade of the hemlocks to a boulder soaked in full sun.

She was dark all right — no mistake about that. Even skin the color of homemade cocoa was dark for our Ridge. Her hair turned under in stiff, shiny waves, laying like uncoiled black licorice on her shoulders, glistening with the heat of the day. Beside her, I felt wan and anemic, like I'd been shipped from the factory without my final glaze and firing.

I remembered, there in the midst of admiring her, how just when you thought the world had gone still and soft, you could be blasted flat to the ground from behind.

More to comfort myself than because I believed it, I whispered to L. J. beside me as we watched the boys swing from the rope, "We're a good generation past . . . you know. Stuff. Right?" Farsanna had already approached the water, dipping her toes in, taking her time.

"Technically, more than one generation," he corrected, "depending on your denotation of 'stuff.' Assuming you're referring to *fatalities* on the Ridge. On the other hand, if you're alluding merely to life-*threatening* violence or legislation significant to racial discrimination —"

"Right. But fatalities, not so much. Lately.

70

So, there's no problem. Right?"

He cut his eyes at me. "Oh *sure,* Turtle. Right."

But I wasn't letting go of my comfort so quickly. "Times have changed, L. J. Right? Even here." I said this with confidence I had to concoct right there on the spot.

He grunted. "Sure, times have changed. Who's there to lynch on the Ridge nowadays? Only a Yankee or two."

I knew that was a jab at my father, of course, and at Mollybird Pittman, who spent twenty years in New York, then came home — but never was quite right after that. We knew all about her not being right, with all the trouble she gave us on a regular basis as we landscaped her yard. Seemed she brought back to the Ridge the kind of attitude New Yorkers were feared for, which she delivered now from under a straw hat encircled by phony red roses. She'd inherited the hat, as well as her house and acres of gardens, from an aunt who, like Mollybird, lived out her days alone on the Ridge.

"I'm just saying," I said.

L. J. turned that sneer on me. "Okay, Turtle." It was the voice he used for his baby brother, Luke. "I'm entirely certain you're entirely correct."

"Shut up, L. J.," I told him. Because I

agreed with him.

Determined to shake off my conversation with L. J., I hit the water at a dead run and, climbing out of the water, shifted my attention to the new girl.

"You can't just wade in," I said to her as I surfaced. "Even in this heat, the water's too cold."

But she had already begun edging in beside our hand-shaped boulder. She nodded toward the chicken fights, which happened regularly near the north beach of the hole. "I would drown, I believe."

"What? Oh, them. That's nothing — just a kind of . . . mating ritual here."

She studied them. "If you wish to join them, please, I have no —"

"Me? Shoot, I'm not —" I could have put her mind at ease by admitting I'd never once been asked to join in. But I left it only at this: "Don't worry about it."

Farsanna toe-stepped her way into the water, so cold it sometimes felt like it filleted the flesh clean off your bones. I sat on the rock, watching her closely. She never complained, or gasped even — and I had to give her credit for that. She edged in more and more, and as she submerged, I saw red bubbled up to her ribs.

For several seconds, I thought she'd been shot. Then I realized it was only the red cotton skirt. But it shook me a little that my mind had slipped there so fast.

And apparently, I wasn't the only one to notice her floating red skirt: The rubble of boys at the base of the sweetgum erupted. In the sweetgum that held up the rope swing, Mort Beckwith and Buddy Buncombe stopped trying to shoulder each other off their precarious perch. They both hung to a limb with one arm and stared.

"Hey, Turtle," Mort thundered. He must've dropped down the trail just after us. He stood there, his shirt off now, his gut-flesh gleaming white, not as heavily muscled as his arms or chest, and rounded out from his waist. There was no rifle holstered from his swim trunks or crooked under his arm, but I reckon I checked anyhow. I flipped on my back, floating, examining the blue circle of heaven above my head. Maybe if I ignored Mort, he'd go away. The sun impaled itself on a hemlock above my head.

"Hey, Turtle!" This time he had my attention — and everyone else's. "So, Turtle, what's that you brung with you? A black dog in a skirt?"

Buddy convulsed in laughter that looked

for all the world like seizures — he'd laughed like that since we were all little, and he'd scared the fifth-grade teacher Miss Buckshorn half into her grave.

All around the Blue Hole in ripples like a stone had been dropped at its center, I could sense bodies rolling up into sitting positions, everyone watching, waiting for me to respond. I could feel Jimbo's eyes on me. And Em's and L. J.'s. Not to mention Farsanna's. Even Welp watched me, and I knew without seeing just how he looked: his acne mottling still darker red as he smirked.

In the blue circle of heaven above my head, a long line of civil rights heroes marched before my eyes: Martin Luther King, Jr., and Rosa Parks and Marian Wright Edelman, and my father's voice describing the Greensboro Woolworth's lunch counter and my mother's asking sweetly, *Now Shelby Lenoir, what do we think Jesus would do?* But so far as I could tell, there was no *we* here — no me and Jesus or me and Martin or me and Momma.

Only me, floating. And wanting to weep for being unworthy of Bo's faith in me. I could feel him compelling me to speak: *Say something, Turtle. Say something.*

But I was that terrified child behind the steering wheel all over again and a truck

74

barreling down. I pretended that I'd heard nothing, and dove under the water.

By the time I'd resurfaced, Bo, at the base of the sweetgum, had crossed his arms over his chest and was shouting to the top of the tree. "You know, Mort, your white done bleached out your brain. And if you'd like to come down here so's I can say that to your face, I'd be happy to wait."

Balancing on his branch, Mort let his snarl crack open, just the tiniest bit. The Beckwiths were all as slow as they were surly, so Mort only changed expressions in jolts and jerks, like a car whose clutch has gone bad.

With a Tarzan yell, he swung by one arm from the rope, and was still whooping when the water swallowed him whole.

And then it was finished. The rope resumed its pendulum rhythm over our heads, and boys dropped into geysers of Blue Hole brown water. A chicken fight broke out near the mud beach's north end. Sunbathers rolled like pork on spits. And some rules got unraveled that day, there by the ragged hem of a pond.

I beached myself and crawled up to the granite palm. And I watched the Blue Hole, now with the sun almost completely below the rim of treetops, grow dim. Jimbo joined

75

me, but his eyes had drifted past me to the new girl, sitting off to the side. My chest ached with the clamor of too many words that wanted out now — *now* — when it was too late. I whispered into the deepening light, and not even to him, the only thing I knew for sure I believed: "I'm so sorry."

Still not looking at me, he slipped an arm around my shoulders and pulled me to him, just long enough for me to smell peanuts, and reach my fingers to the curls at the back of his neck. And then he was standing again.

I caught his hand and had lots I was going to say, all of it eloquent and heartfelt and stirring, beginning perhaps with *Forgive me for my silence? And can you make the new girl forgive me?* But a blowfish had found a home in my throat and sealed off my voice and my air.

Looking down at me for the first time, Jimbo squeezed my hand, and I knew it was absolution he was trying to give me. But I couldn't curl even one finger around it just then.

I sat still and alone and hardly able to breathe in my nearly airless vacuum of not-yet-forgiveness. The granite palm that had always been my favorite perch now felt cold and not sufficiently cupped, like I might be pitched headlong out into the dusk that had begun swelling around us.

Farsanna stayed in the water for longer than I would have guessed — seeing how cold the water always was, and its being her first time.

"Farsanna," I began slowly. "I ought to say . . ."

She looked back at me with that lack of expression I'd seen before. "My friends," she said, "call me Sanna."

I stood, the breath knocked clear out me, not knowing if she'd just accused me of not being her friend, or invited me in. I reached for her hand to help her out of the water. She ignored it, but nodded at me. "Call me Sanna," she said again, looking me in the eye.

She emerged from the water, her skirt all limp from her hips, and her blouse a good seven shades darker from the silt. She took the towel Emerson offered her and let him wrap it around her shoulders.

Em held his towel on the new girl's shoulders like it might slide to the ground if he didn't anchor it there with his own hands. I watched the Blue Hole watching Em, but my brother was focused on Farsanna's wet shoulders and didn't seem to notice or care.

He tipped his head close to hers, and then

allowed Farsanna to hold the towel for herself.

I wanted to shake Em. To rattle some sense back into my brother. To tell him how he was looking just then, and what people might think if he kept standing like that with the new girl. At the far side of the Hole was Mort Beckwith, watching it all. The right side of Mort's mouth was lifting back into a snarl.

I turned to Jimbo — he always knew what to say. Bo was watching the two of them too. But saying nothing. And not looking my way.

As we gathered our things to leave for the day, it seemed to me that murmurs rose from the banks of the hole in a tide all around us. But then it backwashed into flotsam, just a whisper or two, floating there, unmoored and harmless. So how bad could it have been? That's what I told myself every few feet of the way back out of the Hole: *How bad, how bad, how bad could it . . . ? Harmless, harmless, how bad?* I didn't look back to see if Mort was still watching. But I knew that he was.

4. Hog Wild

Extracting yourself up from the Blue Hole's hollow was always the trickiest part: Having finally been cool for the first time all day — maybe all week — you had to climb real slow, just below sweat-speed, back out of that bowl with the sides of slick clay and slate. Sanna examined us laboring up, hand on root over foot on rock, then swung herself into the steep. Once, maybe twice, but not more, she accepted the hands that Emerson and Jimbo both offered to help. Mostly, she climbed on her own, jerking that skirt out of the lift of each foot.

"That's right," I told her once, because she deserved some kind of praise, her climbing nearly as fast as I did and her in a long skirt. And her not taking the hands that the boys offered. I was liking her better.

At the top, I bent to retrieve my flip-flops, and still barefoot, I sprinted to the pickup, arriving first, beating L. J., who generally didn't think too highly of girls — which made it worth breaking a sweat again. We piled into the truck bed, all of us flesh-heavy and quiet, this time not caring whether or not we rested our legs on mulch and manure.

Emerson's truck bucked its way out of the woods and back onto paved roads.

Lifting his head a few inches from the metal floor, Jimbo was the first to trouble himself with talk. "Hot retching road kill, I can smell Steinberger's from here. Who's in?" He was our social chairman, in charge of judging when we might extend our play at the risk of missing the dinner our mothers had warned us to be home for.

L. J. cast his vote without stirring. "By all means, if you could refrain from unsavory allusions to maimed wild life, I'd say let's attend to digestive demands. I'm utterly famished." But his mother was out of town, and his father would work late at the Feed and Seed, so he was hardly popping up courage. I didn't say this out loud, because he was family.

"We got to. I'm starved," Bobby Welpler said. "All those gonna stick with the pack, raise their hands." He looked straight at me, like it was me who might spoil things by reminding us all to get home. And then he stared straight at Farsanna, and that look spoke for itself too, reminding us all who wasn't a part of the pack. Then his little melon-seed eyes, wide set and without much sign of intelligent life, settled on me. "All those got to get home to their mommas can hop off right here."

"Yeah," I came back, "but *your* momma wouldn't notice one way or the —"

Jimbo was shaking his head real small at me. I stopped there. But I'd already treaded a little too far. *We were all thinking the same thing, even Welp,* I wanted to shout, defending myself. *He knows what his momma is. Everyone does.* And that was true. Only Jimbo mostly saw things out his own porthole, he liked to say, and you could count on his judging people a whale of a lot either better or worse than they looked to everyone else.

Welp turned his face to the woods and shot air through his teeth. Whatever he said, to me or to his mom or to himself, he finished his thought into the wind, still hot off the side of the bed.

Emerson swung his pickup off the highway at Stonewall Jackson Pike.

"A half mile down here's Hog Wild," I told Farsanna. I pointed to the sign ahead: a pink pig gone sassy in a miniskirt and cowboy boots.

"This is a . . ." Farsanna squinted down the road at the low-slung log cabin with an arrangement of picnic tables out front, ". . . a restaurant, no?"

"An establishment. A joint," L. J. corrected. " 'No shirt, no shoes' is entirely customary, if not entirely hygienic." He swung himself out of the truck before it came to a stop. The rest of us scurried to follow, and even the Big Dog pawed open her passenger-side door before Emerson had properly parked.

Emerson pulled a quarter from his shorts pocket, and we flipped to see which one of us would call our mother.

"Tails, you call," I said just before it spun to a halt, "heads, I do."

We both bent over the coin.

He sighed. "I always call Momma."

I patted my brother's cheek. "She likes to know a man's in charge, sugar."

"She'll be ticked, our missing dinner."

"Not if you charm her."

Even Emerson had to agree. Our momma believed in men. And our momma believed in charm. He stalked off, quarter in hand.

Sanna stood watching, maybe waiting for someone to explain. I stopped myself just short of pointing, and nodded to the man taking orders behind a screen mesh. "Steinberger owns it. Hyme Steinberger — that's him there — Steinberger and daughters. They go to our school."

Jimbo motioned us all to a table and bowed, like he was the maître d'. "Steinberger hickory-smokes his pigs for three squealing-free days. Don't got no competition in all Carolina." He bowed again and grinned at us all in a sweep. "Wet shells and welcome."

Bobby Welpler lowered his voice and elbowed Farsanna. "Steinberger don't eat the stuff himself; Steinberger's a Jew."

We all looked at Bobby.

"And," Jimbo said, "he cooks one almighty mean pig." He led the way to our favorite table — Steinberger himself called it *our* table.

Welp turned to the new girl. "What about you? You worship cows where you come from? What if there's beef in this here barbecue? You afraid you'll eat up one of your gods?" He snickered through lips he always kept closed when he laughed — Welp's front teeth were brown at the gums and one incisor was missing.

"Shut up, Welp," I said without looking at him.

Emerson pointed to the pick-up counter.

"Go fetch us some Cokes, Turd Face."

Welp was breathing hard, his arms flexed. "She ain't," he growled over his shoulder as he turned to obey, "answered my question."

Jimbo rolled his eyes and went to call his mother next. When he returned, Welp following behind him with Cokes, he dropped down on the picnic bench next to Farsanna. "Ma said to tell the mangy pack howdy."

Now this couldn't have been true, not exactly. Regina Lee Riggs never said howdy — she was much too refined. She would've asked, in deep Virginian, to *convey mah regahds to y'all's mangy pack.*

Jimbo stabbed his fork into barbecue. "And the good Reverend Riggs," he tipped his head toward Farsanna, "that'd be my daddy — was receiving his weekly word from the Lord." Bo reached for the hot sauce, the one marked with the flames, and raised it to Emerson and me like a toast. "He's calling it 'Rescue the Perishing and *Yeah,* That Means You.' "

"Bo's referring to our father," Emerson said to Farsanna, who sat beside him, between him and Bo. "Dad's what you might call the village atheist."

L. J. nodded. "Every village benefits from a modicum of intellectual dissent."

Welp nodded too. Though he probably

hadn't heard what he was nodding about.

Emerson jerked his head in my direction. "Me and Shelby Lenoir take after the faith of our father, you might say."

For a moment, L. J. stopped sneering. "Which reminds me," he groaned, "have you all seen my daddy's new sign?"

I leaned in to my brother. "What sign?"

"Outside his daddy's Feed and Seed," Emerson answered, laughing. "It's a new marquee, three lines, a good five feet across and lit up so as the blind couldn't miss it: "Fresh Bait —"

His head dropping to his chest, L. J. supplied the next line: "Cold Beer —"

Jimbo snagged the last line for himself: "Jesus Saves!" And Bo began the lines again, chanting with Em: *Fresh Bait, Cold Beer, Jesus Saves!* He gave L. J.'s shoulder a friendly shove. "Me and the good Reverend Riggs drove by it yesterday, and even he chuckled up some."

L. J. shook his head. "Your daddy laughed?"

"Said he reckoned you'd be embarrassed as Kentucky Fried Cherubs."

"Well he's right. He said that?"

" 'Least that's what he *meant.*"

That went without saying. The good Reverend Riggs, we all knew, *never* said

85

what he meant, for fear of offending — but, now, that didn't make the opposite true. Nobody doubted he meant what he said, his sermons all variations on being nice because God was so nice. But Truth was something the Good Reverend liked to hand out soft and slow and sweet-smelling — which, some people said, was why the Baptists had kept him so long, their having run off the preacher before who'd liked his iced tea and his gospel unsweetened.

Bobby Welpler leaned across the table to Farsanna. "What about you, Sri Lanka? Your daddy got himself forty wives and a girl god with snakes for hair?"

L. J. covered his face with both hands. "Good Lord, the ignorance one has to endure here." He turned on Welp. "Sri Lanka primarily practices Buddhism, and secondarily Hinduism. Although," he cocked his head at Farsanna, "although . . ."

"My father's family," she offered quietly, "are Muslim. And Moor. Although we do not regularly —"

Welp interrupted: "What do them Arabs call their Bible?"

"Sacred text," L. J. corrected, one hand massaging his forehead. "And it's called the Koran."

"Yeah. Koran. Or maybe your daddy's

done some of that island voodoo, huh, Sri Lanka?"

The new girl received this without flinching. "This," she told him, "is for us home now."

Just like that. No explanation.

But Welp muttered, "That don't make no sense," and I'd no intention of agreeing with him in public.

Jimbo was gnawing his way through his third corn on the cob, this last one from off my plate. He shrugged cheerfully. "You got a God-given right not to make sense in the Home of the Brave — what makes this country so big-dirty-dog great. Don't nothing got to make sense, and our Constitution protects it."

Welp pouted. "She still ain't answered my question."

"You," I said to Welp, "haven't asked one worth answering yet."

Emerson slapped two quarters on the table. "Welp, Big Dog here's needing a drink." She grinned and drooled beside him.

Sulking, Bobby Welpler slumped his way back to the screen mesh window.

But by the time he returned, the sulk had lost its hold on his face, sliding down to only his mouth, his eyes having cleared up out of their half-lidded glare. And a few baby back ribs later, the sauce basting his nose, the sulk had slipped from his face altogether — ribs'll do that — and showed only in his shoulders.

We wiggled our bare toes in sawdust as we talked, with barbecued beans and butter from the corn greasing our noses, our cheeks, our chins. Our napkins untouched in a stack, we licked the sauce, heavy with maple syrup and brown sugar, from our fingers and lips. And we took turns letting Big Dog finish our sodas. Her teeth gripping the cans, she tottered on her hind legs to toss back the dregs. She preferred Dr Pepper but would settle for Coke, and because she turned her nose up at Tab, I kept the pink can to myself.

The new girl offered the last bits of her shredded pork to Big Dog, and Emerson turned his cap a full revolution in thanks, while Big Dog slept on Farsanna's feet.

"The time that is the next," Farsanna told them, "I will bring with me the dog at my house."

Em scratched his golden retriever behind the ears. "That'd be nice," he said to Big Dog, like he'd all of a sudden gone shy about lifting his head. Farsanna crouched down beside Em to stroke Big Dog's broad, happy back.

It was the same touch Farsanna had used for readjusting her mother's headscarf, small fingers deft and light now smoothing Big Dog's ears. The new girl smiled up at my brother, who managed to return the smile.

Jimbo cut in. "It's a little-known fact that Big Dog has always harbored a hairy fondness for," he held up his palm, and placed his other fist down and to the right, "Sri Lanka."

Farsanna considered this for a moment. Then, rising, she lay one hand lightly, quickly, on Emerson's arm, and one on Jimbo's. "Then it is Big Dog I have for the kindness to thank. Please tell her for me that I am most grateful."

My brother and his best friend looked not at the new girl and not at Big Dog, but at each other.

"Well," I said, changing the subject, "seemed pretty clear to me that Buddy made the best jump from the rope today." And just as I'd hoped, the male egos present locked horns.

Em snorted. "Then you clearly missed my triple back." He turned to the new girl. "Farsanna?"

"I saw it," she smiled at him. "It was indeed splendid."

Em turned back to us with a self-satisfied smirk. "What did I tell you? *Splendid.*"

"But," Sanna added, with the first sly glint I'd seen in her, "the long spin of L. J. was also most impressive."

My cousin readjusted his horn-rims and pretended to snap suspenders on the John Deere T-shirt that served as uniform in his daddy's Feed and Seed. "I call that my Cyclotron Extraordinaire. And I thank you for observing the perfection with which it was executed."

I waved this away. "I still think Buddy's drops showed more guts."

"Turtlest, Sweetheart," Jimbo put his hand over his heart, "you wound me! Did you not witness the full Dirty Harry with a half twist I delivered, just for your viewing pleasure?"

"Was that the time you slipped off the branch and fell headfirst?"

"Ah, I see you were fooled by my clever display of wit and athleticism."

"I was worried you'd bust your fool head open on one of those lower branches."

He leaned in toward me. "But tell us the truth: You'd miss my fool head, if it was to bust open."

"I would miss," I said sweetly, reaching my fork to his plate, "your sharing your fried okra with me."

We dug our toes deeper in sawdust.

I leaned in against Jimbo; he leaned against me. I could feel his landscaping muscles still taut from the day. I lay a head on his shoulder, he draped an arm over my back, and all was right with the world.

Even Welp settled in to something that crept past civil and almost to warm.

After dinner, we began to stagger our way toward Emerson's truck, arms draped around each other's shoulders. I turned my head back to Hog Wild, satisfied, and glimpsed Mort's truck in the corner of the dirt lot. Wiping the last of barbecue sauce from his mouth with his forearm, he must've been there at Steinberger's some time already and we'd just not seen him and they must not have seen us. He and Buddy, their bulky backs to us, were walking away from the picnic tables and toward Mort's truck. They were sauntering first, and then Mort lifted Buddy's wrist for a look at his watch. They both broke into a run.

I nudged Jimbo, who was beside me, his right arm over my shoulders, his left over Welp's.

"What do you suppose," I whispered to Bo, "the two of them are off to this time of night?"

Bo shrugged. He could be irritating that way, his not getting worked up when worry seemed rooted in nothing but air.

By the time we stopped by Dairy Queen for chocolate-dipped cones on the way to drop Farsanna off, the fireflies had already begun damping their lights for darkness to tuck the town into sleep.

Sleepy and no longer hungry, we curled up next to each other like kittens, and Em's engine purred for us. My head resting against Bo, I idly pedaled the warm air with bare feet.

"What could I grow up and do for a living," I murmured into his shoulder, "and never wear shoes?"

His eyebrows crumpled together in one long, shaggy line. "Well, lemme cogitate now. There's surfing. And pearl-diving. And there's professions I can't pronounce in the presence of ladies."

I nuzzled in closer. "Hmm. What else?"

He ran a hand down my hair. "Or we could keep doing this."

"You think," Bobby Welpler wanted to know, "that we could?" He looked, I thought, about four years old just then, his mouth gone all round and hopeful.

Bo closed his eyes, nodding. "Day in, day

out. Day up, day down. Day good, bad, and ugly."

"How 'bout," I whispered, "we just skip all the ugly?"

He rested his chin on the top of my head. "All right, then. We'll skip all the ugly."

"Hey . . . Bo?" I whispered.

"Hmm?"

"You don't reckon . . ."

"Don't reckon what, Turtlest?"

"You don't reckon Mort's gonna do anything with that gun, do you? I mean, anything besides cart it around like he's always done?"

Bo tightened his arm around me. "Shoot."

"You . . . don't think he will, do you?"

He chuckled into my hair. "Shoot *no's* what I meant. His kind's all blam and no bullet."

I thought about this. "But . . . Bo?"

"You plan on ever letting a man sleep?"

"Bo, you may be right about Mort all by himself. But what about as a group?"

"Mort's big enough to be his own group."

"I meant . . . you know how wild dogs, by themselves, wouldn't do much harm but eat trash, but once you let them start running in a pack —"

"And then you got trouble." His chin still on the top of my head, I could feel him nodding. That was all the reassurance he offered just then. But just then, it was enough.

Jimbo was right, I had decided. Mort was mostly a loner, except when he ran with Buddy. And Buddy only followed whatever Mort did. Mort himself, Jimbo had said and I was believing, was all swagger and snarl. Him and his gun for a security blanket.

Everyone's eyes were closed by that time except mine, and I'd like to think Emerson's because he was driving — and maybe also the new girl's, whose head was turned toward the white wake of taillights behind us that sometimes washed red. We rode in silence down the Pike, Em pulling his truck onto back roads that led to the Look. Slowing, he followed the two-lane road without guardrails that traced the edge of our mountain. Far below, the lights of the valley below winked back at us — those of us who opened our eyes to see them. L. J. was snoring by now against Welp's shoulder, and I made a mental note to abuse L. J. tomorrow for that. Welp himself came to long enough to see where we were and then squeeze his eyes shut, like Emerson might be on the verge of missing a turn and sending us all plunging over.

I watched the lights in the Valley and felt Jimbo's chin on the top of my head and tried to feel safe. Although without guard-rails and at night, the point where our mountain ended and the Valley began was not clear to me.

The whole day, in fact, had been unclear to me: just where the point was when someone goes plummeting over the edge, and whether you get to see that coming before it happens, or whether sometimes the edge is under your wheels before you find there's no reverse gear.

Em's truck eased off the side of the road on the thin strip of grass before the Look dropped off into air. He parked, startling us, and we all sat up, L. J. snorting awake and rubbing his eyes.

Emerson unfolded himself from the cab and joined us back in the truck's bed. "Pretty, isn't it?" He said this to the new girl.

She nodded, pointing. "What is there?"

"Nothing but valley," I dismissed it. You can't be raised on a mountain without growing a good, healthy disdain for the piti-ful souls who live on flatland and closer to sea level.

Farsanna's head was cocked toward the Valley, the clusters of white lights, and the lines of red and blue glowing pinpoints way out toward the airport. She waved a hand across the clusters of white. "And . . . ?" she said.

Innocent as this hand gesture and one word might've seemed, I knew it for the challenge it was. The new girl wasn't accepting that so many clusters of lights could be only nothing.

"Nothing worth seeing," I persisted, a little peeved now. "And it's dangerous at night anyhow."

The new girl waited for me to explain.

"Nobody goes downtown at night, and it's late." I reached for the Mickey Mouse watch on Bo's wrist. I'd hoped it would announce we were nearing eleven, our summer curfew, but it was still only nine-thirty. "And anyway, it's rough and dirty, not at all safe this time of night and it's crowded. . . ." I stopped myself there, irritated that *crowded* and *nobody* might seem to contradict each other, when in fact we all knew why they didn't.

My own cousin didn't help matters any. "There are some splendid examples of Victorian architecture from the late nineteenth and early twentieth centuries on several streets. They're desperately in need of rehabilitation now, but someday perhaps someone will have the foresight to fix them back up. And the lights down by the river aren't half bad. It's predominantly ware-houses now, but someday . . ."

Welp spit off the side of the truck. "What Turtle here was trying to say was the Valley ain't safe at night, not in town anyhow, because there's a certain *kind* of nobody lives there."

It was, in a way, exactly what I'd been say-ing. And hearing it bounced back to me, all crawling with ugly from Welp's mouth, meant I had to switch sides. "It's worth see-ing," I contradicted myself, quickly and loudly. Which I meant not one bit, but it had to be said.

The truck radio, fuzzed in static but on Em's favorite station, introduced the next band, Kool and the Gang. Emerson cranked up the volume.

Then he and Jimbo, the two tallest of us, looked at each other over the tops of our heads and had clearly reached some kind of agreement without speaking.

"Hang on, then," Em called as he slammed the cab door behind him and U-turned onto the two-lane road that looped down our mountain. Welp clutched the side of the truck as if he'd been loaded into a carnival ride with the safety bar gone. "*What?* Where we going?"

5. THE WAY OF THE WORLD

Bo leaned back against a six-bag pile of mulch and manure and laced his hands behind his head. "Wherever the spirit leads and the road rolls is where we're going, Welp."

Welp crouched as if he would leap. "No. Not to that part of town, we're not."

Bo looked at him and grinned. "You driving from back here?"

"I ain't going down there tonight. You hear?" Welp stood up straight then, not seeming to care that the truck was already moving at near full speed.

Bo dove for Bobby's legs and buckled him down into the truck bed. "Are you *nuts?*" Jimbo banged on the back of the cab. "Em, man, swing Bobby by his house." To Farsanna, Bo added, "He lives close by. Won't take but a clip of a minute."

She nodded, looking more relaxed than I'd ever seen her. And more relaxed than I felt, or she should have been, had she known where she was headed.

Welp sat sulking as the truck tunneled into the dark of a back road that connected the Look with the Pike, a road so obscure that no one but Bobby and his mother lived there, so far as I knew, and no zoning laws could apply.

At the foot of Welp's drive, L. J. roused himself for a moment. "Anyone home at the Taj?" The Taj was Jimbo's name for Welp's mobile home, which even for an ancient single-wide trailer was in sorry condition. But L. J. had said it out of kindness, even if it was L. J. We were grown up, almost, but still of an age that our mommas liked us not to be home all alone for too long, and we looked out for each other.

Welp shot me a look. "Ask Turtle. She'd be real glad to tell you: Is there *ever* anyone here?" He'd swung out of the truck before Emerson's back wheels had followed his front into the drive.

Emerson let the truck idle there at the head of the drive till we saw a light go on in the trailer. "You'd think," I said then, "that I made a habit of slamming his momma. Or that she didn't do nothing to earn it."

As Em drove off, I could feel the truck engine and the bumps of the old road beneath us. I closed my own eyes and let the last few miles of our Ridge disappear under the tires without my having to watch. Then the road that left the backside of our mountain pitched downward and switched back on itself again and again in a long, slithering snake whose tail petered out in the Valley.

We reached the snake's tail in a few windblown minutes: Our record down was fifteen, but that was by daylight. Farsanna was rubbing her ears from the rapid descent. And I was nauseous from the dozen switch-backs and getting swung side to side in the truck bed. But it had been my suggestion, these lights down here in the Valley being worth seeing after all — my suggestion that I didn't even remotely agree with. So I wasn't saying a word.

Em steered the truck toward downtown, and then exited onto Seventh Street. I pounded on the cab window, but he ignored me.

Seventh Street was the border of the neighborhood of Victorian homes L. J. described. And while I'd never thought twice about them before, I could admit if I squinted and imagined fresh paint and new front porches and turrets that weren't collapsing into bare yards, maybe there was something attractive about them — like the black-and-white sketches in children's versions of Dickens' novels, his young ladies of good family who'd fallen on hard times and were hungry.

But Seventh Street also housed a number of bars and lounges and long lines of shanty houses whose roofs slumped in tired, half-hearted attempts at protection. The bars throbbed with music, their walls seeming to pulse and push those inside out into the street. Unlike our Ridge, where after nine at night, most house lights flipped off so inhabitants could retire to bed respectably early, Seventh Street blazed with light. The bars pulsed with neon carnival color, bold red block letters and yellow floodlights and green cursive words, "Appearing Nightly" and "Live Music." But the houses, too, spilled out bright yellow light from every window and door, flung open to the night air, and from cracks between planks, as if their being so small meant their flimsy walls couldn't contain all the life pent up inside.

On a corner where our truck pulled to a stop at a red light, a group of young men huddled just outside one of the buildings, metal bars over the neon of its windows. Their arms around one another and their heads tipped toward the inside of the circle they'd formed, they looked like they were waiting for a quarterback to shout them their plays. I shrunk tighter into my corner, watched the new girl's face for signs of abject terror at being stuck at a stoplight in this part of town, where white people, we'd been told all our lives, were not welcome and, God knew, not safe. Sanna's face registered, so far, that she didn't understand the danger we were in, a truck bed full of white teenagers, and one new girl from someplace we'd only recently learned to find on a map, all of us with no doors we could lock.

But she was leaning out over the side of the truck. And so was Bo. Trying to listen.

I suddenly realized what she was trying to hear. The young men — at least ten of them circled there on the Seventh Street sidewalk — were singing. One of them bent first forward and then back, lifting a fully extended trombone toward the sky. A saxophone flashed, red neon reflecting off its brass, and a trumpet flared high and clear about the melody.

"One would surmise," L. J. said into my ear, "they were too hot inside. With which one can sympathize." He nodded toward the low-slung building where bodies pressed into each other as they squeezed through the door and emerged, swaying, hands on each others' waists, following the band into the night.

The red traffic light was just turning green, but Emerson kept the truck where it was. The musicians ignored us, each of them finding his part, breaking into harmonies and half-harmonies, falsettos and rhythms I'd heard nothing quite like. Not in person at least. Their knees bent and straightened in time to the beat so that the whole huddle sank and rose to their tune.

I was alone, I took a ride, I didn't know
    what I would find there.
Another road, where maybe I could see
    another kind of mind there . . .

I waited for the young men to notice us staring at them from the truck, until I realized their eyes were closed, most of them, and the ones that were open were not watching us. They'd been swept into their own music and swam there still, feeling the rapids and steering together. We were nothing but far-off spectators on shore, irrelevant.

Jimbo snatched up a shovel and put its handle to his mouth as a mike. He leaned forward over the edge of the truck bed in time to supply the Ooohs of the next lines.

I leaned in toward L. J. "Beatles," I whispered, recognizing the song and savoring a moment of superior knowledge. "This is their song."

L. J. cut his eyes at me. "Earth, Wind and Fire's covering of this song is the far superior version, as demonstrated by this group's rendition. Complete," he nodded toward the band, "with homemade kalimba." He pointed toward the wooden box someone had nailed metal spoons to, and now strummed with his thumbs.

A group of five women slipped out onto the sidewalk from another one of the shacks. They looked middle-aged, one of them heavy, another one of them tall and stalk-slender, and she tucked her own arm under the heavy one's for support. They were well dressed, the tall one in heels and the heavy one in a floral print dress with a wide scoop of lace at her collar. At least three of the ladies carried books under their arms that maybe were Bibles. I'd noticed once the way Jimbo cradled his own; there's a certain way people carry them, gingerly, like there was something inside they were a little scared of, something that might go off if you treated it roughly or ignored it too long.

For a moment, I expected the ladies to

charge through the huddle of young men and into the bar and clear it of all iniquity. Or maybe to turn to us in the truck and tell us how much we didn't belong here. But they stopped there on the walk just beside us in the truck, just beside the singers, and listened.

The heavy one nodded and kept time with one hand patting her purse. The slender one turned to smile at us.

Joining the brass that had gathered us all in to them, several of the band's listeners added their own instruments. One grabbed a metal pipe from the ground to tap on the concrete. Another drew the long neck of a bottle over the crenellated top of chain-link fencing. Another cupped his hands into a horn.

The heat of the day still clung to the pavement, trapped in canyons of concrete and brick. The white lights of the streetlamps, the red and green neon of the bars, the yellow lights of the houses all throbbed through the heat, making the human forms on the sidewalk seem almost transparent, unreal, like a mirage that would soon flicker back into unbroken night.

I felt at that moment like a medical student who'd just seen inside a living body for the very first time, and realized he'd only ever *thought* he'd seen a person before — the lips and the eyelashes, the painted nails — till now, seeing the heart swelling each beat. The Valley I thought I knew, the department stores on Market and Main where our mothers dragged us for school clothes, the steak place we went to on birthdays down by the river, the city we made sure to leave before dark, the smoke-stacks and back alleys and shanties that lay far beneath our mountain, beat all along with a life I'd known nothing about. But now I felt drawn to it, the lights and the music and the sway of the forms on the sidewalk, the deep, throaty laugh of the tall singer, all tugging us in like a tether.

The band had modulated to another key, and the brass turned toward one another and cut swaths in the dark. Me, I couldn't take my eyes off the guy with the trumpet, his long fingers rolling over the keys, his wide shoulders hunching then broadening back with the effort of a high trill, his arms keeping the instrument's mouth pitched above his head and rocking right to left in perfect time with the trombone. I'd hardly noticed there were words to the next song until it was well begun.

. . . looking back we've touched on sorrow-

ful days
Future pass, they disappear

The stoplight turned red, and then back to green, Seventh Street empty of cars, and our truck had not moved. We sat and listened. And the young men sang on.

A child is born with a heart of gold
The way of the world makes his heart grow
   cold

The women walked on toward us, all of them staring at us but not hostilely, just amused, maybe, and curious, our Pack lolled in the back of an old pickup and all of us turned audience. Big Dog and Em with their heads out the passenger window, both with their mouths open and smiling, Em with his Sox cap, Jimbo and the new girl leaning out over the side, Bo drumming the beat now on the metal side of the truck. Even L. J.'s head ticked side to side with the sway of the brass.

Then Jimbo pulled Farsanna to her feet and spun her around. The Baptists on our Ridge frowned on dancing, but never quite managed to frown on Jimbo, and even with the size of his feet, he danced well. From the dip he dropped her into, Sanna laughed up at him. L. J., severely lacking for partners, pulled me to my feet. He was clumsy at dancing, but so was I, and bags of manure and mulch in the way served as excuses. Emerson opened the cab door like he might join us, and Big Dog strained at the passenger door. One of the young men in the band offered a hand to the tall lady in heels, and she took it, twirling in toward him and laughing.

A car from far down the road was approaching. But Seventh Street was four lanes at this point; the car could sweep past our truck idling there at the light, so we ignored it.

The car, though, was approaching too fast. It shot through the intersection a block north of us without so much as a tap of the brake at the red. Swerving, it came on.

Someone was shouting. It might have been someone on the sidewalk, or the shouts might have come from the car. Maybe both. And something long and thin jutted out the passenger window.

I remember thinking the car was a Gremlin, orange and awkward and already sounding like its transmission was grinding its last. The car's design was distinctive — in the way of the memorably shoddy. And I recall wondering why a big stick poked from its windows.

Until it was clear it wasn't a stick.

Gunfire shattered the night into jagged pieces of screams and flying glass. The music of a few moments ago had become the screech of rubber melted on asphalt and more shots through the dark and a street-lamp hailing its white light and glass onto our heads, and more screams. Stomping on the accelerator, Em sent the whole truck bed of us slamming back toward the tailgate, its latch faulty and held with nothing but thin-gauge wire.

The truck swerving, its tires screeching, we tore through one red light, then two, fleeing from the direction of the shots and from the streetlight raining white light and glass down on our heads, and from the bedlam as those on the sidewalk dove for cover and the front windows of Seventh Street shanties dissolved into shards.

The Gremlin came tearing behind us, its occupants hooting and throwing bottles. The lights of Seventh Street blurred like a spun pinwheel as the pickup's engine roared over the sharp report of the rifles. As Em threw the truck to the right and the pickup took a turn on two wheels, I groped frantically for the side of the truck to keep from being thrown clear out of the bed. My hands met with nothing but air. I felt my body lift off the metal floor, and I knew I was flying over the side.

But Sanna, her legs pinned underneath fallen bags of mulch, snagged the hem of my T-shirt, yanking me back to the floor just as Em threw the truck into a sharp left. The pickup winged into another curve.

All of us in the truck bed plowed against its right side, as the wheels screamed — our bodies flailed. As if in slow-motion replay, I can still see the lights whirl all around me, still see the blood that had pooled underneath me on the truck bed. Then my head slammed onto the white metal floor, and the spin of lights snuffed out.

6. Blood on the Truck Bed

"Is she bad hurt?!" I heard a voice say.

I had clearly fallen in the truck and passed out, and the world was just taking form again over my face. I assumed he meant me, if I was okay. The voice was my brother's.

Followed by Jimbo's voice: "There's blood enough here coming from her head to float Dracula's castle."

"Typically," L. J. spoke now, quickly, "the cranium does bleed excessively."

I felt my head for the gash that they must be speaking about, and could find nothing. Except for a large bump on my forehead.

I could see their faces now. And they were not looking down onto mine.

Jimbo and Emerson and L. J. all knelt over the new girl. *Fine,* I thought. *Well that's just fine. I'm here with no doubt a concussion and internal bleeding, and they're not even watching me die.*

My head throbbing, I sulked on my back

for a moment, alone. I let my head roll to the side and felt my hair stick, warm and wet, to my cheek.

Alarmed, I sat up, pulling back the wet hair from my face. It was blood. And lots of it. Apparently not mine or the boys'.

Farsanna lay flat on her back, her eyes open, her face entirely red and blood still pouring from the right side of her head.

"You're *sure*," Emerson pressed L. J., "it's not grazed from a bullet? You're sure it's just where her head hit the side of the truck?"

L. J. shook his head in disdain. "You've watched far too much *Big Valley*. This, my friends, is nothing but a flesh wound." He chuckled at his own Monty Python allusion and adopted a bad English accent: "Only a flesh wound." None of us laughed. "Look, she's fine, all right? We can take her to a doctor for stitches, but he'll only tell us she doesn't need them. Look closer."

I saw then he was using someone's T-shirt to dab at her head and stanch the wound, and that Jimbo was shirtless.

My brother leaned down closer still to the wound. "I'm so sorry," he whispered.

Farsanna shook her head slightly. "You are not the one at fault, no?"

"I slammed on the accelerator when I saw

the idiots swerving and heard the first shot," Em moaned.

Bo lay a hand on Em's shoulder. "So you, good man, get credit for saving all our lives." He tousled Em's hair. "I, on the other hand, failed miserably. Despicably. Unforgivably." He, too, leaned further in. "I failed to protect the ladies among us. I dove for them, like a good human shield, but only knocked Turtle upside the head." The boys shifted their joint gaze toward me.

"Don't y'all worry 'bout me none," I snipped at them. "I'm just *fine* over here with a knot on my head the size of . . . of my head." That sounded a bit selfish, even to me, given the amount of blood, not mine, in my own hair. But I was annoyed with the boys. So I crawled the three feet to Farsanna. "How are you?"

"Only a flesh wound," she mimicked in her own island accent. And she smiled up at us, weakly, and gave a fleeting thumbs-up.

"You need to see a doctor," Em persisted.

"No." Farsanna's jaw squared and her eyes went black, liable to smolder.

My brother wouldn't let it alone. "You need to — ?"

"My head is fine. L. J. has said."

"But —"

"And the doctor visit means for me that my father will know what happened tonight. And my father will fear."

"Well," L. J. mumbled to me, "maybe your father has reason to fear."

"And," she continued, "I prefer for him not knowing that we were here."

Bo drew his long legs up to his bare chest and scooted closer beside her. "Your momma gave you permission to go riding with us. So they'd not be so hop-along happy to hear you'd been cruising the streets of the city."

Farsanna nodded.

Bo nodded back, then looked up at us. "Well, then, that settles it. We say nothing to nobody about this."

L. J. raised an eyebrow. "And when the civic authorities pursue their inquiry into what happened tonight on Seventh Street?"

Farsanna rose to her elbows. "Tonight, what *did* happen?"

It was then I heard sirens. Emerson must have driven us blocks from that corner of Seventh, but we were still in the city, and the city's concrete and asphalt echoed with their wail.

Emerson spoke first. "I only saw in the rearview mirror everyone diving for cover, and screaming like us. I think, though I'm not sure, I think the guy driving was too drunk or too nuts to give a straight aim to whomever was shooting."

"Whomever?" I said. Even in the face of near-certain death, my brother couldn't let go of grammar.

My brother ignored me. "At least it's possible no one was hurt terribly badly. As far as I could tell, the shots, most of them, were going high and wide."

"So," L. J. pulled a hand over his chin's growth of peach fuzz as if it were a full beard, "so perhaps that little display was primarily for the purpose of show. Let's conjecture a moment: What if it were only a tactic of intimidation?"

"Directed at . . . us?" I asked.

My cousin shrugged. "Perhaps. Or perhaps blacks in general, just a little reminder of who calls the shots."

"Or fires them," I muttered.

Jimbo's arms were crossed over his chest, a sure sign he was paying attention. "Or both."

L. J. nodded. "Or both. Yes, one might conjecture that."

Emerson pulled a quarter from his shorts pocket. "Let's conjecture that somebody needs to call and report them at least. Like right now."

"The sirens . . ." I pointed out.

"I mean not just report there was trouble, but report what we saw. I'll make an anonymous call from this pay phone. They do that sometimes now in cities, you know. I'll report the car we all saw, and I'll say we saw . . . that we saw. . . . Did any of us see the guys driving?"

Silence.

L. J. rolled his eyes. "Stupendous. At the very least, they'll inquire whether the perpetrators were black or white. Or —" He stopped, glanced sideways at Farsanna, and left off there. "They'll want a thorough description."

Emerson looked from one to the other of us. "Did anyone see what they were?"

"White," I offered at last.

"You're sure of that, Turtle? Did you recognize faces? No need to be frightened now."

"On the contrary," L. J. put in, "there's every reason to be frightened of thugs who roam city streets inebriated and armed."

"No faces," I told him. "And the Gremlin you and I saw, I didn't recognize it as belonging to . . . well, to anyone whose car I know. But I think . . . I think the faces were white. Yeah, I'm sure of it. I think."

L. J. put the hand back to his forehead.

"Inebriated and armed *and* unidentified. Great. Just great. Not so much as an eyewitness to contribute to the cause of justice."

And so we contributed nothing that night, nothing except to each other, to a sense of belonging, perhaps. And to a load of guilt we shouldered together for saying nothing to anyone else.

"We did," Em reassured us, and himself, "hear the sirens. Which meant the police had been called. Which means they're going after the guys. Which means they'll catch them."

I watched L. J.'s face as Em said this. "You just rolled your eyes, dear cousin. So what are you thinking?"

"That's my default demeanor." He shrugged. "Just contemplating whether anyone will actually *try* to catch them."

In the one open gas station we found, I asked the man inside for the key to the ladies restroom, and Farsanna met me back in the shadows, her face still covered in blood. We washed her hair and her face, and staunched the wound with the remaining white of Jimbo's T-shirt. We arranged her thick, heavy hair over the wound, which, once it stopped bleeding, lay nicely disguised.

"Good as new," I pronounced her. "You

feeling okay?"

"My wound is obvious, no?"

"No. Really. You're looking gorgeous as ever. Just maybe a little . . . shaken, that's all."

"You do as well." She smiled, and her dark eyes crinkled at me. "Gorgeous and shaken."

We left the gas station and reached the summit of the road up the back side of our ridge well before midnight.

I scooted along the truck bed and settled in next to L. J. "Can I ask you something?"

"You're going to regardless of my giving consent."

"Right. So, listen, I know I'm not always real fair to Welp, so Jimbo wouldn't be happy with me if he heard this. But did it occur to you that he wasn't with us? I mean, does it bother you any that he left before we went down, that he said he wouldn't go down there *tonight?* You think he knew anything?"

L. J. raised an eyebrow at me. "You impress me, small cousin. I thought no one but I had caught what he said about tonight. Yes, it occurred to me. Though that's circumstantial, at best. Wouldn't hold up one moment in court."

"Except that we know how he can be. And how Mort and his crowd could sweep Welp along into most anything."

"We also know that wasn't Mort's car. And that none of us saw him, or Welp either. And that none of us witnessed anything substantial at all. That we have now agreed upon collective silence. And that we are in effect less than useless, if not actual aids and abettors of crimes committed tonight."

"Right," I said, and slumped so low my chin touched my chest. Then I sat up a bit straighter.

Emerson pulled the truck from asphalt, pocked as it was, into the trenched gravel of Farsanna's driveway and stopped close to the carport. Its metal supports, I noticed, seemed weary of holding its roof. Or maybe that was only my own weariness, and now this new thing to carry, this secret of what we had seen, and hadn't.

For no good reason, we all stood in the back of the truck. Emerson emerged from the cab. Farsanna ignored Jimbo's hand to help her and swung down by herself. Bo and L. J. and I landed beside her. Her gaze gone into searchlight, she looked from one of our faces to the next.

In all times of crisis, we let Jimbo speak for us, as he did then. He held up his right hand, flat to the air, and placed his left in a fist beside the right thumb. Emerson did the same thing, and so did L. J. and then I did. Farsanna was last, and most slowly.

It then became our Pack's secret hand-shake — though not a handshake at all. From then on that summer, in moments of tension or crisis, or when someone needed to laugh or loosen up from a fit of the grumps, or cheer up after a parental rebuking, we would form Sri Lanka with a palm and a fist, and define our own little culture. Years later in a college class called "Social Deviance," I studied subcultures and gangs. Primary-source research told me what I'd learned long before in the back of a pickup: that subcultures gravitate toward ways of symbolizing belonging. And that summer, whether we liked it or not, we belonged to the Pack. And the Pack had its own sign, its own grasp at exotic and secret.

With the white dust of the new girl's gravel still clouding around us, Jimbo raised the fist that he'd placed by his palm. "*This* would be Sri Lanka."

Farsanna reached for his fist, covered her own hand around it, and pulled his down. "And this," she told him, raising herself to full height and motioning to her house, to the truck, to the block of bare lawn, "would be home." And maybe because this met with incredulous stares from us, she added,

"Home is for us here now." She looked from one to the other of us, her eyes somehow darker than even the night and her face set into its mask that said nothing of what she was thinking. I waited for the *no?* that should've ended that sentence, and for once it didn't come.

It was so utterly absurd, her choosing this day, this night, this moment, to announce this place as her home. It flew in the face of what anyone could have expected, of what she ought to have done, and been afraid of.

"So . . ." I offered. And I almost met her eye — but not quite. "So, we'll . . ." We'll what? Nothing came to me then. I was hearing Earth, Wind, and Fire punctuated with gunshots, hearing the hail of shattered streetlights and shriek of truck tires. Just then even the sound of the "we'll" sounded false to my ear.

"We'll see you tomorrow," Em finished for me. "For the Blue Hole. We got to have you there with us. Okay?"

I never thanked Em for that, for saying what I never did. It struck me at the moment, though, that I liked him, my very own brother, liked who he was — not something I'd have said to his face.

Em snatched his towel from the cab and flung it over Farsanna's shoulders. "You look cold," he muttered.

She didn't look cold to me. Or scared. Though she had to have been, seeing what we all had seen.

Jimbo and Em walked with her almost to the end of the drive, where she nodded to them, but that was all before walking away.

We watched Farsanna tenderfoot the rest of the way to her door, her feet bearing witness to her first time down the slope to the Hole. She turned once, knelt to pet the stray, who'd fallen asleep on the stoop but rose to lick her feet. She looked right and left, seemed to listen a moment. Then, clutching Em's towel tightly around her, she opened the door and let the dog in. I pictured her momma inside, stiffening to hear the door creak open, limping to greet her daughter, both hands stroking Farsanna's hair.

Her hair. I held my breath. Farsanna's hair was dry now, blown in the wind off the truck. But there was the gash underneath. Even if her momma couldn't see well, or at all, would she be able to feel what had happened? Would she ask questions?

Farsanna turned as she closed the door behind her and lifted a chain to lock it. I put up my hand in a wave, and so did the boys.

■ ■ ■ ■

We dropped off L. J. next, then rolled up to Jimbo's just after midnight.

Em craned around from the driver's-side window. "Bo, you want me to cut the lights before we pull in?"

"Yeah. And the horsepower, if you don't mind, my good man. The good Reverend hadn't lost his hearing as fast as his boyish figure."

Bo had a policy of complete honesty with his parents. If they asked him what time he came in, he told them, right to the minute. But if he slipped in without waking them, and they never asked, he came and went sometimes in the wee hours without the slightest restraint.

Emerson and I walked Bo down his drive. We never walked Bo to the door, but this night we were in no hurry to let go of each other.

Em motioned with his head to the side of the drive. He mouthed, "Whose truck is that?"

I'd been lost in my own thoughts and intent on sticking close to the boys, and not noticed the green truck parked at the walk.

Bo shook his head, shrugging. He reached

for the screen door, then yanked his hand back and waved us all down. We jumped behind the rhododendron and crouched there as the screen door swung open.

"Order," a man's voice was saying, "is what we'd be after, preacher. Just law and order. Reckoned you could help us with that. We don't want to let nothing get too out of hand in this town, now do we? We reckoned you'd see it that way."

Bo yanked on our T-shirts and we all ducked still lower just as the porch light flipped on.

"Well," said the good Reverend Riggs, as he let the porch door swing shut, "good night then."

Several pairs of legs lumbered down the stone steps from the screen porch. I raised my head just inches to look for a face, but Bo yanked me back down by the ponytail.

"But — !" I whispered.

Bo put his forefinger against my lips. I sat then, saying nothing, and let his finger stay where it was.

7. LIKE AMOROUS BIRDS OF PREY

Frosted Flakes wilting in my bowl, I paced our kitchen floor, my brother reading the paper and trying hard to ignore me.

"Explain to me one more time why Jimbo wasn't more bothered by those guys coming out of his house last night?"

Em talked out the side of his mouth, his cereal squirreled up in the other. "I told you already, Turtle. Number one, Bo said himself there were trillions of reasons they could've been there. Unconfessed sin, maybe."

"Right."

"Seriously, they could've been there to talk about anything. Anything besides what you thought."

"And you don't think what I do? You can sit there and tell me Bo's daddy wasn't being threatened by those guys? And worse, that the good Reverend didn't seem to be telling them where to get off?"

"I told you: Bo just said his daddy doesn't think like that, doesn't agree with that sort. At any rate, Bo wasn't much rattled by it, so maybe you and I shouldn't be either."

"Is that why your forehead's scrunched up into a knot? Because you're not bothered?"

My brother put a hand to his forehead to feel. "Okay, look. So, it bugs me a little. But you know how Bo practically worships his daddy."

I toyed with my Frosted Flakes petulantly. "Well. I reckon there's something on the front page about what happened last night in the city. What's the front page say about it? Emerson?"

He lay down the paper. "I heard you."

"So? What did it say?"

He frowned and shoved the paper to me across the Formica. "See for yourself."

I scanned the page. "I don't see it."

He nodded. "Exactly."

"What?"

"Try page seventeen."

"Seventeen? A car full of drunk white boys goes on a shooting spree and . . . ?"

"You only thought they were *probably* white."

". . . Goes careening through a city and shooting at people, and it's buried underneath the state fair and somebody's award-winning *turnips?*" I skimmed the four-paragraph piece on page seventeen. "This says the police have located no suspects. That some of the witnesses have reported they were white guys, and there's some suggesting they're *black!*"

"Read carefully. None of the witnesses said they could have been black. Apparently the police are just looking for black guys or white, either one. If they're looking at all."

I read the article again. "Nothing more than minor injuries. And property damage . . . It doesn't say much about property damage. But that one streetlight shattered right on our heads, and —"

Our father walked in just then, still half asleep and groping for his second cup of coffee before the morning began. My brother and I exchanged glances, wondering what he'd heard of our conversation.

"Heads?" our father asked us.

"Would roll," I said too quickly. "I was just telling Emerson here that it seems like heads would roll, you know, seeing as how some idiots went racing through town shooting at people."

Our father shook his head, wearily. "No, they weren't shooting at people. I was at the city editor's desk last night when the report came in. Apparently, some unidentified guys in a car were just shooting out lights, having a bit too much to drink, causing a general disturbance. Not admirable behavior, I'll grant you. But nothing murderous in its intent anyway."

Em and I looked at each other.

"But," my brother ventured, "it seems as if it might have been. I mean, shooting that close to where people . . ."

"And the property damage," I added.

Our father glanced up from his coffee and narrowed his eyes, first at me, then at Em. "Well, aren't you two the civic-minded pair this morning? The property damage was minimal. And in that part of town, the city might not even bother to fix the lights for a while. That's the assumption. It's generally viewed as a way of punishing a certain sector of the population for getting so far out of hand."

"But they didn't — !" I blurted.

"A regrettable attitude, I'll grant you. But typical, and perhaps not just of the regressive South," he said.

"But what if the damage was done by . . . by not the people who have to live with the damage?"

Our father looked up again from his coffee. "You'll find, children, as you grow, that our justice system waits for facts until it proceeds. And lacking facts, or suspects in custody, this case of disturbing the peace and probably some sort of unlawful discharge of firearms will have to be dealt with by people more experienced with urban crime than you or I. But this part of downtown hasn't exactly been known for its calm and quiet."

Our father opened his briefcase and stuffed the newspaper into it. He would be out the door any moment.

"What if," I began, "what if the guys shooting weren't from there at all? What if they were white and what if — ?"

Our father eyed me carefully as I'd seen him do his note cards when he was having trouble deciphering his own print. "Then this would be a racially motivated incident, possibly with intent to harm. And if not dealt with well, could escalate into more racial unrest."

I stirred my drowned flakes.

"Shelby Lenoir?"

"Yes, sir?"

"Do you and Emerson have anything you'd like to tell me?"

"No, sir," my brother said, "except . . ."

"Except have a good day," I finished for him. And we both manufactured big, perky

129

smiles for our father, a skill we'd learned from our momma.

Throughout those next several days, while the heat raged unabated, we combed the newspapers. We drove some nights after dark to the Look, where we could see another downtown block blazing, abandoned buildings set fire by what the paper called "angry black youth." The police had found no one to blame for the shooting, and one officer's quote implied the force had little interest in pursuing the case, given that no one was killed or permanently maimed and there'd been "minimal material damage." With all these reports, our parents warned us vaguely about "disturbances" down in the city and forbade us to visit, no matter the time of day, until things settled down.

So that summer, whole blocks of the city burned in the night and bricks found their way through plate-glass windows downtown.

I watched Bobby Welpler for signs of involvement or at least knowledge beforehand of the shooting spree, but his eyes had always looked shifty to me, and his slumped posture, always guilty. So that was no proof at all.

We waited to see what — or who — would ignite up on our Ridge.

And meanwhile, we returned to the Blue Hole: my brother and me and my brother's best friend, one cousin, one Welp, one remarkably chubby golden retriever, and the new girl on Pisgah. And sometimes her dog, which Jimbo named Stray, tagged along too. He was as sweet as he was homely, and Bo made it his new role in life, when not working or swimming or flying from the rope swing, to keep one of Stray's long, silky ears flopped across his thigh.

Unlike in past summers when Emerson's pickup played trolley, collecting random friends and kin as we went, we no longer stopped along the way except at each other's houses, and at the Feed and Seed. Emerson made sure we always parked right under L. J.'s daddy's new sign. And while L. J. climbed in, we always made sure to read it aloud, all three lines of it.

"Fresh Bait!" I would begin.

"Cold Beer!" Emerson and Welp and even the new girl would call out, and laugh.

The punch line we saved for Jimbo, who rendered it with gusto and hands over head: "Jesus saves!"

And every time, L. J. would sink against the side of the truck bed, push his brown plastic horn rims up his nose, and moan. It was our own little litany, that sign was, and it lifted us up and sometimes around through the fear that some days snagged at our hearts.

Late one afternoon, Farsanna and I lay side by side sunning ourselves after a swim. I disliked that, though not so much because I disliked her straight-out. She was smart, I had discovered — we all had. That didn't take long. But unlike our L. J., she had a way of not pointing it out. She liked to ask questions — or maybe liked to make you think that she liked it. And off you'd go, spinning out dreams of your own, stitching together — out loud, even — a future you'd never heard yourself think. And only way out into your tangle of answer would you realize she'd never said much of herself, just coaxed the silk out of the spider.

"And how is it about you, Emerson?" she asked, for example, just out of the blue as we all sat one day on the bank, all of us sun-seared and still warming back up from a swim in the Hole. "When you have more years, what will you be?"

"Books," he told her — before he thought not to. "I'll find a way somehow for someone to pay me to read. Read all day every day."

Bobby Welpler snorted. "I tell you what,

you wanna spend your life with your nose in dusty old books when you could be making time with the ladies? I tell you what." He held up the stick he'd been whittling, now in the form of a voluptuous woman.

"Stand up, Bobby." Em rose to his feet.

"I was just kidding you, man. I don't want to fight . . ."

"Not gonna punch you, Turd Face. Just stand up. Okay, now kneel."

Welp did as he was told, still clutching his pocketknife and his stick. Em knelt beside him, then motioned Farsanna to rise and join them.

"Observe," Emerson instructed. He took Farsanna's hand in his and gazed up into her eyes and spoke softly:

"Now therefore, while the youthful hue
Sits on thy skin like morning dew . . ."

Gently, he brought her hand to his cheek, then slowly rose.

"And while thy willing soul transpires
At every pore with . . ."

He lifted her hair and ran one finger down her neck.

"Instant fires,
Now let us sport us while we may
And now, like amorous birds of prey . . ."

His right arm slipped around her waist.

"Rather at once our time devour

Than languish in his slow-chapped power."
The other arm closed the circle.
"Let us roll all our strength and all
Our sweetness up into one ball . . ."
He drew her closer to him.
"And tear our pleasure . . ."
He brought his cheek to hers, almost, not quite touching.
"With rough strife
Through the iron gates of life
Thus, though we cannot make our sun
Stand still . . ."
His face turned into hers, his lips sweeping her cheek.
"Yet we will make him run."
We all sat staring. Except for Sanna, who stood — but I'm guessing just barely. Me, I could feel my cheeks set to broil. I leaned in toward Jimbo. And he leaned back in toward me. But he wasn't looking at me.
"What," said Bobby Welpler, who dropped his knife and stick, "was that?"
"Dusty old books," Emerson said, and sat down.
It happened that way every time: Farsanna asking one of us a question about ourselves, something I'd have sworn we all knew, and then out would come some revelation, some peek into some part of a soul we hadn't known we were living beside. Sanna would

nod like she understood, like whatever it was you'd said made sense, and lots of it. She had that way about her. Those hard-edged eyes of hers probed like a screwdriver blade leveraging off a paint can lid, and out would come more and more and more, before you knew you'd begun to spill your insides. And you were grateful somehow to her, like she'd given you some kind of gift that was only yourself, but pictured from the best angle and held up in a frame.

"And what," Sanna asked Jimbo when his turn came, "will you someday pursue?"

"Money," he announced earnestly. "Cold, hard cash."

And we all laughed, our legs dangling down into the Hole from our favorite finger of rock.

"The day you care a flying flip about money," I said for us all, "is the day I wear a pink satin bow on the top of my head."

Em shook his head. "Jimbo, man, why do you think I don't let you collect for the Big Dog Lawn business? You'd let all our customers walk away without ever paying. *Poor Miss Pittman's had a hard week. Bless little ol' Charlie Barker's heart, he's on a fixed income now and his kids don't hardly ever come to see him. The Dooleys got eight kids and one on the way — don't reckon they ought to have to worry about one more expense here lately . . .* Lord, we'd have gone broke in a week!"

Jimbo nodded, clearly agreeing. "All the more reason to make money — so's to have fun getting rid of it as fast as I can."

"You could arrange it," L. J. suggested, "in piles untended in the back of the truck. And you could drive in your typically pell-mell fashion down the Pike. That would disperse the wealth rapidly enough."

Jimbo looked hurt. "Now what the Helsinki'd be the point in that? Why would you want it landing on folks already too loaded to stand up straight?"

I pulled his head toward me and ruffled his hair. "It's why we all love you, dear Bo."

"What Turtle means," Welp snickered, "is her. She means *she* loves you, Bo."

Once again, Bobby Welpler had come far too close to echoing what I hadn't meant to be saying. But no one except Bobby caught how I turned pale and desperate just then.

L. J. leaned out over the Hole to address Farsanna at the end of our line of dangling legs. "Excuse me, Sri Lanka. But since you're currently garnering information about America, take heed: The particular specimen you see before you," he motioned to Bo, "would *not* personify the American Way."

Farsanna's small feet kicked a circle of froth. "This," she asked L. J., but she was looking at Jimbo, "is not to you so attractive?" We all stared at her feet and the froth, then at Jimbo, who grinned at the ground.

We laughed at the blood that was rising from Bo's neck into his cheeks.

Farsanna was speaking again. She'd shifted her focus to L. J. "You will make much money?"

"Most assuredly I will. And not by selling cow poop and pine bark to octogenarian gardeners."

The new girl leaned forward to listen. "Tell to us how you will make it." It was not a challenge but a question, a real one. And that was the thing about her: Like steam rising from her steady simmer of anger or worry — whatever it was — came this need to know — almost desperately — how the rest of us thought, how we saw the world and chose to handle what it might throw at us.

L. J. sneered. "If Emerson can find someone to pay him to live the life of a bibliophile, I'll find someone to pay me to be unpleasant. It's what I do best."

"Well, friend," Jimbo laughed with the rest

of us, "you already got that goat good and roped."

"You wait. The world shall reward my skill. Hey, what about Turtle? We've not yet been privy to her professional aspirations."

Farsanna leaned past Emerson, sitting close beside her, to look me in the eye. "An American woman may do as she wishes, yes?"

Em tugged on the fringe of my cutoff shorts, then on my ponytail, wet and limp and weighted with Blue Hole silt. "Fashion model, no doubt."

I bounced up to my feet and pretended to walk a runway, pausing to show off an imaginary ensemble. "Note the lines," I emceed myself, "the detail, the exquisite proportions of this one-of-a-kind creation."

My brother, bless him, clapped for me.

Jimbo, better still, catcalled and whistled. "Wearing," he announced into a microphone-hand, "designer duds from the exclusive Big Dog Lawn and Garden Beautifiers."

Bobby Welpler hadn't spoken to that point. But then: "I'm sayin' Turtle here's gonna be an erratic dancer."

"Erotic," L. J. corrected, laughing. "Or exotic."

I felt my spine shrinking down into my heels.

"Yeah, right," Welp roared, framing a marquee with his hands. " 'GIRLS, GIRLS, GIRLS — AND THEN THERE'S TURTLE!' "

It was a direct hit at my figure — my figure that wasn't — my baggy T-shirts and ratty shorts, my big flop as a flirt: my not being a girl, as girls go.

Then "Can it, Welp," came from Em and Jimbo together, but it arrived late and Bobby, smirking, knew he'd scored a hard hit, which was when Farsanna pulled herself to her feet, small-boned and yet somehow gianting just then over Bobby. "And when you have many years more," she asked him, "what will *you* someday become?"

But Welp didn't answer, focusing instead on his knife and his stick. Under the smolder of Sanna's black eyes, Welp's gloat shrank into a sulk.

Like her quiet gift for making us feel larger and grander, we witnessed that day Sanna's talent for the opposite, for decimating anyone who failed to observe the bonds of loyalty or affection. I waited until the boys were back in the water, and I stood beside her.

"Hey, Sanna," I said. "Thank you."

She waved this away. "It is nothing. You would be protective of me, no?"

It wasn't a question. And yet I wondered: *Would* I do the same for her?

8. BEAUREGARD

I think that was the day I decided the new girl and I could be friends. For a girl, Farsanna Moulavi was not at all bad. But she was still a girl, and sometimes, even with her, I was reminded why I'd never much liked my own kind.

Her swimming in clothes quickly became impractical, so I gave her one of my old swimsuits, one I'd never much liked. The first time at the Blue Hole she lifted her blouse and her skirt to reveal my suit underneath, L. J. tripped over his feet and Welp ran smack into a tree and Emerson dropped the truck keys into the water when he was aiming them for his pants pocket. He even removed his Red Sox cap, and then returned it to his head backwards, bill forward.

Jimbo was the only one of them who said anything, and that was only to me.

"Well, *remember me at Christmas*," he

whispered, all hoarse.

I pretended I didn't hear and dove off my finger of rock.

Farsanna was short and dark so you wouldn't have guessed it, but the new girl looked good in my suit.

"Your daddy approve?" I asked her later. Reckon I was feeling a little vindictive.

"In America, girls who are good wear a bathing suit, no?"

"Even good girls, you mean, wear bathing suits. Sure," I muttered, and wondered if maybe she might catch a cold soon and not be able to join us sometimes at the Hole — and wouldn't that just be a shame. And I was trying to recall why I'd passed on my old suit to her. "He's a real sucker for anything American, huh? Your dad, I mean."

Emerson's Big Dog snoozed on her side on my left, the Stray on my right.

I was feeling sleepy myself, a rock for my pillow, when Farsanna offered, "In my home . . . in Sri Lanka, some Muslim women even do wear bathing suits since the 1950s or so. The expectation for the hijab has been somewhat relaxed, although some women prefer to keep the hijab."

"Like your mother."

"Yes, like *Mata.* She says that women are responsible for not tempting men. American

142

women do not believe that, no?"

I lay on my back thinking of the new girl in my suit, and of the boys' reaction to her. I pretended not to hear her question and stroked Big Dog's pudgy stomach. Here was a creature everyone loved, especially Em and Jimbo, and she was no picture of perfect proportions.

I turned my head toward Sanna. She probably didn't deserve to be punished, I was trying to convince myself, for looking good in my suit.

"And Shelby . . . who does . . . are you asleep, Shelby?"

"No . . ." It occurred to me then I might tell her to call me Turtle. But I didn't. Not yet.

"Who does Jimbo . . . ? Does he . . . prefer . . . someone?"

"You mean prefer, like, *prefer*?"

"Yes. Jimbo."

Sanna's tone sure sounded casual-like — that's what I reckoned, lying stone still, my eyes closed. Maybe if I pretended to have drifted back off, the question would die right there where it had got itself born — breach, and not right in the head.

But she propped herself up on one elbow and leaned over me. I could smell curry.

I told myself that the metal tacks mambo-

ing on my insides wasn't fear for myself —
only concern for her sake. For her mistake.
I opened one eye. "You know," I began
slowly, "his momma named him after a Civil
War hero, some great-great-great-something
or other in the family. *Beauregard.* Which is
how she got accepted into the Daughters of
the Confederacy, real active member." I
shut that one eye and waited.

Farsanna did not budge.

I opened the other eye this time and tried
another sail into the wind. "Jimbo's never
been one to go out much just for the sake
of something to do."

"Then he is . . . dating . . . no one?"

Now she was making me mad, her not
understanding, not even trying. "Jimbo?
Shoot. Who'd go out with Jimbo?" I lifted
my head to see her looking at me, and
returned my head to its rock. "He'd rather
spend an evening reading *Consumer Reports*
on fertilizer and pulling ticks off the Big
Dog. Not," I told the beast beside me, "that
there's anything the matter with that."

I could feel the new girl's eyes on me and
the dog. "He is nice for looking."

"Big Dog's a girl."

"No, I —"

"Who . . . ?" I shielded my eyes with my
hand. *"Jimbo?"*

"Yes. You do not think — ?"

"Shoot. *No.*"

It was partially true anyway. Jimbo Riggs was not handsome, not really. Dark hair stuck out over his ears in crow's wings because he never could remember to keep it clipped. His two front teeth stuck out slightly and just barely crossed; his nose was a little too large; his eyebrows, a little too bushy. Like a koala bear cub, Jimbo Riggs was one of those irresistible creatures who meet not one single standard of beauty.

And then, too, Jimbo Riggs' green eyes always looked up to mischief — mischief he himself probably knew nothing about. His way with language was the only form of rebellion he'd ever practiced: All the fathers on the mountain trusted Jimbo fully with their daughters, a reputation Jimbo preferred not be publicly known.

"Em," I once asked my brother as we rocked on our front porch. "You and Jimbo are both still virgins, aren't you?" I'd never used the word — outside singing "Silent Night" during the annual Methodist church pilgrimage my mother forced on our family. But I was feeling grown-up that day, and worldly.

Em's fingers froze on the neck of his guitar. "Where'd my kid sister learn to talk that kind of smut?"

"Well, aren't you?"

Jimbo was there on the porch too, sprawled deep in the hammock. "Now Turtle, my girl," came from inside the hammock's green folds, "what comes to make you think that?" His hands were dropping peanuts into the glass neck of a bottle — the way he liked his Cokes best.

"It's what people say, is why."

Jimbo sat up slowly. He and Emerson exchanged glances. "Well, sweet tea and Jesus," Jimbo said.

Emerson thrummed a mangled chord. "Lord, Bo. It's even worse than we thought."

And then there were Jimbo's dimples: Whether or not they'd got the consent of their owner, they said flattering things girls wanted to hear. Even a best friend's little sister could see the attraction. Maybe especially a best friend's little sister.

Though I chose not to say so to the new girl.

"I don't know that Jimbo's your type," was what I managed instead.

Sanna propped herself up on one elbow. "And your brother?" she asked. "He is not either my type?"

I could feel her inspecting my face. I could feel the air between us, hot and humid, unstable, like summer had reached a rolling boil.

But she said no more of Jimbo Riggs that day. Or my brother Emerson, either. So I told myself there was no need for me to explain. Things happened around Jimbo, and at the Blue Hole, that didn't make sense, not given how the rest of the world worked. I told myself she ought to know by now about lines, and about boundaries and walls. " 'Good fences make good neighbors,' " Em had quoted from one of his poets to me months ago. It was during a dispute over the bathroom we shared, but I thought now how that was true. Sanna surely understood about how things could go only so far and no farther.

A "Bridge Over Troubled Water" was all well and good in its place, and we all sang along on the front porch when Em or Jimbo thrummed out Simon and Garfunkel on the guitar. But some waters couldn't be bridged overnight, or at all, and she ought to be able to see that.

9. IN THE HEAT OF THE NIGHT

Down in the Valley, police had yet to turn up a suspect in the Seventh Street shootings. One of the victims, whom the paper described as a fifty-year-old black female, was released from the hospital. The area of her shoulder that a bullet had grazed had become badly infected.

"Hey, L. J.," I said as we slid down the final drop to the Blue Hole. Maybe it was the descent that reminded of me of our trip to the Valley, or maybe it was the eerie red of the twilight that was settling into the rim of the Hole that reminded me that darkness was coming, and how arson fires still burned most nights down in the city. "L. J., you read this morning's paper?" Of course he had: He was L. J. I didn't wait for his answer. "You know the article on the search for the perpetrators of the Seventh Street shooting, how it mentioned one of the victims was finally healing well?" Dusting himself off from the slide, he nodded and let me go on. "Well, how come we didn't even know she was hurt in the first place? I mean, do you remember the paper's ever mentioning a bullet actually made contact?"

L. J. pushed his horn-rims up his nose and examined the water. "First, we weren't fully cognizant because we didn't go back to check."

"You think we should've gone back?"

"What do *you* think?"

"I think our parents would've tanned our hides if they'd known we were there in the first place."

"Beside the point. And secondly, we didn't know because the paper only informed us of what we wanted to hear: that no one was seriously injured, no reason for concern."

"But . . ." I felt contentious. Something about L. J. always made me take the other side of a subject. "But her shoulder *was* just grazed."

My cousin let his glasses slide down the sweat on his nose so he could give me a look over the top of the rims. "If the group of women on the sidewalk had been you and Farsanna . . ." He stopped there, reconsidered. "If *you'd* been the one on the walk and a bullet brushed by your shoulder, and the guy firing might have been drunk and

149

might have been black, do you think it likely that our legal system would have tracked down at least one suspect by now?"

I felt the wet red clay rise between my bare toes. I might have answered, eventually, but L. J. grew tired of waiting — if he even expected an answer — and rose, leaving his glasses folded alongside his towel. By the time I'd thought of a way to respond, L. J. was upside down on the rope swing, his legs flailing back over his head in a slow roll whose final flourish, a loud, full-belly flop, earned him applause and hoots from the boys lined up at the sweetgum.

On the way home from the Hole that evening, after ice cream, we stopped first at Sanna's, which was closest to the Dairy Queen. In the house, one light burned in the living room, unguarded by curtains. I thought I saw the top of a head, or perhaps the mound of a rounded back.

Farsanna must have noticed my squinting to see better.

"My father is making a prayer," she offered. But only that. And even that, the word *prayer,* pronounced with a kind of a warning, told me that she would not willingly offer more.

I nodded, to let her know I'd no desire to

go panning for more — which was true. Religious practices of the truly faithful have always made me nervous — maybe because I've lived my life outside the glass with my nose pressed against it. Those who water their beliefs down to weak broth I tolerate better, maybe because I can scorn them.

But a man with his face to the floor in that red box of a house was not something I needed to know more about. I wondered what he was praying about. If I'd been in his place, knowing what I knew about where he'd moved his family, I'd have prayed for safety from a whole band of heavenly hosts — anyone they could give me.

"I was under the impression," L. J. mused, his arms crossed over folded knees, "that your family were not practicing Muslims." It was a real request for information, and lacking several layers of his usual sneer.

Farsanna sat in the truck bed, apparently in no hurry to exit. "The parents of my parents follow more closely," she returned. "My parents do not follow completely all . . ." She felt for the word.

"Are not devout," L. J. corrected.

She nodded. "Yes. However —"

"Which is evidenced," he continued like it was an additional mathematical fact required to solve this equation, "by your being allowed to run around virtually naked."

We all scowled at L. J.

His face torched red underneath his glasses. "That is, scantily clad. At the Blue Hole, at least. Naked, I mean, only relative to female populations among devout followers of Islam."

I'd never seen my cousin so rattled, and I was enjoying the show — though it occurred to me to be hurt that no one had ever accused me of looking practically naked when I'd worn that same suit.

L. J. was trying to dig himself out of his hole. "That is, naked not in any epistemological sense, but only in a comparative . . ." Wisely, he shifted direction. "I believe you mentioned Sri Lanka was Buddhist."

Farsanna didn't seem to be much offended. "In Sri Lanka, it is not most common to be Muslim. Nearly seventy percent Buddhist is the population. Fifteen percent Hindu. The Moors, my people, speak Tamil as our first language, but are not of the Tamil people. We support the Sinhalese government. However, we wish most to be left in peace."

L. J. nodded, looking relieved to be back on the firm footing of world politics. "You've faced discrimination, then?"

Sanna glanced up at us. "Yes." She shifted

in her seat and played with Stray's ear.

"So," Bobby Welpler interjected from the corner of the truck bed where he'd been sulking in a tight, curled-up ball, "you folks just plain don't belong, huh? Nowhere. Reckon your people would be just like old Stray here."

I hurled a handful of loose mulch toward Welp's corner. "Stray belongs with Sanna. Sanna belongs with us. You got a problem with that?"

Bo squeezed my leg in approval. But Sanna's face didn't register that she'd heard my heroic defense of her. She directed her response to Welp. "It," she said slowly, "has been sometimes difficult."

From his corner, Welp's eyes were glowing like a cat in a closet. "So what do you people do? Worship rocks? Or trees, maybe? Line up behind your daddy and his fifty-nine wives and bow west?"

"East, idiot," was L. J.'s contribution.

Jimbo motioned for Welp. "Bob, you got something on you. C'mere."

Welp leaned over for Jimbo to see, while Jimbo wiped his own filthy thumb in two swipes, down and across, over Welp's forehead.

"Ashes to ashes," Bo said. And that was all.

■ ■ ■ ■

After dropping off Sanna, we passed the Pump and Run, and Jimbo put his hand up in greeting. Mort Beckwith was there filling his tank, and, moving in his usual slow motion, his big head swung up from where he'd been staring at the gas nozzle and focused in on the back of our truck only once we'd passed by.

At the end of Fairview, where my cousin lived, L. J. swung himself out of the flatbed.

Welp stood too. "Reckon I'll come spend the night again."

L. J. never turned his head. "No," he said, his Keds already crunching up the gravel drive. "Reckon you won't." With his hand held above his head in a quick wave — more of a chop — but his face never turning, he disappeared behind the screen door.

Bobby Welpler recoiled into his ball and did not speak until we reached his mother's drive, two parallel dirt tracks between which knee-high weeds flourished. No lights glowed from the trailer, not even the faintest pulse of a television screen that, it occurs to me now, I'd always seen as its weak, flickering heart.

His eyes on the dark trailer, Welp paused

for moment just before he lowered himself to the ground. There, too, he stood looking, his hands on his hips.

"Anybody home, you reckon?" Jimbo asked gently as Welp began his approach, not once turning to look back over his shoulder.

Bobby did not turn back, but only barked over his shoulder. *"Beat it,"* was Bobby Welpler's benediction to us.

On the next Saturday afternoon, punctured to useless by thundershowers and drizzle, Emerson and I stayed home to read. I'd just discovered a third Brontë sister, Anne — Emily and Charlotte had been my favorites the summer before — and I was busy helping the heroine escape with her son from the demon of a husband who'd just installed his mistress as the son's governess.

Tucked inside the *Sports Illustrated* swimsuit issue, *The Complete Poems of John Donne* was open on Emerson's chest. I knew better than to let out I knew it was there.

Emerson and Jimbo had just that week determined to look more official and paint their business's name on the cab doors of the truck: Big Dog Lawn and Garden Beautifiers. Jimbo had phoned that morning.

I answered. "Maynard residence. Shelby speak—"

"Hey, lady," Jimbo said.

"Hey."

"Tell that guy who claims to be your brother he ain't half as good-looking as you, and that I got to paint the truck door with our name, so I can't make it to the Hole today. Got to design the sign — design the sign this time in rhyme —"

"In *rhyme?*"

"Naw. Just got going and couldn't stop."

"But it's supposed to rain, Bo."

"Who the whom says?"

"Me. Look at the sky."

"Then tell him I gotta de-lice my nose hairs and can't make it."

"I'll tell him, but —"

"So we'll go tomorrow, okay?"

"I'll tell him. But, Bo —"

"You be good, Turtle."

"Hey, Jimbo?"

"Yep?"

"You know, did I ever tell you I'm not real fond of that name."

"Of *Turtle?*"

"Yeah. Turtle."

"Me either. Corn-shuckin' shame you got stuck with it."

"But it was you who gave me it, Bo."

"Poor Turtle-Girl. Didn't your momma ever warn you 'bout hanging with the wrong crowd?"

L. J. called after that to say he and his brothers had to help their daddy at the Feed and Seed unloading bales of pine straw. "I have been unavoidably detained" was actually how he said it, but the few of us who liked L. J. even a little back then tried to help cover for his talking funny. So L. J. couldn't go to the Hole either. Emerson made a point of calling Farsanna — *we gotta at least let her know that nobody's going today,* he explained — but nobody was home.

I don't recall if we thought to call Bobby Welpler.

It was nearly dinnertime when the sun came out and my novel's husband-villain was finally killed off. I had decided along with Anne Brontë that they were all villains — all husbands, I mean, maybe all men — and I turned to Big Dog lying beside me for comfort. I stretched out full length in the hammock I'd been curled in for hours, and raised my head slightly toward Em. "You hungry? Wanna go out?"

Emerson lowered his *Sports Illustrated,* its tell-tale weight in the middle making it slip from his hands. Real hastily, he tucked John

Donne back beneath a tanned, busty blonde in a chartreuse bikini — it was college before I learned how much John Donne would have liked that.

"Where?" It was a rhetorical question. Pisgah Ridge in those days had only two restaurants: Hog Wild and one other, a brown daisy linoleum kind of place called the Home Plate Special. But with its all-you-can-eat buffet of fried okra, broiled liver and onions, black-eyed peas, and corn-bread, the Plate was the exclusive domain of folks who cut coupons and remembered the Great Depression firsthand. There was, okay, maybe a third place to eat, a concrete box fixed to the side of our one gas station — what Jimbo never called by its name, Pump and Run, favoring something close and a bit cruder — but their sandwiches stank of brake fluid.

Emerson and I borrowed our mother's car, since Jimbo had kept Emerson's truck to paint their new name on its door. We swung by the Riggs' parsonage on Elm, twelve blocks away. At first, no one answered the door.

"Hey, Em," I launched out, making a point of inspecting the brass dogwood door knocker, "does Bo prefer . . . I mean does Bo . . . you know . . . *like* . . . anyone?"

My brother stared at me. "Well, I *know* you're not asking for yourself, since I *know* Bo's like another brother to you, and only Alabamans get funny that way."

I swallowed hard. "Don't be weird. I meant, like, you know, anybody. Like maybe Neesa or Haley, that crowd. Like, does he think they're . . . you know . . ."

"Like they're *what?*"

"Like they're . . . good-looking . . . or something."

"Well, sure."

"What?"

"Sure he does. You think the man hadn't got eyes? And if he could make out with 'em and leave without having to try to actually *talk* with them, he'd do it, I reckon. But as it is, he'd just as soon spend his evenings with me. Or Big Dog. Or you."

I didn't have time to digest this before the door opened.

The Reverend Riggs was wearing his ill-fitted suit, the one he always wore. I wondered what he wore to bed. Or maybe, I thought, Baptist preachers never risked going to bed.

"I thought my boy was with you kids." Jimbo's daddy beamed at us — he also always beamed.

"No, sir." Emerson shook his head. "You

got any idea where he might be?"

"I sure thought he was with you kids." He opened the screen door wider. "Can I help you children somehow?" I sometimes wondered back then if he saw us — in the flesh, I mean — or saw us only as more people he needed to try to please into God's kingdom. So, around him, I always kept moving, even if slightly, for fear his big preacher-beam would one day hook and swallow me up.

"No, sir," Em tried again. "He didn't say anything about where he might go?"

It occurred to me then that I'd never heard the Reverend say the word no. It wasn't in his constitution. Even now, when he so clearly had nothing to offer in the way of whereabouts information, he nodded. "I surely did think he'd gone out looking for you. Reckon he didn't say exactly, now that I come to think of it. Would you two like to come in?"

We shook our heads, thanked him, and began backing down the stone stairs.

"I don't know as I can think," Jimbo's daddy was saying, "of anyone else Jimbo'd be out fetching here around dinnertime." But even as he said this, I thought I saw the opposite thought flicker across his pale globe of a face — that he'd just then latched onto something or someone specific. His

160

smile flickering and now forced, he continued nodding at us.

"Children?" he began. "I'm wondering . . ." His lips formed into an "o" that seemed to have no other plans to form other shapes.

We waited, then backed up one step at a time. The circle of Reverend Riggs' mouth, stuck in whatever it was he couldn't find the words for, and the circle of his balding blond head and the circle of his corpulent self all reminded me of the Weebles we'd played with as children.

Em thanked him again, and we crawled back into the car.

"Hey, Em. You got any idea how come the good Reverend is Jimbo's hero? I mean . . . you know what I mean. Sometimes he strikes me as sweet. Sometimes as silly. And sometimes I think maybe it's more like . . . scary somehow. Like . . . Hello? Emerson?"

Em's eyebrows had formed a dark line that dipped in the middle, like a preschooler's pencil-drawn bird in flight.

"What is it? You know where Bo might be?"

Emerson nodded, but said nothing.

"Tell me."

But Emerson drove on without looking at me.

Neither one of us spoke, though I knew exactly where we were going when we turned off the highway onto the old logging camp trail that led through raspberry thickets and pine woods down to the Blue Hole. The honeysuckle had blossomed, and even with the wheels churning dust into the air, its little white stars winked through a gritty dusk.

It was the honeysuckle, in fact, that I noticed first when we reached the Clearing up above the Blue Hole — honeysuckle strewn like confetti all over the seat of Emerson's white truck, sitting empty. Em reached in one hand, swept it clean to the floor, and kept walking. This day, his truck was the only one there.

My brother and I paced through the clearing without speaking.

Not that I didn't try: "I don't get —"

But each time, Emerson held up his hand.

At the top of the steep path, where you went barefoot or not at all, two pair of shoes sat side by side: a pair of size 14 sneakers, muddy and worn, and a woman's small brown sandals.

There went the tacks on my insides. My mouth hung wide open and I had no way to cover my looking kicked in the gut.

But Em wasn't looking at me. He'd

yanked off one sneaker before I grabbed hold of his T-shirt.

"Cut it out, Turtle. Come on."

I'd no idea what I wanted to say. I only knew that there was no way, *no way,* I was going down there. When I came up with words, I surprised even myself with what I choked out: "It's just a shame, is all."

"What?" Emerson looked up.

"Just that it's too bad we couldn't ever find him."

"Look, Turtle —"

"Too bad we couldn't find Jimbo."

Em stared at me.

I tried on a shrug. "Just a shame, is all I'm saying."

Emerson stood there, one Converse in hand. Then he rammed it back on. We limped back to the clearing together and paused by the empty pickup. Then we folded ourselves into our mother's sedan.

"You know how Bo is," I said. "Always looking to be nice. Not leaving anyone lonely. Or scared. Maybe she let Mort's games with his gun, or the shooting on Seventh, or the stares she gets around town — all that — start to connect in her head. Or —"

"It's not like Bo to beg off hanging with us. You name me one time he's ever done that. *Ever.* Till *she* came along."

I was stuck on the *You name me one time,* because I couldn't.

"Hey. Turtle." Emerson slammed the car into gear and spun the radio dial. The Eagles were belting out "Heartache To-night." He smacked the radio into silence.

"What's up?" I said then, casually, my way of asking how I could help him without letting him know I knew he needed help. And my way of covering for the tightness in my own chest.

"So what do we do?" he asked me.

"We make like nothing happened."

"Nothing better not have happened."

"Likely nothing has, Em."

He scowled as he drove through the parking lot. "Right. And Bo always takes a pair of little brown sandals with him when he blows us off and goes alone to the Hole, taking my truck without me."

"I mean maybe it doesn't *mean* anything. You know Jimbo. He's Mr. Everyman's Friend."

"I'm not saying anything *happened.* I'm saying . . ." He didn't finish running down that path. "It's one thing for us all to run in a group. But you know as well as I do that in this town if word were to get out —"

"How would it get out? Nobody knows

164

anything but you and me."

He clubbed the words: "What's there to know? What's there to say?"

"Hey, I'm on *our* side, remember? That was my point: There's nothing there to know." I was beginning to sound convincing even to myself. Which was helpful to the well-being of my insides.

"Somebody's got to talk to her." He rolled down his window. "Somebody could get hurt."

"What's wrong? Don't you like her?"

He shot his glance my way. "Who says I like her?"

"No, not *like* her. Don't be ridiculous. Of course you don't *like* her. I mean just like, just think she's all right. Look . . . nobody's attacking you here. What's the matter with you?"

Emerson stuck his arm out the window and waved it through the air. "Fine. So nothing has happened," he said, without looking at me. "Nobody's gonna get hurt."

"Nothing." I nodded. "And nobody." Though for no good reason I pictured the size fourteen sneakers and the little brown sandals so close beside them.

"Roll down your window, Turtle. I need more air."

I cranked the handle and did not say what

I was thinking: *Me too. Can you not see that? Me too.*

10. A House Maybe Divided

All the way up the old logging camp trail, Emerson kept his head faced forward.

"Movie," he said, and that was all.

"How 'bout if we stop first to eat?" We were just passing the turn onto Stonewall Jackson Pike, and I could smell hickory smoke. "I'm hungry, remember?"

"Popcorn," he said.

"*Really* hungry."

"Big bucket. With butter."

"But —"

"I'll buy."

I sat back and sighed. Pisgah Ridge had no movie theaters, so we were committing ourselves to a trip down to the Valley and back before getting our barbecued beans.

"You think," I ventured, "Momma'd mind our going down off the Ridge? I reckon if we stayed clear of downtown and Seventh and just stuck to the theaters. But has it been long enough after what happened?"

It was how the adults on our Ridge referred now in past tense to the Seventh Street shooting: "what happened." No suspects had even yet been apprehended, and our father had written an eloquent editorial for the paper on how regrettable this was. But in general, the sentiment aired in hushed tones was a kind of dismayed clucking over the inadvisability of boys' drinking themselves into misbehavior, as if naughty toddlers had Magic Markered the living room wallpaper.

Emerson made a sound deep in his throat. "I reckon the 'disturbances' are over. For now." He whipped the car onto Falling Creek, a two-lane dirt road that dropped off the back side of our mountain like a bulldozer had lost its brakes and cut its own path, careening first right and then left and then back, plowing down pines on all sides as it went.

A few minutes later, we stood side by side, gazing up, before the theater marquee. Even the Valley's choices were limited: one cinema, three screens, all second-run.

"*The Good-bye Girl,*" I read aloud. I turned to my brother. "Welp and somebody — was it Welp? — saw it and said the girl he was with liked it a lot. No . . . couldn't have been Welp. Anyhow, supposed to be a sweet story. I've been wanting to see —"

His feet planted apart, his arms crossed over his chest, Emerson stood looking up — not at the marquee, though, but past it. Up toward the backside of our ridge.

"Or," I read on down the marquee, "or then there's *The Deer Hunter.*" I waited. I sighed. "Vietnam war flick. Every girl's choice."

We paid for our tickets. The black couple in front of us in the line turned to look at us — and the girl's gaze dropped to my shorts. I was wearing the cutoffs, my favorites, and they weren't overly clean. She had on French-cut jeans, an avocado shirt that covered only one shoulder, a chain belt, and platform sandals, every inch of her sleek and well heeled, straight out of *Seventeen* magazine. I waited until she turned back to her date to wrinkle my nose at her.

We'd already missed the previews, and also the opening scenes. Not that I cared. I closed my eyes and kept them closed mostly — peeking only to reach for the popcorn and Coke, and occasionally, unintentionally, see a man's forehead blown open. For the most part, I sat in the dark, and sometimes covered my ears. I opened one eye for the closing credits.

"Hey, Turtle." Em rose and stretched.

169

"Thanks."

"Hey, Em, you're welcome." I slipped an arm around his waist as we left the theater. "You owe me big-time."

Squeals speared us from behind. Haley Foreman and Neesa Nell Helms were hailing us from across the parking lot. Hailing Emerson, I should say. They waved and bounced over to us — to him.

Neesa ran her fingers along his shoulder and bicep. "You *are so sweet* to bring your *sister* to the movies. *So sweet.*" In a white peasant blouse that she wore off the shoulder, she looked sweet herself — in that way of a milkmaid bent on seduction. She blinked her blue eyes, made so big behind navy mascara that they'd overtaken her face.

Em glanced at his watch. "Awfully late, isn't it, for you girls to be running loose down here in the Valley?"

"Loose," I muttered close to his ear, "would be the operative word."

Neesa answered my brother by shifting her shoulders and ever so slightly brushing against him. "Must've lost all track of time," she purred.

Swinging her attention to me, Haley pivoted on one heel of the spiked red Candies she wore with her jeans. "Where's your friend, Shelby Lenoir?"

It might have been a question; it might have been a taunt.

I just shrugged.

Neesa dropped a hand onto Emerson's forearm. "Bless her heart, that Shelby. I think it's awful sweet of her." She shifted her weight from one hip to the next and back again.

"What?" Emerson asked, not looking too much at her — at her face. The rest got his attention just fine.

"Making new friends. Your sweet little sister." Neesa's hand brushed down his arm. She rolled her hips into reverse, signaling their exit. Both girls waved.

"Call me," Neesa shouted from the little MGB whose top she kept rolled down most of the year round.

Emerson waved back.

He opened the sedan door for me — a first. And, come to think of it, last. "You know, Turtle, you're not half bad."

"As girls go," I added for him.

"As girls go."

11. Coming to Blows

"Shelby! Shelby Lenoir!" It was Momma's voice, which was usually sweet and soft as moss, except when she cranked up the volume — then the sweetness grew serrated edges.

Our house was old and graceful and large: the only inheritance — along with a sizable stash of sterling silver platters and pickle forks — from my mother's mother's side of the old Carolina aristocracy. Or that was how Momma's family was billed to us — by Momma. Besides the front porch, which wrapped three-quarters of the way around, my favorite feature of the house was its ceilings, ten feet high and crowned with crenellated molding and carved ceiling medallions above crystal and brass chandeliers. If I wanted to imagine myself a misplaced princess of the plantation South, I had only to look up. Looking down was less helpful, the wood floors having been covered eight years ago in a long gold and green shag that snagged Momma's high heels.

From a top floor window, my mother was calling, stopping me cold mid-leap into the back of my brother's truck.

"Shelby Lenoir, sugar, a phone call for you!" She smoothed her voice back to its purr. She had visitors that morning, the Pisgah Ridge Garden Club ladies. Taking stock of how many of the ladies might have seen me leap in and back out of the bed of the truck, she called less loudly, "Honey, you're *not* going with your brother to work again, are you?"

"Wait for me?" I begged Emerson.

He rolled his eyes, but shifted the truck to idle.

Taking the stairs three at a time, I panted into the phone: "Hello?"

"This is Farsanna Moulavi."

That was like her, adding her last name. How many Farsannas did she think we kept on the Ridge?

"Hey," I said. "We're just leaving for work. We'll swing by for you later on the way to the Hole."

"Yes. However —"

"Okay, then, see you —"

"I am asking if you would like at my house to spend Wednesday night."

Her house. I pictured the warehouse-brick rectangle. And the mother, heavily draped in her hijab and fear, and the father, dark and short-statured and somber, whom I'd only seen from a distance through the plate-glass window. And I smelled the curry, wafting on hot currents of air. Wednesday night — tomorrow night! — was still hours away. Maybe I'd find myself accountably stricken with a temporarily incurable disease.

"Hold on," I said, and I covered the mouthpiece. "Momma!"

She appeared at the door of the kitchen. "You needn't shout so, dear. I wasn't in the Congo."

"Can I spend tomorrow night with . . . someone?" I prayed she would say no if I were just vague enough.

She looked startled — but not so startled she couldn't ride herd on my grammar: "*May* I."

"Yes, ma'am. *May* I. I reckon that's probably not a very good time, being . . ."

But Momma looked pleased. I never had sleepovers. Except when Emerson and I had Jimbo sleep over — that happened lots. But that didn't count, my being a girl. "Why, of course, Shelby, honey. Of course. And do come out and say hello to the ladies."

"I, um," I stalled into the phone, then

sighed. "Great. Sounds great." It wasn't true, not really, but it had to be said.

"Great," said the new girl.

"Great," I said again, and wrinkled my nose. "So, then . . . so I guess I'll see you later today. Bye."

I dropped the phone in its cradle and grabbed the screen door handle.

"Shelby, *sugar?*" Momma called. It was the kind of *sugar* that works like a yank to a leash.

"Yes, ma'am?"

"Who is it? Which of your girlfriends asked you to sleep over?"

Bless Momma. She said this as if there were legions of girls waiting to ask me to their houses, and as if I got calls every day from girls with exotic accents. I caught the screen door before it slammed shut behind me, which Momma could not stand — the slamming, I mean. "The, um, the new girl," I said, not quite meeting her eye. Though I could feel the Garden Club — Mrs. Regina Lee Riggs at its center — listening intently.

"The new girl," Momma repeated.

"Yes, ma'am."

"You don't mean the sweet little girl from . . . where is she from, dear?"

"Yes, ma'am. Sri Lanka."

Now, all white Southern women keep as a

weapon against an uncouth world a certain smile that can be whipped out of storage and tacked up in an instant, covering over a multitude of too-candid moments. My mother's face, whose upturned mouth never moved, registered confusion, then fear — then landed where I expected: that steely, doggedly cheerful resolve of a smile.

She was at least quick with her calculations, and I watched her face, its sweetness thickening, hardening, like warmed syrup cooling: She was considering, I knew, that the Garden Club ladies were gripping sweet tea beside her, but also what Jesus would do. "Well, now," she murmured. " 'Turn ye not away strangers, lest ye entertain angels unawares.' Isn't that right?" Momma looked to the wife of the good Reverend Riggs.

Regina Lee Riggs had been poorly assigned, I'd always thought, as a small mountain town's Baptist preacher's wife. Slender and sleek, she wore her brown, shoulder-length hair in a ribbon headband that each day matched her dress and her shoes. She was blue-blooded — and Virginian-First-Family-blue at that, which runs several shades deeper. Besides the Beauregard she'd passed down to Jimbo, she had the Lee in her name, as in Robert E.

But besides Regina Lee Riggs being more elegant, there was something else about her presence, always so gracious, always so tense, something high-strung and caged there, like a white tiger pacing behind her smile. I sometimes wondered if she secretly hated going to church or had some private gripe with her husband or God.

"Yes, ma'am," I said, though Momma still wasn't looking at me. "Yes, ma'am." I stuffed my hands deep within the pockets of my cutoffs. The pockets were full of holes too. "May I go now?"

"I'd no idea you all were such . . . *chums.* You and the new girl."

"We just go swimming together is all."

"Go swimming? You mean at that place you all go?"

"Yes, ma'am."

"You mean *all* of you all?" Momma asked. Regina Lee Riggs lowered her tea.

"Yes, ma'am."

"You mean you and this new girl and — ?"

"Just Emerson and them. Nobody special."

Regina Lee Riggs watched my face.

I grasped for a distraction: "And Welp, most of the time."

Regina Lee Riggs followed that path:

"That little Bobby Welpler, you mean?" She and Momma exchanged glances. "Bless his heart," Mrs. Riggs said, "is his mother still drinking, do you know, Shelby Lenoir?"

"Yes, ma'am. I reckon."

"Well." Momma concluded the interrogation in just those two syllables — two when Momma pronounced it.

But Regina Lee Riggs followed me past the screen door to the front steps. "I suppose, Shelby, that my James goes too. 'Course I know he goes swimming. And you all run together, of course?" It was a question.

For once Momma fussed over my hair, smoothing a lump and tucking a lock of straw behind my right ear. "You could run fetch a barrette, Shelby Lenoir," she began.

"That's all right, Momma. I need to go —"

"You know you could try just a little, Shelby Lenoir, honey."

I motioned with my head back toward Emerson. "I'm sorry, Momma. Emerson's been waiting for me. You know how men are when we're late."

And with that I was down the front steps.

Momma did know men, and knew they must not be kept waiting. She let me go. "Your Jim," I heard her say to Mrs. Riggs, and loud enough too for the Garden Club ladies in general, "is just the sweetest thing this town ever did see. Regina, you must surely be proud." Momma waved to her own boy there in the truck, and then even tossed out an extra wave to Big Dog, whom Momma'd never cared much for, her shedding too much on the carpet.

Emerson had propped a *Sports Illustrated* on the steering wheel and appeared to be reading it — though there was no telling what kind of steamy, seventeenth-century seduction one-liners hid underneath.

I leapt into the back of the truck and snapped open the cab window.

"What the heck took you so long?" Emerson growled at me as he slammed the truck into reverse.

"Well, now," I said in a voice low and sweet, just like our momma's, "guess whose kid sister is bunking up in foreign territory tomorrow night?" I held up my right palm, my left fist right beside it.

Jimbo was waiting at the end of the parsonage drive when we pulled up. I was certain he showed no signs of being anything but the Jimbo he'd always been — and I told myself this over and over that morning, to make sure it stuck. The good Reverend

Riggs was there too, one leg already inside the cab of the beige El Camino that carted him around to his flock.

He beamed at Emerson and me. "You children off to work bright and early?"

"Yes, sir," we said together.

"That's nice. So you can be done early. Big believer in that myself. Early to bed, early to rise." He wobbled, one foot still inside the El Camino, one foot on the street, his tentative smile balanced above them — precarious, as if he were asking us to like him.

"Except," I couldn't help adding, "I reckon you have to work some nights." I pictured that knot of men emerging from the Riggs' screen porch door, the men whose faces we couldn't see. But whose voices had been demanding, some kind of threat behind the studied calm of the words. "Some nights maybe real late."

Emerson mouthed from behind Jimbo's head, "Cut it out, Turtle."

But the good Reverend Riggs only looked pleased, "Well, now. I reckon I do, when I'm needed." He patted his boy on the shoulder.

"Well now, you children take care of each other, you hear?"

Bo slung an arm around both of our

shoulders with such force, Emerson's and my forehead slammed together. "That's what mangy packers do best," Jimbo assured his daddy.

"And . . . son?"

"Yes, sir?"

"You don't go . . . don't go *looking* for trouble, you hear?"

Bo cocked his head, his green eyes big and innocent. "Trouble? No, sir. Hadn't never heard the word."

The three of us waved to him as we drove off. It looked to me like the Reverend might've had more on his mind, like he might be just starting to speak, but Emerson had the pickup out of the drive and onto the road, so the good Reverend Riggs only waved. Big Dog stood in her passenger seat and wagged.

Emerson waited until our lunch break to open the flap of what I could tell had got camped out in his brain.

"So we saw a movie last night. Me and Turtle."

Jimbo's mouth bulged with jelly and banana on white bread, his favorite, which he washed down with the usual: Coke studded in peanuts. He ignored Emerson's tone, less like a here's-what-we-did than a right hook to the jaw. "Yeah? What flick?"

I made a face. "*The Deer Hunter.* I just *insisted.*"

Jimbo patted my leg. "You're a good man, Turtle."

Emerson grunted, but Bo ignored him.

By late afternoon, we were drenched with sweat. I was wet straight through till my skin didn't know itself from my shirt. Momma would've insisted that as a young lady, I was only *glowing.* Reckon it looked and smelled like more than glow to me. We'd sprayed each other and Big Dog down with the hose any number of times, and still the sun broiled us on down to the bone. Big Dog, bless her heart, didn't budge from under her dogwood tree, where her tongue spilled out of her mouth and puddled on dirt. The pickup's eight-track player sang to us all day, but Diana Ross and James Brown together *in person* that day couldn't have lifted us up out of that heat.

At one point, Jimbo leapt up onto a bound of mulch bags in the truck bed, the shovel in his hand serving as microphone. *Ain't no mountain high enough,* he lip-synced down to us, *to keep me from you.*

I lifted my trowel to croon back to him: *Ain't no river wide enough . . .*

And the two of us twirled and swanked

and grooved among bags of mulch and manure and partially weeded flower beds and half-mown lawn, both of us turning to point and address Em on the chorus's punch, *To keep me from you!*

Emerson waited until the song finished. Then only this, sullenly: "When you're through messing around, we got work to finish."

"You know, Turtle, this is why Diana ditched the Supremes," Jimbo said, winking at me as he jumped from the truck bed. "You people ready," he asked, leaning on his shovel, "to make like hounds for the Hole?"

"Any reason you got to quit early?" Emerson snarled. But he switched off the mower.

"It's after five, old man. And over five hundred Fahrenheit. What's been eating your gizzard all day anyway?"

"Nothing."

"Uh-huh. So it's nothing."

"You heard me."

One bushy eyebrow raised, Jimbo looked my way.

"Don't ask me, Bo. I just got born into the same family."

"Hard luck. Tell you what, Turtle, we'll dip him seven times in the Hole and see if he ain't some better then."

"And then what?"

"If he ain't all good-as-better by then, we'll just hold him under the last time."

Emerson circled the tools on the ground three times, then paced to the pickup and snatched up a saw. I watched him scramble up an old pear tree and begin to trim out dead branches, working the saw with gusto.

Bo returned to change his shovel for trowel, and he slung a bag of manure up onto his shoulder. "Em, man, you plan on leaving a trunk on that tree? The way you're hacking —"

Em climbed back down the tree and hurled his saw to the ground. "Oh, *I'm* the one hacking, am I? *I'm* the dangerous one here, that it?"

"Whoa. Haul back on them reins, man. Who slipped a burr under your strap?"

Emerson stood up on his limb. "You ever stop to think about what you're doing? You ever stop to think about somebody else besides yourself? Last night, what you went and —"

"I been meaning to talk to you about last night. 'Cause we talked."

"Yeah, well, what you . . . Who's *we?*"

"Them," I said, supplying what was not very helpful.

Jimbo stepped toward the half-massacred

pear tree. "Me and Farsanna. About us. About all of us."

I was stuck on the *Farsanna.* Funny how her name could still sound so strange to me. But there it was, pronounced all careful and particular by the guy who'd flunked a straight flush of our high school's foreign language classes.

Sadness sloshed around inside me like rainwater that kept rising, rising.

"No nickname for the new girl?" I asked, instead of crying.

"Give me time," Jimbo said, and he smiled, one of those smiles with whispers behind it. Which was why, maybe, Emerson leapt at him from the tree, knocked him flat.

Bo lay there, sprawled like just-shot wild game in the grass. "Did I . . . miss . . . something?" He went to stand, when Emerson hauled back and slugged him.

Jimbo was back flat in the grass. He hiked one of his feet in the air right as Emerson dove for him, and my brother took a size 14 in the gut.

But even before Em had leveraged himself upright, he was lunging again for Jimbo.

"Em!" Bo blocked a blow to the head. "Man, *talk* to me. What —" he rolled right, just missing another lunge for his head, "is *wrong* with you?"

Emerson pulled back his right arm again. Jimbo's gaze, just ever so briefly, shifted over to me, running to them. He looked back at Em's fist, colliding then with Bo's face.

It was my fault, I figured right then, Bo's not relocating his face in time, the distraction of me running at them. I dove for Emerson's wrists, clawed into the one I caught, and pinioned it around to his back.

"How *dare* you," Emerson bellowed at Bo, "put her in danger for nothing but your own — your own —" My brother's free arm flailed, and I held tight to the other one, in hopes of preventing another swing.

The free arm drew back and aimed, then dropped to his side, hung useless, unhinged. Big Dog had risen from her place in the shade and whined by my side.

They stood, the two of them, staring at each other, both of them panting and filthy, both of them bruised, Jimbo bleeding.

Bo nodded, like they'd just completed a whole conversation I couldn't hear. "It's okay," he said.

His shoulders hunched, Emerson was shaking his head at the grass. "Don't do this to her."

Bo reached a hand and lowered it to Em's shoulder, lightly, like it might topple off. "To her?" he asked. "Or to you?"

There it was, out where we could see it: My brother was in love with the new girl too. *Too.* My brother *and* his best friend were in love with the new girl.

The one fruit of its kind in a whole garden of showy, available Neesas, and they both had to want the forbidden.

"No." It was all I could manage from my seat on the grass.

So they were in love, both of them at the same time, with the same girl. Two boys who'd always shared everything: their landscaping business, their peanuts, their Cokes, Bo's tape collection, the truck, and Big Dog.

Until the new girl and the map we'd all learned to make with our hands.

The little boat they'd paddled, Jimbo and Em, for so many years — and with me in the hull — had run up on a rock, and I could feel us all rocking there, the keel bending, misshapen. We'd hit trouble head-on, crashed straight up on top of it.

Em's hands twitched at his sides, his face spasmed up like the mad might break loose from under the skin. "Don't you care a *thing* about her safety?"

"What?"

"It's one thing for all of us to run together, be seen like that. But just her and —" he choked on the next word, *"you!* Why do you think I've left her alone? Huh? Why do you think? You *JERK!*"

"Maybe," Jimbo said, just hardly above a whisper, "I don't think less of her than you do, cowboy. Maybe I think a little more of this Ridge."

"*This* place? Are you nuts?"

"You sound like L. J."

"Well, maybe he's right."

"Well, maybe I got faith."

"Faith in what? You got faith in Mort? Seventh Street? What?"

"In change, maybe. In maybe . . . redemption, you know?"

Em blew air through his nose and looked as if he might take another swing. "Right. And I got faith in sunshine and daisies. You got any evidence anything's changed so much here?"

"Nope. Just scraps of the holy hoped for, that's all."

I must've moaned then, or somehow made myself known. For the first time since he'd leapt at Bo, Em looked over at me. I felt like crying — though I ducked my head fast so maybe they couldn't see my face crinkle. "What's wrong with you?"

"Me? Oh, I don't know. Just enjoying a ringside seat at the fights."

"Well, pull yourself together, Turtle."

188

"Right. You're obviously the emotionally *stable* one in the family."

Jimbo grabbed his watch, the plastic Mickey Mouse band he'd won at Six Flags. "Hey, we got to git! It's quitting time and the Hole's waiting on us to fill it." He brushed away what Emerson was about to say. "Look, you might wanna know what the fair lady said about us."

Em snorted again. "Oh, yeah. I been dying to hear what she said about you and her —"

"Not me and *her,* Spud-Head. Me and *you.* And . . . her."

Emerson turned slowly to face his best friend.

Bo shook his head, his dimples beginning to show. "I thought that might get your attention. Look, you wanna hear the whole putrid truth?"

Em folded his arms over his chest. "Maybe."

I lay back on the grass and wished I could cover my ears.

Bo walked up to inches from Emerson's face. "Goes something like this. Her Ladyship Fair likes *us.*"

"Who's *us?*"

Bo shrugged. "Us whole mangy pack. And, romantically speaking, the lady finds herself asundered."

"Asundered?"

"Ripped clear to shreds by the pain of competing passions. For us."

"Who's *us?*"

"Me and you. She likes us both. Although . . ." Jimbo's dimples deepened. "She does find me a particularly irresistible specimen of manhood."

"She said that?"

"Didn't have to. I could see it in her eyes. She could barely keep her hands off me."

Emerson brightened a bit. "But she managed, didn't she?"

The approach of Mollybird's ancient Buick, thunderous, with the occasional ping, announced her return. The roses on her straw hat bobbed as her head jerked side to side, forward and back, surveying our work. The Buick rolled to a stop, thundered and pinged for several long moments, then proceeded on to the back of the house. We exchanged relieved glances: At least for today, our work had been approved and Mollybird would fetch her sweet tea to the screen porch rather than charge into the yard to list which of her wishes we'd carried out inadequately.

Jimbo turned to me and pointed to the grass stains across his chest. "How d'I look?

These match my eyes, Turtle?"

The grass stains did, in fact, match his eyes, and I suddenly, desperately needed to tell him just that, at that moment the most urgent fact in the world.

But Jimbo didn't stand still to hear me say so.

12. Ropes and Threads

As we pulled up to the Feed and Seed, Bobby and L. J. were unloading a shipment of mulch and had just finished helping out for the day. Uncle Waymon waved to us from the office and turned back to the cash register. The boys swung into the flatbed.

"We stopping for that new girl?" Welp, all edgy and frowning, was wanting to know. He was wearing his jeans with unfrayed slits in the knees.

Jimbo eyed him up and down. "Reckon we stopped off for *you,* Wonder Welp."

Because I wanted one — needed one — myself, I handed the boys Cokes from the cooler. L. J. produced a bag of peanuts from his pocket and we passed it around, each of us popping into the bottles our required number. I always preferred five, and no more. Jimbo, on the other hand, liked to get the bag last so he could baptize all those remaining.

The new girl was waiting at the plate-glass window, her long, red cotton skirt hanging a little lower — and maybe more ragged at the hem than it used to. Behind in the dark sat her mother, only an oval of face-flesh showing out of a swaddling of scarf. I watched Jimbo as our new passenger boarded. He greeted her warmly, as usual — but nothing out-of-the-way warmly for Jimbo.

I raised my Coke to her, my greeting, and fished through the ice for another. L. J. passed her the peanuts — what few Jimbo'd left.

Bobby Welpler, I noticed, sat still and sullen. But then he'd always been given to fits. "We can't be stopping here," he spit out as Em pulled us into the drive.

"How's your momma?" I asked him. I was feeling malicious.

If he heard me, he didn't let on, just stared past my ponytail into the woods.

And I remember wondering then, at that moment, if Bobby Welpler — pimply, tag-along Welp — were capable, ever, of any real harm.

Neither Farsanna nor Jimbo showed any

signs that day of anything having changed between them, or with any of us.

There was one time when we were all stomping our shoes off at the top of the footpath's slide down: They bumped against one another. But even then they sprang apart, like they'd both just brushed a wall of broken glass.

Jimbo was in rare form on the rope swing, performing flips with full twists so close to the sweetgum tree, I closed my eyes more than once. Each time he narrowly missed hitting the tree — but the closer he came, the harder he laughed.

Emerson's mood required not seven, as Jimbo had threatened, but a single good headfirst plunge into the icy waters.

Jimbo nodded cheerfully from beside Emerson's water-crater. "That ought to knock the puke out of him good."

Next to where I'd planned to sun myself in silence for the remainder — and there wasn't much — of the afternoon, Farsanna spread a towel: the same threadbare scrap of white terry cloth she brought every trip to the Blue Hole. It looked like the one my father took from a one-star motel whose hot water was broken — took it to even things out, he said — then bequeathed it to Big Dog for baths. The new girl's towel was like that but thinner.

I'd grown sleepy, and though I could hear Farsanna shifting restlessly beside me, I was content to listen to the splash and thrash, and then the steady lap, lap, lap of the Blue Hole and its everyday business. Warm, well-fed for the moment on peanuts and Coke, fully and completely content, I wished only to be left alone just then. Perhaps, I thought, if I kept my eyes closed . . .

"Shelby?"

I opened one eye. Wearing, as she always did these days at the Hole, my old suit, Farsanna was sitting up straight, her usual ramrod posture, and studying intently the boys on the rope swing — but not, so far as I could tell, any particular boy.

"Yeah?"

"Why is it only . . . them?"

"Where?" I raised my head groggily.

She pointed to the pendulum swing of the rope.

I shook my head. "What . . . them?"

"Girls are not open to it?"

"It's not open to girls," I corrected. "But it is. 'Course it is."

"Why do you not fly on the rope, then?"

I sat up, shading my eyes. "Me? Shoot. Why would I want to do that?" I shrugged and would have lain back down had I not gotten a good look at her eyes. I should have known better by then. She was prodding with them, as surely as if she'd poked me in the chest with a sweetgum branch. I watched the rope swing, where Buddy Buncombe and his sizable self were hurtling down toward brown water, a sizable hole when he hit. "Why would I want to do that?"

She said nothing, but I knew without looking she was still staring at me.

I wrapped my arms around my knees — though my thighs looked fat in that position. I frowned at the brown water — though the frown was intended for her. "I do what I do because I want to. Not because of any bunch of any boys. There's some things they can just *have*." I lay back down.

"*Mata,* my mother," she said flatly, "expresses similar views to that of yours."

I sat back up. All I'd ever seen of her mother was a dark circle of face deep in the shadows of a hideous house. A woman draped in cloth from head to toe. A woman I imagined bowing to her husband as she sprinkled curry over rice, and over the table and chairs, the floor. . . . I was not pleased with the comparison. *"What?"*

"Yes."

I heard myself snipping the ends off my words: *"I'm* like your mother?" The rock beneath my towel had become harder, sharper, and I shifted position.

"In this one way: There is for men a realm, as well as for women one. A good woman does not wish for what belongs to men."

"Oh, come on. That's not what I meant at all."

Her stiff, licorice hair moved as one piece when she turned her head back toward the brown water. "It may be that I did not understand you," she said.

Farsanna stood up without pushing off with her hands. "You are coming?" she asked, not taking her eyes from the sweet-gum.

"Oh, come *on.* So what if they've got one little ol' rope to themselves? So what?"

She stood where she was.

I threw my hands up. "Look, girls just don't go off it, all right?"

"Then it is not to girls open . . . it is not open to girls." Her eyes were on the rope.

"No, it's just . . ."

She turned to look at me.

"Look, it's — *Jeez.*" I dropped my head in my hands and groaned.

"You are coming?"

I rolled onto my knees and — clumsily — stood. "Yeah. I'm coming."

We leapt from rock to rock, landing at last

by the base of the sweetgum tree, already pretty high above the water. Sanna didn't stop to look up. I, on the other hand, grabbed hold of the trunk of the sweetgum to steady my legs. Smirking, the boys stood in a loosely slip-stitched line, edging aside to let us pass.

"It *would*," I moaned, my face to the bark, "have to be that high."

One brown leg already on the first branch and the other on its way to a board nailed into the trunk as a step, Farsanna bowed her head down towards me. "Perhaps I should have let you proceed first?"

"No." I'd only begun the climb up, and the ground was already starting into a spin. "No, it's okay."

When she reached the branch — a good twenty, maybe thirty feet up it seemed at the time — from which the boys snagged and mounted the rope swing, Farsanna waited for me to catch up. I did not look down.

I clutched the trunk with both arms. "So you came to America for this?"

She smiled — that smile with the splash in it — and for a moment I forgot I was standing more than two stories above the earth in a tree with a rope as my only means of escape. And then before I forgot to forget,

I looked down and saw faces fixed on our branch: Emerson and Jimbo and L. J. and Welp. There they stood, all in a line, all on firm earth, all of them laughing at us — no, not quite. Not Jimbo.

Jimbo stood, I recall, a little off to the side, his hands on his hips.

Mort Beckwith was next in line for the rope. He stood, one hand on the branch above him, the other reaching far out to snatch the rope on its return. Rope in hand and resting on his gut, he turned to Farsanna.

"Reckon you think we're gonna just move out of the way for you, do you?" He threw back his shoulders, sucked in his gut, and held his free arm well out to his side as if the swell of its muscles wouldn't allow it closer. I had an image suddenly of Mort as a tank, a circle on top of his flat, crew-cut head opening and closing with a metallic clang.

Farsanna's spine stiffened, I could see from behind. But if she said anything, I couldn't hear it.

"You know," Mort told her, moving a step closer, "I've eaten meals bigger'n you."

Her whole body, not just her eyes, turned toward him slowly. "In Sri Lanka are trained elephants more clever than you."

Some boys at the base of the tree snickered.

Mort Beckwith did not.

I could not watch. Could not look down. I turned my face back into bark.

Someone was yelling below. And only then did it hit me that the Blue Hole was silent. Silent, except for one voice. Jimbo was calling to us — saying what, I couldn't tell, like my hearing had shut down when my heart rate took off.

"Wha— ?" I tried to shout back, but stopped. Even projecting my voice threatened to throw me off balance. I clung to the tree.

Mort was looking at the new girl. "Ol' Jimbo there says you can't swim too good, huh?" He toyed with the rope. "Girl, you either got yourself a good-sized chaw of brave, or you ain't just real bright."

Sanna held out a hand.

Looking suddenly confused, Mort held out his own hand.

She shook her head. "Please, I would like the rope."

"Let go too shallow," he went on, embarrassed, "and you'll put your feet out your ears."

She waited.

Mort curled up one side of a lip at her —

it wasn't exactly a smile. "You're gonna jump anyhow, ain't you, just any old way come into your head."

Again, Sanna held out her hand. As Mort gave her the rope, she let go of the branch above her head to grasp the rope with both hands.

Mort Beckwith arrested her swing by grabbing her arm, nearly throwing himself off the branch. "Listen. I'm tellin' you, don't be droppin' any later than 'at finger of rock if you like walkin' on legs."

She nodded again, and this time he let go her arm and she threw her whole self into the air.

I turned my face from the bark to see her fly into red, the last of the sun just spilling off the rim of our world. *It will be dark in just moments,* I recall thinking as I watched Farsanna clutching the rope above her dark head, her hair all in place.

And then her hands were slipping, the pull of her body at war with her grip. Down several feet her hands slid, her body stiff as a pillar, arcing out over the Hole. Then her hands reached a knot in the rope and for a moment retained their grip.

And then I saw that she was trying now too hard to hang on. The instinct not to lose her hold had rattled her concentration of when to let go. She swung out over — far out over the finger of rock.

From the height of her swing, her toes pointed nearly to the tops of the trees that skirted the pond. And then she was falling back down.

From where I stood clutching the sweet-gum trunk, I could see that her release was not perfectly at the finger. Farsanna had dropped way too close in to the shallow.

And then there were splashes, one after the other, one just below me.

I'll never know, I don't reckon, if Mort fell like he claimed or jumped off that branch. I did know, even with my eyes closed, that Jimbo and Emerson both dove in from the shore.

When Sanna emerged, she was already walking up toward the bank, her shoulders breaking above the water before anyone was within yards from her fall. Maybe it was her being so short and so little that saved her. Maybe it was just her being her.

Em was the first to think to hand her the tissue of towel as she calmly climbed up the bank. She seated herself on a rock, her back and legs a right angle.

Tentatively, Emerson squatted beside her. He lay one hand on her shoulder and leaned in to speak in her ear. She turned her head toward him — maybe she smiled — and he sat down beside her.

Which was when I went limp. In the midst of watching, I'd failed to catch the rope on its return. This I knew was the cardinal rule of the rope swing: You must catch the rope. And I didn't.

My cousin was the first to break the Blue Hole's silence. "Hey, Turtle," L. J. called up to me. "Make the family proud." And then he saw — like everyone else then — what I'd neglected to do, and he sneered.

He did, though, break off a long branch of a dogwood tree, then stand on the bank and swat at the rope until at last one of the boys who stepped past me in the sweetgum could finally snag it.

My legs gone to rubber and useless, I straddled the branch and eased myself out. Someone placed the rope in my hands. Perhaps someone else gave me a push.

The rope burn I gave myself that day stayed with me for at least a week — maybe two. I slid down the rope inch by inch as it — and me with it — ticked back and forth, back and forth. And not until the rope nearly stilled and my feet nearly touched the water's surface did I finally let go.

I swam underwater nearly the entire way to shore, and when my face broke the surface, Emerson hurled my towel at me.

Welp kicked a rock out near me, into the Hole.

Jimbo, at least, was waiting to shake my hand. "You're a brave one, Turtle." And then he drew my head close to his mouth. I felt his breath on my ear. "My first time looked a little like that." And then came a kiss — only a brush of a kiss on the top of my head. But it left me unsteady.

"I hereby herewith heretofore proclaim this Ladies' Night. Dr Pepper's on the house," I heard Jimbo announce — from several feet away now. "That's Steinberger's house."

Like the fall of a theater curtain on the last act, dusk dropped onto the Blue Hole. Pink smudges still glowed from behind the circle of trees at the rim, but in our hollow of earth, darkness came early. That evening, darkness came like a friend, warm and humid and close, wrapping my chilled skin like a blanket, with little weavings of light where the fireflies were venturing out. The deep woods were damp from a hard rain the midnight before, and I could smell the chestnuts and hemlock and soil.

I found myself thinking of the book Emerson had left open at the breakfast table a couple of mornings before. I'd caught only a couple of lines of what he'd highlighted before he'd caught me reading and scooped it up in *Sports Illustrated*. But the ones I did see stuck with me: "All will be well and all will be well and all manner of thing shall be well." Stuck with me, let me be clear, because it was completely and hugely ridiculous, and when I'd asked Emerson about it, he'd mumbled about its being a fourteenth-century Julian of somewhere I didn't catch, and then he stalked off.

"Fourteenth?" I yelled after him. "Dang, Em, you're just falling farther and farther backwards."

That evening, though, at the Blue Hole, the scents of the pines rising around me, the crickets commencing their gig, the boulders beneath me as familiar and firm as old friends, it occurred to me suddenly that if — not that it really could be, but *if* — this could ever be true — *All will be well and all will be well and all manner of thing shall be well* — then, well, *here* was the place.

Emerson and Jimbo sat on either side of the new girl, all three of them watching the next swings off the rope and laughing. Bo turned to motion me over, and I came. Maybe because I was cold from my drop in the Hole and needed to feel warm skin beside me. Maybe because Sanna and Em turned and motioned me over too. Maybe because it suddenly seemed all clear to me, all good. Just as Farsanna had made us speak about our futures, somehow we would all make something fine and noble and good of ourselves. I could see that just then. The future suddenly rose up before me as clearly and strong as the hemlocks rising up from the base of the Hole. Maybe hurt couldn't find its way to us here.

The pink smudges washing to gray, the last of our light to climb out, helped us keep time. And clearly, it was time to go.

The last I saw of Mort Beckwith that day was his struggling up the opposite bank, where other swimmers were gathering their things and beginning the trek up the path. Bobby Welpler came alongside him, for no reason I could imagine. Welp stood with his back to the water, and to us on the far side of the Hole, so I couldn't see his face. Mort Beckwith, though, shook his head and nodded, shook his head again, and then turned and looked straight at me — I was sure it was me. Then one of the girls who'd been sunning herself on that side of the Hole slipped her arm around Mort — what little of his girth she could cover. He smirked down at her, and when she lifted her face up to him, I saw she was Neesa. The two of them turned from Welp toward the path.

I spun around for Emerson, to see if he'd seen. But he and the rest of our crew had already started the trek toward the path.

Only Sanna hung back to be sure I was coming. "You are not hurt?" she wanted to know.

"Naw. You? Shoot, you had me scared stiff."

She held up her palms to show ropeburn. I held up mine.

She cringed. "You please will forgive me, Shelby? It is my fault, no?"

"No," I laughed. "Hey . . . um . . . Sanna."

"Yes?"

"You know . . . you can call me Turtle."

Single tree trunks were now only barely distinct from the mass, the deep woods. Jimbo paused at the bottom of the footpath. "Hustle up your shell there, Turtle. Hey . . . you two lovely ladies all right?"

Sanna only nodded at him, while I said we were fine. Even then, though, I knew he was not waiting to hear my answer, but was watching the new girl begin her climb up. Even then when Sanna nodded but did not answer him, I saw that she'd had to think about not speaking, had to concentrate on moving up away from him, hand over foot over hand up the path.

I saw Emerson watching her, saw her smile back at him. Saw her keep her distance from him, too. And I saw that in the fifteen feet between them — a distance which all day I'd taken as a positive kind of nothing — lay the early spinnings of a thread connecting them, the three of them bound together in their careful distance apart.

Me? I tried not to watch. Tried to tread water above the loneliness that broke over me in a wave.

13. SRI LANKAN *Sambol* AND ICE CREAM

Like it or not, I was on my way the next day to Farsanna's rectangle of house to sleep over.

I rummaged through my T-shirt drawer for some appropriate thing to sleep in at a Muslim house. Or a family whose parents' parents had practiced Islam, at least. And from what I could see of Mr. Moulavi's boulder of a back there through the plate glass, visible clear out to the road after dark, he must be still hanging by one hand onto something religious. Seemed to me nobody prayed with their face to the floor just to sniff out the carpet.

My cousin dropped by in the midst of my search.

"You know they don't drink alcohol," L. J. said, as he approached my room.

"Who?"

"Muslims."

"Oh, that. Yeah, well, neither do you

Baptists. But that's why you always take two Baptists fishing, right? You take one, he'll drink all your beer."

"No, I mean Muslims *really* don't imbibe. Not just talk about not."

"I'm underage anyhow. Remember?"

"Nevertheless."

"What?"

"Read me your T-shirts, Turtle."

"Captain Jack's Beachfront Bar," I said. "Myrtle Beach Grand Strand Cocktail Hour, Press the Flesh Spring Fling . . . Fine, you made your point. I'll take the football jersey."

Though maybe, I thought as I packed, it didn't matter all that much, not really. If I couldn't cover up clear down to my wrists — and I knew I couldn't, not in this heat — maybe there was no sense in trying not to offend. And besides, if Mr. Moulavi allowed his daughter the kind of freedoms he did, what could they expect of some tomboy American girl who'd stumbled into a friendship with her?

I watched L. J. leave the room and looked down at Big Dog, who stood next to me. "What if," I said to the dog, "she wants to talk about . . . them. Either of them." I sighed.

The Big Dog whined in female solidarity

— or maybe she was begging for barbecue scraps.

"Either of whom?" It was Emerson, standing there at my door.

"You weren't supposed to be listening."

"I live here. Remember?"

"So that's why the sink's always gunked up with shaving cream?"

"So what are you gonna do if she wants to talk men?"

"That'd be fine. I just don't want to talk about boys. Not any boys I know anyhow."

"Think she'll make you her confidante?" He leaned against my doorframe and crossed his arms.

He looked so sad and vulnerable just then, I wanted to hug him. But I didn't.

"She's not . . . Farsanna's not a gabber, Em. Maybe that's why I can put up with her. I s'pose she'll talk if she wants to."

"You're not gonna ask questions?"

"Not a chance."

"How come?"

" 'Cause I don't want to know."

"Why?"

I zipped closed the athletic bag I used as an overnight case. Then turned and patted his cheek. "Why do you think? If she was partial to either one of you over the other, I'd have to hate her forever."

Em patted my hand patting his cheek. "You know . . ."

"Know what?"

"You're not bad, Turtle."

"As girls go."

"Or even in general."

"Nicest thing you ever said to me."

"Yeah, well. Don't let it go to your head."

Jimbo, Em, and I worked together all day mowing lawns and trimming garden beds, mostly with their usual good cheer spiked with peanuts in Coke, but now and then in a silence that was brittle and sharp as old tin. Em and Jimbo together dropped me in front of the Moulavi house. Because I'd insisted I needed the wind in my face and the Big Dog beside me — which was not true in the least — the boys shared the cab. I knew they needed to talk, and I knew I'd rather not ride with Bo just then. I wanted to punish him — though he didn't seem to be suffering without me like somebody deprived.

Those two didn't speak a single skinny word to each other the entire trip out to the far end of the Ridge. Emerson pulled into the Moulavis' drive.

I readjusted the Big Dog's collar and put my face up to the open cab window. "I wonder what's for dinner?"

"Man cannot live on key lime alone, you know, Turtle," Jimbo assured me. "Hard-boiled octopus'll do you good."

"Thanks. Y'all on your way to the Hole?"

"No," they both said without checking to look at the other.

"No? It's hot as blazes today — like that's a change. I'd sure go if I didn't have a dinner date."

They both looked at me, and not at each other. Then both turned to watch the front door.

I tried again. "Game on tonight?"

Em shook his head. "Nope."

They both kept their eyes on the front door.

"Well," I said brightly, "I reckon I'll run their dinner late if I sit here any longer."

Scowling, Emerson crossed his arms like a barricade over his chest, like he had to hold something in. "You ladies have a nice time."

Jimbo leaned forward, squinting at the house. "Tell her howdy." He nodded towards the driver's seat. "From both of us."

"Yep." I threw my legs over the side. "See *both* of y'all tomorrow."

I don't know much about what I ate that night, but I do remember fumbling for my water between each bite, and not asking to know what I was eating, or where it swam or crawled or slithered in life. The curry alone would be with me for days. There were white fleshy chunks that must have been some sort of seafood, and white rice, and chilies — and Farsanna mentioned the coconut milk.

"It's *sambol,*" Sanna told me. "Like this is the way you must eat it." She scooped it up with her right hand and pushed it into her mouth with her thumb.

I braced myself for another bite but stalled, thinking up what Momma would have said, and then making myself say it: "Your mother must be considered a marvelous cook in Sri Lanka."

Farsanna nodded and watched me.

"My father works often late," Farsanna offered, a few moments into our meal. "Tonight also he will not join us for dinner."

"His job worked out then? That's good news."

"Not," she said slowly, "the job for here we moved." She shook her head. "Not the job for which we moved here."

"Say it too right and you'll sound all wrong, like L. J. Just *the job we moved here for.* So this isn't the same one?"

"The one that was promised," she looked across the table at me, and I had the sensation of her punching the words, "seems no more to exist."

"Not to exist?"

"Not to exist. For *him*." She raised her eyes, and I had to fight the instinct to duck.

"Oh. That's not such good news." I waited.

She stabbed at her rice.

"So then," I asked, wondering if I shouldn't, wondering what Momma would say, "where's he working?"

She found things to stare at in her rice. "At the paper mill is where for my father there is work."

"Way over in Clive? That must be thirty miles away!"

"Yes," she said. "It is. And he comes to here with a degree from the University of Sri Jayewardenepura. My father is a smart man."

I sat, rearranging the *sambol* to appear substantially nibbled. Mrs. Moulavi limped back through the kitchen door to refill our water glasses and our rice. Rising, Farsanna caught her mother's arm. "*Mata,* you must not need to serve us. Sit. Rest your legs."

But Mrs. Moulavi shook her head. Her head was slip covered, as usual, but if that was supposed to hide her good looks, it didn't much help: seemed to me it put a frame on the face and lifted it off the dark of the wall behind her. One hand on the table and helping her balance, she straightened a little. "I am not tired." She kissed her daughter on the top of the head and stroked her daughter's hair. My breath snagged on my throat as I wondered if she could feel a knot or gash where Farsanna had been wounded on Seventh.

Sanna adjusted her mother's hijab. "You are never saying you are tired. But sometimes I know you are tired."

Mrs. Moulavi turned to leave. "I am worried only," she whispered.

"Doesn't your mother," I suggested when the folds of gauzy fabric retreated, "want to come sit down and eat with us?"

"She will wait for the return of my father from work. Then eat in the kitchen."

I was at a big, empty loss for anything gracious to say that would make that information seem normal. "Yeah?" was the best I could manage.

"My mother prefers for herself the old ways of our — of Sri Lanka."

And then, as if she'd been listening, Mrs. Moulavi appeared in the doorway.

"Well," I said when it was clear she had

no plans to speak, "thank you for the delicious dinner."

Chips of charcoal looked out of her face. They were like Farsanna's, those eyes, at least in color and shape — but the mother's looked like they might already have burned out, couldn't any longer catch fire.

"How do you like your new home?" I asked, trying the tone Momma would've used at that point.

Mrs. Moulavi's eyes, whatever she could see from them, lay on her daughter. "Our home is Sri Lanka."

"Oh." I shifted in my seat and had to unpeel my hot, sweat-damp skin from the metal folding chair. "How do you like it *here?*"

She rotated her gaze to me, and then to my legs sprouting out from the frayed bluejean growth of my cutoff shorts. Perhaps she could see at least that much.

"American women . . ." she said vindictively almost, her accent thicker, murkier than her daughter's.

"Mata!" Sanna put in, a warning, effectively truncating at least that one sentence.

There was no tablecloth to cover my legs, skinny and bare, and they stuck out from me, obscene.

"At the store," Sanna's mother continued,

217

"spices I do not find."

I pictured the Piggly Wiggly shelves. Were there not plenty of spices? Cinnamon, allspice, cloves. Lots of brown sugar.

Farsanna rose from the table with an upheld palm for me to remain seated — a sign that reminded me of the map she made with her hands. She and her mother gathered dishes in a single sweep and disappeared into the kitchen.

Their voices collided, hard-edged syllables gathering speed, driven at each other head-on, and crashing.

When Farsanna appeared at the door, she wasn't smiling, wasn't pretending anything other than that I'd heard every word. That I'd understood not one word didn't matter, and she knew it. I'd understood plenty: that Sanna and her mother had been arguing over me — and what I represented.

She swiped at one of her own bare thighs below her khaki shorts, like she was dusting off dirt I couldn't see. "You would perhaps like to walk?"

For a second, I thought she was asking me to leave. And then I saw her reach for a fistful of coins left on a rickety stack of veneered shelves, and realized she meant we *both* might need a walk.

"Where to?"

"You did not like your dinner."

"I —"

"Possibly you'd like ice cream?"

It hit me suddenly she'd been using contractions here and there. "But," I tried pointing out, "there's no car —"

"The Dairy Queen's down the road, not very much far."

I pictured the thin-shouldered highway outside her house, imagined the day's heat, stored and heaved back at us from the asphalt. But I considered also this hot cave of a house, and Sanna's mother so full of worry and sharp-sided regret. I felt for change in my pocket, and nodded. "Okay."

Stepping out the back door, she patted her thigh and the Stray appeared at her side. She scratched him behind one ear, and I did the other as we attached a makeshift leash to him and set off.

Dusk had dropped gray sheers over Stone-wall Jackson Pike and fireflies pin-pricked the gray. The occasional eighteen-wheeler thundered by us as we walked on the road's shoulder, but other than that the highway was not heavily traveled that night.

Sanna glanced at me as we walked. "You will please forgive that. My mother," she began.

"Please." I held up my hand. "I understand how mothers can be."

"My mother is sad for leaving Sri Lanka. She did not intend meanness."

"I reckon most of them don't — mothers, I mean. Most of the time. And *still!*"

"Still," she agreed.

And we smiled at each other.

"My mother," she said, "didn't like to come to America."

"It was your dad's idea, huh?"

"*Only* my father's. For many, many years, my father's."

"Your mom's objection was what, mainly? All the skin we show here?" I lifted one bare leg — bony, but at least freshly shaved — for demonstration.

"My mother does not like American women. Perhaps fears. For me. For my sake."

"Why? Because we're all tramps?"

"You must understand: Rape among my people . . . among my parents' people, people of my grandparents' religion is almost unknown."

"No kidding."

"There are many reasons. It is the same with men and women who wish to love each other. To marry. They do not first undress."

I nodded. "So that's good, I reckon."

"These things to my mother make sense." She glanced my way to see my reaction. So I nodded again.

"And also," she added, still watching me, "to me. Much of the old ways make sense, no?"

"So how come," I asked, "you don't wear a headscarf like your momma?"

Farsanna may have shot me a look then, though I couldn't have seen it. She waited a moment to answer. "It is your opinion that I should wear a hijab?"

"Me? No. That is, I don't care one way or the other. It's just that your mom . . . and you seem . . . that is, you never seem embarrassed that she's wearing one."

"It is not right for a daughter be embarrassed by her mother, no? She is her daughter. That is enough. My mother was raised in Sri Lanka, a Muslim. My father wishes for me to be raised in America."

"And your family is not all that devout, but without the headscarf, the hijab, don't your parents worry about . . . you know. Boys? Your being looked at by boys?"

"And American parents, they do not worry about the boys?"

"Yeah, but —"

"You must tell me," she said, her voice dropping lower, "what means Beau —" she stopped and corrected herself, "what does Beauregard mean?"

"Mean?"

"You said to me that Jimbo Riggs' name . . ."

"Well, yeah. It is." I would've liked to have left it right there. But she stopped walking and waited. I doled out a little more, and even that was whittling away at my own insides. "Middle name. His ancestor was a Civil War hero. That is, depending on whose side you're on."

"Whose side you are on?"

"I mean *were* on. Are on. Same difference, I reckon. You know. The war. Civil War. *The War.*"

"The war," she repeated.

"What Bo calls The War to Make the Confederacy Comfy for White People." It didn't come out sounding anything like what Momma would have said just then — and so maybe shouldn't have gotten said at all. "The Mrs. Reverend Regina Lee Riggs," I added, "doesn't much like his calling it that." I'd meant this to help. But there the awkward still sat, heaving between us like a sick cat. And me wondering how to swat it out of the way.

Farsanna stared straight ahead. "This Beauregard — ?"

"Confederate general. Real smooth with the ladies, people said. Reckon he passed that on down the line."

She looked at me, her face telling me nothing.

"Yes," she said. And still nothing.

I'd no idea what my face, which had never been loyal or discreet, might tattle to her about me. So I studied the way the pavement petered out into clay, which surrendered to weeds, which infiltrated the asphalt in cracks.

Soon we were within sight of the Dairy Queen, its fluorescent swirl corkscrewing up into the dark. Several Jeeploads of teenagers were just piling themselves in for departure, their vanilla ice creams frosting each other's hair as bodies squirmed for position on floorboards and seats.

A white pickup that looked a little like Em's from the back was parked just beneath the glowing cone.

Farsanna nodded toward the truck. "That is your brother's, yes?"

We'd neared the parking lot by that time to see that the white pickup had red lettering on its door. I didn't need to read "Big Dog Lawn and Garden Beautifiers" to know she was right. The Stray had already leapt to greet someone he'd sniffed out as familiar.

I saw Em, his back to us, standing in front of someone unreasonably blond — a shock of yellow showing behind Emerson's brown.

I stopped in my tracks, my arms making a knot. "Well, what the heck does he think he's doing?" I inspected Farsanna's face for twinges of jealousy — or maybe she'd not seen the shock of blond — then took her by the elbow. "Come on."

Neesa's hot pants were as tight as they were short, and her orange halter top with daisies plummeted into a canyon of cleavage.

"Jeez," I muttered as Farsanna and I approached. "What is he *thinking?*"

"Something is wrong?"

"That something's name is Neesa." I checked again, real quickly, for signs that maybe Farsanna felt threatened. Sad. Jilted. But her face told me nothing at all.

"Something's wrong with this Neesa?"

"You mean besides the fact she can't spell her own name?"

Farsanna studied her from the distance quickly decreasing between us. She nodded, accepting my judgment, but asked, "Why is she stupid?"

"Because she's pretty."

Farsanna frowned, unconvinced.

I tried again. "Because boys like her that way: stupid. At least all Southern boys do."

Farsanna considered this. "All?"

I halted, my hands to my hips. "You got the ugly truth right there before you. I reckon they do."

She gazed off into the woods, then shook her head. "I cannot think all of them."

Maybe as a protection against the possibility of losing his share of the new girl's affections to his best friend, Emerson must have decided to drown his sorrows in Old Seasick Hips. Maybe, I thought, just like small children find comfort in hollow milk-chocolate bunnies, men find comfort in figures alone, without caring if there's nothing inside but air.

"My own brother," I sighed.

"But if your brother prefers . . ." Farsanna suggested.

I shook my head. "Don't ask. Come on. We can at least slow down her frontal assault."

After buying our ice cream, I elbowed a place in their circle for Farsanna and me, right beside Emerson, and nibbled at my cone slowly. I turned to Neesa.

"Emerson here *loves* seventeenth-century poetry. I bet you'd want to know that,

Neesa, may be some sort of something in common between you two."

My brother looked from Farsanna to Neesa to me and looked as if he might lose the two scoops he'd just eaten. "Cut it out, *Shelby Lenoir,*" he hissed in my ear. "Quit trying to make Neesa look dumb."

I whispered back, "If it wasn't so easy, I might could resist. You know I can't stand stupid girls. Or you making an idiot of yourself just because you're jealous of —"

He began to respond, but Farsanna was speaking.

"In my school, my old school, in Sri Lanka, we read *Paradise Lost.* To practice the reading English. Is that of the same time?"

Em beamed at her and nodded.

"Ever had *sambol,* Neesa?" I purred to my right.

"Do what?" Neesa was eyeing the Stray at her feet, her glance weighing Em's friendly welcome of the dog with her own obvious discomfort. "Does he bite?"

"Not too awfully often," I told her, pretending to pause a moment and count on the hands of one finger. "At any rate, *sambol's* a Sri Lankan delicacy. Ever had it?"

Neesa's eyes stayed on the dog. "What? Where?"

"Sri Lanka. Where Farsanna comes from. It's in South America."

"It's —" Farsanna protested.

I stopped her rising arm. "On the West Coast. Next to Kenya."

Emerson turned his mouth to my ear. "Cut it *out*, Turtle." He called the Stray to him and held onto the dog's collar.

Reassured, Neesa took a deep breath and swung her blond hair to the right and the left. "Never been there myself. Like my daddy says, ain't too much point in travelin' when you like where you are just fine."

"You know, I never thought of it that way myself. What about you, Em?"

Emerson wouldn't look at me.

"Or," Neesa added, shifting her hips in Emerson's direction to brush up against him, "when you like who you're with."

I smiled just real sweetly. "*Whom.* Right, Em? *Whom* you're with."

Emerson researched the ridges of his cone.

Neesa turned to me. "Why, Shelby Lenoir, don't tell me you're already *drivin'* already. Or wait, don't tell me you *walked.*"

"We *walked,*" I told her.

"Well, *get* out of town. What in heaven's name is there around this little ol' nowhere place to walk from?"

"My house." Farsanna put that in. And I

liked her for that.

Neesa peeked out from under a canopy of mascara. "Well, isn't that *sweet.* Are y'all staying up late?" She waited until I met her eye. "You spending the night with the new girl there, Turtle?" The canopy lowered at me. "You always were the sweet little ol' thing."

I patted my brother's shoulder. "We gotta run. Things to do. Em, sugar, that was good of you, helping Momma that way, bless your heart. Comfort to have a strong man around. I know unplugging that upstairs commode was *some* kind of chore."

The slow, constant sway of Neesa's hips, always seductive, even when she was standing in place, jerked to a stop. I'd done some damage at least.

Already beginning to back up, I blew my brother a kiss. "You have a nice night, Emmy, honey. Run on home now and be good."

Em stepped forward and reached to catch hold of Sanna's arm but she'd already turned and patted her leg for her Stray.

"Sanna —" he began.

Maybe she didn't hear him, her attention having turned to the dog.

And, just as we turned to leave, a truck parked near the back of the Dairy Queen

turned on its lights and started its motor —
not that it struck me as strange at the time.

"For Emerson to like her," Farsanna asked
as we walked along the gravel shoulder in
the dark, "you don't want this?"

It was another contraction, like maybe her
speech at least was settling in. It occurred
to me then that I liked that about her, the
fact she was trying so hard, slowly scratching the exposed roots of her heart into our
granite-soiled Ridge.

I shrugged. "Men are generally idiots, you
know. But the good ones don't want to be
all the time. They need our help not to be."

She laughed. "This is much as *Mata* would
say."

"Yeah," I joined her in the laugh. "My
momma too."

There was a pause. "And your brother . . .
he is one of the good ones, no?"

I patted her arm then. "If you promise not
to tell him I said so: yeah. My brother is
one of the good ones."

As we walked, the night seemed too quiet
to me. Our feet on the road's shoulder
crunched as if we were grinding the world
as we knew it into powder. I wondered if
this was how blind people felt, their senses
heightened so that every crack of a twig or

beat of a wing sounded alarm.

Sanna, who'd been less occupied in the business of ruining my brother's evening, had long since finished her cone. I was gnawing the final stump of mine when headlight beams swung out from behind us with the open-throat roar of a gunning engine.

I turned and saw the bright parallel beams level out at my face and fly forward, lighting up the shoulder where we stood.

The last thing I remember after that moment was grabbing for Farsanna's arm to pull her with me off the road and into the woods. But Sanna wasn't beside me.

I dove for the ditch — a decision I hardly recall making. Gravel from the highway's shoulder sprayed over my head and pelted me down. And I tumbled from the road's shoulder down a steep bank toward the woods.

And then the roar seemed landmasses away, far up on the road and retreating. Where I lay down at the edge of the woods was impenetrably black and silent, like someone had pulled the power cord to my world.

14. PEARL OF THE INDIAN OCEAN

When I came to, I lay still for a moment testing my limbs for signs of life. Everything seemed accounted for and functioning.

"Sanna?"

Nothing.

"Farsanna?"

Still nothing.

Now I was screaming. *"Sanna! SANNA!"*

Then there were footsteps. My heart threatened to hammer its way out of my chest.

"Sanna? Is that you?"

Without speaking, she hooked her arm through mine, nearly scaring me clean out of my skin. "Hey," I said, when I could speak. I stepped away, glad I couldn't see her face in the dark. Especially thankful I couldn't see her eyes. "Hey, you all right?"

She didn't answer.

I could hear the question, the What Happened, that neither one of us said, there between us, those words sapped of their strength lately for us. I pulled a row of thorns from my forearm and waited to know what to say, know what to think.

I tried to lay a hand on her arm.

"My Stray?" she asked then. The panic in her voice pushed it higher.

"I . . . he hasn't . . ."

She whistled. We waited.

Something moved close beside us, something slinking out from the woods.

Then Stray touched his nose to our calves. He'd emerged, apparently, from wherever he'd been blown from the road. The dog sat at Sanna's feet and she threw both arms around him.

The relief of his safety and Sanna's gave me strength to say what surely couldn't be true, but needed saying. I took a deep breath. "I reckon maybe somebody was playing." It seemed the thing to say just then to build a seawall against the fear I could feel swelling.

"Playing?" She didn't believe me.

I didn't believe me either.

"Or," I tried again, "or just, you know, not watching where they were driving. Maybe switching out tapes and looking up almost too late. But not aiming. Not aiming for us. Not even to scare us."

She would not speak after that. The air between us vibrated with the sounds we weren't making.

We walked the remaining stretch of highway back to her house in silence, sticking close beside each other, Sanna's dog close by our feet. Every far-off growl from a motor or the woods sent us ducking for cover.

For the first time I could remember — and maybe the last — the Moulavi house looked attractive up ahead, its curtainless plate-glass windows' yellow rectangles we ran toward like beacons of safety. Mr. Moulavi was kneeling, I could see, on the living room floor. Farsanna, still trembling, touched my elbow and we both skirted toward the back door. She knelt to stroke the Stray, and let him kiss her cheek and nose and chin. She may have been crying again, but she seemed not to want me to see, so I didn't look. I bent to stroke his back and was startled to find his coat soft, homely as he was.

Sanna put a finger to her lips. Glancing right and left, she cracked open the back door and let the dog go in before us. Apparently not unused to this liberty, he skirted the one light thrown from the living room, and keeping to the shadows, padded down the hall.

Her mother nodded as we entered, and I held my breath waiting to be called upon to recount what had happened on the highway. If she saw the Stray slip past, she said nothing.

And Mrs. Moulavi didn't ask if we'd had a nice time, and her daughter didn't volunteer anything. Kissing her mother on the forehead, Sanna walked through her bedroom door that lay just off the kitchen. I nodded and cranked up one end of my mouth in an attempt at a smile and followed.

Watching Sanna's *mata* limp back through the kitchen, I closed the door and collapsed on Sanna's bed. I wriggled my legs between the sheets, rough and pilled, like I was tired, hoping maybe my body would take the clue. It didn't. I lay awake in the dark, my head hurting with the crush of too many thoughts.

Sanna had lain so still and so quiet I'd assumed she'd long been asleep. The Stray certainly was, his snores rising and receding from the end of the bed. But Sanna rose and walked quietly to the window. Maybe sleep felt like a distant, unreachable place for her, just like it did for me. When she glanced once over her shoulder, she seemed as if she were checking to see that I wasn't awake.

"What are you looking at?" I asked her.

She jumped a little at my voice, but didn't take her eyes off the black outside her window. "Tonight, the moon is like a pearl." She must've had a better view of the sky than I did, still huddled in bed. "Like the Pearl of the Indian Ocean."

I could barely make out what she said, her face turned away like she was whispering words off a black screen.

"What?"

"My home. Sri Lanka is called the Pearl of the Indian Ocean."

Her pretty face — I caught myself thinking how pretty it was — had gone hard, like she'd been whittled from onyx. "I miss the Pearl. I miss my home, Turtle."

Her accent hitting my name like rapids at a rock stopped me cold in the midst of whatever flip thing I'd have said just then. With that one word, her *Turtle,* we'd passed somehow to a different place, crossed some threshold of understanding or trust — not one I was sure I wanted to cross. But there it was, already passed and no turning back.

"Hey, Sanna. . . ." I began as she sat down on the bed. "Lemme ask you something: How come you hardly talk about Sri Lanka?

Not even when somebody asks you, like L. J.? I mean, if you miss it so much —"

"*Because* I miss it so much."

"Oh." I thought about that.

"My father," she said, her face toward the window. "My father said everything would be for us different here. In America, everyone is equal. In America, everyone is free. In America, everyone does as he wishes, and no one for stopping."

"Hmmm," I said, not sure when, or if, I was supposed to agree.

"When my father was young, he loved a Sinhalese girl. Her parents were wealthy and the Goigamas caste, the highest."

"But I thought the caste system was . . . Never mind. Go on."

"They wouldn't allow with him marriage."

"Because he looked . . . Arab? Or because he was Muslim? Or didn't have enough money?"

"All."

"Oh." I thought about this. "That's rough. So what happened?"

"So —" Her eyes stayed on the window. "So he said his daughter must be," her voice curdled, "an American. *Free.*"

It was the kind of statement Momma would've assigned to the care of a hug. But I said: "Reckon it's not always so great for you here."

She had her face towards the moon again
— which was just fine with me. "What do
you think for me it is like?"

"You always look like . . . like you don't
care *jack* what anybody thinks. You always
look, you know, like, like you don't give a
rip about public opinion. I've always liked
that about you."

"To pretend — this is for me to survive."

I watched her profile, still and hard, which
told me nothing. I followed her eyes to the
moon.

"Is it beautiful?" I asked after several moments' silence. "What's it like, your home?"

She shrugged, a habit she must've gotten
from me — and didn't much suit her. "Colombo, the most big city, is full always of
many people, and loud. And hot often. The
roads are buses, cows, people in bare foot,
bicycles, tuk-tuks —"

"What's that?"

"Like a taxi, with three wheels only. The
gutters are full. My father was a shopkeeper.
But sometimes we traveled to the most high
point, Mount Pidurutalagala."

"What's that like?"

"Waterfalls. Forests of big trees, old trees:
pine, mahogany, ebony, teak. Women sold
by the road cashews. Little villages I saw

there. Very more cool than Colombo. At the end, we moved down the coast near to Beruwela. A very old mosque is there."

"Your father got a better job?"

Farsanna shook her head. "My father rented to tourists equipment for sports in the water."

"Oh. But you got to live at the beach. That must've been nice, huh?"

She leaned against the window frame. "I loved the rattle of the palms. Everywhere coconut palms. We drank from them, from coconuts, with straws. Everywhere was fruit: pineapple, watermelon, papaya, mangosteen, guava — you have these here? We, I mean. We have these here, no?"

"Some, I reckon. Nothing much exotic."

"There are many rocks. The water was everywhere clear. And blue. So blue."

I put on feigned surprise. "Bluer than our Blue Hole?"

She smiled, still gazing outside at the moon.

"Sounds like paradise." That part I said more gently. "No wonder you miss it."

"My family could not make a living there." She turned toward me then, but seemed not much to see me. "No place on this earth," she said, "is paradise."

And over and over again that night, as I stumbled toward sleep, I slipped into faded dreams of Stray's silky ears across Jimbo's thigh. Of the screech of Em's truck tires on Seventh Street as we tore away from gunfire and hailing streetlights.

I tried counting sheep, and then ticks of the Blue Hole's rope swing with nobody on it. But then there was Mort's face leering from the top of the sweetgum.

I tried smelling the sunbaked hemlock and decaying wood of the Hole, but I smelled instead the exhaust of the good Reverend Riggs' El Camino as he, one foot on the running board, one foot on the road, straddled, indecisive, his intention to go.

As I crept closer to sleep, I saw Farsanna and me laughing and eating ice cream. And then came truck headlights like battering rams.

And I was reminded again that maybe things were worse than we thought, than we'd any of us been willing to say.

Those last words of hers swelled in my mind and wouldn't leave room for sleep: *No place on earth is paradise.*

There was more, I was sure, that she

hadn't told me. Something more that had happened out there on the road.

No place on earth is paradise.

That's what I heard, propped up beside her against the pillows, both of us leaning a little in towards each other, staring down the blank face of the night. And that's what I heard as I finally fell toward a sleep that was like tumbling down the slope toward the Hole: *Paradise . . . I miss my home, Turtle . . . No place on earth . . .*

15. SHADOWS IN THE SHAPE OF A COWARD

Farsanna had been asleep for maybe an hour, her breathing becoming a tide. The same almost-full moon we'd earlier used to guide our way down the Pike now taunted me outside Farsanna's one small window, which faced the woods behind her house. I rose to look for some kind of blinds to yank down.

I stood at her window a moment, startled by the sheer size of the moon, impaled by a tall, dead pine trunk like in a ghost story. As I looked out, a shadow flitted across the bare strip of backyard. It didn't at first strike me as strange. But no other shadows were moving. The shadow lengthened. And moved on two legs.

A breath logjammed in my chest. I ducked by the window, its sill even with my nose.

The shadow was approaching the house.

Dropping lower, I crawled on all fours to the kitchen. The only phone I'd seen in the house hung beside the stove.

But who could I call? I crouched beside the stove a moment — but only a moment — thinking. And felt the slam of my heart nearly rock me off balance.

I stood only long enough to find seven numbers, counting out their position in the dark and waiting for the everlasting spin-back of the dial. And then I squatted again, one hand cupping my mouth at the receiver's mouthpiece.

The chances of Emerson's being home, I knew, weren't too good. There being Neesa involved. I was already wishing I'd dialed out Jimbo's when the phone rang a first time.

I saw out the kitchen window the figure crossing the backyard again, moving from the far woods near the driveway towards the back kitchen door, not ten feet from where I crouched.

The phone rang again.

There was no jack in my parents' bedroom, only the upstairs study and the kitchen downstairs. So only if Emerson were not still out with Neesa, and only if he were not already asleep in his room and only . . .

It rang a third time.

Of course he would still be with Neesa. I pictured her little white hot pants again, and the plunge of her halter.

I stretched my arm to hang up the phone but froze: Someone had bumped up against the Moulavis' back kitchen door. He was on the back stoop behind the kitchen.

"Hello?" Em's voice cracked through the receiver I was holding above my head. I jerked it down.

"Em!" I whispered.

"Turtle? What — ?"

"Em, you gotta come."

"What?"

"For real. You gotta come now!"

"If this is your way of making sure Neesa —"

"You gotta get here! Somebody's outside."

"Outside? Outside *Farsanna's?*"

"And he's acting like he wants to come in! Em, hurry!"

The line's going dead told me my brother was already halfway out the screen door.

Creeping as silently as I could to the kitchen window, I watched the figure retreat again towards the woods by the drive. But he'd already slipped that way once before and come back. I crossed the living room to the front door, which was locked.

I'd no idea what to do. I slipped through the front door into the warm black of the night, my skin gone clammy and cold.

The figure was approaching again from the far woods by the drive. Keeping close to the block of a house whose warehouse brick I couldn't see in the dark, I slipped along the front of the house to its side, then dropped to my stomach and slithered, like I'd seen men do in the army movies I watched with my brother. My elbows dragging the length of me across the dead grass and bare clay, I reached the edge of the drive closest to the house, then slunk quickly across its gravel arm to the opposite side, to where the weeds had grown long enough to help hide me.

Not only could I see better from this position — this struck me as real brave of myself — but also I was closer to where Emerson would pull in his truck — and maybe take me away. So if I was brave, it was still splintered with scared.

I lay still while the figure slipped back towards the woods.

In that instant he turned, and just before he ducked again into shadows, the pearl of a moon shone full on his face.

I heard myself gasp — maybe more of a gag, a scream that I muffled.

I knew the face, and knew I'd made no mistake, not even in the yellow of a carnival moon.

There was the round form and face of the good Reverend Riggs.

16. OVERHEARD IN
THE DARK

Its headlights off, Emerson's truck crept to a stop on the gravel shoulder in front of the Moulavis' house — as quietly as a Ford can growl across gravel, which isn't very quiet at all. I leapt for the driver's-side door, yanked it open, and dove across him into the passenger seat with Big Dog, who licked the back of my neck.

"Em!" I was panting myself. "You can't believe . . . It's not what —"

"First off, calm down."

"Calm down! Em, I saw who it was! Who it is — he could be back any minute!"

"You saw who it was?"

I clutched my throat with my hand to keep my heart from slamming its way up through my neck. "It was . . ."

"Who?"

"It was the Jimbo's, the reverend good daddy, the good Rev— !"

Emerson stared at me a moment before

speaking. "What'd you have for dinner, Turtle?"

"Stop it, Em. I know what I saw."

"Right."

"Stop it! I saw his face!"

"In the dark."

"By the moon. I know his face when I see it, 'bout as well as I do yours."

"Come on, Turtle, why — ?"

"Didn't say I knew *why*. I said I *saw* him. That's all."

"All right, all right. Look, let's get out of the truck. Which way'd you see him go?"

I pointed.

Em backed the truck several yards up the wide slash of the gravel shoulder so that it was parked well off the road, partly hidden by woods. We scrambled out and crept back through the front yard without speaking, skirted the side and knelt in the depths of the dark where the moon's light didn't reach, there near the back door's kitchen stoop.

I tucked my hands in the fold of my legs to keep them from shaking.

When Emerson saw what I had, I could feel the air go dead around us and the stars batter down on our heads. Knowing my brother had now seen what I had made it more real than before, a key piece of evidence that perhaps after all the world was not a good and safe place, perhaps there were things — and people — you simply could not count on, despite what you'd been reassured, perhaps the sky would in fact fall. It was as if in one night, my childhood dropped away forever.

And then there were voices. We'd seen no one else — at least I hadn't. But there must've been men, at least a couple of them, there further into the shadows of the scrub pine beyond the reach of the moon. I caught only snatches.

"It'll save more trouble in the long run's what I'm saying. . . . You don't want to see nothing bad happen to these folks, now do you? Or to that mighty fine boy of yours?"

We couldn't hear what Jimbo's daddy said then, his back to us and his voice inclined to be soft. But whatever he said must have been short, or interrupted, since another voice picked up from there.

"You know how the boys can get to having themselves some fun and get a little toe over the line now and then. I been able to hold the boys back so far. But I said to them, 'Now . . . fellas, we don't want no trouble. . . . A little more friendly pressure on these here folk — for their own good, you understand . . . help them find their own kind down in the Valley.

Or back wherever it was they come from.' 'At's what I told them."

At one point, Reverend Riggs' arms went up over his head as if he were shouting, although we heard nothing. The gesture reminded me suddenly of Jimbo's way of throwing his arms over his head when he delivered the last line of our litany, the words of L. J.'s daddy's new sign.

But whatever the Reverend said or didn't, the only voices we could hear in the dark were the others:

". . . Why, even tonight the boys was making a ruckus about wanting to just, you know, have themselves some innocent fun, not let nobody. . . . Just be making some points is all. . . . You just looking the other way is all I'm sayin'. To be keepin' the peace, you understand. . . . People got to be brought along slowly. . . . Keepin' the peace. . . ."

"That sounds," I whispered, "like Mort's daddy."

Em elbowed me hard to be quiet. But then put a hand on my arm to let me know he agreed.

Whether Reverend Riggs responded at all, I don't know — I couldn't hear. What I saw was his walking away, his shoulders slumped forward, his round body sunk down into itself so that I'd have sworn someone had

249

taken a shovel to the top of his head and pounded it into the round flesh of his body. And he staggered, like he'd been given a load too heavy to carry.

"Oh, Em," I whispered, thankful my brother couldn't see the water that spilled on my cheeks. "Jimbo will die. He'll just die."

"Yeah," came his response, my brother's voice ragged. "Yeah. He will."

Emerson and I sat there together with ragweed and clay the color of blood the only thing left holding us up.

17. YELLOW SPHERE
OF A MAN

Best we could tell, Reverend Riggs and the others left soon after Em arrived. But the two of us sat in the pickup for a good piece of the night and dozed in between keeping an eye on the Moulavi house. And when it looked like dawn might be trying to gnaw into the night, I crept back into the house.

I dozed off once more in the bed beside Farsanna, and woke up in a sweat — not a glow, but a sweat sure enough. The house was swollen with sound, with notes — were they notes? — that wriggled and chanted and shook themselves loose of language.

"What language is that?" I asked from inside my pillow.

Farsanna was sitting straight up in the bed. "Arabic."

Turning my head, I squinted at her. "He's praying?"

She nodded.

I sat up too, groggily.

251

"I thought he didn't observe all the . . . you know . . . I thought it was his parents — who were devout."

She looked at me. "This means he cannot then pray?"

I thought about this. "What's he saying?"

" 'I testify there is no God but God.' "

I waited. "What else?" I could hear there had to be more.

" 'God is great.' " Here she turned and nearly smiled at me. "And 'It is better to pray than to sleep.' "

"Oh," I flopped backwards, "I could never convert."

And then I remembered what I'd witnessed outside Sanna's house in the night. And I lay there thinking that maybe I'd only dreamed it. And praying I had. And wishing I knew how to pray.

I was home the next day by mid-morning — and would've been thankful to have left sooner. Farsanna's mother had fixed "hopper" for breakfast — a cooked egg burrowed down in a pancake. And likely it wouldn't have been bad if I could've eaten.

At nine, Emerson swung by — without Jimbo — to pick me up, and I was fidgeting by the front door, my *thank yous* already said.

I was hardly through my front porch door before Momma was calling for my help with stuffed eggs.

"I'll let you run these lunches out to the boys, sugar. Did you have a nice time?"

I gave her what she'd not wanted to hear, but still would expect: "Yes, ma'am."

"I do believe Emerson said they'd be back at Miss Pittman's again today. Bless her heart, she's a little different, wouldn't you say, hon? Shelby?"

"Yes, ma'am." I was wading through my own weariness and confusion to get a clear thought. "They can't come in and pick lunch up themselves? The boys, I mean."

My mother turned, hands on hips. "Well, I swan. This is a first, your not just jumping at the chance to tag on after those boys — you and that ridiculous retriever of Emerson's. Is something wrong, honey?"

I shrugged. "I'm . . . just tired, I reckon."

"Well then, Shelby, hon," Momma told me, "you can help me do three dozen more of these deviled eggs — hand me the paprika, sugar — and take them to the picnic supper over at the firehouse. And then you can get yourself some good beauty rest."

I resolved right then that no matter how tired I felt, I'd be with the boys at Mollybird Pittman's until the end of the day.

Mercifully, Miss Pittman appeared only once that day, marching out in her big straw hat just long enough to list our shortcomings — including the fact that Jimbo slouched sometimes when he walked — and then tooled away in her brown Oldsmobile for a trip to the doctor. We all three of us bent into our shovels and hoes and were careful not to meet her eye.

We worked hard and long that day. Though summer in the South is hardly the time to plant anything, there've always been those who think they can force the seasons to their own will — and Mollybird Pittman was one. Big Dog Lawn and Garden Beautifiers thrived on this type of person.

After the twelfth magnolia sat smugly settling into its hole, my back muscles were shredded.

Splayed on Mollybird's fescue, I groaned for anyone who would hear me, "Got to get to the Hole."

By four, we'd finished a six-pack of Coke and a full bag of peanuts. We packed up our tools and left to pick up the Pack.

We picked up L. J. first at the Feed and Seed, where he had just finished loading bales of pine straw into old Mrs. Barker's trunk. We hauled new bags of cow manure, peat moss, lime, and cedar mulch into the back — then L. J. himself. He dropped to the floor of the truck bed. "So, Turtle . . . what's new?" he asked, almost cheery. Heading toward the Blue Hole had that effect.

I felt Emerson listening through the window of the truck cab. He and I had agreed late last night to wait to say anything to anyone else about what we'd seen and overheard at the Moulavis' until the two of us had a chance to talk and sort things out. It looked real bad for the good Reverend Riggs, and we knew we were dealing with Jimbo's faith in his daddy, his dogged faith in his faith, and its power to change people and things, against all the evidence everyone else could see to the contrary.

I shrugged at my cousin. "Since yesterday, nothing." A total lie. "What's new with you?"

He shrugged, and we were done being nice. Which is the good thing about family: You don't have to draw these things out.

We arrived at the Moulavis' house, and through the plate-glass window, I could see Sanna's mother limp toward the front door. Mrs. Moulavi held out her arms for her daughter.

It's all she has here, I was thinking, watching Sanna's mother stroke my friend's hair as if she were afraid to let go of her girl.

"Mm-hmm," Jimbo said, nodding.

"Did I say that out loud?"

He squeezed my hand. "Reckon so. Least-wise, I heard you."

Having found no one at home at Welp's trailer, we made our way to the Hole and swam hard and lingered that day. I'd no idea what we would be telling Jimbo, or how, about his daddy. But there at the Blue Hole, the granite palm warming my goose-pimpled skin back to smooth, the craters of water thrown toward the sky, the rhododendron in layers of green reaching up to the rim of the world, the waves of terror I had felt swelling all day over confronting Jimbo slipped back now to only a slow current of worry.

I scratched both dogs' ears as they stretched on the rock. *All will be well,* I told them, not convincing myself. *And all will be well, and all manner of thing will be well.* They drooled their thanks on my hand.

On the way back up to the Clearing, Bo asked to be the first to be dropped off.

"For some reason," he'd shrugged, "the good Reverend requested my presence this evening. Who knows."

"Look, Bo," Em began, "Turtle and I need to tell you —"

I landed an elbow square in his ribs. "That you're welcome to be the first to get home." I mouthed to Em, *We said we'd tell him later. Not with anyone listening.*

Em shook his head at me, but left it alone.

When we reached Jimbo's house, Reverend Riggs was sitting on the porch.

"Hello there, children." The Reverend approached the truck as Jimbo jumped out of the truck bed, with his hand held out, but without the usual beam. His suit was rumpled, his shoes off.

He offered his hand first inside the driver's-side window. "One of these days you'll have to join us again in church, Emerson, son. We've missed you and your sister. When was the last time?"

I knew then the good Reverend was thoroughly muzzied. He always invited us to church when he was at loss for something to say.

"Vacation Bible school," Emerson said. "It's been a few years. I was ten. Turtle might've been eight. We made Noah's arks out of popsicle sticks. Turtle still has hers."

"Too long," Jimbo's daddy was mumbling absently to Emerson, even as his hand offered itself to mine.

Against my will, I shook the Reverend's hand. I was unsure about Jesus, but I knew it was what Momma would've done, and I could think of no other way to get his hand out of my face. I spoke too, but as coldly as I could manage: "Evening."

He focused on me then for the first time, then turned — with a perceptible start of surprise — to Farsanna.

He looked from Bo to Sanna, then from me to Sanna, then Em to Sanna, his eyes always coming back to the new girl, and apparently startled each time she was still there. Slowly, the Reverend held out his right hand. "Reckon I'm not acting very neighborly." With his left hand, he wiped the sweat that had sprung up on his forehead. "I'm Reverend Pete Riggs."

Farsanna held out her hand in return. "I am Farsanna Moulavi."

Reverend Riggs shook her hand, his pale eyes flickering up to hers, and then quickly away. His hand fell back by his side. "I been meaning," he said, "to get by your house. Been meaning to pay y'all a howdy. You and your folks."

The Reverend's eyes, still lowered, shifted to the threadbare white towel Farsanna clutched about herself. "Well, now," he said. I couldn't read the expression on his round face. "Well, now, so here you are on Pisgah Ridge. You folks adjusting all right?"

The new girl tightened her scrap of a towel around her. She didn't blink — though she didn't immediately answer either. "My father's work is not to him open now," she said finally.

"You mean," I asked, "he still can't find anything in his field?"

She did not look at me. "The position that was open when we spoke of moving is now closed when my father arrived."

Reverend Riggs studied the truck's tailgate held shut with wire. "Well then," he said. This seemed not to satisfy him as a pronouncement. "Well then, that's not good news." We all stared at him, waiting for more. He moved to the tailgate and idly tugged on the wire holding it up. "I'm real sorry to hear that," he told the tailgate. He lifted his eyes just once more to us.

I loathed the man.

Reverend Riggs placed a hand on Jimbo's arm. "Well then," he said. "Reckon we ought to be saying goodnight."

Bo kissed his father on the top of the head and followed him through the parsonage screen door. The Reverend turned back and reopened the door as if he might say something, but turned back again and walked inside.

I spit off the side of the truck like I could rid myself, rid us all, of whatever had happened so far, whatever was yet to come. Jimbo would have to be told, and so would the others. But for now, I contented myself in hating the yellow sphere of a man.

18. New York Yankees Alibi

The next day, with me in the back as ballast, wedged between bulky bags of mulch and plastic-wrapped cubes of peat moss falling onto my feet — Big Dog smiling and comfortable in the passenger seat — Emerson picked up Jimbo for the day's work.

I looked back to greet him, and Bo smiled, winking. I wished all of a sudden I'd changed shorts like Momma wanted. Or brushed my hair better. I bent over, pretending to inspect a hole in the peat moss plastic, and pulled out from my ponytail a few wisps that maybe would frame my face. I could hear Momma's voice: *Must you wear your pretty hair so severely, Shelby Lenoir? There's no call for ears to go sticking all out, is there, sugar?*

"Top of the mornin' there, lassie." Bo handed me a Pop-Tart. "Gourmeted it myself just now."

"Hey, Bo," Emerson called back from the

cab, "how 'bout we watch the game tonight at my house?"

Jimbo's voice went decidedly weaker. "The Sox are playing?" Bo always knew when a game was on, if only because he was Em's best friend. He was stalling for time.

"What do you mean, *Are the Sox playing?* Of course they're playing. The Yankees. Remember? What's *wrong* with you?"

"Just forgot what dadgum day was all."

Jimbo reached to scratch Big Dog behind the ears. Then he pulled a Coke from the cooler and began popping peanuts, one by one, into his mouth.

Emerson glanced back over his shoulder. "Bo?"

"Yeah?"

"You fall out back there? You wanna watch the game or what?"

"Me and Turtle's just hitting the bottle early today." He fished out a Coke for me and pried off its top with his teeth.

I took the Coke, but just held it — real tightly.

"Didn't you hear, Em?" I called out, already regretting what I was about to do. "Poor old Parson Riggs doesn't get to see many games with his boy." I watched Jimbo's face squint in confusion. "He's planned for a father-son time just something like this."

Jimbo met my look and raised one eyebrow.

Emerson turned his hat bill forwards on his head, which always meant trouble. "Ah, come *on,* Bo. It's the *Sox* and the *Yanks.*"

I swung at the pitch myself, wishing Bo would just stop me. Wishing my gut feeling was plain wrong. But he let me go on: "What better time for a father and son? The Sox and the Yanks."

Em scowled at me over his shoulder, but left it at that.

Just barely audible over the motor — to me, but not to my brother at the wheel, Jimbo said, "I don't rightly recall planning to lie."

"I know you didn't."

He patted my leg and squeezed it.

"But I didn't see you jumping to tell him the truth, did you, Bo? That you got other plans? That you got a date?" I kept my head up.

His hand rested there on my knee. "Well, now, I don't know as I'd strategized out my day much past this Coke. . . ." He winked and grinned at me then, his green eyes squinting to slits.

We arrived at Mollybird's place and discovered her waiting for us, all impatient for the spraying, fertilizing, pruning, and general all-out pampering of her precious hybrid tea and climbing roses.

In a black cotton dress — likely a remnant of the Big Apple years, since no one back home wore black outside funerals — Mollybird wreaked vengeance on us that day by joining us there in the blazing heat. Her straw hat — likely *not* from Manhattan — held silk roses in a black band at the crown and they bobbed as she peered over our shoulders at every prod of the trowel. She shook her head each time I measured the pellets of rose fertilizer.

"Wouldn't it be faster," I whispered to the boys, "if she just did it herself?"

Jimbo was more sympathetic to her: "Now, what'd be the fun in a general's having no troops to boot in the bodacious?"

By five, having labored all day in the heat, we'd exhausted not only our bodies but also her imagination for what else we might do with magnolias and roses.

She held up a blossom for us as we packed up our tools. "This one's gone pink," she accused.

"Yes, ma'am," Emerson said. "It's grown a little different from the rest. Kind of nice, don't you think?"

Mollybird's look assured us that no, she did not.

Jimbo hauled a shovel back out of the flatbed. "How 'bout I just dig up that pesky old rebel for you, Miss Pittman?"

"See that you do that, young man."

Em reached for his clipboard, which was his subtle signal for payment. "And where would you like us to transplant the rose, Miss Pittman?"

"I do *not* care for pink, Emerson Maynard. I do not care for pink." She turned and strode toward the house, her hat's roses — *red* roses — nodding emphatically. "You may bill me," she said as the screen door slammed shut.

I helped Jimbo ease the old rose into a black plastic nursery container. I lowered my voice to imitate Mollybird Pittman's root-cellar range: "I do not care for pink, young men. Must I tell you again? I do not care for pink!"

Jimbo braced the rose with two bags of manure. "What *pink* you reckon bit her in the Mollybird?"

"What do you reckon," I asked him back, "they *did* to her in the North?"

Up to full speed on the main road — Em's truck strained at fifty — we passed the

Moulavi house without comment. I watched Bo's face, but he only winked and passed me his Coke. When we pulled into the parsonage drive, my heart idled, real roughly, as Jimbo's daddy waved from the porch. For a moment, I thought he would walk out to greet us. And for a moment, I half wished he would, and lay bare Jimbo's plans for the night, because whatever they were, they weren't with his daddy — to me that was stark naked clear. I was wondering why I'd handed Bo his alibi, just like I'd wanted him to hand it back to us.

But Jimbo just patted my knee and scrambled to unload himself and a half bag of peanuts.

Em snarled from the truck cab, "Just you recall there, Riggs, nobody ever got let into heaven rooting against the Sox."

"Fenway be dyed pink," Bo retorted cheerfully from the porch.

The Sox tanked in the last inning.

When Em's muttering turned to abject despair, I looked up from the novel I'd opened to read during time-outs.

"What's wrong, Big Brother?"

"Nothing. Why should anything be wrong?" He glowered at me. "We need pecan pie at Steinberger's. Now."

266

I closed my novel only halfway. "*If* you can be nice."

"I can be nice."

"*And* if you're paying."

Em whistled for Big Dog, who appeared, retriever-grinning, the truck keys in her mouth. He grabbed the *Paradise Lost* he'd been smuggling inside *Field and Stream* all week, and glanced to see if I'd seen. I had mercy on him and pretended not to.

It was just after dusk. Slowing on Elm, Bo's street, Em nodded toward the dark, lifeless windows of the parsonage. "Now what do you make of that?"

"What?"

"That. Nobody's up."

"Asleep, maybe," I said. "Game just ended. The good Reverend Riggs' been looking whooped lately — the kind of late-night prowling he's been up to can take it out of a man, don't you think?" Em shot me a look.

Big Dog, circling on the seat between Emerson and me, recognized the house and whined. Emerson drove on, slowing again before the Moulavis' house. "You wanna see if Farsanna wants to come with us? Tell her we won't be out but a minute."

I pointed to the naked plate-glass window. "Her dad's got his face to the floor. I'd be scared to disturb his . . . him."

"C'mon, Turtle. How 'bout you just knock on the door."

"I don't see you volunteering."

Em just looked at me.

"Yeah," I finally said. "Well. He looks busy. I'm not going in. Drive on, Ralph Waldo. It's just you and me tonight."

Emerson, eying me suspiciously, drove on to the restaurant.

Fumbling nervously with a serrated knife, Steinberger shook his head from behind the mesh screen. "We got only key lime left tonight."

"Great," I said. "We'll have two slices."

"You sure, Mr. S.?" Emerson persisted. "I had my taste buds all set to pecan."

The old man leaned in close to the mesh. "Your friend," he said, "ate me out of pecan." He cut the two pieces and handed us our Styrofoam plates.

"Jimbo?" Emerson asked, not reaching for the plates. "Jimbo was here?"

Steinberger nodded.

I pushed past my brother for the plates. "Okay, well, thanks. You have a good night. Let's go, Em. Big Dog here's getting bored." The golden looked up at me and grinned.

My brother ignored me — and her. "Was

Reverend Riggs here too? With Jimbo?"

Steinberger turned his back to the screen, busying himself with the coffee machine. I watched him pour out a pot that smelled like he'd just made it, shaking his head, distracted. "Hard to say. Been busy tonight. So many coming and going."

Emerson waited for more. More didn't come.

Mollybird Pittman was there, her head for once uncovered. She sat alone — no surprise there — at a table in the farthest corner, nearly into the woods. In front of her perched a piece of key lime pie, still unscathed by the fork that hovered over its stiff meringue hat. We often saw her there — often saw most everyone on Pisgah Ridge at Hog Wild some time or another. But the sight of Mollybird tonight made my back ache again.

Because we weren't with the whole Pack, we skirted past our usual spot. Shoehorning ourselves into a picnic table whose benches had been built too close, we sat with our backs to the dirt parking lot.

Footsteps on sawdust and pine needles make little sound. So we never heard the trouble that was approaching us from behind.

19. GENERAL MOLLYBIRD

Big Dog must have sensed something wasn't quite right, because from underneath the table, she whined.

"Don't cry to me," I told her, bending to show her my pink soft drink can under the table. "You don't like Tab, remember?" And as I sat up, the hand on my shoulder made me jump and drop my can. I turned to see Mort, leering.

Just behind Mort, Buddy Buncombe leaned over our table as Mort wedged himself in beside me and put his head close to mine. My insides clenched with the stench of tobacco dip and two-day-old sweat. I turned my head to the side and scooted away, but Mort pressed himself closer. "Just wanted to say, Turtle, Emerson, just wanting to let you know how we was hoping to help."

"Help?" Emerson asked this, his voice hammered thin.

This time I knew to keep quiet.

"Y'all's trouble," Mort repeated.

Emerson shook his head slowly. "We aren't in trouble."

"We heard you was having yourself some trouble."

"Thanks. But we're not." Em reached for his keys. "As a matter of fact, we were just leaving."

But Mort and Buddy flanked us as we walked to the truck. "We heard," Mort drawled, "that you was being forced to keep company with . . ." from his distended lower lip where he was dipping tobacco, he sent a stream of tobacco in a long arc just ahead of our steps, "the wrong sort of folk."

"We reckoned," Buddy put in, "me and Mort did, we should warn you to be shed of the wrong sort."

"Anybody can make that kind of mistake." Mort held his rifle with his armpit while he lit a cigarette. *"Once,"* he added, his lip curling up on one side.

Em stepped past Mort's rifle to make his way to the driver's-side door. "Reckon we'd be just fine as we are. Don't need any help; don't need any warnings."

"Unless," I added, drawing courage by swinging myself into the passenger side, Big Dog at my feet, and slamming the door, "by the wrong sort, you're meaning *you.*"

Buddy guffawed, then, his head always engaging in jerks and jolts, seemed to remember something he'd wanted to say. "Hey. We saw, me and Mort did, your pal Bo here tonight. Just him and y'all's . . ." He looked to Mort to finish the sentence.

"Friend!" Mort spat, sending brown juice onto the cab seat, laughing when I flinched. But there was brown juice splattered on the truck cab now, and a general film of filth from the way he'd pronounced that last word, something far worse than obscene the way it came out of his mouth.

Mort held up his cigarette. "Y'all be careful now, playing with fire. Y'all don't wanna get hurt none. And associating yourselves with the wrong type could put you smack in the middle of nowhere you wanna be." He spread his fingers and let the cigarette drop to the ground, a snake of smoke rising from the sawdust and pine like it was charmed.

Mort and Buddy stayed where they were, beefy arms braced on each side of the truck cab. The cigarette butt in the sawdust and pine sputtered and hissed, then sparked into a flame. Mort bent down for a small pine branch whose end had caught fire.

Em had the keys up to the ignition, but Mort's arm was already inside the driver's-side window, the burning pine branch in Emerson's face. "Sometimes," Mort drawled, "playing with fire can get people hurt. And it'd be an awful shame, a real awful shame to see the two of you hurt."

Em grasped Mort's wrist to try and wrench the branch from him.

Buddy pointed to me, backed to the far corner of the passenger side, and he snorted. "At least Turtle here knows to steer clear of fire."

At that moment, a voice shrilled from the other side of Steinberger's hut, startling us all into frozen mid-motion. The voice didn't bother itself with a name: "You, cousin. Come here, boy!"

We all looked at Mort Beckwith. Mollybird Pittman was his mother's second cousin — all Pisgah knew that — which made him once removed.

"Yes'm," he called back, not looking at us, but withdrawing the branch from inside the truck cab. He let it drop to the ground and, without looking down, stomped the last of the flame out with his boot.

"Boy, do you plan on bellowing at me from there to here," Mollybird ripped into him, "or you plan on walking over here to me like something civilized?"

Mort Beckwith tucked his gun under his

arm, and, grudgingly, lumbered her way. Em and I, and even Buddy, craned our heads back to watch.

"You and your daddy haven't been to call on me lately," Mollybird Pittman was saying, even before Mort reached her.

"Yes'm."

"Not for years, would be my reckoning."

"Yes'm."

"And your momma comes only twice a year or so, bringing me a pie — like because I don't have a husband I can't bake one myself."

"Yes'm."

"You agreeing with that?"

"Yes'm. I mean no'm."

"You as dense as you are big? You in school yet?"

"It's summer."

"Lord, it's 200 degrees. I believe I know summer when I feel it charbroiling me, boy. I meant *college.* You planning on college?"

There was a pause. "I don't rightly know. I got one more year yet to be figuring."

"What's that there under your arm?"

Mort looked under his arm like he was surprised to find anything there. "That'd be my gun."

"Lord have mercy, I know a gun when I see it. What's it doing *here* with you? You using the barrel to eat with instead of a fork?"

He lifted the rifle toward her, for her to admire. "I reckon I carry it with me sometimes."

She knocked it away. "I reckon you can get that thing out of my face."

When Mort retreated from General Mollybird, he marched straight back to his truck and sat waiting for Buddy, the engine snorting and ready to go. Buddy nodded good-naturedly to Em and me, like he'd been paying us a friendly call, and he ambled over to join Mort.

I thought maybe I saw one more boy, small and wiry and awkward, crouched there on the hood of Mort's truck, hunched in the middle like a hood ornament nobody thought to mount right. The hood ornament bore some resemblance, I thought, to someone I knew. And then as the figure scrambled from the hood and into the cab with Buddy and Mort, I thought maybe I'd seen wrong, its being so dark at the far side of the lot and our headlights facing away.

I scratched Big Dog on the head to keep my hands from shaking. The lights from Mort's truck dissolved into the dark. We sat, not talking, Em and me. And then when the crickets' calls to each other clattered against the quiet, I took a deep breath. "We better go."

Em was staring out into the woods. "So the jerk was here."

For a minute, I thought he'd spotted the same slinking figure on the hood of Mort's truck. "You saw him too? Was it Welp?"

"What?"

"With Mort?"

"What're you hallucinating about, Turtle? I'm talking about Bo."

"Oh." I understood. "Well, maybe they were hungry." And then I wished I hadn't said *they.* Em frowned at me and started the engine.

We took the long way home, swung by the Look. The lights of the Valley blinked like fireflies suspended in black. I stopped myself just short of reaching to catch one. Em shut off the motor when we arrived at the edge of the ridge, and we crawled out on the rock that sat three thousand feet above the Valley.

"You s'pose," I wondered to Emerson, "it's as peaceful down there tonight as it looks?"

"From down there it likely looks peaceful up here. Reckon we know from personal experience wouldn't either one of those be right exactly."

I lay back, breathing in the clover and pine that had baked all day in the August sun.

"Hey, Em? You reckon you'll live all your life here?"

"Not college."

"Well, 'course not college." We understood the bargain our parents had struck: that our father had allowed Momma to have us christened in the Methodist church, and in return we would be sent North to college. For our father, it was a kind of Faustian selling of souls — only to the opposite team. "I mean come home after. Later, I mean. After college."

Emerson didn't answer.

And I wasn't expecting an answer, since I didn't have one myself.

After a long while of sitting in silence, we stumbled several feet in the dark back to the truck.

"Em?"

He looked up from thumbing through his keys.

"Emerson, we gonna tell Dad? About Mort and them. And Seventh Street. And . . . everything. All the stuff we've kept saying doesn't mean anything." I asked this even knowing the answer, knowing we wouldn't.

Em met my eye, briefly, then swung himself into the cab. "What do *you* think, Turtle?" he asked, not really asking.

"I think we just may be in a world of trouble, and it's too late to start explaining ourselves to anyone now." I pulled out the first tape my hand touched, Martha and the Vandellas, and we listened, not speaking, as we drove home.

When Em and I reached our own porch, he side-hugged me goodnight, walked up to his room, and shut the door.

Still fully dressed, I climbed into bed and lay awake for what seemed like hours. I finally did fall asleep, though, which I knew for two reasons: one, my pillow the next morning was damp with drool. But second, I woke up still tunneling out from a dream: The Blue Hole was filled with bathing elephants and crocodiles and ringed with palms bearing coconuts the color of my hair. The rhododendrons were in bloom again like they'd been in late spring, but this time they weren't pink but a brilliant, brutal red, like Mollybird's roses — like the place had got set on fire. And there was Reverend Riggs in the midst of it all, wearing his ill-fitting suit — only it had gone white and the pant legs had widened so that

they fluttered and flowed. Almost like a
sheet.

20. BRUISED AND BROKEN

The next afternoon after we'd finished our work, Em, Bo, and I had piled into the pickup to gather the others, including Sanna. All through the day as we'd shoveled and weeded and hacked and trimmed, neither Em nor I had mentioned Mort's warning, although I'm guessing neither of us managed to chase his words from our heads or the look in his yellow eyes for more than ten minutes together. I'll confess this much: It occurred to me how much easier things would've been if I'd never suggested stopping for Sanna that very first day. But she'd become part of our Pack, and there was no changing that now.

Just after picking up L. J., Emerson called back to me, "Turtle, before Sanna joins us, tell these madmen about last night."

I started with Steinberger's and ended with Mort Beckwith's driving away. And then I added: "And I think I saw Welp there too. Sitting on the hood of Mort's truck, it looked like maybe. Although it was dark."

"What was he doing?" Jimbo asked.

"Not even sure what I saw. Mollybird Pittman tearing into Mort like that had me a little distracted."

Em shook his head. "On the other hand, Turtle here mighta been seeing things. Too much emotional stress what with those hyenas circling."

I scrunched my nose at him. Then gathered my breath. "And also . . . although it's probably not worth mentioning . . ."

The boys sat waiting for me to go on.

"Well, it's just that the night I spent at Sanna's, on our way back from the Dairy Queen there on the Pike . . . but really it was probably just one of those things."

"*Which* one of those things?" Em wanted to know.

Bo leaned in more closely. "What is it, Turtlest?"

"Just that the two of us nearly got hit, seemed like, by some crazy truck barreling down. It didn't hit us, understand, and probably just happened to swerve at the wrong place. . . ."

I stopped there, watching L. J. ram his horn-rims back up his nose, him and Em and Bo exchanging glances.

"You guys," I protested, "think I'm a baby for even bringing it up."

"On the contrary," L. J. corrected, "we think you're a moron for just now mentioning it."

We arrived next at Welp's, and when he didn't appear at the door just after Emerson's honk, Jimbo threw his size fourteen feet up and over the side of the truck.

Jimbo held out his hand, signaling me to join him. "I think I'll be needing my partner in crime, just in case Bobby's momma's alone in there." I grabbed his hand and approached the trailer with him.

The aluminum door of the single-wide was left dangling open, drunk on one hinge. As we eased up the three wooden steps, two of them already caved in, we could see through the living room down a short linoleum hall to a king-sized bed at the trailer's far end. I was vaguely aware — or thought I was later — of hearing another truck growl into the drive beside Em's.

Jimbo had one-eightied already, looking shaken, and dropped off the steps before I registered what I was seeing. Roach clips trailed from the front door clear on down to the bed, its pink floral spread littered in bottles and cans and a body, a woman's, that didn't seem to be real awfully clothed — not near enough anyhow.

As I scrambled back toward the stairs, I felt a meaty bare arm drop onto my shoulder. Mort Beckwith had landed his big self beside me, and the top step, the only one remaining intact, cracked through the middle.

"Welpler!" Mort bellowed through the door, smiling crookedly at me, then shouted again. "Get your butt out here! HEY! Welpler!"

This roused Bobby's mother, there on the bed. She lifted her head.

Jimbo had turned back to restrain him. "Get off of there, Mort. Go on, now. *Get.*"

Mort Beckwith stayed where he was, but still hadn't peered into the trailer. He roared at Jimbo, "What's eating you, Buckwheat?"

Jimbo leapt to the foot of the rickety steps. He grabbed Mort by one leg and one dangling hand. "I said *get off!*"

Welp's momma, her back still to us, was just wobbling to her feet, beginning to turn.

Mort's neck craned to the far end of the linoleum hall. He let out a whistle and licked his bottom lip, distended as always with a big dip of tobacco. "Turns out our little Bobby's got himself one good-looking whore of a momma. Reckon he'll mind if I have a go?"

It was then that Jimbo heaved Mort, whole, the whale of him, to the ground.

Jimbo waited until Mort had staggered up, cursing, to his feet, then Bo punched him.

The blow, Bo's very hardest left hook, sunk deep into Mort's foam rubber gut. Mort looked surprised but not at all pained. He pulled back his arm and caught Bo's nose on the upswing.

I spun around to shut the trailer door, keeping my eyes down on the clip-littered linoleum and not on the woman, by then up on her bare feet.

"Bobby?" she called. "You, Bobby!"

I pulled the door to, heard it click, and looked frantically for a way to lock it from the outside. I saw my hand shake on the aluminum knob.

"Bobby!" she wailed. "Bobby, you get back here!"

I could hear her pinballing against the walls as she made her way down the hall. Grasping the front door with both hands, I threw my weight against it. She tried the knob, then began pounding the door.

"Bobby!" she shrieked. "BOBBY! You let me out, you hear me? BOBBY!"

I held to the knob. "Get away from the

door!" I yelled in to her.

She pounded and kicked, scratched at the door.

I hauled back on the knob, my whole weight against it. "Go back to bed! You don't have your clothes on! You don't — !"

I saw my knuckles go white as I clung to the knob, and I heard myself, like from a long ways away off, sobbing into the aluminum door.

Welp's momma crumpled, exhausted or maybe passed out, onto the floor.

I turned back to see Mort, shaking his square, crew-cut head, standing over Jimbo. Landing a last kick to Bo's head, Mort lurched toward the door like maybe he'd march in there if he wanted, then he spit to the side, threw his head back, and laughed. He swaggered back to his truck, adjusted the rifle Jemima on her back windshield rack, and turned to survey the damage he'd done.

L. J. and Emerson, each on one end of Jimbo, lugged him to the bed of Em's truck.

With the back of my hand, I swatted away what was left of my tears.

"Bo all right?" I asked L. J. and Emerson.

Jimbo opened his eyes. "Next time, Turtle, remind me up good, huh?"

I stationed myself by his head, and stroked

his stubbly cheek. "What, Bo? To do what?"

"Remind me to stick up for the bad guys. They're always bigger."

"Our poor sweet Bo. Someday you'll grow into those feet and —"

"And then I'll get Goliath good."

"Sure you will, Bo. You sure enough will."

And then his eyes closed, and I pulled his head in my lap, him and his tenderized face.

Emerson slid into the truck cab and waited, his fingers batting the keys already in the ignition, until Mort had started his engine. Then Em swung his pickup ahead of Mort's, blocking the one-lane dirt drive. Mort raced his engine and leaned on his horn. Em thrust his head out the window, then both his arms, and seemed on the point of leaping out altogether.

But Welp's momma's old Pinto appeared at the head of the drive. And there at the wheel was Bobby Welpler himself.

"Get on over here, Welpler!" Mort roared over his engine. "Time you ditched these nigger-loving losers."

Jimbo had gone limp in my lap, and it was Jimbo who always knew what to do in a crisis. We all — all but Bo — looked at Welp, but nobody else spoke.

Welp abandoned his car in the tall grass beside the head of the drive, and sprang out with his skinny arms empty, though I could see a Piggly Wiggly grocery sack on the seat with a gallon of milk, tipped sideways on the shredded upholstery, beside it. He hesitated a moment, shifting his weight toward one truck, then the other.

"Welp!" L. J. called to him. "In this heat, don't forget, your milk will undoubtedly sour and be unfit for imbibing. Welp!"

And for some reason just then, I pictured Welp's momma where she'd passed out, her soured-milk skin against the cracked linoleum floor.

Welp swung himself up into the truck beside Mort and didn't look back.

Jimbo always gave the rescue instructions, but Jimbo was out cold. Both the sideways gallon of milk and the woman passed out in the trailer we left where they fell — hoping, maybe, somebody else would find them and know what to do.

We drove to Sanna's house, slowing to see her father's station wagon just pulling into the carport propped up at the right of the kitchen. Farsanna herself was just unfolding from the back of the wagon. She turned to her parents, both emerging more slowly, and to whatever she said, her mother shook her head no. But slowly, real slowly, her father

287

nodded.

Without waiting to see if we would in fact stop, she disappeared into the house.

"What do you do all day in there?" I'd once asked her as we sat with our feet dangling down in the Hole.

"Read, mostly. And study. And sometimes I cook. *Sambol,* for example." Her eyes cut toward me, and her lips smiled at one corner.

"My favorite."

"Yes. Your favorite." The smile gained height, then sank as she added, "I would like to receive a job. To help my father, our family. But I don't have yet documentation for working."

I'd opened my mouth to tell her I didn't have any particular documentation for hauling manure, but I left it alone.

By the time we'd pulled up to the carport and nodded to her father who stood silently at the door, Farsanna had returned, the straps of my old bathing suit showing from under her clothes. We had Sanna with us and were well out of her drive before the screen door had slammed behind her father.

Her eyes wide on Jimbo, she sank to her knees beside his bruised face — beside my lap. One of Bo's eyes was beginning to swell shut and his nose was still leaking red.

Sanna looked from L. J. to me for an explanation.

"This is twice Bo's been slugged since you came," I said — before I thought to keep my mouth shut.

"Twice?" L. J. asked.

With his one eye still open, Jimbo looked at me, pleading.

"That is . . . the other time was nothing but these two playing." I pointed to the cab, to the back of Emerson's head. "Reckon Em just played too hard that one day."

Farsanna nodded but kept her eyes on me like she was waiting for more, for maybe the truth. I reached for the cooler and passed Cokes all around.

Then Sanna's head whipped around. "The Stray! I did not call for him to come!"

We were a couple of miles away from her house by then. "He'll be just fine," I shouted into the wind off the truck. "He's probably just as happy lounging around the yard, don't you think?"

Persuaded, Sanna poured peanuts into a bottle for Jimbo, then held the cold glass up to his head. Seemed to me nobody needs peanuts in their Coke to unswell a black eye.

Seemed to me nobody needs a face down close enough to suck out your air.

L. J. sat across from me, his jaw gone slack just staring at them, and then sometimes at me — like there'd been a lit sign like his daddy's right there in the truck all along, and he'd only just then learned how to read it.

Me, I couldn't watch anymore, so I shifted my gaze toward the road, trying to focus on the trees swishing by.

We kept to ourselves mostly that day. None of us except Sanna felt much like swimming. So we sat on the rock palm in a tight little knot, our ankles dangling into the water, while Sanna waded in, quietly soaking in the cool water.

After awhile, she emerged from the water, and Jimbo wrapped around her shoulders a towel, a thick burgundy thing, plush and new. For a moment, I was too busy noticing the towel that must've replaced the white excuse for terry cloth to focus on the way Bo reached tenderly to brush a strand of Sanna's black-licorice hair from her face. But when the rest of the Blue Hole went quiet, I knew right then what everyone else must be seeing. Or maybe feeling: the stripped-wire charge between Bo and Sanna that jolted the banks.

It had been a simple gesture, Bo's flinging

the towel, so maybe it was the look in his eye. Or in hers. Or maybe it was when his hand brushed her shoulder. Or her one finger held up, tracing the swell of his eye.

But there it was, the two of them — gone public by letting everyone see how shut out we all were. Shut out tight from them and the place they made private with just a fling of a burgundy towel.

"Oh, man," I groaned — not exactly to L. J., but he frowned over at me, and he nodded.

L. J. and I climbed the trail together, though I turned now and then to check on my brother behind us — he at least had Big Dog beside him, licking his hand. Me, I only had L. J., and no way would he be licking my hand.

Em waved me away every time. "You go on, Turtle. Go on. Leave me be."

"What's eating him?" L. J. asked. At least he didn't ask about what might be eating me.

"You know," I whispered to him, "for a real smart guy, you don't notice too much."

He ignored me the rest of the climb, though we kept close together, our arms and legs pumping hand over hand, pulling us up, our legs dragging us the final flat of the path. We reached the Clearing at the same time.

Side by side, we stopped there at the head of the trail and stared.

And then, side by side, we broke into a run.

Smoke was pouring from Emerson's truck cab.

21. An X Marked
the Spot

I reached the truck first and peered into the passenger's-side window to see what was causing the smoke. Two sticks were crossed at right angles and bound with blackberry vine. Flames leapt up from them.

I swung my wet towel through the open window at the thing, and L. J.'s towel followed close behind mine. The fire suffocated under wet terry cloth and mud. We fell against the truck, both of us holding our chests.

With the sleeve of his T-shirt, L. J. wiped the sweat from his nose and pushed his horn-rims back into place. "What in God's name was that?"

I unpeeled my towel and his from the seat, both of them charred and in pieces. He picked up the bound sticks.

"L. J., don't tell. Okay?"

"*What?* Why not?"

"Just . . . don't."

"You don't expect your brother will per-ceive there's been some alteration to his upholstery? Be realistic, Turtle."

"The truck's in bad shape. Maybe he'll — Big Dog's not here yet to sit on it even . . . Okay, yeah. He'll notice. Just don't."

The others were emerging from the woods.

"You win," I said loudly to L. J., and picked up a tape from the pile on the floor where Emerson stored them. "We'll listen to Little River Band on the way home." I edged away from the cab, and without meeting Em's eye moved toward the bed.

"Hey, Turtle." Emerson grabbed my arm. The air was heavy with heat and gas and burnt cloth.

"Hey, Em."

"You got something to tell me?"

"Me?"

He nodded toward the seat. Big Dog, her chubby hind hips needing Emerson's lift to mount the passenger seat, had her front end strained forward, her nose in the burn, and was sniffing and whining.

"What, that?" I asked.

"Yeah. That."

L. J. stood to one side. "I told you he'd notice."

Jimbo and Sanna were just reaching the

head of the trail that opened onto the Clearing.

"Not everybody needs to see it, Em," I pleaded. "Wouldn't you say?"

"What, you didn't think I'd see a cross charbroiled on my vinyl?"

"It's just an X."

"It's a cross."

"It's nothing but an X. *Now* who's being overdramatic? L. J., what do you say it is?" I demanded.

L. J. raised one eyebrow at me. "It's a cross."

I shrugged. "So what if it is?"

"If it is — and it most decidedly *is*," L. J. pronounced, "well, then —" but he never finished.

Jimbo and Farsanna approached the truck.

I shook my head at Emerson. "Don't mention it to her —"

"Why not?" he demanded. "How come you're so all-fired bent on not telling anybody anything?"

"How come you're so nasty with that tone of voice? I just don't think anybody needs to jump to conclusions is all."

"Look, enough fun and games here. I'm saying we got to tell someone about all this. We've been kidding ourselves that all this didn't mean anything."

Jimbo elbowed his way between us, and we both fell suddenly silent. "By all means, club, maul, or mangle each other," Bo offered, "but just relocate y'all's family feud to somewhere I ain't so likely to starve standing up."

We were all in the truck but Farsanna, and she was just swinging in when Bobby Welpler slipped out from the path that led to the Hole into the clearing with Mort.

I mouthed at L. J., "So if Mort's here . . . then who?"

"I know," he mouthed back.

"So who could've . . . lit those sticks? Did they loop up here and back down?"

L. J. shook his head and his shoulders twitched up and back down — it was the closest I ever saw to his admitting that he didn't know.

Mort tipped sideways to whisper something to Welp, and the two of them laughed a little too hard and too loud, like people do when nothing's particularly funny. Mort had left his gun in his truck, but he retrieved it now and caressed its long, shiny barrel like he'd missed it and needed to make up for lost time.

Then, looking up, he let out a whistle. "Looky there, Bob, it's Turtle's *friend* up there in the truck."

I didn't turn my head.

"Or should I say *Jimbo's* friend? Hey, Bob, looky how fine them black apples is ripening up this season."

Farsanna's leg, which had frozen just in the process of leaping up and over into the truck, must've failed her just then. She dropped back down to the ground.

Jimbo stood up in the truck bed, his face already pulped blue.

Mort swung his square-column legs up into the cab of his own truck. "Lordy, Bob, would you look at that? Mm-*mmm!* Ain't saying I'd keep me a black cow of my own, y'understand now. But I swear I might could be talked into borrowin' theirs for a good time."

I remember Mort's mouth making the shapes for the sounds as much as I recollect the words the sounds made: his jaw dropping and rising, dropping and rising onto his chest, where his neck ought to have been.

Jimbo was out of the truck then and on the ground, my brother right beside him.

Barricading himself in with the driver's-side door and waving for Bobby to join him, Mort reared back to deliver his finishing touch: "I tell you what, Welpler, that there girl is put together nearly as good as your momma!"

Welp's snicker strangled on itself. Already trotting to jump in Mort's cab, Bobby Welpler stopped where he was.

"Shoot, Welpler, don't get no ideas to stick up for your old woman, now, just because she lies around the house buck naked. Got me a look — no thanks to choir boy there — and, *son,* I'm saying your momma, especially when she ain't got no clothes on, is some kind of something. Woman could teach the new girl here a few lessons!"

Bobby Welpler's pink face went purple, the acne across his nose a mountain range on a topographical map. His fists sprang up, small and gnarly. He swung at Mort.

Mort reached out one meaty arm and locked the heel of his hand on Welp's forehead, so that Welp's swings, and even his kicks, whiffed into the air. Mort laughed and looked at us to be sure we saw that Bobby Welpler was crying. With a snort of disgust, Mort pitched Welp aside.

Welp swung around again. One hand whipping his knife from his pocket, Welp threw himself, blade first, at Mort Beckwith. Who just laughed and pinioned Welp by the wrists.

Jimbo stormed toward them, and by the rage in Bo's eyes, I knew for sure what was going to happen: Jimbo would pulverize Mort.

Mort, reared back and, laughing, released Welp. He lumbered back to his driver's seat, motioning to Welp, "C'mon." He revved his engine.

But Jimbo did what I could not have guessed. He lifted Bobby Welpler by the armpits, tossed him clear to Em's truck, right at my feet. Emerson dove for Mort's door handle and nearly got pulled under the wheels as Mort spun out from the clearing.

Em scrambled up from the ground where Mort's truck had flung him.

Jimbo reached for Farsanna's hand, and she grabbed at it this time and half hauled herself, half let herself be hauled up into the truck bed.

Welp curled up in a ball and sobbed.

22. ROADBLOCK WITH RIFLES

Jimbo, in the proper order of things, spoke first after we'd ridden a couple of miles away from the Hole. He propped himself in a sitting position, his face swollen and blue. "Steinberger's?"

No reply.

He tried again. "Steinberger's?"

"No!" That was little Bobby Welpler, suddenly come out of his ball.

"Welp, my man," Jimbo told him, "I reckon you got a right to figure your snout's got stuck in the cactus. But —"

"I ain't hungry," Welp sulked.

"Then come along for the fine talk and fellowship."

"Just take me home."

The word *home* croaked out unsteady, like he didn't expect us to hear it any more than he'd meant what he'd said.

Welp raised his head to glower at us, meeting no one's eye, but letting us all in on the sweep of his fury. "I ain't going. And I'm telling you what, don't you go neither."

Jimbo reached to share L. J.'s Coke and added more peanuts. "Don't what, Welp?"

"Don't call me that name!"

"It's a term of endearment, my man. Look, Mort's making a pair of pig's slippers out of himself. You know that. Your momma —"

"You just drop me off, you got that? And don't be going to Steinberger's. Or if you do, drop *her* off," he stabbed a finger towards the tailgate of the truck where Farsanna sat still, staring out toward the woods. "And that's all I'm saying. You got me?"

Jimbo crossed his arms and nodded, real slow. From the driver's seat, Emerson cocked his head, trying to hear. The Big Dog whined softly.

Bo spoke up at last. "Bobby, my man. Seems to me you got to stay on board this ship for your own good tonight." He banged on the cab window and motioned for Em to keep going.

Welp yelled up to Emerson, "Maynard, you drop me off! You got that? You drop me off *now!*"

Em ignored him.

Muttering, Welp resigned himself to a sulk and kept his eyes on the side of the road.

Bo looked at me. "Turtle? What do you think? You hungry?"

I shrugged.

He turned to Sanna and asked quietly, "How 'bout you?"

"Oh," Welp fumed, "so *she* gets escorted home if she wants, that it?"

Farsanna crossed her arms. "I will stay."

"Well," L. J. said, "we could theoretically patronize another establishment."

"Like what?" I asked. "The Pisgah Ridge Four Seasons?"

"Like, maybe just calling it a night," he tried.

I reckon all of us were thinking our mothers wouldn't so much mind our being home once for dinner. But none of us felt like dividing the day or our group or ourselves any further. I had the sensation of spinning, needing to clutch on to the people beside me or not be able to stand, the feeling of nearly being spun off into the night. *Ashes, ashes we all fall down.*

"We could," L. J. tried again, "purchase sandwiches at the station."

Jimbo wrinkled his nose — and that seemed to hurt his injured face enough to rouse him from his reverie, at least. "If you got a taste for motor oil with pimento cheese, maybe."

So the whole Pack of us, including a seething Welp, shuffled our way through the sawdust up to Steinberger's screen window. The old man was pacing behind the counter.

"Just closing down, kids!" he called, yanking the electrical plugs out of their sockets. He lowered the hinged wooden door behind the mesh windows.

Em looked at his watch. I looked at the sky, going ruddy between the pine fringes. We all looked at each other. It was well before closing time.

"Well," said Jimbo, "I'll be dyed amber."

Wearing her black dress and straw hat and sitting on a picnic bench with a plate of barbecue, Mollybird Pittman had risen for a refill on her drink. "Levi? Levi Steinberger, what's going on here? Levi, I want more sweet tea!"

The wooden door lifted a few inches, maybe a foot. Steinberger's hand appeared briefly, shoving out a Styrofoam cup of iced tea and seven cans of soda, including my usual, Tab, and Big Dog's Dr Pepper. Then the door dropped into place, and we could hear the hooks locking into their metal eyes.

Mollybird blinked at her tea. But then she plopped her plate in the round metal cans by the hut and stomped off to her car.

Jimbo tossed us each our can. "Might as well go, mangy pack."

"What's with the old man?" Emerson asked. "What's with everybody today?"

We turned.

Steinberger dashed around the side of the hut. "You kids got that new girl with you tonight?" His eyes darted right and left as he spoke. My eyes followed, seeing nothing but trees and picnic tables — and Molly-bird Pittman stomping back through sawdust to retrieve the purse she'd forgotten under a bench.

Bo jerked his head back toward our table. "Sure, we got her with us, Mr. S. As ever and always."

Steinberger peered out to spot Sanna. "So you do. Well now, so you do. Look kids, I don't want to be inhospitable. . . ." He stopped there. "And I'm not going to be. Just . . . look . . . just be careful. And get on out of here soon, you hear? And turn left when you leave. That's very important. And . . . just . . . you kids stick together, you hear?" Then he disappeared again. It wasn't until the Volkswagen Rabbit he'd left idling behind the Hog Wild hut started to move that I saw his head poke from the driver's-side window. "And turn *left!*" he called as the Rabbit darted into the road.

"Turn *left?*" I called back. "But —"

Steinberger couldn't have heard me, though, his already pulling left on Stonewall Jackson Pike.

"He's taking the long way," L. J. observed. "Take him three times as long."

We all looked at Welp. He stood, arms crossed, refusing to meet anyone's eye.

Emerson nodded toward Mollybird, just pulling onto the Pike — and turning right. "But she's headed the usual way."

I pursed my lips, thinking. "Maybe she doesn't know."

"Doesn't know what?" Emerson asked.

I shrugged. "Whatever it is we don't know either."

We stood by the truck and watched Mollybird's taillights launch into the dusk.

Jimbo spoke then for the first time in some minutes. "Reckon we got to fish and cut bait."

"That's fish," L. J. corrected, "*or* cut bait."

"Not in this case it ain't."

Jimbo offered me a hand, like he always did, to help me into the truck — and this time I took it. And I didn't let go.

As we rounded to the right on Stonewall Jackson Pike, ignoring Steinberger's strange warning, the first thing I noticed there in the deepening gray, streaks of pink still stringing together the pines, was Mollybird Pittman's taillights, which should not have been there. Having left Hog Wild a full five minutes before us, she should, in theory, have been long gone. Emerson pulled behind her lights, and we squinted into the dark.

The barriers blocking the road were nothing but orange-and-white-striped metal barrels armied across the stretch of asphalt just before Stonewall Jackson Pike met the main highway that formed Pisgah's spine. Em's truck could easily have nudged one barrel, maybe two, out of the way. On their own, they would have signaled only that potholes were being filled there by daylight, and the warm tar was hardening by night.

But the figures in white that swept among the striped barrels signaled what I already knew: This was no construction site.

I don't suppose I'd ever seen any Klan members before — in full regalia, I mean. No doubt I'd seen them in daily life, knew who they were in their jeans and their T-shirts, their wingtips and ties, and yet not guessed at who else they might be. I'd only ever heard stories of the Klan all dressed in their white, and of their hauntings, and of the horrors they'd brought down, years ago, upon the heads of dissenters in the Valley below.

Up on the Ridge, understand, we'd mostly been above all the mess — no problems with buses or houses or seating at all — having no one of the wrong sort so much as staying the night. Old Man Steinberger had been threatened, I'd heard, when he first opened for business, but he'd never pushed himself forward, never talked of his rights, never asked anything but to be left alone with his daughters, to provide a service, three days hickory smoked, that no one could match, no one in three counties. So they'd let him alone.

But they'd not gone away, and we knew it, just ignored it. Now and then over the years, my father had written an editorial that sketched them, them and their hoods, as silly.

And if I'd only seen a snapshot of them in, say, a history book or microfilmed newspaper photos, I'd have said silly myself. On first glance, sure, they looked like somebody'd gotten just real tangled up trying to put the sheets on the line. And they cradled their rifles — like nursing infants. And the eyeholes of their hoods didn't always line up just real straight with their eyes. So you had to wonder how much trouble they could've caused if they'd tried.

They billowed back and forth the width of the Pisgah Ridge Crossing, tripping occasionally over their long gowns. And in the arms of those not cradling rifles rode family-pack chicken-and-biscuit buckets brimming not with dinner but with donations.

These donations they'd been gathering, it seemed, with the method they were inflicting upon Mollybird Pittman. A group of three approached the driver's-side window, tapped on the glass, and slid the mouth of a rifle into the car.

Then asked for a contribution.

It was when they drew near I knew that my father must never have seen them — never in person. All the movies and old newsreels that show them as clowns, as silly, ludicrous, laughable, have missed all their power, have misunderstood. The rippling white, the fire-red crosses in circles emblazoned on some of their chests: They approached like a battalion of childhood horrors, and I knew then that my father was wrong, that this was not some ridiculous redneck costume ball, a gaggle of old men clutching their gods, some Technicolored past that never existed.

They were all that too, I could see, but they were more.

The pale figures surrounding Mollybird's car that night, and then Emerson's truck, snaking around us, were specters of my own darkest fears, grim reapers in white, with loaded deer rifles standing in for a scythe. They didn't think this was play. Black and vacant behind slits in pointed hoods, their eyes were hollowed, King Lear's after his blinding. But they could see: They lowered their buckets and rifles together inside my brother's window.

This was not play; this was business. The human heart gone to rot.

23. The End Does Not Hold

Mollybird Pittman burst out of her Buick with her hat gripped in one hand, swatting at white hoods. And Mollybird was shouting.

"You bunch of inbred potbellies! You think I got time to sit here and play your little games?" She smacked a hooded figure across the eyes with her straw and silk flowers. "You think anybody asked you boys to play in the street and clog up a public road?"

"Calm down there, Molly," one of them said, reaching to grab her arm.

She swung her hat at him. "That's *Miss* Molly to you. I don't have time for your messing around — do I make myself clear?"

"Reckon you oughta know, Miss Pittman, we ain't got no gripe with you. We just —"

"No? Well, I got a gripe with *you*. A lady like me likes to think she can live in a town and get from one place to another unmolested. She —"

"Miss Pitt—"

"— Likes to think she can move around safe without a bunch of two-bit yellow-bellied ruffians threatening her on the road, asking —"

"Now, Miz Molly, we don't —"

"— For what little fixed income she has to put bread on her own table, with no man to help her. Just her by herself. And no one to help her —"

"We ain't asking —"

"Without anybody coming along like highway robbers, like the thieves on the road to Samaria to take what little she has!"

"Now, Mrs. Pittman —"

"It's *Miss,* and I'll thank you not to forget it. You think I don't know your voices? You think I don't know your names? You think I won't report you to the IRS for trying to tax me twice?"

At this, the line of white hoods cracked, pried open by the sheer force of her rage.

Mollybird was back at the wheel of her Buick, her battering ram. She gunned the engine and blasted forward a foot, and then another, slamming her brakes each time just as her bumper made contact with white.

"Well, I'll be cut and curly fried," Jimbo whispered to me. "It's like the breath of the Lord done parted the sea."

"What?"

"Moses had his rod; Mollybird's got her hat and fake roses. Oh, sweet Jesus, hang on . . ."

A wave of white surged toward Mollybird Pittman — just as she let off the brake for good and stomped on her gas.

Welp shrieked as he stood to leap from the truck, but Jimbo grabbed him again by the T-shirt and hauled him back down with us.

White gowns were lunging, some to the side and some toward her door, as Mollybird Pittman's brown Buick roared into and over and through. Orange-and-white-striped barrels leapt into the air, slammed to the ground, and rolled off to the side. Pale figures flew behind them.

One of the white hoods called from the side as he dove out of the way. "Hey, boys! Ain't that the truck we was looking out for?"

More hoods turned, some of them running now not just away from the Buick, but towards us.

"She's here!" one of them shouted, pointing to Sanna. "We got her right here!"

I saw Em look through his rearview back at Sanna, right before he stomped on the accelerator, sending the five of us in the truck bed slamming against the tailgate.

Remembering Em's broken tailgate latch and how too much pressure would spill us out on the road, I screamed.

L. J. and Sanna grabbed for the side. I grabbed for L. J. And we all grabbed for Jimbo, holding to the bottom fifty-pound bags of manure. Welp clawed for a hold on my leg.

"We're gonna die!" I cried into the night.

"Eventually," I heard L. J. mutter as he and Sanna held to the side and I held to L. J. and Welp held to me and we all held to Jimbo — to a belt loop, a pants leg, his arm.

"Don't let go!" I called out — maybe to L. J., maybe to Bo or to Sanna, and likely to the wire holding the tailgate.

White billowed by us like we'd launched into the sky and clouds scuttled out of the wind of our passing. Bo's belt loop was holding and so was his hand. He clawed for a better hold on the bottom bags of manure.

We cleared the roadblock, their flashlights dueling with our taillights as we screeched past the last of the barrels and broke free down the Pike.

I recall my head falling back, recall seeing Big Dog's head poking out from the truck cab's back window, recall hearing her bark, hearing Jimbo's big feet smack into the tailgate.

And then the wire no longer held — and neither did we.

24. Leaning In Together

We were still holding on to each other when we landed, splayed like truck-struck possums across Stonewall Jackson Pike.

Emerson must have felt the lightened weight in the flatbed, or maybe Big Dog's barks. I could hear the shriek of his brakes, the pads already worn thin, and smell the Pike's new skin of rubber.

The darkness throbbed around me, through me, inside my head.

And I thought of the Blue Hole, and thought how nice a final image that was before death. I knew I wouldn't go to heaven myself, not believing in it, but Jimbo at least might find heaven to be a big swimming hole, sunk down into hemlocks and rhododendron in bloom. And I wondered if maybe angels took turns on the rope swing — and if it was only boy angels.

And then I saw legs slowly lifted into the air, like they were testing themselves to see whether they worked. I marveled at how I hadn't commanded their moving, and that they still functioned at all.

Jimbo wobbled up, his yellow Coors Light T-shirt rising like a drunken sun. And I saw it was his size 14 feet attached to those lifting legs. Which meant they weren't mine.

By then my head was a timpani, the pain drumming in time with each pump of panic and blood. And it occurred to me this was good news: that I still had a head to hurt.

Em lept out of the cab, Big Dog right behind him. Her wet nose sniffed us for signs of life. I could hear L. J. moaning beside me.

The skewed beams of the truck headlights illuminating our tangle of limbs, Em knelt by my head, and the hand he lay on my shoulder was trembling. His other hand reached for Sanna. "I thought," he said, "that we were all dead."

"You and me both, cowboy." Jimbo stepped gingerly on each of his feet, like they were clown's shoes he was just trying on. Sanna had leveraged herself up and stood, unsteadily, between Em and Bo. Bo knelt over me then. "You crack your shell, Turtle?"

"Only my head." I felt in the dark for L. J. "Laban Jehu, you okay?"

"Address me in that fashion once more, Turtle, and I'll have you stewed."

"He's all right," I said up to the others. "Mean as ever, and knows his own name, Laban Jehu does."

"I thought I directed you, Shelby Lenoir —"

"Just had to be sure."

"Welp?" Jimbo asked, helping Bobby to stand. "You survive?"

Welp grunted back.

"Good. Because we'll be waiting for you to tell us all about how you knew something was up."

"I swear," Welp whined, "all I knew was to steer clear of Steinberger's. And . . ."

He didn't add the *"her"* that meant Sanna, but we all heard what he didn't say.

Jimbo helped me up and Em helped up L. J. and the five of us, Welp lagging yards behind, linked shoulders to limp to the truck.

Em glanced back repeatedly over his shoulder, toward Welp in one direction and the roadblock on the other. "You do realize they'll come after us."

L. J. nodded. "Although maybe not right away."

"And maybe not us — exactly," I added.

The boys looked at me.

"I mean not us only. Not only us." This only made matters worse.

My brother popped me on the back of my head. "So, Turtle, *now* do you think maybe Sanna's and your little incident on the Pike, getting blown off the road, might've been on the intentional side?"

"Okay, so maybe I'm a little slow to add up the numbers. At least I don't get all hysterical and jump to conclusions."

"You're slow," my brother came back, "to admit there *are* numbers."

"I reckon," Jimbo began, "one thing's got itself clear."

We stopped. My back hurt. My head hurt. My tailbone for sure was broken to bits. *Nothing* was clear. I waited for Bo to go on, and he did.

"Reckon old Welp was trying to hook us on up out of trouble."

I rubbed my head, then my tailbone, and wondered which was in the worst shape. "If you ask me, he didn't try very hard to tell us."

"Maybe he did all right for Welp," said Jimbo.

I dusted off my legs and backside — gingerly. Every square inch of my midsection hurt, wrenched and bruised and battered. "I say next time we listen to Old Man

Steinberger, even if we don't know what he's talking about."

"Well?" L. J. asked, wiping blood from his knee. "How to proceed? Emerson, any more speedways on which you'd like to deposit us next? It's a veritable miracle we weren't dismembered entirely."

"Look, I was just trying to save all our necks from the bedsheets back there. Y'all could've held on a little tighter, you know."

"To what?" I demanded. "The exhaust?"

Jimbo put a hand across all our shoulders. "Now, men," he nodded my way and Sanna's to include us, "we got to lean in together — else we fly all apart."

Our little regiment stumbled to the truck, with Welp stumping a few feet behind us.

Bo paused before crawling in. "We got to check Sanna's folks."

Em already had the truck rolling. "Way ahead of you, man. Get your butt in the truck."

We scrambled, including me. It was the last place I wanted to go just then. Which was, I suppose, precisely why we were going.

When Emerson's pickup eased to the head of the Moulavis' driveway, three more trucks were already there — just leaving, in fact, their wheels spewing gravel and dust and, like cornstarch dropped into gravy, they turned the hot, humid night air into paste.

We sat in the back of Em's truck without making a sound, without moving even.

I choked on the paste that was passing for air and watched, like the others, in silence as their taillights disappeared up the road. One of them set off his horn, which hooted the first line of "Dixie."

Plenty of truck horns in our town played "Dixie," but I recall that night hearing those first notes, *Oh, I wish I was in the land of cotton,* like a spray of grapeshot through the pines as the trucks disappeared down the road. It seemed to me not at all unlikely just then that boys in gray, Confederate gray, would appear next, armed but shoeless, crouched and ready to fire out from the line of loblollies behind the Moulavis' house.

We all recognized one of the trucks, Mort's gun rack empty. Farsanna seemed not to notice the trucks — she was staring out to the woods behind her house.

Like a prison camp searchlight, Em swung his headlights in a swift arc to the side of the Moulavi house, over the parched, treeless lawn, and then back to the right in another sweep of the woods. The light swept so fast, but I thought I'd spotted something other than trees in those woods. Then I saw through the cab's back window my brother's profile, his jaw set tight. He must have seen what I thought I saw: In the scrub pine to the right of the Moulavis' house, something — or someone — hung from a rope.

25. What Hung
from the Rope

Sanna was standing up straight in the truck bed before Em had shifted to park. He slid from the cab and joined us at the side of the truck.

"What's happening?" Sanna demanded to know.

"That," L. J. said softly, "was the end of your rainbow."

Em aimed a glower at L. J. *"Visitors . . ."* he said, and he nodded, all earnest, like he was needing to show he agreed with himself.

". . . who left," I piled on the lie. "And likely had the wrong street address."

Farsanna looked directly at Welp, who looked away, then at me, like it'd be me to give her the truth ungussied up.

Em had aimed his headlights away from the woods, from whatever it was at the end of the rope. Maybe he thought no one else saw. And maybe he thought that if only for a few minutes, he might save Sanna that

322

small piece of horror.

But seeing us all sneak glances at the woods, she'd vaulted over the side and was sprinting before I'd untangled my legs to jump out of the truck and follow her.

Jimbo leaped out, right behind her.

L. J. reached the ground next, suggesting to nobody listening, "The headlights require realigning if they're to shed light on the matter at hand." Hands on his hips, L. J. stood there as the rest of us raced toward the woods. All except Welp, who crouched alone, with his knife, in the bed of the truck.

Muttering, "One's judgment is generally impeded by one's inability to *see*," L. J. climbed into the cab and aimed the head-lights back toward the line of loblollies.

In the flood of white from the headlights, we semicircled several yards from the scrub pine whose branch held the rope, and what dangled from it.

Farsanna reached for my hand, my stand-ing closest to her. In the wash of white light from the truck, I saw fear flicker there on her face. Even then, she kept her face set. But her eyes locked on mine, and her eyes asked a question, something ancient and horrific and terrified there.

Her gaze swung toward the house, which sat just as we'd left it, bare and dull, almost violently ugly, but dark now. No commotion. No suggestion of disrupted peace. But also no light. No sign of life.

Pulling me with her, Farsanna stepped toward the rope and what hung there. Behind us, and then beside us, came Emerson and Jimbo and L. J., all of us finding each other's hands and arms in the dark, all of us grasping for something to hold, some way to keep walking forward.

We'd not gotten closer than fifteen feet of the tree when the new girl doubled over and lost all her supper there at the strip of woods by the side of the rectangle house. Even with only a shiny white shard of light, there was no mistaking the long, silky ears that flopped down over the noose.

Emerson knelt by Sanna and lay a hand on her back while she retched. My brother's tears dropped onto the back of Farsanna's bare neck, her thick hair falling forward into her face. I'd never seen my brother cry, or reach as he did now to hold someone's hair back as her whole body heaved.

Me, I collapsed on the ground. I lay back and wished I could throw up too. L. J. sat down beside me and for once didn't try to say something smart. Didn't try to say much at all, and that was as much as I wanted to hear.

Reaching up for the rope and for the soft, still-warm body that hung there, Jimbo dropped his arms back to his sides and I watched his shoulders curl forward and shake. In a moment, he called softly over his shoulder, "Hey, Bobby, we're needing you. And your knife."

"Where *is* Welp?" L. J. demanded.

I answered, not because I could see much, staring into the headlights like we were doing, but because I knew Welp. "He's whittling."

"In the dark? Correct me if I'm mistaken," L. J. growled, "but nobody's *got* to whittle."

"Maybe," Jimbo said, "you do if you're Welp." Bo called again toward the truck, "Bobby! Bobby, we're needing you. And your knife."

Sure enough, still in the truck bed, Bobby Welpler had pulled the pocketknife from his jeans and busied himself with a stick of cedar. Lumbering sullenly from the truck and along the white beam of headlights, he joined us.

L. J. took the knife from Welp then, maybe because Welp stood too long staring at the cadaver. For all his faults, impatience was one of my cousin's best virtues.

Mostly by feel, L. J. cut down the hanged dog.

Welp was the only one who tried speaking, and then only this: "I tell you what, didn't I say that pup didn't know where it'd shacked up?"

None of us bothered to answer.

Bo found his towel in the truck bed and wrapped the limp little body in it. "I reckon we got to bury the poor soul right around here. But maybe back in the woods some."

Bo stood with the bundle inside his towel while Emerson and I fetched the shovels that only a few hours ago had done nothing more morbid than mix peat moss and manure. We moved through the dark, navigating by clutching the T-shirt beside us. And somewhere back well out of range of what we imagined might be the sight lines of the Moulavi windows, we took turns digging a hole into soil that we couldn't even see in the dark.

When it seemed deep enough, Bo knelt with Stray and lowered him into the grave. And even as he bent over the body, I suddenly was fighting the urge to sob — and I couldn't have said why. Like I was seeing another grave and another body, and not knowing who.

I put both arms around Sanna, whose whole body convulsed.

I nudged my brother. "Somebody should

say something — if this is the poor creature's funeral." I suppose I meant Jimbo, since Em and I couldn't have come up with a sermon, or even a verse, to save our pitiful souls.

But it was Emerson who launched in instead, whispering into the nothing around us:

Death, be not proud, though some have
    called thee
Mighty and dreadful, for thou art not so;
For those whom thou think'st thou dost
    overthrow
Die not, poor Death; nor yet canst thou kill
    me. . . .
One short sleep past, we wake eternally,
And Death shall be no more: Death, thou
    shalt die!

I was standing beside Jimbo and could feel as much as see him cross himself then. It's what Jimbo did on solemn occasions, and when none of the rest of us knew what to do, there'd be Jimbo, crossing himself. Seeing how there were only two Catholics on the Ridge at the time, and they at least had the good manners never to go genuflecting or crossing in public, we never figured out where Bo picked up the habit. But he carried it with him like some kind of a sword.

Stepping to where his voice had come from, I touched Emerson on the arm. "That was nice, Em. Very grand."

He pulled on my ponytail and let his arm hang there, limp, down my back.

"That *Sports Illustrated*," I tried, "is good stuff."

Maybe he heard that and smiled; maybe not — it was too dark to tell. But I knew neither of us felt any better.

L. J. cleared his throat. "We, um, we should sing." L. J. had the singing voice of a strangling bullfrog — and I mean that in the nicest possible way — so for him to suggest a song meant it was imperative.

We all looked to Jimbo, who closed his eyes and began in his mellow bass a tune I recognized but not the verse:

Through many dangers, toils and snares,
we have already come;
'Tis grace hath brought me safe thus far,
And grace will lead me home.

L. J. joined in as best he could; the rest of us put our arms around each other's shoulders and just held on and let Bo be our voice. Even Welp let himself be drawn in the circle when Bo tugged his T-shirt toward us.

Sanna leaned hard against me. I tried to stand straighter to hold her up good.

Not a one of us questioned the use of a hymn for the funeral of a stray dog — not even L. J., who could be a stickler for the rightness of things. Because it wasn't just the death of a sweet little beast we were marking; it was the death of what we thought we'd been doing, where we'd thought we were living, the death of being able to believe anymore in our innocence and the existence of goodness around us.

From the final verse of the hymn, without missing a beat, Bo shifted key and song:

When the night has come
And the land is dark . . .

His whole lanky self swaying, he nudged our bodies to keeping beat with his.

No, I won't be afraid
Just as long as you stand,
Stand by me . . .

Em, who'd hauled mulch for good portions of his life to the song, provided backup harmony. We held to each others' shoulders and threw our heads back and sang how we wouldn't be afraid, no, not shed a tear, not even if things crumbled and tumbled and fell, and our cheeks were wet as we sang.

We finished the song to its end, all of us keeping our heads down to hide our eyes from each other.

Jimbo stood still then. "God," he began, before any of us realized he was praying and maybe could stop him. "Well, here we are. I don't reckon we got to tell you things have been ugly lately, and especially tonight. I don't reckon we got to tell you things don't look too good from where we'd be standing here in the dark. But I'll just say it outright anyhow: Things may be even worse than we know. *We* may be even worse than we know, each one of us here. So all's I know to do tonight is ask, just simple: Stand by us. Help us stand by each other. Amen."

"Amen," said L. J. — which I could've maybe predicted, since his daddy had gotten religion.

"Amen," said my own brother, which I couldn't have seen coming, since our daddy had always held out.

We walked Sanna to her door, Welp lagging again a few yards behind, and stayed by her side for a time, promised to meet her first thing in the morning. Then we hugged her good-bye, even L. J., who never hugged anyone. Sanna was inside the door when she turned, and I realized she'd focused on Welp, back in the shadows of the porch light's bare bulb.

Bobby Welpler lifted one hand, only waist high but a definite wave goodnight. Then he hung his head.

Exhausted, we stumbled down Sanna's broken concrete walk toward the drive. Emerson stopped under the plate-glass window and pointed to the one growing thing there in the red clay soil.

"A pink rosebush," he said. "How long has that been there?"

I looked at Bo, who shrugged. "Some time now."

Em turned to face Jimbo. "If I weren't so dog tired and worried about Sanna, I swear I'd punch you again. I reckon you told her the rosebush was from you."

Bo shook his head. "Told her it was compliments of Big Dog Lawn and Garden. Planted it late one night so she'd never so much as know which of us stuck it in the ground. Honest."

Em looked from Bo to the bush, and we followed his gaze, all of us staring at the rose like it might speak.

"It's flourishing there," I finally said.

We waited until Sanna's house lights shut off.

Then Jimbo charged, not back toward the truck, but towards the woods.

26. Found Hidden in the Back Woods

Jimbo called over his shoulder, "If she finds anything strange inside, I reckon she'll let us know here soon enough. Meanwhile, we best go searching for whatever else they almost done but didn't. Or done already did, and left clues."

L. J. followed Bo, and I joined Emerson and Big Dog just behind.

"What? Why?" It came out of me like a whine, and too much like a girl — what Emerson thought of as girls. But my knees had already gone spongy on me.

Reshouldering shovels, we clung to each other as we tromped through the woods. "What exactly," I whispered into what I couldn't see, "are we looking for now?"

No one answered. I don't reckon anyone knew.

"We best split up," L. J. said.

Welp grumbled, but steered himself toward the woods.

Emerson touched my arm. "Turtle, you stay with Jimbo."

I knew without being able to make out all the features that Em had on his big brother face, the kind that says all kinds of outrageous things about superior knowledge and upper-body strength — so I bristled. "I can do it myself."

"Don't be an idiot."

"Too late," I told him in my best grown-up voice.

"Turtle's all right," I heard Jimbo whisper to Em. "Kid can take care of herself."

And I'd have been grateful, except for the "kid."

Truth was, I was feeling chipped and cracked on the inside, what with the poor silky-eared Stray and the shadow he left of what might come next. It was the *mights* and *what ifs* all strung heavy and too close together that were making me wobble a little over my feet.

I tugged once on Bo's sleeve. "Just this one time maybe alone's not so good. But, Jimbo, it's not that I'm scared. . . ."

"Glad *you're* not. I wet my pants twice since we pulled in the drive." Jimbo reached for my hand and we walked into what we couldn't see.

The last I heard of Big Dog before I split

off toward the rim of the woods was her trotting along beside Emerson and whining, her tail straight out and stiff.

"Now and then," Emerson defended her later, "she put her nose to the ground." But I'd lay money she was snuffling out more barbecue.

Groping our way from loblollies back into hardwood, Jimbo and I both kept our outside arms mapping tree trunks and branches, and once, a spider web — which is unspeakably creepy at night, not knowing if you've taken on the spider as a stowaway in your hair, now that you've destroyed her home. With our inside arms, Bo and I kept track of each other.

The other boys crunched on back through underbrush, dead leaves our only radar to each other, and that growing dim. I leaned on one tree — maybe a dogwood by its satiny bark — and listened. Then remembered I didn't even know for what.

We walked on.

"Y'all were lost, is all I'm saying," Emerson would insist later.

" 'Was lost,' " Jimbo sang softly back, " 'but now am found.' " He nodded in my direction. "Aw, give the kid credit. It was Turtle found the Pot of Gold."

"*Lost* was what she was."

Truth was, I'd tripped over the pot — metal can, actually. But it was the smell, too, that let me know we'd found something we'd been looking for and didn't want to find.

"Hey!" I called into the darkness as loudly as I dared — which wasn't very loud at all. "Hey! Guys!"

Bo, right beside me, dropped to the ground to feel out what I'd found with my feet.

By that time, Emerson had returned to the truck where he and Big Dog had tunneled into the contents of an overstuffed glove compartment and found the flashlight Momma insisted all gentlemen's vehicles must carry, particularly those transporting young ladies. But Emerson couldn't hear the not-much-of-a-girl he'd left back in the woods by herself.

Help arrived in a pack led by, of all people, Bobby Welpler, followed by Emerson, his Big Dog, and his light. Em stabbed the beam in my face.

I defended my eyes. "The *ground,* idiot."

The beam dropped to the ground.

The gas can at my feet was rusted dark, but its smell on the leaves was new and strong as could be. And the smell of gas trailed on ahead through the woods toward the house. I bent over and took a deep breath — to be sure what it was, maybe — and for a minute, the vapors unrooted the trees and rocked the ground under my feet.

We stood there. Just staring. And sniffing. And trying not to. And staring. Not at each other.

I'd found the can and figured I ought to speak first, the voice of reason and calm: "Now, it doesn't mean anything. Necessarily."

Jimbo grunted. "Right. This plus the other events of the evening puts us at *nothing*."

"I meant . . . look," I started again, stumbling, my thoughts slow and crippled a little by the edge to Bo's voice. "Look, it could've been here a long time. Long before the Moulavis moved here. It might have nothing to do with . . . anything."

Em lit into me: "Turtle, how many times you gonna make a flashing-light danger sign into a big Welcome Friends plaque?"

I crossed my arms and tucked my head lower into my shoulders. "It's just that some random can by itself doesn't mean necessarily that anybody's setting a fire. Not yet, anyhow."

"Not yet!" It was the first time I'd ever heard Jimbo snap at anyone, least of all me.

"*Not yet* and mowed grass don't last a good week."

I squared up my shoulders, but my words came out wobbly, petulant even. "You guys got better ideas what to do, then you let me know. Y'all just wanna all be the big knights that come riding to save —"

"*You,*" Em came back at me, "just can't admit when —"

Bo lay a hand on Em's shoulder and mine. "Hold on, now. You and me both gotta let her alone. No point in piling on Turtlest Girl just 'cause we got the puke scared out —"

Em shook off Bo's hand. "*You're* one to —"

L. J. reached for the gas can. "That will suffice, gentlemen. *Come on.*"

We fell in behind Emerson's light, all of us prickly and stiff, and L. J. with the gas can and Big Dog, who whined.

Stepping softly through the crunch of old leaves and crushed gravel, we followed the reek of gas through the woods and up to the drive, where it stopped. L. J. set the gas can in the truck bed, and we cleared the tailgate one by one without the usual thunder.

Jimbo paused just before launching himself up and over the side. "Ain't no point in any one of us left hauling the blame all alone. Turtle here's done good to keep calm and not jump to conclusions." My brother opened his mouth to protest, but Bo held up his hand and went on. "Up till *today,* when it'd be time to start jumping away. I reckon it's time now we all posse up on what's going on here. And how we best head trouble off at the pass." One by one, we lifted our heads, met his eyes, then each other's. Even Welp looked me almost full in the face.

I let out the breath I didn't know I'd held.

Bobby Welpler sat next to me and under what little light a splinter of moon and the truck lights gave out, I could see slits, un-frayed, in the knees of his jeans. "You just cut those with your knife?" I asked — for no reason at all, except maybe to talk out the gas fumes and the picture of the pup strung up by his neck, to clear all that out of my head. And maybe so I wouldn't cry in front of the boys.

I maybe didn't intend to be mean, or even to say much at all — just to talk so I couldn't hear myself think. Everyone knew Welp had never slid into a base in his life, that the holes in his jeans couldn't have been there for real, worn through by living like everyone else's. His mom never having much money on hand, he wore his jeans till they got to be flood pants at the ankles, but they never ripped good through the knees. He must have knifed out slits in the knees to look a rugged-guy tough that he'd never been.

He ignored me.

"Won't your momma be mad?" I asked him, then almost wished I hadn't — even if it was only Welp. So I took one step toward what was supposed to be helpful: "Look, hey: It's all right, though — *your* mom won't even notice." Which also was not how I meant it to come out.

His hands dropping over the knee slits, Welp studied the slash pine blurring past in a broad band of black that I knew to be green if it hadn't been night.

L. J. and Jimbo looked at me, and then at Welp, and then back at me. Bo handed me what was left of his Coke, which was his way of passing me courage and letting me know it was my turn to speak.

I took a deep swig of the Coke. "Hey, Bobby, what I said. That was . . . just plain mean. I'm a mean-spirited poop some days. And some nights. And also, Bobby, what I said . . . it wasn't true."

Welp turned from staring into the woods. "Yeah," he said. "It *is* true."

We watched loblollies whip by. I offered the Coke to Welp, and meeting my eye for the first time, he took it, tipped it up straight, and finished it, rivulets running down each side of his chin.

Waymon's Feed and Seed, known in three counties, was on our way home. There the new spotlight that had been installed out front, adjusted full beam on L. J.'s daddy's new sign.

I read it out loud, for something to say: "Fresh Bait, Cold Beer . . ." I waited for Jimbo to deliver the punch line. For someone to say something.

But Bo's head was down in his hands and his mouth making words I couldn't hear.

Not but a quarter mile down, L. J.'s house came first, a green slab ranch skirted by what in springtime was the pink and white chiffon of his mother's prize-winning azaleas. In the garden's raised center, a black garden statue grinned, grasping a lantern. Bounding from the flatbed, L. J. tossed his wet, charred towel across the groom's head, so that only one chipped black hand and the lantern were showing.

Welp stood up in the back of the pickup. "How 'bout if I spend the night?"

L. J. shrugged in agreement, without turning. Welp hopped to the ground, though he snagged one sneaker on the tailgate and had to scurry, half-shod, to catch up.

"Tomorrow?" Emerson called from the cab.

L. J. had the screen door open. "After work. Same time."

"Tomorrow's Sunday, Saint Laban," Jimbo called back.

L. J. winced. "After church, then."

Em poked his head from the truck cab. "We pagans'll wait on you. Same Sunday time then."

I gave a halfhearted salute. "Same place," I said.

"Same whole exact Blue Holing crowd," Jimbo added.

And we all understood what he meant. That no one would be left behind, especially tomorrow.

L. J. lifted his hand, not in a wave, but as a flag to show he'd heard. Bobby Welpler hurled out a, "I'm still sayin' we shouldn't oughta include . . . ?" but L. J. shut the door behind them.

Emerson drove home through a summer darkness that blew thick against my face and stuck in my throat there in the back of the truck. With one hand I clutched the gas can, while the other reached through the cab window to pet the Big Dog, who licked my wrist and whined.

Jimbo scooted in closer to me, or maybe it was me scooted closer to him, but neither one of us talked.

I don't recall thinking that I was about to cry, but then there were tears on my face and Jimbo brushing them away. I'd like to have said they were every one of them altruistic, those tears, born of compassion for the four-legged victim and for Farsanna. Truth was, though, the tears were for me as much as anything, my mourning the group we'd been, the peace we'd rested safe in, the belonging that nobody questioned.

The whole way to his house, or even as he squeezed my hand and climbed out of the truck, Jimbo never asked why I was crying, which was good: I'd never *not* told Jimbo anything, or Emerson either, whenever they asked. But I'd have been ashamed to hear myself say it out loud.

27. Ain't Nobody Gonna Turn Me 'Round

The next morning, Jimbo's voice rattled us out of a shallow sleep, me still fully clothed but curled in a ball on my bed, and Em stretched full length on the floor, his guitar cuddled on one side, Big Dog on the other. I'd have died before I'd have asked my brother to sleep on the floor of my room because I was scared, but the truth was, I'd never have slept that night without Big Dog and Em there with me.

Jimbo turned up the volume on his own song:

Ain't nobody gonna turn me 'round
Turn me 'round,

"Oh, help." I covered my head with a pillow.

Emerson staggered up from the floor. My eyes still crusted closed, I had to paw my way out of bed. Em cranked open my second-story window, just as Jimbo took his song up an octave.

By the time I reached the window, Jimbo had upended himself into a handstand on our lawn, the half Windsor knot of his necktie dangling in his face, and he was handstepping to the rhythm of his song:

Turn me 'round —

Emerson was leaning so far out my window I thought he would tumble into the magnolia for sure. "Bo, give a guy a break up here!"

Bo remained on his hands — or one hand, at least; the other was over his heart as he switched songs, his voice dipping down deep and soulful.

People get ready —
For the train's a-coming —

My brother wasn't impressed. "C'mon, man. It's the weekend. You wanna wake the whole street?"

Still upside down, Jimbo cocked his head. "You people got ready?"

"Ready to come down and beat the tar outta you, yeah."

Jimbo righted himself and ran a hand

345

down both dress shirt sleeves, as if to smooth their wrinkles. Ever since I could remember, he'd crumpled — he said *stored* — his Sunday dress shirts in the same drawer, never closed, that held his favorite T-shirts. Jimbo tugged on his half Windsor, raising it all the way up to the second button, as high as it had ever gone. "Hey, we got to *git* in a bigheaded hat of a hurry so's they don't frisk us for the offering. We're —"

"What?"

"Wanna come?"

"Come exactly *where* with you?"

"It's Sunday morning, Altar Boy. And we're greeting the town head-on. Where the rubber meets the road. Where the pulpit meets the pepper sauce. The whole Pack of us."

Em jerked back so hard he hit his head on the window sash. "Man, are you *nuts?* After what happened last night? You'd show up with us — with *her* — *THERE?*"

Jimbo was buttoning his sleeves at the wrists — something I'd never seen him do, not even in winter. And here it was, the hottest of summers.

Emerson was nearly falling out my window, just like he fell — or leapt — out of the pear tree. "What are you gonna do, march us all down front and sit on the first pew so the whole town can get a good look?"

"Good idea. We gonna let 'em think they got us lily-licked? Gonna let them think they run this whole town? Well, here's one place they don't, and we're one pack they can't mangy up more."

"*Look,* Bo —"

"By the way, if we're late, we'll sure enough have to sit on the first row. You and Turtle better hop-to and get your goose gussied."

It occurred to me then that Emerson and I had never told Jimbo about our seeing his daddy skulking around the Moulavis' house, and the way we'd heard the voices bullying him, and the way he had let them. We'd meant to tell Jimbo. Not just me this time hiding my head, but Em and me both, the two of us putting it off, looking for a moment alone, a moment of quiet, a moment when what we had to say wouldn't have wounded our Jimbo; that moment hadn't yet come. Maybe because talking about it might have made it more real, made it mean something I didn't want it to mean. And here we were marching into the Reverend's own territory with him on the enemy side and Bo not even being prepared.

From the driver's seat of the pickup, Emerson hissed across me, in the middle. I began tying the straps of the sundress I'd thrown over my shorts during the three minutes I had to get ready.

Jimbo smiled out the window.

Emerson pounded the steering wheel in time with his points. "Look, Bo, you know my old man walked with King. It's not like I'm —"

"Since when do you hitch on your old man's train?" Jimbo wanted to know.

"Fine. You know *me*. You know Turtle. You know we're not like . . . some people are. I'm just warning you, for your own good, and for Sanna's. . . ." Em stopped at the name, and all of us stared at the road. "Look, you stopped to think here about all the warnings we've had? The gas can and the pup. Not to mention the men in white sheets acting like ghosts running a roadblock."

"And," Jimbo offered, "the cross that burned Big Dog's place in the passenger seat."

"Yeah, and the . . . How'd you know about that?"

"My momma birthed me with eyes."

"Fine. I just don't think it can be any

clearer, Bo, that these boys've been trying to send us a message."

"Well, yeah. Message received. And back at 'em."

"If you pull this stunt this morning —"

"If we do."

"If *we* pull this stunt. Look, Bo, don't be a fool! Gonna look like you're throwing it in their faces, us showing up there with her . . . Are you *listening* to me?"

Jimbo turned his head towards me and bared his teeth. "Hey, Turtle, do I got jelly toast in my teeth?"

Emerson pounded his head on his window and groaned.

Me, I shook my head no and smiled faintly.

"So," Em asked, his voice without its elastic, "does your daddy know about this? That we're coming? That *she's* coming with us?"

Bo shook his head. "But shoot, the good Reverend Riggs never yet left anybody out in the hot."

I could feel Emerson's eyes real intent on the road, on not looking at me, just like I was making a point of not looking at him.

It was my turn to ask: "So does *her* dad know where you're — where *we're* — taking her? You know that night I spent at her house: I'm telling you, he prays like a man nobody told he wasn't devout."

"Called her this morning. Made sure she talked to her dad, told him right precisely where we was headed."

"And he's letting us take her? I'd have thought —"

"Maybe he just trusts the looks of us. Turtle, you got no faith."

"More like maybe he figures this is an *American* thing, going to church."

"Could likely be. But there he'd be wrong. Why, look at you two specimens: as rank a couple of heathens as ever got hatched."

When we picked up Farsanna, she appeared at her door wearing an outfit I'd not seen before — and I wondered where it'd come from. It wasn't in style; the colors didn't match; the skirt was too long and too full — even I could see that, and I've never been one for fashion.

And *still* the new girl looked good. Beautiful, even.

We all four rode in the cab, the back all full as always of mulch and manure, and now of a shovel with blood on it still. Sanna rode in the middle, her and Em and Jimbo, all three trying not to brush up against each other and all of us crammed in together, so as not to get our Sunday best dirty.

We rode the few miles to the church without speaking. Em and I stared out opposite windows.

As the four of us piled out from the truck in the church lot, Jimbo tilted his head towards my brother. "Man, take it easy. We ain't nothing but four poor ol' sinners paying a front porch visit to our Maker." Jimbo crinkled his eyes at me.

Emerson rubbed a knuckle into each temple. "*Meeting* our Maker's more like it."

I was holding my stomach — like it might calm the churning. I muttered to Em, "You ever have that little heart-to-heart with your best friend, Big Brother?"

"We should've told Bo about seeing his daddy."

"We should've done a lot of things before now," I agreed.

Jimbo Riggs' daddy's church was Baptist, and the largest in town of any breed. And the ugliest, Baptists not having much of an eye for beauty in buildings — I reckoned it was part of their creed. The organ inside was wheezing out the most hideous chords. Even the stained glass inside was no help — chunky pinks and putrid greens that jigsawed a fish.

I plopped myself down on the brick wall just outside the foyer. "I can't do it," I whispered to Em. "Not even for Jimbo. I can't."

"Too late now. I'm not taking you home."

"I can't."

"You pansy," my brother encouraged me.

"Take that back!"

"Pansy."

"I'm not scared. It's the organ. I can't take it."

"Tough." Em jerked me up by the elbow. "You don't have to listen."

I shook free of his grip, but walked by his side toward the door.

Sanna and Jimbo stood just outside the sanctuary doors, which were still propped open. The August sun was stabbing down through the maples that surrounded the church, and the concrete walks already putting out heat. But through the mouth of the church, I could see that its belly was dark, if not cool.

The four of us squared off there at the mouth and stood for a minute — just stood.

"L. J. might already be on inside," Bo said lightly, "waitin' on Jesus to come back and for us to come in."

Farsanna glanced sideways at me. Fingers twisting each other, her hands gripped each

352

other in front of her waist. "Shelby, I thought that you and your brother with churches did not —"

"We don't," I said. "We aren't." She'd called me Shelby again. Not Turtle. With no contractions.

She cocked her head. Then looked from me to Em to Jimbo.

Jimbo flashed his dimples. "They're willing to come only on *special* occasions."

The *special* was what made me stumble on the threshold, like in that one word Jimbo had nudged me — and his best friend — ever so gently to the side.

From the dark mouth of the church, a hand reached to catch me from falling, an usher who propped me back on the stilt-heeled sandals I never wore well. And he offered me a folded paper, the church's picture on front. "You all right, little lady?" he asked.

I nearly told him the truth, that I'd have been a heap better if it weren't for the organ, coughing and gasping and wailing like an old man with TB. But it sounded out in my head like something L. J. would say, so I didn't.

And the usher wasn't looking at me anyway, wasn't waiting to hear what I said. His eyes were on Jimbo, and who Jimbo was standing beside.

The people inside the big belly were already on their feet singing, the organ wrestling the voices for a stranglehold. Couldn't say I remember the hymn, except it talked about suffering and shame. *Suffering and shame* swelled up from a sea of bright, puffed-sleeve florals and avocado green sport coats and too-coiffed, too-happy hair — big hair on the men and the women. *Suffering and shame,* I remember they sang, *Suffering and shame.*

I looked around me for signs of either, or both. But a hot, sticky breeze blew from the open doors at the back of the sanctuary, and signs of sweat were all I could find, on myself or anyone else. I felt hollow inside just like this cavernous room — hollow and hot and likely to be sick any moment.

In Southern gentleman style, Jimbo had taken Farsanna's elbow to guide her to a pew. The back of the belly was all clogged with bodies, the only loose spaces far up to the front.

Jimbo was nodding and grinning to the faces who turned — one by one they all did — heads whipping around like a giant fan had been flipped on from the front.

Regina Lee Riggs was there, on the third row, her headband matching her dress and her purse and her shoes. She had on the same face she'd worn on my mother's front porch with the Garden Club ladies — except those caged-animal eyes of hers looked like something had got loose. They never left Jimbo, her eyes, and I wondered how he could still stand up straight, her skewering him like that.

The people in the pews reached another verse of the hymn, but as voice by voice faltered and fell, the organ marched on triumphant, alone.

An usher approached the front and bent to speak in the ear of the man up on the platform. Reverend Riggs sat on a stage in a chair that looked to me like a throne. His round jaw was moving in time with the organ, but his lips weren't forming words. His eyebrows, bushy like Jimbo's, had crawled high on his face. But whatever the usher whispered to him, Reverend Riggs made no sign of hearing. He was looking at Jimbo, and the girl who stood beside him.

The organ heaved into a victory lap.

The usher returned to the back of the belly — where we still stood. I took hold of Emerson's shirt at the waist.

The usher who'd approached the throne at the front put his head next to the usher who'd kept me from falling. The two of them bookended Jimbo and smiled. One laid a hand on his shoulder and patted it once. One put his mouth to Bo's ear.

Here's what I saw on the faces that watched — they all did, of course. Like snowflakes, there were no two expressions alike. There were some hard looks, I reckon, but also the soft eyes on women who were already seeing the casserole they'd like to serve us for lunch. Mostly there were everywhere the expressions like children lost at the fair and panicked, searching for someone to show them the way home.

The good Reverend Riggs sat on his throne without moving, except for his jaw up and down like a hooked bass hauled into the air.

It was *that* face, his daddy's, that Jimbo was watching.

28. THIRTY PIECES OF LEAD

A belly vomits what it can't digest, and so we got spewed out the mouth into a searing sun.

Jimbo made eye contact only once with the ushers who escorted us out, and that happened only at the threshold of the back door. I couldn't see Jimbo's expression, his back to me, but I could tell by the way the ushers seemed to shrivel right there in their shoes what his face must have told them. Bo never gave them a word. And he never let go of the elbow he held.

We walked four in a line to the truck without speaking. And then stood there, leaning against the truck, taking it in.

There was no breeze, the heat already so fierce it about knocked you down, and I wondered if this hadn't been Dante's seventh circle of hell all along, and we'd just thought it was our mountain home.

We might've stood there for days, might

never have moved, but an old Chevy Impala screeched into the lot with a blat of the horn.

I jumped.

Hands flapped at us from out the car windows.

"So we're not the only ones who're late," Matthew called, with Mark and Luke and L. J. emerging one by one behind him. *The Waymon* of Waymon's Feed and Seed plunged out of the driver's seat, then dove back in and resurfaced with a Bible in hand.

L. J.'s mother blew a kiss in our direction and called over her shoulder, her heels already tapping at the asphalt, "Good morning, dears. See you inside." Maybe inside, at the end of her spindled sprint, maybe then it occurred to her she'd never before seen her nephew or niece at her church.

Maybe it hit her once she'd got inside the belly and felt it still heaving.

But five of the six of my mother's kin were dashing headlong for the door and waving above their heads while they ran.

Only L. J. stood still.

"Well, well," he said. "Well, well, well."

We — most of us — looked at him.

"So," it wasn't his usual sneer — just a question, "what exactly transpired here? I'm conjecturing you've already been in?"

Jimbo was looking at no one, his eyes fixed on the ground. I wanted to touch his shoulder. But didn't.

Sanna's eyes had become again like I'd first seen them, that day by the school water fountain: deep and black, too dark to tell much about — but possibly dangerous. Like a pit that might be storing explosives.

Emerson looked to Jimbo for an answer, got none, so he took up the task: "What do *you* think happened here?"

L. J. sucked a deep breath and pushed at the bridge of his glasses that for once hadn't budged out of place. "I take it they were not enamored of our new, improved mangy pack?" He nodded at Farsanna. "Or simply not too fond of the color black?"

Jimbo cursed and spit on the ground.

We never discussed where we were going when we hauled ourselves into the truck — no need to.

Farsanna sat, her spine flagpole stiff, her eyes straight ahead.

We swung by only Em's and my house for Big Dog and swimsuits — I snatched up two, one for Sanna and me, and Emerson grabbed a stack of shorts for the guys. Bo appeared in Em's room long enough to snag his shoebox-sized eight-track tape player, the one we'd found banged up and cheap at a garage sale last spring. Music at the Blue Hole generally wasn't the norm, partly because you couldn't hold anything in your arms as you slid down or climbed back up out of the Hole, and less so because we valued the quiet. Today, though, we knew we didn't want to hear ourselves think.

All of us back in the truck, Em swung by the Pump and Run for sandwiches.

"Who'll have pimento cheese and petroleum oil?" Jimbo asked grimly, as he tossed us triangles of white bread with little strips of orange between them, suffocated in cellophane wrap. We passed round the Cokes he'd just bought, and the peanuts, but saved the white triangles for the Hole.

L. J. thumped on Emerson's back window. "You going for Welp? I dropped him off at his momma's place early this morning."

Em eased up on the gas and waited for the decision.

L. J. raised one eyebrow at Jimbo.

"No Welp today," I pleaded — directing this, of course, to Jimbo.

Jimbo pressed his big feet against the bed's side like he might push it down. His voice came out only half alive: "Reckon we all of us might ought to get one more chance'n we deserve."

We backtracked for Bobby.

Emerson yanked the truck off the paved road onto a dirt swath that trespassed into the field where Welp's mother rented her trailer. Out behind it, Welp was changing the oil in her car. His face streaked in grease, he rocked to his feet, planted his fists on his hips and his feet in the dust.

Jimbo lay a hand on my shoulder. "Turtle, you go talk to the man."

"And say what?"

"Reckon you'll know when you get there."

"But it's been a long day," I hedged, "and it's not even noon."

Jimbo nodded, his hand still on my shoulder. "You can do it, Turtle." He leaned into my face. It was the first time he'd met anyone's eye since the church. "Don't reckon I much feel like talking." His chin gone to stubble — he'd forgotten to shave, or maybe it still hurt the swelling too much — and his bushy eyebrows scrunched up in a question together that made his green eyes stand out from the bruised, broken lines of his face.

Seeing where we'd just been, I wasn't much inclined to make peace with the world, and Welp was just standing there watching — just being Welp. But Jimbo was giving the orders that day, and I was — we all were — inclined to let him.

I slid out and down slowly, and barefooted my way through ragged grass and flowering weeds to the car. "Wanna come to the Hole, Bobby?"

Welp eyed me, first up and then down. "What's with the dress?"

I saw our mistake. Too late. "Just church."

"Who all here went to *church?*" he demanded.

I shrugged. "It was only church. And we didn't stay."

Welp dropped the oil pan. "Race you!" he called, already sprinting toward the truck. He was like that, a four-year-old boy all over again, his only chance at winning being to pick on Emerson's kid sister.

Without shoes I wasn't too fast, but I gained enough on Welp to lunge for his back and brought him down just even with the truck.

Welp shook me off.

I gave him a shove that was meant to be playful. "Beat by a girl," I taunted.

He shoved back, hard. More like a punch. I hit the ground.

A whetted edge to his voice, Jimbo tore into Welp: "Listen, Welpster. You've had a tough crack at life, I'll give you that. But you don't got to let the bad thrown at you become the ugly you think you got to be."

Bo held out a hand to me and I took it, just enough to get me to my feet, and saw Welp sulking.

He'd hauled himself up one side of the truck, and then froze.

His stare was on Sanna, his melon-seed eyes widened to what almost was normal. "*You* went?" He whirled on Jimbo. "*She* went with you, and you didn't call me?"

"Take it easy there, Welpster. It was planned real last minute. And you never —"

Welp's round face had gone red under the acne. "Y'all *all* went, all of you, even *her,* and you didn't call me?"

I shrugged. "It was nothing but church. And we didn't stay."

He looked straight at me. "Hey, Turtle, how come you don't got any friends of your own, huh? Nothing but *nigger* yonder. How come is that?" Welp nodded toward Sanna. "Reckon she thinks she's coming to the Hole again too?"

I sat there, and, afraid to meet anyone's eye, I looked at the weeds. But I slid a hand to Sanna's back, which had gone straight and iron-stiff.

"Welp," Jimbo's shoulders were rising up towards his ears, like a tiger before it attacks, "I reckon I'll give you one chance to tell me I heard wrong just now. There's a chance I didn't rightly hear right."

Bobbly Welpler stretched to his full five foot six. "I reckon I can call a spade when I see one." His hands went back to his hips. "Or a nigger-lover, too."

Emerson had shot out of the cab by then and even L. J. had climbed up to his feet, one finger pushing up at the bridge of his horn-rims, again and again and again.

Jimbo's hands went deep in his pockets, and then deeper, like he'd better keep them from swinging. His voice took on a rumble, a whole lot like thunder. "Welp, I tell you what, boy: If it weren't for your momma right now, I'd lay you out flatter'n grass, and more green."

But Em didn't have his hands in his pockets, and maybe didn't have Bobby's momma in mind. He had Welp by the throat and then on the ground, rolling. Em landed on top, hollering whole lines of things I couldn't make out, and probably couldn't repeat if I did, followed by, "You got that? *You got that?*"

Maybe because my brother was big, and little Bobby Welpler was not, or maybe because we all had some sort of dad, and Welp did not, or maybe because Welp's face contorted with fear like he was gazing down the gullet of hell, Jimbo and L. J. hauled Emerson off.

Jimbo bent over him. "Welp, I got to tell you: You got some real noble rightness inside you — but I'll be hanged if I know where sometimes."

From the weeds, Welp looked from one to the other of us, and ended on L. J. "You too?"

L. J. looked back. "I share the sentiment."

"That how it is? One of *her* sort got the whole pack of y'all turnin' on your own kind?"

None of us moved. Except Bobby, who fell one step back.

"Yeah? Well, *fine! Fine!* The whole pack of y'all mix it on up! Go ahead! Just go ahead!" He followed this with a string of words, rabid and run together into a froth. Then he swung himself up to the crippled stoop of the trailer, yanked on the aluminum door, and slammed it — a pitiful *tap.*

Em leaned against the truck bed near Sanna. In silence, we all watched her face.

Her arms crossed over her chest just as they'd been that very first day she'd ridden with us, Sanna made sure she looked each one of us in the eye. "Perhaps," she began, her voice low and bitter, "this means for me . . . it is time to go."

I kept my hand on her back, and the three boys huddled in closer. I took a deep breath. "If you're meaning *us*," I began softly, "time for *us* to go, then we're with you."

Jimbo, Em, and L. J. nodded together. Then L. J., of all people, spoke up, his voice gone unfamiliarly soft: "Sanna, I wish we could explicate for you how a town full of charming people could also house —"

"*Idiots*," Em said, rubbing his upper arm where Welp had slugged him.

"*Cowards*," Jimbo put in, his gaze shifting back up the road in the direction of his daddy's church.

L. J. nodded, "Those who are less than charming."

Jimbo's hand brushed Sanna's arm. "You're still coming to swim, aren't you? We can't Blue Hole without you."

She looked straight ahead, her words clipped down almost to nothing. "I would like to go home."

For the flicker of a moment, I thought she meant Sri Lanka, the Pearl of the Indian Ocean. And almost like she'd read my mind she looked at me and tacked on, "To my house."

I tried to look back at her steady, and tried

366

to benchpress my voice into something like reassuring when I said, "Your *home*."

Jimbo shifted forward, right into her face, and whispered, "Come back to the Blue Hole, just this one last time."

We heard the *one last time,* our heads snapping up in surprise. But not one of us gainsayed him that day. Maybe because it was Jimbo speaking. Or maybe because it seemed to us all at that moment that it might turn out to be true.

Sanna nodded finally — and even then not much of a nod. Em nodded back and climbed into the truck cab. In the rearview mirror, I could see his mouth had gone taut.

29. Stand by Me

For once we had the Hole to ourselves, the other regulars being still at church, and then strapped into long Sunday dinners with pot roast and au gratin potatoes and green bean casserole with fried onion topping. In my family we didn't do church — except for Momma who most weeks snuck out for early service at the Methodist church, and most weeks covertly invited Emerson and me, though we always said no — *No thank you, ma'am* — but my father always pretended she just slept late on Sundays, always covered for her like some families hide their alcoholic Uncle Billy. The result was that we were generally free not only of sermons and asthmatic pipe organs, but also of Sunday pot roast and adult conversation never worth keeping your shoes on for. So on this Sunday morning, the Hole was ours.

The chill of the water must've done us some good that day. We splashed a little and floated. Having held eight-track tapes in our teeth as we'd slid down to the Hole, and having strapped the player on Em's back with a towel, we let Ray Charles and Diana Ross ease our pain just a little.

Jimbo, who had come out of the water and was resting on our rock, grabbed up a bottle of the sunblock his momma always sent with him and, standing up, held it to his mouth as a mike: *Ain't no mountain high enough, Ain't no valley low enough,* he crooned along with Diana.

And we sang back to him: *Nothin' can keep me from you . . .*

We ate pimento cheese on white bread warmed in the sun. It did taste a smidgen of gas — and we didn't care.

"I reckon," Jimbo said, his mouth full of bread, "we'll remember this day. Reckon you can say that much for it."

"Anybody miss Welp?" L. J. asked.

Emerson reached for a third Coke. "Couldn't say I miss him. Just seems kind of strange, his not being here."

Jimbo flopped back on his elbows. "What if any of the rest of us was gone? What'd we remember about 'em?"

"About you," I suggested, "your sweet nature." And then, before I could stop myself: "And your pretty green eyes."

He dimpled up in my general direction, but weakly.

"But for certain," I finished, "your platypus feet."

He tossed peanuts at me with his toes.

Later, others trickled into the Hole — it felt like an invasion that day. But the rope took up its ticktocking as usual, and the chicken fights broke out on the north bank. After she'd watched for a while, Farsanna stepped away from our group and waded back into the water. Jimbo hesitated a moment, then followed. They stood with the water up to their knees.

I might have hated her then — no, I *know* that I did — her standing by Jimbo like he was hers. His way of looking at her that closed some kind of door to the outside where we'd all, even Emerson and me, wound up finding ourselves peeking in. And my hating her had nothing to do with my liking her too, at least a clean shot better than any other fifteen-year-old girl I'd ever known. I hated myself, and also was thankful, for asking my brother to U-turn his truck on a day when I was too hot to think straight — we all were. And here's where we'd come: the calm and the steady and the *us* of our world all spinning apart. And somehow also pulled in closer together.

As the Hole gradually filled with swimmers, Sanna and I joined each other on the rock, drying off. We'd sat for a while and then this: "Turtle, I . . ." She seemed stuck on that word, and on the anger I could see in her eyes.

With a sliver of sandstone I drew on the granite beside me. Then I wrote one single word. "Sanna? See this."

She looked at the word I'd sandstoned. "We," she read.

"*We've* got to do something about Mort. About . . . everything that's been going on. *We.*"

She reached for my sliver of sandstone and circled the word. Her arms went briefly around me and she gave me a smile that wasn't one really, but more like a way to say thanks. Then she dropped the towel she'd kept cocooned around herself for some time, and she waded into the water.

I dove from the rock then, despite the water's not being deep enough there. I needed the blast of cold. When I surfaced, Sanna had waded in to a few feet from me.

"Turtle," she asked, not looking at me, "what will happen to . . ." she turnd toward me then. "To us? I'm tired of being . . . afraid."

I couldn't remember her admitting fear until then, even when the rest of us had been clearly terrified, or even last night when she'd been heartbroken by what we'd found at the end of the rope. Maybe she'd been scared all along and too brave to show it.

"I don't know." It was all I could think of just then, even with my looking for the warm, easy words that couldn't be true anymore but wouldn't've been nicer to hear myself say.

But if Sanna heard me just then, she never answered.

Her eyes redirected to the base of the sweetgum tree. I felt more than heard the tremor that went through the Blue Hole just then. I lifted my head to see what Sanna's eyes had locked on.

A group of boys no one knew had gathered at the base of the tree, their collective dark skin emerging from the shadows like a scene from a fantasy film: the inanimate landscape that comes strangely to life. The trees themselves may as well have grown feet onto their roots and begun moving about.

How these boys had found this place I never knew. What possessed them to come up from the Valley, I never heard. But here they were, a whole group of them, maybe as many as five, waiting in line at the tree just like they'd been invited. They pulled themselves up to full height and stuck their chests out and planted their feet.

Mort, who'd retired himself from the rope swing to sprawl on a towel beside Neesa, rose now. He squinted, rubbed his eyes even, and then his forehead, like sunstroke might be at fault for what he was seeing.

Someone punched off Em's tape player, and the Hole sat watching in silence and Mort began lumbering to the sweetgum.

One of the boys from the Valley had already made his way to the jumping-off limb of the tree. It was when he first put a dark hand on the rope swing that Mort charged.

30. REGRET

Buddy Buncombe had been waiting in line at the base of the tree and had backed off in blank confusion when the new boys arrived. But he stepped forward now, catching Mort by his shoulders.

At the opposite side of the Hole, I couldn't hear what those two said. But they both talked at once, heatedly, both pointed toward the sweetgum, both pacing on the red clay bank like two bulls eyeing each other and a red flag. Twice, Mort shook off Buddy's hands as he began charging again toward the tree, and twice Buddy grabbed him again, their voices rising.

Buddy's face was in Mort's. "Not here is what I'm saying!" was the first thing loud enough that I could hear on my side of the Hole.

Everyone stared at the two of them, like the outcome would instruct the rest of us what to do.

The boys from the Valley lined up along the bank of the Hole, their arms crossed over bare chests, their feet well apart, their expressions defiant. Their eyes darted up to the one of their number who stood on the limb and clung to the rope. They knew just what they'd done by coming. They'd never expected to be warmly welcomed.

All eyes stayed on Mort. He shook off Buddy's hands once more in disgust, but this time made his way back to the towel beside Neesa and dropped himself to the ground, where he propped on his side, his skin visibly twitching, to watch. Buddy followed. For several long moments, nobody moved.

Then slowly, Bo crouched down to punch back on Em's tape player. And the music called out for the rope swing to keep time.

Jimbo and Em and L. J. all found their way to the tree, Jimbo and Em lip-synching the words as they waited in line and as they climbed.

The next hour became a blur of black and white bodies hurling themselves from the rope. Higher and higher the rope's end pitched, deeper and deeper the depth of the dives, twists and flips and plunges, each one a dare and a taunt to the next boy in line. Someone spun up the volume on Em's tape player, and the Hole pulsed with the heavy downbeat of a bass and the swing of the pendulum rope. Perhaps there were shouts and catcalls from the shore, but the blast of the music must've covered it all. Black and white bodies, long and lean, danced on the branch of the sweetgum where they waited their turn, and fell laughing, twisting, shouting from the arc of the rope swing.

By the time dusk was finding its way to the rim of the Hole, our fever had cooled, and we all began our departure.

Someone turned off the music. Somebody else yawned as they waded out of the water.

And then, the boys from off of our Ridge lifted themselves hand over hand up out of the Hole. And then they were gone.

On our way out of the Hole, I turned back for the T-shirt I'd left on the rock. Mort was there, his back to me, one hand hooked onto the tree, so that his biceps were hung like big hams for Neesa standing before him to see and admire — or he might have been hoping she'd bow down and worship. She did run a red fingernail over one bicep.

"Reckon you let one of them slip in and the whole herd wants feedin'," he said, his words coming slow, like he'd had to fetch each one from a little grazing herd of vocabulary.

She answered by shifting her hips.

"Don't nobody take a hint no more?" He snorted. "There's guys, you know, older'n me, they been through this back when, and they're — *we're* tired of messing around."

Seeing me, Neesa put a finger to Mort's lips in a hush. And she smiled right at me, like she dared me to tell.

I almost did, almost told what I'd heard.

Whatever else Mort had said, this couldn't be a good thing for any of us, not to mention Farsanna.

Farsanna.

Our peaceful, all-get-along world had little by little been crumbling to pieces, and what did she care? Her and her arrogant no-expression-at-all. She'd come and mangled our Pack, divided us all, nearly gotten us killed by the roadblock and by Emerson's escape from it, chewed up whole days of our time, our keeping eyes out, our cutting down poor little dog nooses, our detouring for her, our being thrown out on our tails from a church with a mute for a preacher. Our not being quite so sold on each other, or on our town maybe, as we'd been before she came. And now what did she care? She seemed happy right now just to have Jimbo's attention. His undivided attention. I decided there was no reason to tell what I'd heard.

Emerson dropped off Farsanna first. She nodded to each of us in the truck bed, and through the driver's-side window, "Thank you."

Em stuck his head out the window this time. "Hey. Farsanna."

She turned.

"You know what? You're an awful good sport. And I —"

She nodded, just slightly, and began walking away.

I lifted my hand and thought about calling out something, but it's likely she never saw me — and there was nothing from me to hear anyway.

Jimbo had launched his big feet over the tailgate and caught up with her before she reached her door. He touched her arm.

She drew back.

I couldn't hear what they said — and, sure, I tried to listen.

But she kept her gaze to herself, and whatever *please* he was plying her with, she seemed not to feel.

Her screen door creaked open, and Jimbo might've followed her in if her father hadn't suddenly filled the door frame. His hands were in his pockets, his face in hard creases.

Farsanna slipped past her father.

Jimbo smiled in that way of his that gave him the air of bowing, and he thrust out his hand. Mr. Moulavi stared at the hand, then stared, still unblinking, at Jimbo.

Jimbo withdrew his hand and found a use for it raking his hair.

He stumped back to the truck, and L. J. offered him a hand to haul himself in. "I perceive he doesn't fancy you," L. J. offered.

"Don't start," I said, and added, "Laban Jehu" by way of warning.

Emerson started his engine, but idled for a moment. "What if something happens?"

"Look," L. J. offered, "they've not enacted anything actually lethal since —" L. J. offered.

We all turned to him.

"Since, what, last night?" Em said. "That's supposed to be a good sign?"

I opened my mouth to agree with Emerson, but was distracted by the movement I saw on the far side of the Moulavis' house, just behind the scrub pine. Was someone watching us? Or watching the house?

"Hey . . . guys?" I piped up then, my eyes still focused on the woods behind the house. "Look, what if there's even more more ugly about Mort than we thought?"

The boys waited for me to go on. It occurred to me that maybe I should have mentioned what I had just heard Mort say. But what was one more threat and slur from a bully like Mort? It wasn't like this was really anything new, was it? I settled on something simple and vague: "Let's just say the guy's got to be stopped."

But L. J. persisted. "These types like Mort are basically cowards. I'd make a significant wager they're done with their pubescent pranks."

Jimbo eyed L. J. suspiciously. "I'll grant you one thing, L. J.," he said bitterly, "cowards is what we're dealing with here."

After we dropped L. J. off, Jimbo thumped on Emerson's back window. "You wanna swing by my place?"

This might have struck me as odd, given that he always was the next to take home and wouldn't have needed to ask Em to stop. But I'd known Jimbo forever, every bit as well as I knew my own brother. I'd known since that morning he wouldn't be spending the night at his house. Not after I'd watched him watching his daddy up in front of that church. Emerson would've known the same thing.

"Better stop here." Jimbo motioned to a driveway three doors down from the Baptist church parsonage. "Maybe swing around the block a couple of times while you wait."

Jimbo's bedroom, the former garage, sat against the kitchen and breakfast room. He'd left one window cracked open.

Emerson leaned out of the cab. "We'll give you five." And we drove away.

On our first circuit of the block, we saw Jimbo gripping the sash of the window, his legs in a deep plié and straining to rise, like an Olympic weightlifter. On our next circuit, Jimbo was still there. On our third circle, we stopped.

"Well, Turtle," Em said.

I sighed and made a face through the cab window at Big Dog, who licked my hand. My being skinny had always made me the logical choice when Frisbees or baseballs or kites needed to be retrieved from tight spaces. Emerson's golden could, on occasion, sniff her way to them, but then, wide as she was, only whine.

The crack in the window was tight, even for me. And I might have been stuck there, teetering on the fulcrum of the sill and unable to wriggle my hips all the way over, if Jimbo hadn't shoved on my feet.

"Ouch!"

"Sorry, Turtle. Had to be done."

"What am I in here to get, anyway?" I whispered.

"Forget my toothbrush — it's in the bathroom, too risky. I'll just use yours."

"No you won't. You want clothes?"

"Just stuff for work. Three days' worth maybe. And cash — it's on the dresser. Underwear's in the top drawer."

In his top drawer were a dress shirt, wadded but sparkling white, three ties, two T-shirts, and a host of athletic socks. "No underwear here," I whispered over my shoulder. "What am I looking for — trunks or briefs?"

"Now, Turtle, I'm hurt. You know the answer to that."

It was true. I did. Though I'd forgotten I did. Until very recently, Jimbo had changed clothes freely with his best friend's kid sister coming and going — though never, of course, with my mother at home. My mother believed in men, but in modesty, too.

My mother, were she in my shoes, wouldn't have known as I did to look for Bo's trunks.

"Try under the bed," Jimbo whispered.

"Wouldn't they be dirty?"

"Only a couple days' worth. Or so."

I turned to wrinkle my nose at him, then

thrust a hand under the bed. Then thought the better of it and lowered my head to the ground to see what I'd be touching.

Two baseballs lived there, and a bat, a pair of flannel pajamas he couldn't have worn, surely, for months — not in this heat — "Aha!" I snagged a pair.

I dropped them out the window to Jimbo.

I returned to his dresser, swept up the cash scattered there, and stuffed it deep in my pockets.

I was just turning to go when I noticed the crack in Jimbo's door — through it, dim yellow light from the breakfast room glowed. I could see only a shoe and a knee, both unmoving. The pants leg looked like the blue pinstripe of Reverend Riggs' only suit.

Softly, I stepped to the door and peered through.

Jimbo's daddy was sitting alone, a book with tiny type spread-eagled on the breakfast room table. Rocking forward and back, he held his head in his hands, just as I'd seen Jimbo do in the back of the truck. Only the Reverend bent over his book and rocked forward and back, forward and back, and he sobbed.

31. THE RED THAT DANCED ON THE LAWN

I slithered back through the window pretty smoothly until — once again — the sill hit my hips. Jimbo grabbed my wrists and hauled the upper half of me over his shoulder, the other half still stuck between sill and sash.

"Hey, how 'bout being careful!"

"Too hard?"

"I might wanna bear children one day. Jeez, you're killing me."

I got unstuck all at once, which sent Jimbo and me tumbling to the grass.

"Turtle, you still got everything attached to what oughta be?" He bent to help me up.

I dusted myself off, but didn't bother to check out the scrapes I could feel down my shins where they'd dragged against the sash. I began softly, "Bo, there's something you got to know." We dashed from shadow to shadow across the parsonage lawn to the neighboring yard where we huddled behind

384

an old oak. Emerson's truck hadn't returned yet.

"What? You don't like the way I keep house?"

"No, it's . . ." I'd intended maybe to say then that I thought Mort and the rest of the boys — the ones who were grown men — might be stirring up some kind of trouble, real trouble, during the night. That maybe the Moulavi family might ought to be warned.

But this is what I chose instead — and it needed to be said sometime too: "You oughta know your daddy was inside. And Bo, he was —"

Jimbo looked past the parsonage, into the trees. Then: "Turtle, I don't reckon there's nothing you can tell I wanna hear tonight about the good *gutless* Reverend Riggs."

"He looked awful upset." *Tortured* was the word I'd had in my mind when I'd seen him, but *upset* was the watered-down version I handed to Bo.

Jimbo wasn't much moved.

"Bo, maybe he's sorry."

"You *think?* For looking like a two-karat coward in front of God and everybody in town?"

"Maybe he was just . . . confused. I mean, he didn't exactly have warning to think over

385

what he'd do."

"Think *what* over? What's there to think over?" We were standing underneath the old post oak in the parsonage front yard. Jimbo's arms shot up over his head. "The man sits up there and says *nothing, NOTHING* — as good as broadcasting to this whole bloody town —"

I'd loathed Reverend Riggs, and not even seeing Jimbo so pained at the spinelessness of his daddy made me want to defend him — but now for Bo's sake, I offered: "Maybe he didn't know what to say — you know, what to do. Maybe he got all kinds of pressure."

"Yeah, well, he made that real abundantly clear, didn't he? That, and how he's got the backbone of Gumby. Wasn't that brother of yours supposed to be back by now?"

"Look." I pointed to the parsonage porch, its one light on. Jimbo's daddy had let the screen door whap behind him, and was pacing now across the front porch, pacing with his arms first behind him, then in front and above him. Back and forth and forth and back he strode, pivoting on the heel of a bare foot. He still wore the suit, but the unbuttoned shirt had come all untucked and the tie flapped loose, one end to his thigh.

I tapped Jimbo on the arm. "Don't you think maybe he might just want to know where you are?"

"You know what, Turtle? He can reckon it out." Jimbo turned away from the porch.

I motioned with my head toward approaching headlights. "Here comes Em now." I was just stepping from the post oak shadows into a white pool of streetlight when Jimbo snatched at my arm, tugged me back.

The lights were, I had to admit, closer together than they should've been, and too low to the ground. Then it swung into the parsonage drive.

A chill swept up my back and I shivered, there in the hottest of summers. "Bo, that car!"

He nodded, moving closer to me. "A Gremlin. An orange Gremlin. Like we needed more pleasant surprises today."

"The car from the Seventh Street shooting."

We watched three men unfold themselves from the car and regiment themselves in a line up to the parsonage porch.

Reverend Riggs continued to pace.

"C'mon, Turtle. There's our ticket out." Jimbo pointed far up the street to headlights. Emerson was standing on the hood of his truck, one hand on his hip, the other motioning to us.

I thought about Reverend Riggs' skulking behind the Moulavis' house. Which fit with these guys. But they were wagging fingers and fists in his face, seemed to be angry with him. "Bo, wait . . . You don't suppose your dad's in trouble with them?"

Jimbo was already walking away, his face and his back set against the parsonage steps. "Piddlin' little ol' pawns don't get in trouble with the chess king, Turtle — didn't you know? Not so long's they're scooting along all quiet and nice in their place. Turns out my daddy's a pawn, Turtle. And not making so much as a move to be anything else."

I lay awake that night for hours trying to make out what Emerson and Jimbo were saying just on the other side of the wall. Now and then, one voice or the other would swell above a whisper, then crash on the undertow of the other's response.

Maybe it was midnight or later when the phone rang. I wasn't asleep and could still hear the tide of the boys' talking in Emerson's room.

I could hear my father's foot-thuds falling in the dark, hear his whispered curses as he stubbed his toe on a door frame and fell into Big Dog. Then he was pounding on Emerson's door.

"Son, Jimbo: *Get up.*"

I heard Em open the door. "Yes, sir?"

"It's Mrs. Riggs on the phone."

"Sir?"

"Wanting to know if we've seen Jimbo. He never came home last night, they said, and they're worried sick."

Then Em must've opened the door still wider.

Or maybe Jimbo spoke up first. "Howdy, Mr. Maynard."

"On the phone?" Emerson asked — he sounded stupid even to me, and I was on the same side of the thing.

"Yes. The *phone.* The instrument we civilized people use to let others know where we are. What do you *mean* not letting the Riggses know where Jimbo was?"

"It was my fault, Mr. Maynard," Jimbo began. "I reckon I reckoned wrong. Figured they'd know where I was."

"Bo, you ought to know by now, you don't assume, you *confirm* these things."

"Yes, sir," the boys said together.

My father sledgehammered his words. "Let me suggest, Jimbo, that you march downstairs to the kitchen and dial that phone and explain yourself to your mother.

If I were she, I might not let you come home, but maybe she is kinder than I. Meanwhile, Mrs. Maynard and I are going back to sleep."

"Yes, sir. Goodnight," the boys muttered.

I waited until my father's door slammed before poking my head out of mine. The boys looked like they were expecting to see me.

But when the door to my parents' room flew open again, all three of us jumped. Momma was standing there in her robe.

"Sugar," she said, reaching to smooth my hair where it stuck out from my ponytail, "I'm real worried about you all."

The boys looked to me. "Worried, Momma?" I began. "Big Dog Landscaping's booming now. Right, Emerson? Jimbo?"

"Huh? Yeah," Bo said. "Uh-huh." Then, remembering Momma, he added, "Yes, ma'am."

Momma eyed him like a squash that might have gone bad. "Did all y'all have a nice day today?" she asked in the tone that said she meant far more than that.

"Today?" Emerson asked, his eyes on the green and gold shag. "What'd we do today, gang? Oh, that's right. Went swimming."

"The water wasn't so cold," I offered, "now that it's end of summer. And it's being so awful hot all these —"

"Mmm," Momma mused, pulling the ponytail holder from my head and letting the coarse sheaf drop on my shoulder. "Because when you left here this morning, your daddy and me still in our bed with the paper, you'll recall you said you all were headed to church."

We looked at each other with our eyebrows gathered, like we were straining to scrape up the distant past.

"I recall quite clearly," Momma continued, "because when you, Emerson, sugar, shouted upstairs you were headed out to the Baptist church with Jimbo, your father spilled his coffee all over the sheets. A wonder he didn't fall clear out of bed and scald himself senseless."

"She's right," I said to the boys. "Momma's right. We did swing by the church on the way." I turned back to my mother. "We were there only real briefly."

"Real short," Emerson jumped in.

But Momma was staring at Jimbo, who managed, "Yes'm. Not hardly time for Jesus to weep."

"I see. Well, then, you kids might not have been there for the disturbance. I did hear, though, that there was one."

"We weren't even there," I offered carefully, "long enough to sit. We did, though, Momma — did we tell you? — see Uncle Waymon and Aunt Jean-Anne and the boys in the parking lot. They sent their love. Aunt Jean-Anne had on that dress we saw in the window of Miller's . . ."

But for once Momma would not be swept into that current. "Shelby Lenoir," she said quietly.

"Yes, ma'am?"

"Emerson, Jimbo, there's no need to slip down those stairs just quite yet."

Our backs against the stairwell wall, we waited for her to fire.

"I just wanted to say," she took the time to look each of us in the eye, "you all have made the stranger in town feel welcome."

"Yes, ma'am," we said in unison, and waited for more. Of course there was more.

"And far be it from me, the one always having to beg and plead with my own family to go just that little old once a year to *my* church, far be it from me to complain that you all would *ask* to be in the house of the Lord."

We nodded together, and waited.

"My concern, though, is that you all might think you're pulling some kind of prank. I would surely hate to think of *my* children — and you know, Jimbo, I've always thought of you as my own — would use a whole church full of innocent people just to see what kind of a ruckus you could cause. I would surely hate to think that — like some people might."

"Oh no, ma'am, no, oh, ma'am, no," we said in a scattershot.

Momma held up her hand. "Now, I've said my piece. You boys go on down to talk with Regina Riggs, bless her poor worried heart. Shelby Lenoir, if you're going downstairs, you'd best change those raggedy shorts."

"But Momma, it's just the phone —"

She raised one perfectly plucked eyebrow at me.

"Yes, ma'am."

With clean shorts on, I followed the boys down the stairs to the phone.

Jimbo stared at the dial. "How the cow hock do I say I didn't call 'cause I didn't *want* to call?" He gingerly lifted the receiver and made a face at us. "Howdy there, Ma." We watched him as he paced back and forth across the kitchen floor in his bare feet and trunks, and scowling as he paced. He raked his hand through his hair, standing it on end. "Didn't reckon I had to explain," he said. "Reckon you all could figure on why, after what happened this morning." That was how he started, and from his tone, he wasn't headed down any friendlier road. I couldn't see an apology peeking out anywhere on his face. A hard-edged "No, ma'am" was as close as he came.

But then, just as he paced past the arch that led to our dining room clear through to the front of the house, he froze on one bare foot, the spiraled phone cord stretched almost to straight. The phone clattered out of Bo's hand, his eyes round and wide under those dark, bushy brows.

Emerson looked up from the bowl of ice cream he'd just scooped himself. "What's wrong?"

Em and I exchanged glances. Jimbo didn't move, not even to reach for the receiver, limp on the floor, Regina Lee Riggs' Virginian blue-blooded voice waltzing out into nowhere, unheeded.

We followed his stare — him already crossing himself. And for a moment the three of us stood side by side, mesmerized, charmed by the red snake that danced on the lawn.

32. Klan's Calling Cards

The cross in flames on our front lawn stood as tall as a man. This I knew for certain because Jimbo flew out the door at it like it was alive and on the attack. And it was only because both Em and I dove for him that Jimbo did not run headlong into the writhing yellow and red. Tackling him to the ground, Em held his waist while I grabbed an ankle, then wrapped both my arms around the leg I'd secured and lay my whole self on top of the leg, even while Jimbo thrashed to shake us.

As the headlights of the trucks bored into the night, one of the horns let fly with "Dixie," its notes hovering on the hot summer night air for a moment, suspended.

From flailing against my grip on his calf, Jimbo suddenly lay quiet there on the grass, and watched white sparks shower the green just inches from where the tips of his fingers reached out toward the flame. He swiveled to a sitting position and reached for my hand to let himself up.

Emerson touched both our shoulders. "I'm going for —" he was yelling as he ran towards the house, his voice disappearing with him around the garage.

My father was already there in the doorway, Momma behind him, a pink satin bathrobe neatly tied in a bow. Her hair lay smooth and tidy, even recently brushed, and her lipstick was bright coral pink.

"A lady, Shelby Lenoir," she had told me so many times, "never appears in public without her face on."

I looked down at my nightclothes — nothing but Emerson's old jersey, really, and the shorts I'd changed into at Momma's demand. My front was a brown stripe of dirt where I'd been dragged several feet by Jimbo's lunge for the fire. And my hair — Lord only knew.

Emerson had raced to the back for the garden hose, and my father, with Jimbo's help, was now training the spray at the base of the flame, which sizzled and spit — and died, waterlogged wood collapsing on grass.

Somewhere behind us, deep in the house, the telephone rang. Momma must have gotten it, her face appearing at the dining room window, whose screens fell forward onto the porch in her haste to call to us out on the lawn.

"Waymon! It's Waymon!" she shouted, her mellifluous voice going shrill.

Momma and her brother spoke often, making a point of meeting at the Home Plate at least every Tuesday for lunch — but rarely did they phone each other.

My father shifted his arc of water to soak a circle around the base of the smoldering wood. He shouted back over his shoulder, "What does he want this time of night?"

Momma's answer stepped out slowly, sound by sound, from inside the house and across our front porch. "He says there's something on fire on his front lawn."

33. A Kiss and Careening

When my brother and Jimbo and I reached
Emerson's truck, my father was still standing with his bathrobe flapping around his
knees and the hose water, reflecting off the
front porch light, was an arc of silver from
his hand. I recall thinking that now that the
danger was past — our house clearly not
about to burn down, my mother safely
inside, the trucks summarily fled — my
father looked . . . almost proud. Can't think
of how else to put it.

Maybe a cross smoldering on his front
lawn was some kind of delayed crowning
achievement, whether or not he'd directly
earned it himself. And it would make great
newspaper copy. I could see he was already
typesetting the headline in his mind.

"We should've told him," I said — to
myself mostly. "We should've told *someone.*"

Jimbo nodded to show he'd heard, and

398

heaved Big Dog in the cab and himself in the truck bed and caught my hand just in time to lift me clear off the ground as the truck rolled out. He didn't let go my hand once I was in good, and I didn't go out of my way to remind him he had it.

My father whirled from the puddle that was forming at the base of the cross. The truck's engine seemed to have startled him out of his reverie and into paternal duty. He gestured for us to come back, and yelled something I couldn't make out but included the words "not safe." But when we pretended not to see him or hear him, he only stood there, watching us go, with his garden hose and the charred, towering wood.

"At least," Jimbo said, "your daddy didn't run off scared."

I shook my head. "Bo, your daddy's not . . ."

Jimbo banged on the truck cab. "Em, you going straight there or stopping at L. J.'s?"

I threw my voice up and over the roar of the engine, Emerson's whipping its horsepower down the Pike. "I thought L. J.'s *was* where we were going!"

Neither of the boys answered me.

Em turned his head to the side to yell, "We'll take L. J. with us, if his place is under control."

"And if things ain't okay at his house?" Jimbo yelled back.

"What are you wanting to hear?"

"That we're gettng to her house as fast as we can."

"That's all I'm saying, Bo. That's all I'm saying."

Of course.

Of course they were right. I was an idiot not to have thought of it first. Of course the bedsheets would go to Farsanna's. If they'd not been there first.

I didn't need to ask about Welp. We wouldn't be stopping for him, I knew. Even if he were home, he wouldn't want to be with us tonight anyhow. And if he weren't home, then he was part of what we were racing against.

"At least," Jimbo was mumbling to himself, "the fire department might show up at L. J.'s."

"What if," I asked him — or maybe I was asking myself, "what if they're just getting things in full swing when we get there?"

"What if why?"

"The bedsheets carry shotguns. You saw them."

He nodded grimly. "I saw them." He felt along the floor of the flatbed and lifted a shovel, which he handed to me, then a pickax. We clutched them, straight up, our shoulders touching.

"We look," I whispered into his ear, "like American Gothic."

And we both laughed, that sudden burst like air pressure released, and nothing to do with mirth. Hot air beat at us in the bed of the truck and churned my hair high above my head as Emerson hurtled us down the Pike. I turned my face into Jimbo's warm chest.

That night was the first time I knew I was in love with James Beauregard Riggs. First time I'd admitted it to myself anyhow.

My face still into his chest, he slipped his arm around me. I could smell the pines we were passing, and peanuts, the salt-sweat of a sweltering August. From the bed of the truck came cedar mulch and manure, dried and mellowed, a kind, gentle, elderly smell, like leather or pipe smoke or wet leaves in the fall. I closed my eyes and tried to picture the Blue Hole, the boulders and hemlocks and layers of pink in late May. The rhythm of life of the pendulum swing. The sun on the cold of a mountain-fed spring.

"I wish," I raised my face up to his, "we were back at the Blue Hole. You were the one called it sacred one time. You remember?"

He brushed the hair back from my face. "Sacred's not the same thing as safe, though."

He kept his face close into mine, our cheeks pressing hard together, my hand slipping to the back of his head, to his hair that flipped up at the back. I knew perfectly well how he meant it, his arm so tight around me. And I knew how I wanted him to mean it. I knew as he pulled me close that he would kiss me, and knew that I wanted him to. And knew just as surely that the kiss would be on my cheek, through my cyclone of hair.

But I knew that night that he loved me, loved me all the way through, in that same bone-marrow-deep and indelible way that he loved my brother — the way that until that moment I'd have sworn I'd loved him.

And I knew, too, that somehow our holding each other just then had less to do maybe with us, him and me, than with what we could feel and hear and see beating in the dark heart of the night, what was already there and waiting.

I held to Bo as we went careening toward rifles and red, toward fire and eyeholes bored into white cotton.

34. WHEN THE SKY TUMBLED AND FELL

Veering sharply, the truck's back wheels flung dust and loose rock as we spun into the turn just past the Feed and Seed and onto Fairview. Though it was well past midnight, a small crowd had gathered in L. J.'s yard. Matthew, Mark, Luke, my aunt, and my uncle milled about with neighbors in the linking rings of light from the front of the house.

L. J. was in the truck bed before I'd even seen him in the yard. He'd been waiting for us. He turned with a hand up to his daddy, almost a salute, Uncle Waymon shaking his head and bellowing to us to stay right where we were, so help him God.

L. J. thumped on Emerson's back window. "Let's go!" He turned back to his father, who continued to shout.

"Things under control back there now?" Jimbo asked him as L. J. settled back — in between Jimbo and me.

Without Jimbo beside me just then, I felt cored out inside, and more frightened than I'd ever been in my life. I wrapped my arms around my knees to hold myself from flying apart.

"Yeah. Daddy's responding moderately well. For a man who believes the viability of the family business has now been terminated. Although the neighbors, good Lord! Mr. Barker's gone ballistic, back there demanding to know what precisely transpired to bring the old boys out of hibernation."

"Fresh Bait, Cold Beer —" Jimbo said, but added before we could finish for him, "Glad *somebody's* daddy came through."

L. J. shook his head. "Those guys created so much disturbance setting the post in the ground — you'd think they'd been constructing a fence — before they lit the fire, they awakened Matthew. Conflagration barely had time to scorch the grass."

"They drive off fast?"

"We'd barely emerged from the house."

Bo nodded. "Reckon that might've been a good thing. Don't know as they take kindly to crashing their dress-up tea parties."

"Bo?" I asked then, not much liking the shimmy in my voice. And it wasn't like my hands to shake, or my legs either one.

"You all right, Shelby?"

It was Jimbo who asked that. Jimbo, using my name.

Even L. J. stopped in the breath he'd just drawn to say what he was going to say. And he looked from me on his right to Bo on his left.

And me, I stared at the floor of the truck bed. I ignored L. J.'s eyes, the tips of two drills.

Jimbo's using my name was the last shadow of what happened — or didn't — between us that night, his way of letting me know he'd remember.

I was finally the one who passed us all into the next moment by managing to push sounds out my throat: "What are we headed into?"

They didn't answer. Not that I expected them to. But it was the closest I could come just then to Farsanna, and what might have happened to her. Seeing Bo's head come up, and his eyes close in a cringe, I knew I'd been noble, unselfish, and brave by mentioning her. I've never often been any of these — and the pain of that moment reminded me why.

The Moulavis' house was dark: no lights outside or in. No headlights raking the gravel drive — except ours.

Emerson eased all the way down and into the backyard, shining the truck lights into the woods. No sign of life.

And, for that matter, no sign of anything else. Relief came for a brief moment, but there was something in the air that unsettled us again, something watching and waiting. I knew, I *knew* there was something I could not name. Something closing in all around us.

I was finding it harder and harder to breathe.

Emerson pulled the truck to the back of the house.

A sole light flickered in the corner of the kitchen window. And even that got doused straight away.

Then a hand reached up to the window to close the blinds.

And in the last yellow of Emerson's headlights before he cut them off, all four of us in the truck saw this, and gasped: The hand was a man's, large and heavily veined, but here was the thing — it was not Farsanna's father's dark skin.

35. When the Mountains Crumbled

L. J. was the first to speak: "So, gentlemen, given what we just witnessed, who might that be in there . . . with them?"

Jimbo leapt over the side of the truck. "Reckon we'll find out right about now."

I ducked down lower in the truck bed, though I peered up over the side, as he tapped on the kitchen window.

"It's me. Sanna, it's me."

She must have recognized the voice, the "me," and didn't need a name. Fumbling with a bolt lock, she opened the kitchen door. Jimbo met her there, looking through the opening for the owner of that white hand.

"Who else is there?" Sanna whispered into the dark.

"Emerson, Turtle, L. J."

There was a pause — maybe she was processing who was missing. "This is not for you a safe place."

But we were following Jimbo, and he didn't pause to ask us for a vote.

We all slipped into the kitchen and stood huddled together, unable to see as our eyes adjusted to the darkness after the headlights. Then I heard — and smelled — a match drawn across its box's rough strip. Farsanna's face swam unsteadily above a sputtering candle.

Behind her, soundlessly, her father and mother stood, staring — not quite at us — just into the dark.

And behind them came Reverend Riggs.

I opened my mouth in a scream, and would've, except for Emerson's hand smacking it closed.

"Children! Brave children. I need to tell you . . . I want to explain . . ." the Reverend Riggs began, his voice hoarse and tired, snagging on something, maybe, that he couldn't say. He lay a hand on Emerson's and L. J.'s shoulders, gently patted my cheek. Then he turned to face his son.

Jimbo did not move. "Why are *you* here?"

"I was afraid —"

Jimbo's eyes had gone hard and cold as two bits of ice, their glittering green frosted over. "Afraid! Yeah, well, that was your problem this morning too, Preacher."

Reverend Riggs received this without

flinching — like maybe he'd been waiting for that. He let the words stand for a moment just as they were: ugly and naked and cold. Then he said quietly, "That's right. I was scared, son. For you, for your momma, for —"

"Yourself," Jimbo spewed. "Yourself and your job, your precious image you got to maintain in this town: the saintly, the *good!*"

Reverend Riggs nodded slowly. "Reckon I was. Scared. For myself. For what people think about me. You said it true, son. You said it true. But also, son, also for these folks here." He nodded toward the Moulavis. "You got to believe that part too. Growing up in these hills, I seen what these old boys can do when they're riled. I was scared bad. And — you're right — I acted like it." He waited for Jimbo to say something, but nothing came. "I been owing apologies to Jesus and to Farsanna here. Reckon now I'm owing you one."

Farsanna stepped with her candle close to Jimbo's face, but her eyes stayed full on his father. "Tonight he came because he was for us afraid. My family and me." She held the candle close to his face, like she was looking for something, about to try something out: "And he has come other nights before this."

Here the Reverend's jaw came undone. "You *knew* about that, child?"

Exchanging a glance with my brother, I stepped into Farsanna's line of sight. "Sanna, *you* knew about that?"

"What?" Jimbo demanded to know. "Know about what?"

The Reverend's look shifted to me. "I suspected you knew, Shelby Lenoir. You and Emerson here."

I stared at him. "You knew we knew?"

From behind me, Jimbo stepped to Farsanna. *"Knew about WHAT?"*

I looked from Bo to the Reverend and back. "About your daddy's creeping around here one night."

Farsanna's head cocked sideways at me, like she'd not understood the language too well, then turned back towards Bo. Her thumb and forefinger plucked at the blouse sleeve of her other arm. "This blouse." Then she pointed at the burgundy towel she'd taken last to the Hole, now folded neatly on a kitchen chair. "That towel. Several towels."

"Towels?" I was confused.

The Reverend was nodding sadly at Emerson and me. "Reckon you children must've seen all them stacks of towels. And, Lord, curtains. Toaster was in pretty good shape. Wasn't that the same night you two were here? I was guessing you saw me."

"Sir?" It came out as a squeak from my nearly grown older brother, but in the South *sir* gets said even to villains.

I could barely see Emerson's expression there in the dim Moulavi kitchen, but I knew he was glaring at me. I was glad we weren't alone.

"Many sheets," Farsanna continued, "Boxes of clothes. Things for use in the kitchen. Twice by the back door they were left. In the mornings we found them. It was our mystery, how they came this way. But one night," she turned now to the Reverend, "one night I thought that I saw your face before you left a large box."

Still ignoring his father, Jimbo turned to Emerson and me. "And you two knew about this?"

We both shook our heads no, which, given what had just got stripped down for the truth, had turned out to be true.

"Not . . . exactly," I said.

Jimbo faced his daddy. "So you think you ought to get credit for carting some charity to these people, that it? Kind of bought your right to keep your mouth shut later? That how you reckoned it out?"

"Tonight, Jimbo," Farsanna said, though her eyes remained on the Reverend, "your father came to my home, to my family, because he was afraid that we were afraid." All our eyes followed her to the Reverend, who was fixed on the face of his son, still too hard to read. Even I couldn't tell what Jimbo was thinking and he wore my second skin, Emerson's and mine.

Sanna motioned for us to follow. "Come."

We trailed in the wake of her candle the few feet across the kitchen to the doorway of her living room. She held the light out at arm's length.

The carpet caught and reflected the flickering, inconstant light, like a sea whose ripples flirt with the moonlight. But this was supposed to be carpet, not water, not waves. The entire floor — what I could see by the candle's halfhearted glow — sparkled and gleamed.

"Glass," L. J. pronounced it.

Emerson stepped toward the shattered window, but stopped when Farsanna laid a hand on his arm.

"Don't," she said. "It's not safe."

"How bad is the damage?"

She held up a rock the size of a softball. "These. Several. After your father arrived."

Farsanna's father raised his arm above his head, his hand clutching a crumpled paper. "And this to one was attached."

412

L. J. reached for the paper. "Court's evidence. Exhibit number one."

"What's it say?" I asked.

Reverend Riggs shook his head, like it wouldn't bear repeating.

But Mr. Moulavi shook his fistful of paper. "It says from here we must move. It threatens the lives of my family. It threatens our home."

Jimbo looked at his father. "You think they mean it? You know these guys. They came to you, right? They came to you to try to smooth over everything, to make sure nobody, including your son, got too out of line. Am I right? Because we saw them, and I told myself that you were helping the situation. Only it never occurred to me you might be helping *them* by keeping your mouth shut when you should've told them —"

"Son, please." Reverend Riggs reached for Bo's shoulder, but Jimbo stepped away with a cringe.

Reverend Riggs shook his head and looked at his feet. "I did try to help, son. In my own way. And I did try to make peace by . . . well, by suggesting they simmer on down."

Bo snorted in disgust.

His daddy raised his own eyes to meet his

son's. "And it's also true I could not have handled it worse —"

"You got that right," Bo said, biting the words.

"Thinking if I kept quiet, it would all go away, or work itself out."

"So *now* what?" Bo demanded. "So now that you've had close, personal contact with these idiots, you tell us what they're likely to do."

Reverend Riggs shook his head. "I reckon they're used to being took seriously, son. Though I couldn't rightly say what that says we should do."

"We?"

"I'm not leaving anytime soon, Bo. I'd like to try not to do twice in one day the most cowardly thing I ever done in my life."

Jimbo did not speak, but the two of them looked at each other across Sanna's candle. And then the good Reverend Riggs reached again for Bo's shoulder.

Bo backed away. "You think this makes up for this morning? For what got done — and didn't — in front of all those people? So you helped these folks when they needed stuff. By cover of night, you played delivery boy. But when the time came to stand up and be shot at, you *ducked,* Daddy. The good Reverend Riggs *tucked tail and run.*"

Jimbo's daddy took this with only a flinch, like he'd been slapped and it stung. He put a hand to his cheek. And slowly, he nodded. "Reckon what happened this morning has got us both ashamed as two people ever were of one. No, it don't make up, son. I can't make up for keeping my mouth shut when I shouldn't oughta been quiet. There's things you can't go back and retread like a tire."

Jimbo gripped the back of a chair and his words came between gritted teeth. "So then you do what, then? Just say *oops* and go on?"

"So you pray for the guts you hadn't got natural. And hope you strap the bull's halter on different next time."

Bo looked steadily at his father, but offered no words.

Farsanna's candle led us back to the kitchen. Jimbo dropped himself in front of the stove.

"So," I whispered to Emerson, "you think the bedsheets might never come back? Ever?"

"Maybe. And they might come back in three minutes. Who knows?"

We waited, huddled on the floor of the kitchen, the candle blown out. Reverend Riggs stationed himself at the doorway to the living room, where through the jagged remains of plate glass he could at least see if headlights were coming.

An hour ticked by — this I knew by periodically wrenching around L. J.'s wrist to see his watch, with green glow-in-the-dark hands.

"It's like being inside the Alamo," I said to him. "Travis. Crockett. Bowie." L. J. wasn't the only one who knew something of history.

L. J. rolled his eyes at me. That is, I couldn't see him do it there in the dark, but knew perfectly well when he did — the misfortune of knowing someone all your life long. "Turtle," he said.

"Yeah?"

"Every one of them died."

Jimbo patted my hand. "Let's us just put Turtle here in charge of something besides cheering us up. Turtle, how 'bout you lead the band in 'A Hundred Bottles of Beer'?"

The chumminess in his voice was back, and whatever else had been there with me — us alone in the back of the truck an eternity or so earlier that evening — was gone, and I wondered if someday, a much later someday way far away, I'd be able to say that was just like things ought to be.

Bo raked fingers through his hair, and I

could see his big hands trembling.

Sanna's parents sat silent, stiff as cadavers. She sat beside them, and though her gaze sometimes rested on one of us, she seemed not to be listening to anyone. She relit the candle and watched its white wax spill onto the floor.

At one point, Jimbo crawled on all fours to her side, drew his big feet up and under himself, and touched her forearm lightly. That was all. No words exchanged. No touch other than that.

And Farsanna looked back into his face. I've no idea what she said to him with her eyes. I understood enough only to know that I wished I hadn't seen. And to see that her mother saw too.

"East!" said Jimbo's daddy, retreating to the kitchen. "I must be for certain. For certain, which way is east?"

Jimbo pointed. And L. J., who liked to think he knew the world, adjusted Jimbo's hand slightly — for accuracy.

Jimbo's daddy knelt on the linoleum floor and held out his hand to Mr. Moulavi, who looked doubtfully at him, but then took his hand and joined him. Mr. Moulavi hunched down over the stone that had shattered far more than just his window. Reverend Riggs hunched there beside him.

And me, I sat wondering what to do. Momma would've served sweet tea and brownies and asked everyone how they, bless their hearts, were feeling. And Jesus, maybe, would've faced Mecca and prayed along with the rumple-suited Baptist and the Sri Lankan invader — though I wouldn't know.

But I just sat there, feeling stupid and rattled and very much in the way.

Without warning, Reverend Riggs stood, then gripped the back of a chair for balance. He seemed to have heard or seen something somehow that we didn't.

"Well, children," he said, a good half-octave higher than usual. "It looks like company's coming."

From out the front window, we saw something leap into flame. And around it, white figures flapped like moths around the light they'd called into creation.

36. THE BOYS IN THE BEDSHEETS

The cross on the Moulavis' lawn looked to me twice as big, twice as white, twice as fearsome as what had been set at my house or at L. J.'s. This one writhed, a frenzied belly dance of flames reflecting in savage yellow-blue shards of the plate-glass window.

Mrs. Moulavi crumpled in one corner of the kitchen. She cried in words I could not make out.

"Tamil," L. J. mouthed to me.

Then she lifted her head and wailed to her husband in English, "Why? Why must we come here?"

Emerson was watching the fire as he spoke: "Where's a garden hose?"

Mr. Moulavi covered his face. "We don't —"

Farsanna took charge. "We have no hose. Something else . . . in here." Her hand paused on the kitchen light switch.

Reverend Riggs nodded at her. "Not much use walking in darkness now." He shed his suit jacket to the floor and like a speedway's checkered flag going down, the jacket set us to motion.

Ransacking the kitchen cabinets, Farsanna tossed out a bucket, a plastic pitcher, some metal pots and pans to the middle of the floor, and as fast we found them, Jimbo's daddy filled them at the kitchen sink. Carrying as many containers as our arms would hold, we began running, slipping, across the wet linoleum floor, across the glass carpet, falling, gashing our knees. Blood ran freely down our legs.

"Please, ma'am, stay here!" Jimbo shouted to Farsanna's mother, curled in her corner of the kitchen but preparing to rise. "Stay where you're safe!"

That word *safe* rang in my ears as I waited for my pitcher to fill, a word already flung out in this place a few times too many, and never anything but a curse. I pictured the strung-up stray dog, and our cutting him down with Welp's knife.

Welp. Was he out there with the billowing smoke and the bedsheets?

Farsanna stopped and shouted to her mother what to me was nothing but sound — maybe it was Tamil or Sinhalese, or maybe English mangled by fire — and she heaved up her filled bucket and ran.

And then Farsanna was out in the yard at the base of the flames and the falling cross.

A couple of the figures in white had already run for their trucks — all pickups, and one orange Gremlin. One of the figures in white raised his hands over his head and was bellowing, "One race reigns supreme. One race made to rule over the others. God has ordained that the white man keeps himself pure from the muddying stain of miscegenation!"

Which was when Jimbo charged out of house toward the fire. A couple of Klan members leapt to intercept him.

But one of them lunged towards Farsanna. I saw him grab her by the waist, his hands moving on her. And through the holes in his white, I saw his eyes, hungry and yellow and swollen.

And I saw her elbow swing up to his eyes, catch him hard across the bridge of the nose. Heard him scream. Heard myself screaming too. And I watched him writhe, his hands rubbing his eyes frantically.

Me, I couldn't move. I stood there at the front door, each of my hands carting water that wasn't getting where it needed to be.

And this has not left me, not for a day: I

stood at the door and I watched. I watched it happen. I did not move. I had overheard Mort — and he was here even now, hiding in white. But I hadn't said what should've been said on the first day, and now couldn't do the only thing left to be done.

I recall seeing Farsanna, free of Mort's grip, grabbing a bucket and tossing its contents at the fire. I saw, from my place at the Moulavis' front door, past the arc of Sanna's water, that someone had jumped from the cab of one of the trucks.

And that he was very short, with holes in his jeans.

Bobby Welpler was not wearing white, no hood and no robe.

But still, he was with them. Bobby Welpler was with them.

37. A GEYSER OF FIRE

Through clouds of gravel dust and smoke, I could see that Welp had grabbed one of the bedsheets by the shoulder and whirled him around. But he was knocked to the ground.

Welp scrambled up, shouting for Jimbo. And he was pointing. "The car!"

He pulled from his pocket a flash of silver, the knife he'd used to whittle, to slit his pathetic jeans. The knife we'd used to cut down the dog.

And then Welp lunged, knife in hand, at a bedsheet who was skulking away toward the house. Welp's tinny voice shrieked, *"Wait! Stop!"*

Jimbo hurtled across the lawn. And to this day, I couldn't say if he was diving for Welp because he'd been with the bedsheets, or because Welp had his knife out and was leaping to use it.

Bo dove for Welp, and Em running too, and the flaming, falling vertical post screamed softly and sputtered where it fell, its horizontal piece collapsing with it.

Some of the bedsheets leapt back. But one — maybe the one Welp had been after — fled, cradling something in front of him as he ran toward the carport.

"Let me up!" I heard Bobby shriek from beneath Jimbo. *"You don't know! You don't know what they're going to — !"*

The boys were rolling on the ground, Bobby's blade flashing firelight at each revolution. I saw as I ran — I could finally move — there was blood on the knife.

I'd almost reached Jimbo and Welp — Sanna and Em were already there — when the bedsheet reached the carport. His white arm whipped back and something flew from his hand at the Moulavis' parked car. As the object flipped end on end through the air, I saw that it was yet another rusty gas can — empty now, its contents having been dumped all over the carport. From another man's hand, a still-burning piece of the cross flew into the carport after the can.

The bedsheets were running, were diving and covering their white-hooded heads, before the lit wood hit the soaked concrete floor of the carport, reeking of gas.

Then a geyser of fire ripped into the dark beside the red brick rectangle house. For an instant, we were slammed, all of us, into a blazing white, blinding chaos. And I wondered if this were the end of the world.

The Moulavis' only car, their station wagon, had sat alone in the carport. And when it exploded, it blew out one wall of the kitchen and engulfed the whole roof of the house in flames.

38. Ashes, Ashes

The station wagon's steel frame still smolders sometimes in my dreams. But those aren't the difficult nights.

On difficult nights, I replay in my sleep Jimbo's sprinting for the house, Sanna's beating him there. I see all over again Mr. Moulavi knocked unconscious where he stood at the sink, Sanna dragging him a good forty feet into the yard.

And I see Mrs. Moulavi, her beautiful hair on fire along with the hijab, her skirts, too, in flames — beneath the burning body of Jimbo Riggs, who'd seen the kitchen wall falling and had dived to cover her from it.

Jimbo's daddy had snatched a blanket off Sanna's bed, already iced in white ash and debris, and threw it over both bodies and then himself on top of that to smother the ravenous flames already devouring the stove and the table and human flesh, even before the kitchen roof had completely caved in.

The smell of the hair and the skin and the gas all on fire knocked me in half. I knelt right there on the lawn between the cross and what was the Moulavis' kitchen. I knelt, but I didn't pray. Instead, I threw up my insides. That's what I did. That's how I helped.

And that's all I see in my dreams — which, I reckon, is a kind of a mercy, given all that came after.

I don't much recall the whole lifetime before an ambulance arrived from the Valley below, or the endless days that followed: the waiting, hour on hour, strung like fake pearls, all exactly alike and none of them precious, outside the intensive care unit, the living on Heath bars and Cokes from the waiting room machines, the trying to read, and trying not to look at the skin of Jimbo Riggs' legs, far darker now than the brown ones that had swung up that first day over Em's tailgate. Bo's legs were black and buckling like old paint, the skin of his arms and his chest the same.

Sometimes I still see in my dreams Mr. Moulavi down on his knees and finding the east-facing waiting room window, his face to the floor and both arms splayed on the ICU waiting room tile. Sometimes I still hear Bo moan in his sleep, or see his school picture posted above his hospital bed at the nurses' request so they could remember the carcass was human, or watch Bo's daddy holding his hand, refusing to budge from the side of Bo's bed, refusing to eat and sleeping only hunched there in the chair as the hours limped by and collapsed into days.

Sometimes I can still smell the stench of charred flesh and infection, and watch all over again Em lifting Bo's head and cranking the volume of the hospital's TV so that the unruly mob of a Sox game might shout down the horror around us. I can hear the gurgle and hiss of tubes and machines as Em put his head down beside Jimbo's, Em's tears wetting the white of Bo's bandaged cheeks. "It's Ted Williams to bat, Bo. It's Williams. Don't you go drifting off again on me, you hear? The Sox can win yet. You hear me, Bo? Don't you go giving up yet."

That was the day Bo used the pen we always left by his hand — because it hurt him to speak — to scrawl this on a notebook: "Not me. Don't YOU give up. On anyone."

The words we tried to trade in the molten center of those days were no good — like they'd been maimed too and never would heal. We knew, those of us who'd been raised there, how to be nice — and that was no good anymore. Whatever words we made then were the same: just debris. Like the litter, the beer cans middle-aged men tossed off the Look. Words worth no more than that.

When Mrs. Moulavi, her gorgeous hair shaved flat to her head, but then scarved, recovered enough to move from the hospital, the doctor discharged her and her daughter to go home — forgetting for a trip-over-truth moment what he knew all too well: that there was no home for them on the Ridge.

That had been the point all along.

And sometimes I still see in my dreams the day we huddled by the side of Bo's bed, his dimples only a memory to us, his face bandaged and contorted in pain. The day we saw whole worlds of agony in his eyes and prayed he would die. All of us held on to each other, Sanna beside me, both of us trembling, the whole Pack of us — all but Welp — having cried ourselves sick. And Bo's parents there beside us.

"If," Sanna said that day, "if I'd never come. . . ."

Regina Lee Riggs, at Bo's head, lifted her eyes, red and glazed over with grief, but said nothing. She lowered her head then, and her hair, not brushed for days, fell over her face.

But Bo's daddy turned from his place by Bo's side. He held out his hand to Farsanna and pulled her close by his side. "No one," he whispered, "*no one* blames you for this, child. There are plenty enough to blame for it, me at the top of the list. Me at the top. But that won't undo what's been done here. And you, child, *you* aren't to blame."

We stood there together and rode the ebb and flow of Bo's moans. Then something changed in his breathing.

Bo's daddy looked up at Sanna, and his voice came out clogged and uneven. "Maybe . . . maybe it's time we told him good-bye."

Sanna bent then and left a kiss on the bandages that were Bo's face.

L. J. bent over him next and then Em, all of us kissing him on the unmarred patch of forehead where his black hair stuck up straight like he'd just raked his hands through it.

" 'One short sleep past,' " Em said softly as he knelt beside his best friend, " 'we wake eternally, And Death shall be no more: Death, thou shalt die!' " He swiped at tears with the back of his hand. "So don't you think for a moment, Bo, that we've seen our last Sox game together. You got that?"

I hunched over Bo last and held tight to his one unbandaged hand. "You can't," I whispered to him, "you can't go. You *can't* go without us. I dreamed about you last night, and you were dancing on the top branch of the sweetgum and James Brown and Ray Charles were playing their tunes at the foot of the tree, and you had a gun and were shooting up at the stars, and they were raining down light. And your daddy, Bo, your daddy was right there beside you, and so were the boys from down in the Valley who came swimming that day. We were all there. And I woke up thinking the dream meant that you'd live. I *knew* it meant that. I told Em. And Sanna. And L. J. I told the nurses, told them all today you would live. And I told your daddy, and he squeezed me till I couldn't breathe. Bo," I begged. "Bo, you *can't* give up now."

My brother took hold of my shoulders and gently pulled me away. "Shelby," he said, holding me as I sobbed. "Jimbo hadn't ever given up on anything in his life. Or anyone. You know that. And he's not starting now."

I lifted my head in time to see Bo turn his face, briefly, toward us. He lifted his good hand, which all of us reached for and clung to.

For a moment, but only a moment, his green eyes crinkled as if he were smiling. And then his eyes closed.

39. Fools

The Moulavis left on a Greyhound just after Bo's funeral, bound for Washington, D.C.

Maybe, I recall thinking, Sanna's father hadn't quite given up his dream of America, and would go searching for it at its diseased but still-pumping heart.

We cried, the new girl and I, and even Emerson and L. J. We'd smelled too many lilies in hospital cells, too many fumes, seen too much skin in black flakes and arms bloody as raw beef beneath and hair turned to brittle black threads. We'd been burned on the insides, by the smoke and the fumes and the cross-frenzied red. And we cried because we'd been welded together somewhere in the flames, somehow part of each other, and yet we never wanted to see each other again. So we circled our arms across shoulders and cried because there was so much and there was nothing to say.

Em made one final map with his hands;

Farsanna put her hand over his and squeezed it.

It had been Emerson's idea that Jimbo's ashes — that was nearly all that was left even before the morticians got hold of him — should be laid to rest at the Blue Hole. I've always loved my brother for that. Bo's funeral was packed, the Baptist church-belly swollen and heaving and sick, this time with grief. For the burial, the whole part of the town that could walk, teenagers and children and grown people, they all kicked off their shoes and made the climb down to the Hole.

Welp wasn't there. Not that I saw. And neither was a single one of the Beckwiths. But Mollybird was. And Mr. Steinberger, and both of his daughters. And a whole town of mourners who slid their way down to where we laid Jimbo's ashes to rest, by the side of still water that wasn't in any way blue.

It was my idea to transplant the pink rosebush that in some cruel kind of trick survived the explosion, singed but alive at the roots. Having come from Mollybird Pittman to Emerson and Jimbo's landscaping business, and from Jimbo to Farsanna, and somehow living through the blast, it struck me as fitting, somehow.

It was L. J.'s idea to take two seared rafters from the Moulavis' kitchen and make a cross out of them for the grave — not a white one, but scorched and half-eaten by flame. And it was the idea of the good Reverend Riggs to take another two charred, broken beams from the site and replace the hanging white cross in the Baptist church sanctuary. They tell me it's still hanging there, the cross so falling apart that when the organ moans out of too many pipes, the cross sheds charcoal and bits of wood onto the choir.

I've never seen it myself, though. At seventeen, I went north to Wellesley, where once they'd got an earful of my accent, they were thunderstruck I could read and write my whole name. I went back south, back home, only twice during college, and then only to bury my parents, their dying of natural causes within a year of each other. And I've never yet been back inside the place where Jimbo's daddy made his son so ashamed, and helped send us all down the road that dead-ended with me standing there, watching it all, doing nothing, and Bo's body caught fire like a torch, lit by the good of his heart.

My father did live long enough to see Emerson go to Dartmouth, but not long enough to see him become a professor of seventeenth-century English literature and live in Seattle — his specialty being John Donne. That much I might've predicted. But I'm still walking around shocked about this: The very month after our father died, Em joined a church — though at least only an Episcopal church, so it could've been worse. He tries to explain it to me: It's some kind of breath to him, some kind of pulse to his life that — I'll be straight up — I just don't understand. And some days — only off days, mind you, or down days — days like today maybe, I'd like to. At least understand. But I will say this: Every time I hear Emerson talk, hush-breathed, using words like *mercy* and *holy,* I picture what Jimbo would do. I see him throwing back his head in a hearty laugh at our Emerson kneeling so earnestly on a prayer bench. And I imagine Jimbo would squeeze right in beside him.

To no one's surprise but his daddy's, L. J. never took over Waymon's Feed and Seed. When Uncle Waymon suffered a stroke, his second son, Matt made a real enterprise of the old place, even took Big Dog Lawn and Garden Beautifiers as a sideline. Bought

Emerson's old truck, too, with the company name Bo painted there on the door. I have to give Matt credit for keeping the name.

The Big Dog herself, overindulged to the end, breathed her last from the shade of an old dogwood tree while she was supervising our spreading cedar mulch just a week before Emerson left for Dartmouth. She was buried, by request of Mollybird Pittman, beneath a particularly large, particularly red hybrid tea rose. Em never even tried to argue that Big Dog needed to be in our yard — maybe he knew, even then, we wouldn't be back, him and me. Not anytime soon anyhow. And in the hole with Emerson's best friend — outside of Bo — we placed an unopened box of barbecue scraps and a full can of Dr Pepper, memorial gifts from Hyme Steinberger and daughters.

L. J. went with the Peace Corps to Togo — or was it Tonga? He eventually became a lawyer in Birmingham and busies himself with pro bono civil rights cases. Pro bono to the extent, he admitted to me when I asked, that he does very little for pay. And his wardrobe looks like it, I assured him last time business brought him to Boston. So he calls when he's in town, and he pounds out the occasional terse, meant-to-be-friendly e-mail. My aunt's Christmas letters hint that she still grieves her son's lack of graciousness and tact, his never, she implies, having made too much of himself.

Me, I moved down the Mass Pike from Wellesley to Boston. And after years of playacting big-city sophistication, I still prefer Emerson's old pickup to my Saab, and Steinberger's barbecue to Legal Seafood's lobster. I still prefer male friends to female — though who has time really for either?

I couldn't say why I chose Boston for a place to prop up my feet — not that there's time for that either — and the weather here makes me wear shoes. Don't hear me wrong: I love this city — as cities go. I love its quirky little streets: Water and Milk. And cobblestone-pocked Beacon Hill — where I live. I love Mike's Pastry's cannoli in the North End and the bookstores, quirky and musty and marvelous, sprinkled through the whole town.

But some nights just before I drift off to sleep, listening to the rumble of car wheels on my cobblestone street, I hear Emerson's voice and his bluegrass guitar, or see Jimbo dangling from the rope swing, one hand on the rope, the other melodramatically over his heart, and singing to Sanna, and also to me,

When the night has come
And the land is dark . . .

And I enter my dreams on those nights hearing banjos and dulcimers and mandolins, all mixed up with Motown, and watching a sea of blue mountains roll out before me, smelling the sun on the hemlocks and damp, fern-carpeted forests, feeling my bare toes sink into warm, wet red clay.

No, I won't be afraid,
Just as long as you stand,
Stand by me . . .

And I am trying, I think, to stay there, to not have to leave ever again.

But even then, sometimes my dreams take a nasty turn, the clay turning to embers beneath me. And I cannot move. Or maybe just don't.

On the way to our first trip back to the Blue Hole, to visit where we'd just buried Bo's ashes, Em drove and L. J. and I shared the cab seat with him and Big Dog, who sat at our feet, her head still and sad in my lap. Not one of us talked as we drove down the Pike. We passed by Steinberger's, then looped left by the Overlook.

There was an old Pinto parked there off

the side of the road that clung to the edge of our Ridge. We all knew whose it was — whose drunk of a momma's it was.

L. J. motioned for Em to slow down.

Emerson tapped on the brakes, but didn't slow down too awfully much. "Nope," Em said.

L. J. motioned again.

Em's head popped around. "NO . . . WAY."

"Don't you think," L. J. asked pointedly, "Jimbo would've wanted us to find Welp? And not give up on him yet?"

That was the problem with our having hung out with Jimbo for so long, his always digging out room for a chance that somebody could change.

There was Welp, sitting with his tires just where our Ridge gives out of strength and lets the earth fall away into cliff, and down three thousand feet into valley. The Pinto was idling loud and irregular, metal pings and heavy, hard thunks that shifted the loose soil beneath it.

Em slammed the truck into park. "You screwed up, Welp," he called out, his hands clenched on the wheel. He took a deep breath and met L. J.'s eye, and I could see my brother was groping for something like mercy. But shaking his head, his hands turning white at the knuckles, he came up only with this, strangled there in his throat: "You screwed up big time."

Welp sat there in his car. He nodded.

L. J. inched his way out of the cab and approached Welp slowly, like the car might just be driven right off the side of that ridge. "Perhaps Welp," L. J. said over his shoulder, "is cognizant of having screwed up." He stood a couple of arms' length from the Pinto.

Welp looked out his driver's-side window, his shoulders starting to heave. "I tried to stop it, right there at the end. I don't know what happened. Me and Mort was supposed to be just having some fun. And then the old guys come along and things got out of control and . . . You got to believe me: I tried to stop it, right there at the end —"

L. J. nodded — real slow, and held out a hand. "You got to put that car in reverse and come on out of there, Welp. Come on out of there now."

"I even wrote a letter. To them. Said I was sorry. So sorry." His whole body convulsed as he cried. "I gave it to a nurse down to the hospital, before they left town. Did you know that? I gave it to a nurse. And I wrote one to Bo, and snuck in one night and read it to him and his daddy."

L. J. moved one step closer. "You did some good, then, Welp. You did some good. You throw that car in reverse now, and you tell us more."

My heart beat loud and heavy and irregular along with the car's engine, the violence of the Pinto's motor shifting the gravel beneath its tires.

Welp sat there, just sobbing behind the wheel and he reached up a hand to L. J., just fingers to fingers, and touched.

"So sorry," Welp said one more time.

Then his foot pressed the gas of his momma's old Pinto to drive off the edge of the world.

"Bobby!" I screamed.

For an instant, Bobby's foot mashed the brake, the car's front tires slipping forward and down.

"Bobby!" I called from the truck bed, and scrambled out as I yelled, "Bobby, Jimbo was talking about you at the last." When the words formed in my mouth, they were a lie, something I spit out to keep a car from plunging over a cliff — a selfish act, really, words to keep us from living through any more death than we already had. But shouted out like they were, echoing there at the edge of our mountain, Bobby's miserable face turning to listen, it suddenly hit me that my lie was also the truth.

The Pinto's front wheels shifted on the loose shale and dead leaves at the rim of the Look. The car's front end sank as the tires lost their grip on firm soil.

"Bobby!" Em yelled, as the Pinto nose-dived into thin air.

When the flashing lights had come and gone, and the tow truck had observed the pile of scrap metal it needed to fetch three thousand feet down, and after the police had finished shaking their heads that Bobby Welpler had managed to throw himself out the driver's-side door before the car had plummeted down, or that he'd managed to cling onto a rock until we could pull him to safety, after all this, we piled in Em's truck. Bobby huddled with us in the bed of the pickup, all of us shaken and numb, and went to the Hole. We sat there by the grave in a huddle, and looked at the water and wept. Even the boys. Even me. Nobody was there swimming, so the stirred-up brown had gone a dark almost-blue.

Bobby lay facedown alone on the granite palm, and whatever he said, to Jimbo or Jesus or whoever it was he imagined could hear — we let him say it in peace. We let him alone until he was done being alone, and then we hung onto each other, what was left of us, on into the dark.

They tell me folks back home still talk about Jimbo and us and that summer, and argue on about just who was to blame, or where the trouble back then really began:

"Jimbo Riggs, if you're asking me."

"You lay off on that boy, bless his sweet heart. He was as good a thing as this town ever growed."

"Sweet on that colored girl was what he was, I tell you what."

"You ask me, it was the fault of them news-paper editor's kids. You just look where both of them ended up if that don't tell you how —"

"I heard Bobby Welpler got hisself mixed up in the thing. Heard that was why he left town and why he come back, and why he built his momma that house."

"I tell you what, it was the fault of that family from . . . where was they from?"

"Then they should've had better sense than to set down here, seeing how they didn't belong — a monkey could tell that by look-ing."

"They shoulda knowed better than be play-ing with fire. Pack of fools, what they were."

But I could tell them it wasn't like that, wasn't Bo's fault or mine or his daddy's or

444

Bobby's — not even Mort's: It was the fault of the Blue Hole, and how it made us forget how things were.

Em still goes back there sometimes when he visits from the West Coast. He says the Hole is most always empty, and the rope swing rotted through. He says the rose still grows where we buried Bo's ashes, and it still blooms every summer, clear through the hottest of months — like it thrives on the heat somehow, or like it's found some kind of home deep in the woods by a pool of nearly-blue water.

Roses grow too in the Public Garden in Boston, perhaps one reason I come here so often. Maybe I'm drawn here by the way the willows tickle the pond and swan boats come swimming by, and though I could do with a few azaleas and magnolias, I'm real fond of its bridges and fountains and roses, its children digging in dirt, just like I loved to do with my brother. My brother and Jimbo.

I was there this morning. Between meetings at the State House, where I work. I stopped at the Starbucks on Charles for the espresso I take into the Garden for an occasional break from my black pumps. I don't ordinarily pay much mind to the folks who pass by: All those baby strollers and diaper bags only make me feel ancient, make me wonder if maybe I forgot to ask for Door Number Three on the way to success. So I take my work with me when I go, and rarely look up except to admire the landscaping, especially the roses, and now and then to pet someone's golden retriever — they're everywhere here.

But this morning two people stopped just in front of me and caught my attention. They were both dressed in business getup, had to be from some convention down Boylston at the Hynes Center. The woman was nodding at whatever the man was saying, but she was gazing away, absently — like women do when they're only tolerating a man. I know the look pretty well.

I was admiring the black — nearly blue — of the woman's thick hair when she turned. Her skin was the color of homemade hot cocoa, and even though she was small in the frame, she held her head high and back stiff, like a queen or a saint or a general — like Joan of Arc maybe. And her deep eyes sent me falling into my past, way back to where the good caught on fire, and the bad started clouding in thick and spinning on up to today.

I don't swear that it was who I thought it

might be. I sat for a long while like a missing person's ad artist and tried to sketch in my mind the lines and hollows and swells that age likes to add. Still I wouldn't swear. People change in twenty-five years.

But here's what I did, sitting there by the Boston Public Garden pond, truly blue, a thousand miles north of the Blue Hole, which wasn't: I scrawled a note.

I was late for a meeting already. Because of the face and the two dreams crashing head on, or maybe just because I was imagining things, I'd spilled espresso all down my suit, and me with a power-point presentation at ten. So I didn't stop to talk — and I know better than to speak to strangers in Boston.

So I just handed the woman with the face and the skin and the eyes and the black-licorice hair a note, and then left. It said only this:

Remember the Blue Hole.

It wasn't a question, or a battle cry either. Just words offered out for the taking.

And I signed it:

Shelby Lenoir

Then I crossed that out and wrote *Turtle.* Because one summer when I was too hot to think straight, she made me her friend.

And at the last minute, I added just this

one more thing:

I'm sorry. So sorry.

Maybe the words, those extra four little ones, couldn't hold up under the weight of what I wanted to say, didn't nearly explain about the nights I still saw in my sleep, me standing in the door of the Moulavi house, and not moving. Watching the sky and the lawn and the world turn to fire. And not moving. Watching the white that billowed and whipped through the night, through the black and the red. And me never moving, not until fire shot up into the dark and the roof — and the world — fell in on our heads.

I'm sorry could never tent over all that, but there it was, at least said. *For things done and left undone,* Emerson would say now — now that he talks liturgy like it was regular English. *Lord have mercy.*

The slip of paper had my office number on the letterhead, but I've been in meetings all day. And somehow, maybe, I'm nervous to check.

Anyway, what are the chances?

Maybe — most likely — I handed the note to a stranger, and she figures she got assaulted this morning by a fool in a nice suit. With coffee stains down the front. And black pumps. And maybe I am one — a fool.

Only a fool would think — and I know

this — that maybe the phone might ring sometime today and the voice at the end would say — and use contractions to say it, "It's all right, Turtle. Turtle, it's okay."

Maybe, back at the Hole, we were all fools — our whole mangy pack that caught one summer on fire and watched our world fall out from under our feet. Fools, dangerous fools.

And maybe Jimbo was right all along: *"There's times,"* he once said, *"a fool's a fine thing, an almighty fine thing to be."*

AFTERWORDS

. . . A little more . . .

When a delightful concert comes to an
end,
the orchestra might offer an encore.
When a fine meal comes to an end,
it's always nice to savor a bit of dessert.
When a great story comes to an end,
we think you may want to linger.
And so, we offer . . .

AfterWords — just a little something
more after you
have finished a David C. Cook novel.
We invite you to stay awhile in the
story.
Thanks for reading!

Turn the page for . . .

• Reader's Guide

- **A Conversation with Joy Jordan-Lake**
- **Resources**

READER'S GUIDE

1. Discuss the scene in which Turtle urges Emerson to stop and pick up the new girl. Turtle quickly feels a hint of regret over her decision, though she couldn't have predicted what it would eventually lead to. Why do you think she feels that twinge of regret so immediately? Can you recall any moments in your life which felt equally pivotal, and how did you react? What was the outcome?

2. Joy Jordan-Lake created a diverse and most memorable cast of characters. Who do you relate to most, and why?

3. Farsanna says, "In America, it is every-where the land of opportunity, my father says . . . 'It is the . . . end . . . of the rainbow.' " Farsanna's journey in this novel reminds her and the Pack again and again

about this rainbow. Discuss how this statement could take on different meanings for each character, and discuss whether you believe there was any rainbow to be found on Pisgah Ridge.

4. How did you react to the scene in Reverend Riggs' church? What do you think is the appropriate reaction for faith-based communities in the face of similar situations, which may have nothing to do with race or ethnicity at all, but instead with differences of all kinds?

5. Mort Beckwith and Bobby Welpler are tragic characters in this story. What are the differences between them? In what ways do you relate to either of them?

6. How did you respond to the way the novel ended? Was what happened to Jimbo a surprise? And, how do you interpret the town's reaction to his death or to the Moulavis' departure from Pisgah Ridge?

7. Various characters in this novel have very different approaches to faith in God, from

Shelby's admitting, in response to seeing Mr. Moulavi at prayer, that "Religious practices of the truly faithful have always made me nervous — maybe because I've lived my life outside the glass with my nose pressed against it" to Jimbo's dogged insistence on "scraps of the holy hoped for." What accounts for the difference in the various characters' approaches to faith or skepticism?

8. Do you believe any justice was served in *Blue Hole Back Home*? And was there any redemption to be found? How, and where?

9. Have you ever encountered discrimination the way the Mangy Pack did in *Blue Hole Back Home*? Did this novel stir up those memories for you, whether in a new — or old but still — powerful way? If you're comfortable, tell your story.

10. Do you believe this kind of racially based hatred still exists today in America? If so, why? How do you think this story would be different if it occurred today?

A CONVERSATION WITH JOY JORDAN-LAKE

Blue Hole Back Home **is inspired by a true story. How does this novel represent your own story, and what ultimately motivated you to write about it years later?**

Honestly, I've felt haunted by this story.

All the characters in *Blue Hole Back Home* are purely fictional, as is the town of Pisgah Ridge, North Carolina, but the story has its roots in several incidents during my own teen years. One of these incidents involved a family from Sri Lanka who moved to our all-white town in the mountains of East Tennessee. I grew up on Signal Mountain, a small town on top of Walden's Ridge just outside Chattanooga. The Sri Lankan family's daughter was about my age, a year behind me in our high school down in the valley, and we became friends. She was beautiful, small-statured and had the thickest, black hair and a smile that knocked you clear off your feet.

I remember her explaining to me that her family had moved to the U.S. because her father was convinced that America was "the end of the rainbow." She just beamed when she said it, so full of trust and excitement. And I recall even then being uneasy. They were the only dark-skinned family living on our mountain, and my friend seemed happily oblivious to the fact that perhaps not everyone thought it was just peachy she and her family had moved to our town. She began attending my church — and in fact, the church still has some old photographs someone snapped of a group of us teenagers together. So far as I know, she was accepted there, at least, without question. Her family had come from a Muslim background in Sri Lanka, but they weren't practicing Muslims, and I'm guessing her father allowed her to become involved with a Christian church because it seemed the American, and certainly the Southern, thing to do in order to fit in.

Then one night my father announced he'd been notified that the Klan was burning a cross on the family's front lawn, and he was rushing there to be with my friend and her family. He and I have different memories of what happened next: whether I went with him that night or desperately wanted to and wasn't allowed. I don't suppose it matters at this point, nearly thirty years later, which one of us is right. At any rate, here's what I recall of what actually happened: the Klan had, in addition to burning the cross on the lawn, also shattered the plate-glass window in front of the house, and burned the family's car — and generally destroyed, of course, any sense of welcome or safety. In the midst of that night's terror, my friend's father turned to my dad and asked, "Which way is Mecca? Please, can you point me toward Mecca?" My father pointed him toward the east, and then knelt beside him to pray.

Immediately after the cross burning, the family decided to move to Washington, D.C., where my own family had moved from ten years before. And when I stood there saying good-bye to my friend, she looked me in the eye and, with tears streaming down her cheeks, demanded, "We thought America was the end of the rainbow — we believed it. Explain this to me."

And you know, I'd like to tell you that I made an inspiring little speech that revived her faith in God and in the United States of America — with freedom and justice for all

— and that I exchanged addresses with my friend and that we've been close to this day, emailing and text messaging regularly. The truth is, I have no idea what I said in that moment as we stood there as frightened teenagers. I just remember being so rocked by the whole thing, so embarrassed, so inadequate to say anything even remotely helpful. I never saw or heard from her again.

So maybe that's why I initially wrote a short story about it that was included in my first book, *Grit and Grace.* The book editor for the Chattanooga newspaper suggested in her review of *Grit and Grace* that I should consider making a novel of that story, "Blue Hole." And I thought, "Yeah, she's right. I'd like to do that. I'd like to have another chance to say, through fiction, what I wish I'd actually said to my friend back then." So even though it took me years to get around to writing the novel, maybe I've been trying to get it right all along, trying to make the story turn out differently, with more closure, more healing, more hope.

Interestingly, though, even in writing what I'd intended as a more hopeful version of the story than the reality, things in the fictionalized world still refused to tie themselves neatly into a bow of perfectly resolved reconciliation. Maybe life is just more open-ended and complex than that.

One of my editors with this book, Nicci, who was fabulous to work with, found it disturbing, I think, that justice isn't really served at the end of the novel — nobody really gets nailed for Jimbo's death — and she leaned on me a little, appropriately so, to make things happen more justly. I took her input seriously, and just couldn't do it. Maybe something inside me kind of rebelled — maybe, not consciously, but maybe I couldn't because historically so many African-American deaths resulting from race crimes went so utterly unpunished.

Any idea what happened to the Sri Lankan girl of your actual experience?

Over the years, I've tried to find her a number of times, but so far haven't a clue. I changed her name for this book to protect her and her family, and also because the fictional Farsanna figure is only inspired by my friend, not a replica. Still, it's occurred to me to dream: wouldn't it be incredible if somehow, someone who knows her now and knows something of her early days having settled in the mountains of East Tennessee. . . . What if this someone stumbled across *Blue Hole Back Home* and gave it to her — and we had a chance to reconnect.

The possibilities are more than a little remote, I realize, but wouldn't that make quite an afterword for a later edition. . . . An afterword, perhaps, more valuable than the story itself.

Your novel involves the Ku Klux Klan and racism in America in general, and evidence that it still exists today. What specific bits of history are particularly relevant to *Blue Hole Back Home*? How did that history drive your characters and storyline? What did your personal experiences teach you about such discrimination?

In addition to the cross-burning, other elements in the novel that were inspired by actual events, and that occurred during this same time period, the late 1970s and 1980, include the Ku Klux Klan roadblock and the downtown shooting spree that injured several African-American women. During the eight or so years that I lived as a young adult in Boston, if I ever ventured to tell my Northern friends any of these stories, they looked at me like I must be about a hundred and twelve years old. They were convinced that the South remained an illiterate, racist backwater, but it still struck them as utterly impossible that someone my age (I was born on the last day of 1963) could have seen an actual Klansman anywhere outside a history book, or known anyone whose yard had been the site of a burning cross.

The novel's scene with the KKK road block was inspired by one my family ran into driving back from swimming on the back side of the mountain. My father was driving. To that point, I'd never seen the Klan in person before, and I recall when we saw these figures up ahead all dressed in what looked for all the world like bed sheets and pillowcases, I thought it was a joke — until we got closer. And they were holding fast food chicken buckets. An utterly ridiculous image, you'd think. But there was nothing amusing about these guys. They were collecting money in the buckets, and they poked shotguns in the driver's-side window to encourage contributions. My father declined to contribute.

At the time, it seemed only natural that he would calmly refuse — exactly what I expected, and I don't recall being as terrified as I probably ought to have been. But as a parent now myself, I realize how frightened he must've been, not so much for his own safety as for the safety of his family there in the car. He was declining to contribute to guys who'd just shoved a shotgun muzzle into a car with his family in it. That had to have quickened the heartbeat a little.

And you mentioned the shooting spree was also inspired by actual events?

Right. The novel's shooting spree down in the valley was inspired by an incident on April 19, 1980 — again, while I was in high school. In response to some Klan members having met with leaders of the NAACP, three local Klan renegades who viewed this as evidence of the KKK's becoming too soft, drove through an African-American section of downtown Chattanooga with one of the three guys shooting randomly at the sides of the street. One of these guys, I'm told, graduated from my high school, though several years before I did. I'm happy to say we've never met.

Four African-American women were shot, though not killed that night, and a fifth was injured by flying glass from the blasts. Incredibly, two of the three men were acquitted, and the third, the one firing the gun, spent only nine months in prison. When the verdict from the all-white jury came down, the city's African-American population erupted, quite understandably. Again, we were well past what could be considered even the broadest definition of the Civil Rights era, and yet here were these atrocities going essentially unpunished. I suppose it made an early cynic of me about racial hatred ever being entirely eradicated from any part of our country — and at the same time, made me someone who is doggedly, even unreasonably hopeful about the potential for individuals and towns and whole regions of the country to admit screw ups and tragedies and brutalities, and genuinely change.

What about one of the chief villains of the novel, Mort Beckwith? Any basis for him in real life?

Actually, yes. His first name is just a play on the French word for death, *morte.* But the last is a point toward Byron De La Beckwith, the assassin in 1963 of African-American Civil Rights activist Medgar Evers whom De La Beckwith shot in front of his home and then watched crawl, bleeding, dying, to his wife and children. De La Beckwith was set free in 1964 by two all-white juries in Mississippi who failed to reach a unanimous verdict. All this I knew, vaguely, from history courses. But in the 1990s when *Ghosts of Mississippi* came out in theaters, I was living in Boston and sitting by my husband watching the movie. In one pivotal scene, a central character insists that De La Beckwith has gone unpunished all these years, living free and easy up in his home on . . . and then the character's voice rises to what I recall as a shout — *Signal Mountain, Tennessee.* Or maybe it only sounded like a shout because of its exploding inside my head.

So the man whom everyone knew was Evers' assassin had been living on our mountain all those years and none of us knew it? And what was it about my beloved hometown that made it a place where he thought — or knew — he'd be safe, infamous as he was? I called every childhood friend I was still in touch with. Like me, this movie was the first any of them had heard of the fact. So if none of us knew as children or teens growing up there, and presumably none of our parents knew, who exactly *did* know? De La Beckwith apparently did begin to talk, even brag, about the murder. Jerry Mitchell, an intrepid reporter for Jackson's *Clarion-Ledger,* worked with Evers' widow to re-open the case in 1989, and finally in 1994, to send De La Beckwith to jail, where he died of heart failure. But even now, if you look up my hometown on Wikipedia, it will tell you, essentially, that this is a remarkably beautiful place with a remarkably high average income level, and that it is the residence of Byron De La Beckwith. It's so sad.

But this wasn't ancient history — these were my growing up years. And I'm not entirely ancient yet, last time I checked. This wasn't just any old racist, decrepit Southern town straight out of Faulkner's fiction; it was our own peaceful, neighborly, dogwood-covered hometown. How could it be that I learned of this particular ugly secret of my hometown thanks to Hollywood speaking through a cinema in New England? Maybe that was when the incidents from my teen years, the cross burning and road block and shooting spree, began to strike me as more than a string of unrelated events.

How did the story behind *Blue Hole* **effect your own journey of faith?**

My teen and adult years have been a spiritual journey with plenty of ugly stumbles, but a journey, at least, of seeking God, of being, on my best days, knocked-over-grateful for grace.

Looking back, I realize how formative — and maybe fragile — those early years were, in terms of forming some kind of idea of who God is and what God is about, and what a faith community ought to be. Although the church I grew up in was all white, I just naively assumed that when I invited my Sri Lankan friend to church, she'd be warmly welcomed. And she was. There were rumors sometimes about someone or another in the church being known as a racist — this was a small town after all, and people knew things about other people, or thought they did. But my friend seemed to feel genuinely comfortable there. I suspect a number of people went out of their way to be sure she felt cared for and included. It didn't seem particularly monumental at the time — and shouldn't have, that a church would welcome anyone wanting to walk through its doors. Wouldn't that be precisely the point?

I imagine that if my hometown church had in any way rejected this Sri Lankan girl because of her skin color, lots of us my age would've rejected anything and everything the church tried to teach us from then on out. Instead, despite what happened there on our Ridge with the Klan, at least this particular Southern church didn't bolt its doors.

The fictionalized church in the novel, though, I depicted more along the lines of how miserably so many other Southern churches behaved during the Civil Rights era, and years after. And the Baptist preacher of the novel, who is initially passive to the point of cowardice, is decidedly *not* based on my own father, who was our church's pastor. One reason I probably pictured the good Reverend Riggs as a round, blonde, balding mouse of a man was that he was diametrically opposed to my own tall, dark-haired, slender dad, whom I watched over the years take a lot of heat for his position on any number of issues.

If anything, the character of Reverend Riggs comes from my own fundamental tendencies to value harmony, as in the lack of conflict or turmoil, over just about anything. It can be a very dangerous trait, and one I'm forever learning to battle. By nature, I just want the lion to lie down with the lamb 24-7 and be chummy so I can relax and digest my food.

I was once privileged to eat dinner at the next table over from Archbishop Desmond Tutu — though he wouldn't know me from the pork tenderloin that was served. He said in his speech that night that taking seriously the teaching of Jesus means becoming not peace*lovers* but peace*makers*. There's an enormous difference there, a difference that calls for active engagement on our parts, for speaking up. Which is why Dr. Martin Luther King Jr., in his "Letter From a Birmingham Jail" reamed out the "nice" white clergy of the South as being ultimately more harmful than the Klan: Letting things roll along for the sake of not upsetting the social order or disturbing anyone's day can contribute more to the perpetuation of evil than all the blazing crosses in the world. It's a word I know I need to hear every day: Are there ways that even today my keeping my mouth shut on an issue — because I am so blasted conflict-averse — actually helped evil along on its way?

How are you like your Shelby? How are you different?

I'm certainly not Shelby, and Shelby is not me. I was never, for example, in love with a Jimbo. Shelby, though, is about the same age I was when my Sri Lankan friend moved to town, and like me at the time, Shelby is skinny and awkward, more comfortable with her brother's friends than girls her own age. In my own early teen years, my own brother, David, let me run around with his buddies, who accepted me for no good reason other than that, I suppose, they respected my brother. Maybe Shelby partially comes from the more cynical, skeptical side of me, the side of me that screws up and then refuses to feel forgiven. And I suppose I share in common with Shelby that while she is capable of being fiery and feisty, she can also clam up just when she ought to speak out — and she despises that about herself.

What about the Blue Hole itself, where the novel's teenagers go to swim, and to be together and escape heat and the tensions of the outside world? Is there a real Blue Hole?

The Blue Hole of this novel is loosely based on two swimming holes in my hometown, one actually called the Blue Hole and another reached by a trail that descends sharply at Rainbow Falls near Signal Point. The natural beauty of the mountain is stunning. Now that I live in the Southeast again, I love going to visit.

What do you hope most for your readers to glean from this novel?

I'd like to think that any story of bigotry or blind hatred or deceit reminds us of the ugliness any of us are capable of — not just actively perpetuating it ourselves, necessarily, but sometimes choosing to look the other way and let it continue. I also hope this is a story about the possibilities that always exist for complete and total transformation, against all the odds. The history of racism in the United States is a tragic one, no doubt about it. But I'm always fascinated by the individuals or groups along the way who, despite what they'd been taught to believe, despite how everyone around them behaved, held to an ideal of equality in God's eyes, and couldn't be shaken from that.

Why set the novel in the late 1970s, rather than, say, the '60s, better known for racial turmoil?

For one thing, this was an era I remember well from personal experience, whereas I was a young child in the '60s. And it was important to me to set this novel in 1979, at a time that was supposed to be safely beyond the horrors of slavery, or of early twentieth-century lynchings, or of mid-twentieth-century legally segregated buses and sidewalks and school systems. The summer of 1979 was beyond that, yes — yet racially motivated ugliness was still far from underground. I hope this story suggests our taking a serious — and maybe intentionally skeptical — look at the not-so-distant past, and our own era.

You are a beautiful writer. Have you always been a writer? What turned you into a writer?

That's awfully kind of you. I've wanted to write ever since I learned to read, I think. And the more I read, the more I wanted to write, and keep reading, and write better.

I remember in fourth grade, my teacher Mrs. Gross read aloud to the class a poem I'd written about having spotted a buck in the snow. Now, I don't know that I'd ever seen a buck in the snow before, and it was probably an atrocious poem. But it was a turning point, letting my imagination create this scene, then creating that scene for a group of other people, and having the teacher hang up my poem for everyone to see. I was never the kid who could knock the kickball clear out of the field, so it was a real gift to be noticed that way. For days, I'd pass my poem hanging there on the bulletin board, and just couldn't believe anyone else had taken notice of it, or that my words had actually connected with other people. In fifth grade, my teacher Mrs. Buckshorn quietly left me an article on my desk one day and whispered, "This is for you to read when you grow up and become a writer." I don't know that I'd told anyone about wanting to be a writer, and I've always been pathetically insecure, so, again, her insight was an enormous affirmation.

I have times of wishing I didn't enjoy writing so much, since unlike lots of other professional endeavors, there's not necessarily a direct correlation between how much time you put in and how far you get in the field. I enjoy teaching on the university level, too, and I often try to convince myself that since I dedicated all those years to gathering the proper credentials, I should simply, and only, teach. But teaching, if you try to do it well, often crowds out time to write, and I become . . . well, out of balance, off kilter with the universe when I can't write. I just want to snarl and snap at anything that moves. So it's probably best for all concerned that I try to write on a regular basis.

And what else have you written, and what intrigues you for future novels?

Blue Hole Back Home is my fifth book. I've written a nonfiction book, *Working Families,* on navigating kids and career; a collection of stories, *Grit & Grace;* a collection of reflections, *Why Jesus Makes Me Nervous;* and an academic book, *Whitewashing Uncle Tom's Cabin,* that looks at nineteenth-century women novelists' responses to Harriet

Beecher Stowe. That era, nineteenth-century America, continues to fascinate me. I've worked off and on for several years on a trilogy of novels set in Charleston, South Carolina, and Boston, Massachusetts, during the Underground Railroad, and I'd like to return to it as my next writing project. Or maybe on a contemporary novel set in Charleston. . . .

RESOURCES

The lyrics on page 103 are from the song "Gotta Get You Into My Life," written by John Lennon and Paul McCartney.

The lyrics on page 106–107 are from the song "That's the Way of the World," written by Earth, Wind & Fire.

The poem on pages 133–134 is "Amorous Birds of Prey" by John Donne.

The lyrics on pages 182 and 369 are from the song "Ain't No Mountain High Enough," written by Nickolas Ashford and Valerie Simpson.

The poem on page 327 is "Death Be Not Proud" by John Donne.

The lyrics on page 328 are from the song "Amazing Grace," written by John Newton.

ABOUT THE AUTHOR

Joy Jordan-Lake, who holds a PhD in nineteenth-century American literature as well as a masters from a theological seminary, lives in Tennessee with her husband and three children. Raised in the South but having lived a good portion of her adult life in New England, she often writes about issues of race, and of redemption. Her other books include *Grit and Grace: Portraits of a Woman's Life* (Harold Shaw, 1997); *Whitewashing Uncle Tom's Cabin: Nineteenth-Century Women Novelists Respond to Stowe* (Vanderbilt University Press, 2005); *Working Families: Navigating the Demands and Delights of Marriage, Parenting, and Career* (WaterBrook, 2007); and *Why Jesus Makes Me Nervous: Ten Alarming Words of Faith* (Paraclete Press, 2007).